# THE DARK HEART OF THE SEA

PIRATES OF THE ISLES BOOK TWO

CELESTE BARCLAY

OLIVERHEBERBOOKS

Published by Oliver Heber Books

❦ Created with Vellum

*Behind every strong man is a great woman.*
*To all those women who are a source of strength and support to their partner, you make both of you better people.*

*Happy reading, y'all,*
*Celeste*

# SUBSCRIBE TO CELESTE'S NEWSLETTER

Subscribe to Celeste's bimonthly newsletter to receive exclusive insider perks.

Subscribe Now

# PIRATES OF THE ISLES

*The Blond Devil of the Sea*
*The Dark Heart of the Sea*
*The Red Drifter of the Sea*
*The Scarlet Blade of the Sea*

# CHAPTER ONE

Ruairí MacNeil opened the door to the Three Merry Lads and tried not to curl his nose in disgust. The overpowering odor of too many bodies, stale beers, and burned food created a cloud of stench inside the tavern. Ruairí scanned the crowd as he stepped inside and immediately noticed that many members of his crew were already settled, a pint in one hand and a woman in the other. His ship, the *Lady Charity*, had docked an hour earlier. With their most recent bounty already stored in the nearby cave, Ruairí had granted them shore leave. He nodded his head once to his first mate, Kyle, who was the only sober one in the lot. Ruairí made another visual sweep of the room, checking whether there were any other sailors who might be less enthused to see him come ashore. When he was satisfied none of his rivals were waiting to stab him, he attempted to make his way to the bar. As he pushed through the standing-room-only main room, he noticed a tavern wench attempting to carry a tray of empty mugs to the bar. She was a sturdy sort, but short when compared to the mountainous Highlanders and Hebrideans who made up the patrons of the Lads. Ruairí couldn't help but smile as she tried to twist and shoulder her way past men who blocked her on purpose to give themselves more time to ogle her body.

It was rare that Ruairí felt mercy, sympathy, or compassion for anyone, let alone a woman, but there was an odd twinge in his heart as he watched her try to maintain her smile as she became more frustrated. The woman swatted away a hand that dared come too close to her modest neckline. That observation caused Ruairí to quirk a brow and inspect the woman. She had on a clean white blouse—a rarity in this tavern—and it fit loosely over her entire bust. It left much to the imagination, and Ruairí found his was alive and well. Her skirts reached her ankles instead of hiked up on either side like the other women who worked in the tavern. From what Ruairí could tell, she looked more like a farmer's wife than a tavern wench. She didn't fit in.

Ruairí's sense of compassion grew alongside his annoyance at not being able to make his way to the bar. He began to elbow men around him, and the crowd parted. Between his size and reputation, Ruairí MacNeil was a hard man to ignore. He grasped the top of the woman's hips and propelled her forward. She attempted to look over her shoulder, but she couldn't make out the man who was either her captor or her protector. When they made it to the bar, the woman set her tray down and spun around.

Senga MacLeod couldn't believe the man who stood before her was real. He was more Adonis than man. Her eyes swept over his sun-bleached blond hair, taking in his broad shoulders, the ring in his ear, and the cornflower-blue eyes. He wasn't the largest man she'd ever seen; after all, she lived near the Highlands. But he was somehow the most imposing, which made him the most impressive. There was a smirk that twitched at the corner of his mouth as he watched her assess him.

"Am I not what you expected, lass?" The deep timber felt as though it vibrated through every fiber of Senga's body, wrapping around her like a warm woolen plaid on an icy winter morning. "Or am I just what you hoped for?" His second question snapped Senga out of her glazed stare. She frowned as she appraised him. "You're exactly what I expected, and far less than I could hope for." She exchanged the dirty mugs on her tray for full ones.

"How could you've known what to expect when you couldn't see me?" Ruairí asked, amused.

"A man who assumes he can put his hands on me and do as he wants with me? Shockingly unexpected. An arrogant pirate with an earring, even more surprising." Senga once again turned away.

"You seem to know me so well, lass, but you're an enigma to me."

"An enigma? A pirate who can do more than curse. You are full of surprises."

"And you're as prickly as a thistle, but then, they're among the most beautiful flowers."

Senga turned to stand facing Ruairí once again. "If I'm prickly, it's because I've learned to take everything men say here with a barrel of salt," she huffed out. "But I can at least be gracious enough to say thank you for helping me through the crowd. I wasn't making any progress on my own."

Senga lifted her tray and dove back into the crowd as Ruairí watched her waist-length black braid swish close to her backside. He couldn't help it when his eyes were drawn to her trim waist, broad hips, and ample bottom. He'd already noticed her eyes were a deep shade of brown shot through with light green lightning strikes. It made her eyes luminescent, and he suspected they'd change color with her mood. A consuming desire to discover what hue they became when locked in the throes of passion heated his bollocks.

Ruairí watched her throughout the evening as she wove

her way through the crowd, avoiding clawing hands that tried to roam over her or attempted to pull her onto the lap of a drunkard. Each time he was ready to stand and come to her defense, but she'd pull a drying linen from the waist of her apron and snap it across those daring hands. All the while, Senga served the men with a smile plastered to her face, but even from a distance, Ruairí could see the strain around her eyes and how her smile stretched her cheeks taut. He admired her calm and patience, but his blood boiled as he watched patrons manhandle her. He couldn't understand where these feelings of sympathy and possessiveness came from. When he initially approached her, he found her form appealing. When she faced him, he was interested, and when they matched wits, he was intrigued. It had been a long time since any woman intrigued him past what she could do in bed or against a wall. He found he wanted her to come back so they could talk again, but she never did.

Senga felt overheated and could feel her shirt sticking to her back. Her backside was sore from an overly firm slap. She forced herself to continue smiling, but her cheeks ached along with her head. Senga never acclimated to the noise and smells of the tavern, and she left every night with a sharp headache. She was relieved when her uncle sent her to get two pails of fresh water from the well. Senga moved into the kitchen and grabbed the buckets before making her way to the side door. She sensed the pirate's attention all night, but he didn't seem as lecherous as the other men. Instead, he seemed almost protective, which she found puzzling. She chortled to herself as she thought about their brief exchange. He'd frightened her when she first felt his hands grip her waist, but his touch had been gentle even as his stride was determined. It was the first time since she began working at the tavern that she could make it to her destination without being stopped or pawed, and the men had made no lewd comments. She had to admit she appreciated it, but the man's attractiveness had stunned her too much to remember her manners. Then he spoke. His arrogance raised her hackles even though she could tell his comments were made in jest. She couldn't keep her eyes from shifting back to watch him as she worked the thirsty and rowdy crowd.

The fresh air was a balm to her sweaty skin. She gulped a breath of unfettered air as she flushed the tavern funk from her airways. She looked to the well and picked her way along the uneven path.

Ruairí watched Senga walk out the back door of the tavern. He scanned the crowd as his senses fired. These were the same instincts that kept him alive throughout his years of sailing and pirating. He watched three men elbow one another before they made for the side door. Ruairí was on his feet, but the tavern was even busier than when he arrived, and not as many people were willing to clear a path for him. Some didn't care; others had nowhere to move. He walked past his crew's table but shook his head when several slammed their mugs on the table and began to stand. Ruairí made his way through the crowd, even throwing two punches when a man had the audacity to smirk. He barreled through the door just in time to see Senga pressed against the wall of a nearby building. She swung an empty bucket against the ribs of one of her assailants as she tried to knee another, but her skirts kept her from connecting. Her other hand scratched at anything it could reach as she headbutted the man in front of her. She was quick to duck when a fist came at her, forcing it to smash into the brick where her head had been only a moment ago. A hand attempted to go over her mouth, but she snapped her teeth onto the fingers coming toward her. The man howled and wrapped his hand around her throat.

Ruairí catapulted himself across the open space and launched himself at the men. His shoulder collided with the first man, and the momentum knocked the other two over. Ruairí was swinging his fists before he was on his knees.

"Run!" he called out to Senga. He heard her scramble away as he rained down several more blows before rising to his feet.

"Do you know who I am?" His voice was soft and menacing as he glared at the men still on the ground. "I am Ruairí MacNeil," he bellowed.

Senga paused when she heard the name of one of the most feared pirates to sail the Hebrides. He and his cousin, Rowan MacNeil, were infamous for their bravery and their cruelty. She tucked herself behind the corner of a building and leaned around to watch. She was in awe as she watched the men scramble backwards on their hands and backsides as they tried to get away. Clearly, they recognized the name too.

Ruairí took one step forward and placed his hands on his hips as he bent over them. "Don't touch women who aren't willing. There are plenty of whores inside to keep you going for a month of Sundays. You don't need to force the only one who clearly isn't a whore."

"But Captain, that's what makes her even more appealing. She isn't used up like the others, and she taunts us with her smile and hints of a body made for sin. It's not our fault."

Ruairí roared as he lifted the man by the collar of his shirt and shook him like a rag doll before tossing him aside. "Consider her under my protection. Do. Not. Touch. Her." He punctuated each word with a hiss.

Ruairí watched as the men stumbled away from him and from the tavern. He hoped they'd learned their lesson, at least for that night. There wasn't much he could do once he sailed out of port, but he could save her this evening. He turned back to the tavern, but he knew he wouldn't make it all the way back without stopping.

Senga tried to sink back into the shadows of the building as Ruairí walked toward her. He'd told her to run, and she had, but she knew he meant back to the tavern. His manner of fighting didn't give rise to fear; rather, his ferocity eased the terror she experienced while the men attacked her. However, now a bone-deep sense of trepidation came over her as Ruairí prowled toward her.

"Come out, lass. I know you're hiding."

# CHAPTER TWO

Senga took a deep breath before squaring her shoulders and lifting her chin. She stepped out of the shadows and rushed into a wall, one that happened to be broad and made of muscle. Ruairí's hands shot out to catch her as she stumbled backwards, but he pulled a little too hard, and she tilted back toward him. They stood there, with Senga's cheek against Ruairí's chest and his arms wrapped around her. Neither of them moved as they took in what was happening. Senga could hear Ruairí's steady but rapid heartbeat, and it soothed her in a way she hadn't been calmed in many years. Ruairí held her, and for once wanted to console rather than seduce. Senga's hands crept to his waist, where she held onto his billowing leine before easing her arms around to hold him too. He kissed the top of her head, and she was sure she'd dissolve right where they stood.

"You were supposed to go back to the tavern. Believe it or not, you'd be safer there. Why didn't you listen?"

"I was going back, but then I heard your name, and well, I--" Senga stammered and squeezed her eyes shut, chiding herself for sounding addlepated.

"And what did you think when you heard my name? Did it

freeze you and frighten you into hiding? Is that why you're still out here?"

"No. It made me curious. I never would have thought you the type to rescue a damsel in distress."

"No, I wouldn't say I am. Admittedly, I haven't met many damsels in distress, but I had a sick feeling when I saw those arses pass through the same door I'd seen you use."

"I count my blessings you were watching me. It might have embarrassed me earlier, but it saved me."

Ruairí kissed the top of her head again as he stroked her hair. He couldn't remember ever being so gentle with a woman; the last time he'd been so tender was when he cared for his younger sisters. That was half a score of years ago. There was something about this woman that brought out every protective spark within him, even though her attempts to defend herself impressed him.

"You fought valiantly, and had there only been one or maybe two, you would've gotten away," he murmured.

"Perhaps."

They stood in silence for a long time before Senga pulled back and looked up at Ruairí. His face was cast in the moonlight, and she reached up to caress his angular jaw. "Thank you, Ruairí," she whispered and pulled away.

Ruairí caught her hand before she stepped around him. "You know my name, but I haven't a clue about yours. I never heard it inside."

"Senga. Senga MacLeod."

Ruairí couldn't hide his shock, and his face revealed it because Senga laughed as she darted back to the tavern. "Which ones?" he called after her.

She paused at the door before calling back, "Lewis."

She ducked inside, and Ruairí stood there shaking his head. Of course, the woman who mesmerized him would have to be from not only a neighboring clan, but from the rivals to his own clan. Ruairí grew up on the isle of Barra, where men and women were born to the sea. Their Viking heritage showed both in their looks and in their innate ability to sail. Ruairí grew up sailing with his father as they traded along the coast, and he was captaining a boat by the time he was four and ten. He was tall and strong for his age, so none of his clansmen questioned his ability to sail, and he was a natural leader. His neighbors, the MacLeods of Lewis, were as renowned for sailing as the MacNeils of Barra. They were rival merchants and, at times, raiders.

Ruairí puzzled over how Senga came to be on the tiny isle of Canna. There wasn't much here other than caves below Carn a Ghaill, or the Cairn of the Stranger, where pirates often hid their smuggled and stolen treasures. Ruairí weighed anchor there just after sunset, and his crew unloaded the hold before they sailed around to Suileabhaigh, the wide bay near Sanday. They came ashore here and made their way to the Three Merry Lads, which Ruairí now entered for the second time that night. He once again watched Senga navigate her way through the hoard of men, who were drunker than when they stepped out not even a quarter of an hour earlier. He wondered again how a MacLeod of Lewis ended up working in a tavern on one of the smallest Hebridean isles.

"She's my niece, so don't get any ideas in that pirate head of yours," said a colossus of a man who was suddenly standing across the bar from Ruairí.

"Shamus Sorley! How are you, my friend?"

"Well enough, I'd say. But I'd be a far sight better if you stopped watching my niece like she was a rare gem in a pile of dung."

"I don't know that I'd let her hear you make that comparison. But I ran into her earlier, then I watched three men follow her out to the well. They attacked her in the time it took me to get through these heathens and make my way outside."

Ruairí watched as Shamus's already ruddy cheeks turned a dark shade of magenta. The man was old enough to be

Ruairí's father, but a lifetime of owning a tavern didn't make for a weak man. He looked like an irate bear.

"Who?" he growled.

"I don't know. They ran in the opposite direction after I roughed them up."

"I thank you for watching over Senga. She's a tough one, but she's no match for three men."

"She's your niece?" Ruairí asked. "She said she was a MacLeod."

"She is. She's my niece-by-marriage."

Ruairí felt the air whoosh from his lungs as though he'd taken a poleax to the gut. He was certain he saw stars dance before his eyes. "Marriage?"

"Aye, she married my nephew, Alexander, may God rest his soul," the older man made the sign of the cross. "And she stayed on after he and their babe died five winters ago. A fever. It wiped out a third of the island."

"I remember that. We had to find somewhere else to stash our goods that winter."

Ruairí turned back and watched Senga again as she made her way back to the bar, but she went to the opposite end from where Ruairí and Shamus spoke.

"She stayed on rather than go home?"

"She didn't have much to go home to. Her parents had already died, and while her uncle was the laird, he had no use for another woman in his household. He turned her out when she married my nephew, told her she wasn't welcome back if she didn't want the arranged marriage he planned. Some MacLeod from Skye for some alliance or another."

Shamus shook his head as he wiped down the bar and moved on to help other customers. Ruairí looked over to his crew, half of whom were passed out drunk while the other half were still entertaining whores. Ruairí considered finding one for himself, but his gaze drifted back to Senga, and the idea soured. He chided himself for letting one woman ruin his plans to get sotted and bedded. Just as he was about to leave and return to his cabin, a woman he recognized from a visit earlier that year approached.

"She won't have you, you know."

Ruairí put on a look of confusion.

"She doesn't have anyone. Refuses to dirty herself as though she's too good to earn a few extra coins. She'd rather live in the shack she calls a cottage than lay on her back for a good rogering now and again."

The woman, whose name Ruairí couldn't remember if he'd ever learned it, pressed her ample breasts against his arm.

"She might not have you, but I would. Again."

The whisper was none too quiet, and Ruairí wanted to cringe. The whore's stale breath wafted across his face, and he realized he'd smelled mint on Senga's breath when they embraced.

"Not tonight, love. Perhaps the next time I'm around."

The woman sneered at him before flouncing away. Ruairí saw her march over to a man in the corner and whisper in his ear. The man left without looking back, and the whore went back to work. Something warned him to stay after all.

# CHAPTER THREE

The evening wound down as men stumbled out of the tavern or passed out where they sat. Ruairí had been sipping his ale all night, never one to overindulge when on land. He moved to sit with his men after the whore—whose name he still couldn't remember—propositioned him. His first mate, Kyle, was still mostly sober and awake, so he and Ruairí discussed their plans in hushed tones. They knew roughly where they intended to sail next, but the final decision would depend upon the weather. Senga walked past as she pulled her apron over her head and hung it on a peg by the kitchen entryway. She pushed her hair from her face and lifted her long braid as she wiped the back of her neck.

"I'm going home now, Uncle Shamus. I'll see you tomorrow eve."

"Take care, lassie. I heard what happened earlier." Shamus stuck his head out from the kitchen. "Bar your door when you get home."

"I will. Goodnight."

Senga walked out the main door of the tavern and looked around. She was prepared this time and pulled a dirk from each of her pockets. Had she not carried two buckets earlier, she would've had a dirk in at least one hand when the men attacked. She learned years ago to walk to few places at night without having a weapon at the ready. She hadn't needed it, but she'd heard from the other women what happened to them when they were unprepared. Senga shifted her gaze continuously as she walked home, just like she had countless times in the last five years. Even though she was alert, her mind wandered. She wondered how she'd never seen Ruairí before when he sounded as though he knew her uncle. She'd overheard them when she returned to the bar to refill mugs. They were friendly and seemed familiar with one another. Senga rolled her eyes when she realized she'd never seen Ruairí before because he probably went directly abovestairs rather than milling about. She saw Agnes brush up against him and had wanted to bash her over the head with her tray. She knew it was an unreasonable reaction, and she'd assumed Ruairí would follow Agnes upstairs. But when he turned her away, Senga realized she'd been holding her breath.

When Senga reached her door, she paused as she always did and looked over her shoulders. When nothing stirred, she pushed the door open and stepped inside. A hand covered her mouth as another hand squeezed her breast without mercy. She swung one dirk wide as she tried to stab backwards with the other. The man behind her howled, and his grip on her breast only tightened.

"You will pay for that, bitch."

He moved his hand from her mouth in an attempt to squeeze her wrist hard enough to make her drop the dirk. Senga ground her teeth as she refused to release the weapon. She once again swung her free arm in a wide arc as she tried to keep the other two men away.

"Where's your hero now?" one of them mocked as they dragged her to the table in the center of the room. "No pirate captain to save you, huh?"

"He broke my bluidy nose because of you. You're nothing more than a whore who thinks too highly of herself. You'll be just the same as the others once I sink my cock into you."

16

"Then you should have picked one of the others," Ruairí roared as the door slammed against the wall. He took in the scene before him. Senga was stretched on the table as two men held her wrists and rubbed their groins while the third man stood between her legs with the ties of his leggings undone, his hand down the front.

With little thought, Ruairí whipped a blade from his wrist bracer and threw it at the man about to assault Senga. The knife embedded in the assailant's neck, and blood squirted like a geyser. It was the distraction Senga needed as she rolled to the right, jerking one man off-balance. She broke free and pulled a dirk from her thigh, which was only an inch from being discovered when her attacker pushed up her skirts. She came onto her feet beside the man who was now pulling and twisting her wrist and stabbed him in the throat. He grabbed her hair and grasped her neck, but his strength was already draining from him, and he collapsed. Senga spun around as she heard a howl of pain, and then the table toppled over as the third man crashed to the floor with a dirk through his eye. Before she could register the gruesome sight, she found herself hauled against the chest that had offered her protection earlier that night. Ruairí held her against him until he was sure she wouldn't be ill or faint, then swept her into his arms and turned toward the only door inside the cottage. His mind flashed to the tavern wench's snarky comment about Senga's home being a shack and chalked it up to jealousy. The cottage was spacious and cozy from what he could see. He carried Senga into the bedchamber and sat her on the edge of the bed before stepping back. The last thing he wanted was for her to fear he'd molest her after saving her once again.

Senga stared blankly at the door Ruairí kicked closed. She ran her hand absentmindedly over the bed cover before looking with vacant eyes to Ruairí. He approached her with caution and kept his hands where she could see them. He came to squat before her.

"Lass?"

"Aye, I'm well enough. They didn't have a chance to do any real harm."

Ruairí reached out but dropped his hand before he touched her.

"Really, I'm all right, just very startled," Senga assured him.

"Startled? That's how you'd describe being attacked twice in one night, once in your own home?"

"Would you like me to wail and pull my hair? Am I not hysterical enough for your liking?" Senga spat at him.

Ruairí pulled her into his arms as they stood. He held her and felt the shuddering breaths as she tried to keep from falling apart.

"It wouldn't surprise me if you did, since that's what I want to do myself. Nothing ever frightened me more than when I could hear male voices yelling while I was still a fair distance away. I wasn't sure I'd make it in time. I never want to see you held against your will, and I've seen it twice tonight. If I hadn't been so frightened you might get hurt in the middle of a fight, I'd have done far worse to them."

"You were frightened?" Senga's hoarse words barely reached Ruairí, even though she still stood in his embrace.

"Terrified. Though I was supremely impressed to see you plunge your dirk into one of their throats, and I saw a gash across another man's side. You fight like a wildcat."

"And like one, I'd rather chew my leg off than remain caught in a snare."

"If I hadn't been so enraged, I would've been awestruck. I'm proud of the way you fought them both times. I just want to know what manner of place you live that men would attack you like that twice."

"It's a tavern on a small isle. It limits the choices for women. I refuse to whore, and so some men think I mean to offer a challenge. I saw Agnes send her younger brother outside, so I should've known her older brother would be back to finish what he started."

"Who's Agnes?"

"The woman who seemed to remember you quite fondly."

Ruairí felt his cheeks burn from embarrassment for the first time since he was a lad. He didn't know what to say, so he opted to stay quiet.

"Her brother has been hounding me for weeks, so it didn't surprise me to see him when I was at the well. I just hadn't expected his two friends would slink out to help him. I didn't think they'd come here after the way you handled them, but they wanted revenge for the beating as much as they wanted to rape me."

Ruairí swallowed the lump in his throat as he listened to Senga's detached assessment of her evening. He wanted to carry her away from this cottage, the tavern, and the blasted island. Instead, he continued to hold her and ran his hand over her back. She relaxed enough to step back. Senga looked around the room and sighed. Nothing had been the same since her husband died. Even though their marriage was brief, she'd been happy. Now she had little to look forward to.

"Why do you stay?"

"Where else can I go? I heard Uncle Shamus tell you my uncle won't have me back. I tried to return after the illness passed, but he wouldn't let me into the bailey. Turned me away in front of my entire clan. I boarded the birlinn and returned here that night."

Senga looked up but saw that Ruairí was looking past her. She knew what he'd spotted, and her heart pinched. Senga had almost forgotten the cradle that sat covered in the corner. She walked to it and ran a hand over the curved end.

"It's one of the few things I have from my childhood. My da carved this for me before I was born. My aunt smuggled it to me just after I married." Senga held her breath trying to keep the tears from falling. "It's stood empty for a long time, but I've nowhere else to store it."

Ruairí stood behind her, and she could feel his heat against her back. When he cupped her shoulders and pulled her back against him, she didn't resist.

"It's not too late for you to have a family one day."

Senga's laugh was hollow if not bitter. "You saw my choices tonight. I will die alone just as I live alone. My chance for a family came and went."

"Shamus said it's been five years since they passed. You must have loved your husband to not have found some other option."

Senga shook her head as her fingers continued to trail over the cradle covered by a bed linen. "I was only five and ten when I married. My parents died a few years earlier during a raid, and I was desperate to get away from my uncle. He had plans to marry me to the old MacLeod laird. The man was old enough to be my grandfather. I met Alexander when we were still children and his father came to trade. We were fond of one another, and as we grew older, we were attracted to each other. Along with that came curiosity. When he asked for my hand, I agreed, and we wed within three sennights. Alexander had the banns posted here, so my uncle wouldn't hear of it. I got with child two moons after we wed, and they were both dead two moons after I delivered our son."

Senga rested her head against Ruairí's chest as his arms wrapped around her. "I loved Alex just as any girl my age would have, but I don't know that I'd still love him as the woman I grew into. I loved the idea of being loved, and he loved the idea of being a protector and provider. He was three years older than me, and he was a good protector and provider. I was happy here as a farmer's wife. That life just wasn't meant to be." Senga took a deep breath and squared her shoulders before stepping away from Ruairí. "I've been remiss in thanking you again for coming to my rescue not once, but twice this evening. I don't know that I'd be alive right now if you hadn't followed me home." Senga's brow creased. "What made you follow me home?"

Ruairí looked around the bedchamber and saw chemises

and nightgowns folded neatly on a shelf, and a fresh blouse and skirt hanging on pegs. He'd walked past a chest at the end of the bed when he followed Senga to the cradle. The room, much like the rest of the cottage, was spacious, but it held the bare minimum. He could only describe it as sparse, and his heart ached for the umpteenth time that night as he thought about Senga and what she endured.

"I don't know for sure. The same feeling that has warned me of an impending attack at sea told me something would happen tonight. Nearly everyone was passed out at the tavern, so I knew it wouldn't be there. My intuition screamed to follow you, so I did. I learned long ago to listen to that voice, and I'm glad I did."

Ruairí knew it was the middle of the night and he should let Senga go to bed, but he felt unsettled. He wasn't sure if it was she who made him feel off-kilter or if it was the events of the night, but he didn't feel ready to leave.

"You must be exhausted. I should let you get some sleep, but I don't feel right leaving you alone. I could sleep by the hearth, if you'll let me. I'd feel better knowing you're still protected, and I could clean up."

Senga had completely forgotten the three dead men in her home. She shuddered to think how the village would react to learning the men died in her home, at her hands and at the hands of a pirate. "I'll help you."

"Lass, you don't have to do that. I'll go back to the tavern and get some of my men to help me. You should rest."

"You think I'll be able to sleep knowing there are three dead men in my cottage or when you and your men are moving about out there? Carrying away those bodies? I think not."

Senga walked to the door but turned back to Ruairí. He was only a few steps behind her, so she waited until he stepped near her. She stood on her toes and kissed his cheek.

"I know your reputation. I know what people think of you, and I'm sure much of it is true. But I haven't seen that side of

21

you tonight, and I'm grateful. I won't tell a soul how kind you've been, but I doubt I'd be standing here in one piece without that kindness. I'd either be dead or a puddle of tears." She kissed his cheek once again.

Ruairí's arms itched to hold her again, and a look of mutual desire passed between them. Senga made the decision easy for Ruairí when she embraced him. He'd spent his adult life angry and bitter about his past and vengeful for the course his life took. For the first time in years, he didn't feel those emotions. Instead, he felt hope.

"Lass--"

Senga cut him off when she leaned back and tugged on the front of his leine. She lifted her chin and parted her lips, and Ruairí needed no clearer an invitation. Their lips fused together on a sigh that exchanged breaths. Ruairí swept his tongue over her lips, and she opened wider for him. She flicked her tongue and lured him in where they dueled and tangled until she gently sucked. Ruairí growled as his cock strained against the front of his leggings. He forced himself to cradle her, not willing to frighten her, but she ran her hands down his back to his buttocks. She pressed against him as her mound grazed his aching rod. Her moan echoed his growl as she shifted restlessly. It had been years since a man touched her or aroused her desire. Ruairí's touch made her combust as a need coursed through her stronger than anything her husband had stirred. The events of the evening melted away as Ruairí replaced fear with passion. A small voice in her head warned she was insane for kissing a man only minutes after those men had attacked her a second time, but a much more strident voice told her to keep going.

Ruairí was lost to the raging storm of emotions, floundering like a wind-tossed boat. His bollocks screamed for him to hike up her skirts, wrap her legs around his waist, and sink deep within. His head told him to slow down before he frightened her. And his heart demanded he care for her that night and all the ones to come.

22

Senga felt the ache low in her body take hold as she clung to Ruairí as though he was the only thing keeping her from floating adrift. He anchored her to the spot, both physically and emotionally. She didn't want to ponder the connection she believed they had. She didn't want to set false hopes, but she knew his need matched hers, and it wasn't something she'd ignore.

"Ruairí," she breathed against the stubble that abraded her swollen lips. "Make me forget the past, forget tonight."

"Are you sure, Senga?"

"Aye."

The one word of consent was all they both needed before they ripped the clothes off one another and tumbled onto the bed. Ruairí was careful not to crush her small frame under his much larger one. His feet hung off the end of the bed as he slid lower to take one of her breasts into his mouth. His tongue whorled around her nipple as he alternated breathing warm and cool air over the puckered flesh. These were the nipples of a woman who had nursed a babe, and he found he enjoyed having more to suckle. He turned his head and worshipped her other breast before switching between them. He nipped and pulled with his teeth as his hand kneaded the opposite breast. Senga's back arched, and she cupped her breasts in offering to him. One of his hands trailed from the dip in her throat, down between her breasts, over her belly until it came to the thatch of raven curls at the apex of her thighs. He ran his fingers through them and tugged gently. He used one finger to slide over her bud and between the folds until he was sure she was as eager as he imagined. Her sheath drenched his finger as she moaned, unsure whether to raise her breasts or her hips in offering.

"Shh, little one. I'll take care of all of you. What do you want?"

Senga looked into his blue eyes and moaned again.

"You inside me. Hard."

Ruairí's chuckle rumbled across her body, and she tight-

23

ened her grip on his hair. She hadn't even realized she'd pulled his queue loose and tunneled her fingers in his blonde waves.

"We'll get there soon enough, but I won't rush us. What do you want?"

"Your fingers then. I want, need, some part of you there."

"Where? Can you not say it?"

"Cunny. Quim. Pussy. I can say it, but I don't want to talk."

Ruairí once again chuckled, but it was cut short when he groaned as he thrust three fingers into her channel. Her hips lifted off the bed, and for a moment he worried he'd been too forceful. She was no virgin, but it had been years since she was with a man.

"More," she panted. She pressed his hand further into her sheath. "Harder. I need more, and I won't break. Please."

Ruairí plunged his fingers into her over and over, and as she watched, he inched down to blow cool air over the heated flesh.

"Yes," she mewled.

His tongue whipped out to lave her pleasure nub before sucking it into his mouth. Her knees fell wide before trapping his shoulders. He slid his hands beneath her and lifted her hips to his feasting mouth. His tongue replaced his fingers as he brought her close to climax over and over. When her moans of need turned to ones of frustration, he once again plunged his fingers into her as he sucked her nub. She exploded around him, screaming his name.

Ruairí lifted himself over her and before he could guide himself in, he felt her wrap her hand around his leaking shaft. She stroked him thrice before aligning him with her entrance. She locked her ankles around his waist as she pressed him into her. He needed no further instructions and surged forward until he was seated to the hilt within her tight sheath. He groaned as he dipped his head to once again suckle her breast, but it wasn't enough. Ruairí looked up at

Senga and saw her watching him. She stroked the hair away from his face, and a tenderness that would normally fizzle his desire made him want to possess her. Their lips came together with the same force and need as their hips. Ruairí held her as he thrust into her over and over. Senga pressed her heels into the bed to help her meet him each time he rocked forward. Theirs was a rhythm of give and take that felt natural, as though they'd always been lovers. Ruairí sucked in what air he could as he tried to slow the growing need to climax. He refused to finish so soon. He didn't know if he'd ever join with Senga again, and he wouldn't let it be over yet.

Senga's hands roamed over every part of Ruairí she could reach. She brushed his hair back as they kissed, then scored her nails down his back as his thrusts drove deeper still. Her fingers dug into his backside as she felt her release rip through her.

"Ruairí!" she screamed again as he pushed her over the edge once more.

"*Mo bhòidhchead.*" My beauty. "I'm close, but I don't want this to be over yet. Can you keep going?"

"Yes. Oh, Ruairí. Don't stop."

Those were the last words spoken for some time as they moved together toward completion. Senga found her release twice more before Ruairí could no longer fight his body's need. He pulled free and watched as his seed painted her belly. Never had such an image called to him. He couldn't cease the thought that this marked her as his. He knew it was ridiculous. Ruairí would leave in the morning and never see Senga again, but even that felt more outrageous than the idea that she was his. He watched her for a long moment as she, too, stared at his seed. He wasn't sure of her thoughts, but her face relaxed as though she liked what she saw. Ruairí climbed from the bed and found a cloth beside a pitcher of water. After wetting it, he returned and sat beside her as he cleaned her. Senga tried to take the cloth, but Ruairí batted her hand away.

"Let me," his hoarse voice was almost unrecognizable to him as he leaned forward to kiss her nose. "I want to."

He'd never in his life done such a thing for a woman. When he ceased his ministrations and prepared to stand, Senga snatched the cloth from him as she sat up. She reached forward and ran the cloth over Ruairí's cock. It twitched beneath her hand. Senga dropped the cloth to the ground and wrapped her hand around the already lengthening rod. She stroked it as her breasts pressed against his shoulder. Ruairí turned his head to look at her, and Senga leaned in for a kiss. This was slow, sensual, and filled with a different need. Ruairí couldn't believe he was hard and aching to be inside her again already. He hadn't recovered that quickly since he was a green lad.

Senga pressed his shoulder until he laid back, and she slid from the bed to kneel before him. She continued to stroke him as he came to his elbows. Propped up, he watched her stare intently at his cock as though considering her means of attack. Her tongue whipped forward and circled his tip before flicking its head. Ruairí growled as his head fell back. Her lips slid down his length and closed around him. He jerked forward when she began to apply pressure. The suction made him want to thrust, but he was careful to keep his hips grounded to the mattress. He knew he was a large man in length and girth. He neither wanted to scare her nor choke her, but Senga continued to sink lower onto his cock. It mesmerized him to see how much she could take in before she could go no further. She cupped his bollocks and rolled them in her palm as he scooped her hair off her sweaty neck. He watched her head bob as he had with so many other women, but it felt entirely different. Whores rendered a service, and while some pretended, or even genuinely liked the task, Senga seemed to revel in it. She worshipped his length as she alternated licking, sucking, and stroking until Ruairí thought he might lose his mind with need. He felt his release gathering at the base of his cock, and he had no intention of holding back this time.

"Senga," he grunted. He pressed on her shoulder, but she wouldn't release him.

"Senga," he said more forcefully, and she looked up at him, her translucent hazel eyes locked with his deep blue ones. "Let go. I want to see my seed on you again."

Ruairí couldn't believe his own ears. He hadn't intended to speak that thought aloud, but Senga released him at once and leaned back on her heels. Ruairí stroked himself several times before the jets of seed splashed across her chest and onto her breasts. Once again, Ruairí felt he'd marked her as his own, and she smiled at him as though proud to bear his release. She trailed a finger through the viscous fluid and licked her finger.

"I wonder if I taste as good to you as you do to me," she purred.

Ruairí thought he might climax again at her seductive words. He looked into her eyes once more and saw curiosity rather than seduction, and he realized she was being truthful in her musing. He reached beside her for the cloth and once again cleaned her, then himself. He pulled her from the ground and lifted her onto the bed before stretching out beside her. Ruairí ran his hand over her flat belly where he could see tiny, fine lines that were a testimony that she'd carried a child. Her hand covered his, and he watched embarrassment redden her cheeks.

"I called you 'my beauty' for a reason, little one. Every part of you is beautiful. Don't hide from me."

She looked at him for so long, Ruairí wasn't sure what she would do next, but she let her hands fall away.

"Kiss me again, please," she whispered, and Ruairí was only too happy to indulge her request. Once again, this was slow and languid, unlike the consuming need during the first time they coupled. Ruairí ran the calloused pads of his fingers over her belly, and when they broke apart, his eyes spied the cradle. He continued to run his fingers over her belly as a vivid image of Senga round with their child came to his mind. He saw her first standing at the prow of his ship with the wind

27

blowing back her hair, then standing beside the cradle as she checked on their other sleeping child.

*Other?* Ruairí thought to himself. *I've known her a night, and I'm imagining us with not one but two bairns. Well, one in the cradle and the other in her belly. Bluidy hell. What is wrong with me?*

Ruairí looked down at Senga again, but her eyes were closed. He knew she wasn't asleep because her fingers were running over the tattoo that covered the entire left side of his chest before wrapping over his shoulder and covering his left shoulder blade. It was a Celtic design of knots and twists with a water serpent slithering from his back to his front. The fine lines that had marred her brow and cheeks all night disappeared, and she looked serene. His heated palm rested on her belly, and she covered it with one hand before opening her eyes. They gazed at one another, both searching for something they couldn't identify but recognized.

"Come with me, Senga."

Her eyes widened, and her mouth formed a perfect oval. Ruairí's cocked twitched as he remembered her lips on his cock, but he forced his body to relax.

"It won't be safe for you here, whether the men's families retaliate or other men try to finish what they attempted. You've said you've nowhere else to go, and I think you're lonely here alone. Come with me."

"As what? Your mistress? One good bedding doesn't make us compatible to share a cabin."

"It's more than that, and we both know it. There is something here. Something between us too special to ignore."

"And if it turns out it was only one night of wonder, what then? You return me here where everyone will know I'm a whore. That doesn't seem better than what I have now."

"You're not a whore," he growled. "If you use that word again to describe yourself, I will turn you over my knee." Ruairí worried he was too harsh, but he saw desire, not fear, flare in her eyes. He whispered against her ear, "Do you like that idea?"

Senga only nodded. Ruairí cupped her breast as he rolled her nipple with his thumb. "Has any man ever spanked you before?"

"No. It wasn't something my husband ever considered."

"But it was something that intrigued you. Something you wanted." She nodded once again. "Senga, I'm not an easy man to live with. I demand obedience from my crew. I'm brutal and violent during battle, and I show no one mercy. No one until you. I've never been kind or gentle with anyone, but I find a calmness and peace with you. I can let my guard down and not be the dreaded pirate captain. I can just be Ruairí. I find I like it, and I don't want it to end with tonight."

Senga rolled toward him, so they both lay on their sides.

"I also find myself protective and possessive of you. I've never felt that way about anyone. The closest I've come is how protective I am of my cousin, Rowan. I've never felt this toward a woman before. It must mean something."

Once more Senga stared into his eyes, searching for something Ruairí prayed she would find. He began to grow nervous the longer she looked, but she cupped his jaw and bussed a kiss across his lips.

"I'll go with you."

There was little to keep Senga here but old memories that haunted her nights. She knew the risk she was taking, sailing away with a man she'd known for less than a night, but a feeling buried deep within her urged her to take that risk, to make a new life, even if temporary, with Ruairí.

The kiss they shared differed from the others. It was filled with promise and anticipation, not of their next round of coupling, but for the future.

"Know that if you're unhappy, I'll take you wherever you want to go. I'll do what I can to help you establish a new life. You could go back to Lewis, even if not to your uncle's keep. You could even go to Skye. I'll never force you to do anything you don't want, and that includes remaining aboard my ship."

"Thank you, Ruairí."

She laid back and opened her arms to him. He settled his upper body over hers and kissed her forehead, nose, and each cheek before sinking into another languid kiss. He rolled them so she was draped over him. The soothing sweep of his hand over her back and bottom had her dozing within moments.

Ruairí watched as her eyelids fluttered closed and she sighed, her hand resting over his heart. He covered it with his own as his other rested on her backside. He knew of the trust she was placing into his hands, and he prayed for the first time in years. Ruairí prayed he'd remain worthy of that trust. He'd do all that was in his power, but he knew she'd face danger and see sides of him he wished he could hide. His trepidation at her seeing him as the pirate captain almost made him wake her to rescind his offer. He'd spent almost all his adult life harboring a simmering rage for what happened to him and his cousin. People knew him for being cold and aloof to most women, earning the name Dark Heart for that, among other sins. None had seen the side of him that he so willingly showed Senga. Women enjoyed him for what he could do to their bodies and the coin they earned from what they could do with theirs. But most women avoided him if he wasn't tupping them.

Senga hadn't avoided him at all. She'd worked as was expected of her, but she hadn't avoided him. Ruairí wasn't sure if her lack of fear came from his softheartedness toward her, or if it was the other way around. They seemed to understand one another on an elemental and intuitive level. Ruairí didn't feel angry or bitter when he was near Senga. His earlier anger was directed at the men who dared to defile her, but it evaporated each time as soon as he knew she was safe. He hadn't realized how exhausted he was from carrying the burden of his hatred until he found respite in Senga's arms. His own eyes drifted closed for a brief time, but he didn't sleep.

# CHAPTER FOUR

Senga stirred and felt a man's body beneath hers. For a moment, she thought she was dreaming once more of Alexander, but everything was different. The man she laid upon smelled of saltwater and pine, and he felt different. The chest was broader and smooth, unlike Alexander's barrel chest and light smattering of hair. All Senga did with Ruairí flooded back to her as she remembered him rescuing her when the men attacked her in her own home. The tenderness he showed as he brought her into her bedchamber, and the eventual passion that erupted between them. She ached between her legs from still unspent desire along with soreness from muscles that had laid dormant far too long.

"Did you get enough rest, little one?"

Senga looked into the eyes that were once again cornflower blue but had been a shade of lapis lazuli as they coupled.

"Enough to face the world," she replied, her voice raspy from sleep. She realized she must have slept more deeply than she realized. She had a sudden moment of worry that she snored.

"You slept like the dead, even if for only an hour."

"That's all? It felt longer. Did you sleep?"

"Dozed."

Senga wasn't sure if she should believe him. She doubted he lowered his guard enough to be vulnerable to sleep.

"Pack what you'd like to take with you. I can arrange for Shamus to protect your cottage if you think you might want to return, or I can have him clear it out. Your choice."

Senga took a deep breath before blowing it out through her nose. "If I return, it will be to visit. I'll never live here again. Uncle Shamus can do as he wants with the cottage and what it contains."

"Very well. When you're ready to leave, I'll take you back to the tavern and Shamus while my men and I deal with the bodies."

Ruairí watched to see if she grimaced or showed fear at the mention of the dead men in her cottage, but her face didn't change. Instead, she sat up and looked around. When she spotted her clothes from the night before, she considered whether to put them back on or wear fresh clothes. Since she had no idea when she might bathe or launder her clothes, she opted for fresh ones. She moved to the wash basin, and Ruairí joined her as they went about their morning ablutions in silence. It surprised Ruairí at how quickly she packed. The chest at the end of the bed was empty except for two plaids, one in the MacLeod colors and the other in the Sorely colors. Senga packed the fresh chemises, stockings, and a nightgown in the trunk and then carried two fresh blouses and skirts from a shelf Ruairí hadn't noticed the night before. She took a sack from the peg her clean skirt hung on and stuffed her clothes from the day before within it. She cinched it closed and placed it at the top of her chest. Senga was ready in less than five minutes.

"Is there anything from the other room you would have me fetch?"

"Only my sewing basket and a carved wooden cross that sits before the window. My da made that, too. There is nothing else. I burned the linens after I buried my husband

32

and son, and I didn't need more than one set. It's just me who lives here, so I don't have a need for much more. The bowls and mugs don't need to come, so no, there's nothing else," Senga shrugged.

Ruairí had dressed while she packed, and he moved to the door with his hand on his sword. He exercised caution as he pulled it open, even though he'd heard no one and nothing enter the cottage while they dozed. He was honest enough with himself to admit the roof could have fallen down around their ears and he wouldn't have noticed while he bedded Senga. Ruairí tucked her against his side and turned her face toward his shoulder.

"Don't look," he whispered as he led her to the front door, but she couldn't help but pause and look back. Even though it was easy to walk away from the cottage, it had been her home for six years. The home she shared with her husband and bairn. She nodded once before stepping outside.

The morning sun blinded her as she looked around. Nothing seemed out of place, but several of the village women stood with their mouths agape to see Ruairí exit with her. It was only a moment before Senga saw the women buzz with gossip.

*I'm a merry widow now I suppose. I believe I've earned the right.*

Ruairí guided Senga back to the tavern, never removing his arm from her shoulders. His claim was obvious to all and sundry, and they both were fine with it. When they reached the tavern, Ruairí nudged and kicked his crew awake before turning Senga over to Shamus with clear instructions he wasn't to leave her alone, even for a moment. Ruairí led his crew outside and began issuing orders for those who would go to her cottage with him to remove the bodies. He sent his first mate to find the priest. Kyle looked toward the tavern and raised an eyebrow before looking back at Ruairí.

"Just a funeral today," Ruairí answered Kyle's unspoken question.

Ruairí sent some men to ready the dinghies that would

33

carry them to the *Lady Charity*. Kyle found the priest easily enough, as he'd just concluded matins, and brought him to Senga's cottage. The priest crossed himself several times as his eyes darted between the dead bodies and Ruairí.

"They attacked Senga twice last night. They got less than they deserved," Ruairí bit out.

The priest jumped and nodded. He hurried to say last rites before leaving to summon the men's families. Ruairí wasn't looking forward to this, but he wouldn't allow a single person to have any doubts as to the men's culpability and the cause of their deaths. He and his men waited outside as a group of villages gathered, several women crying. They couldn't silence an angry woman. It was Agnes from the tavern.

"You murdered my brother. You believed a whore instead of an honorable man. She's the one who deserves to be dead."

Ruairí stepped forward, pushed his chest out, and towered over almost everyone in the crowd.

"I caught those men attacking Senga outside the tavern and then inside her home. They deserved the fate they asked for. I warned them when I found them pressing her against a wall, but they chose not to listen. If anyone doubts my words are true, step forward now."

There were murmurs among the crowd, but no one stepped forward to speak against the Dark Heart. The look upon Ruairí's face showed it was the pirate captain they faced.

"I'd be careful who you call a whore considering you spend most of your time on your back, Agnes," Ruairí sneered at the woman who now cowered before him. Ruairí looked around before shifting his gaze to the priest. "It seems you've the men you need to carry these sacks of shite from here. My men and I are done."

Ruairí tilted his head toward the shore and muttered to his men before the crew filed down the path after him.

34

Senga waited in the tavern and ate a bowl of porridge Shamus offered her. Shamus, his wife, and his daughter came out from the kitchen, and Senga was saying goodbye when Ruairí returned. He looked at the three women. Senga's aunt-by-marriage was teary eyed and looked sad to see Senga leave. Senga's cousin-by-marriage looked bored before she noticed Ruairí, then jealous, while Senga looked like she wanted to run. Shamus pried her loose from his wife's embrace and gave her a warm hug, which Ruairí was relieved to see she sank into. He appreciated knowing someone had cared for her, and that she'd had someone to rely on. When she stepped back and looked at Ruairí, he held out his hand to her. She approached and entwined her fingers with his. Ruairí felt a shock of electricity surge up his arm and when he looked down at Senga, he was sure she felt it too. Neither missed the rightness of holding hands. It felt natural.

Ruairí guided her along the path to the beach and swept her into his arms before wading to the small boat that would ferry them to the *Lady Charity*.

"I'm not afraid of getting wet, you know."

Ruairí's tongue darted out and flicked her earlobe. "I know, but that isn't the kind of wet I want you to be."

Senga moaned before leaning her head against the crook of his neck. She smattered the tanned skin with feathery kisses.

"In that case, know I'm already wet," Senga whispered as they arrived at the dinghy. He settled her on the seat before climbing in next to her and barking an order for his sailor to row with haste. Ruairí had every intention of getting her to his cabin, stripping her bare, and taking her on every surface they fit. His need flowed to Senga, and her nails bit into the back of his hand as they'd joined them once again.

"I know there are things you must do once we are aboard, but please don't keep me waiting too long," she murmured. She hoped her words only reached his ears. But when the oarsman couldn't turn his head quickly enough to hide his smile, Senga felt her cheeks burn.

It was a short row to the ship, and Senga surprised Ruairí with the ease in which she scampered up the rope ladder. She stood with perfect balance in the dinghy, tucked her skirts into her waist, and was up the ladder before Ruairí could offer her help. Once she rolled over the rail and landed on her feet, she looked back at Ruairí, who was climbing over the rail.

"I'm a MacLeod, remember?" she teased, this time for his ears only. She arranged her skirts before looking around. A moment of real panic spread through her, and she wondered if she'd jumped out of the frying pan and into the fire. The motley crew before her was intimidating at the least and downright terrifying at the most. As she looked at each man, they looked at her. Some seemed shocked, others glared back with disdain, and far too many leered. Ruairí saw what she did and stepped in front of her. He tucked her behind him and crossed his arms with his feet planted wide.

"Well, out with it."

This would be his crew's only time to voice dissent, but they knew it would do them little good, so many grumbled under their breath.

"Bad omen."

"Be the death of us."

"Anger the sea gods."

"Foul luck she'll bring."

Senga heard all the comments, but they didn't faze her. In truth, she'd heard them all before, either about other women aboard a ship or directed at her when she'd sailed with her father when she was younger. Ruairí took a step forward, but Senga grasped his leine at his waist, out of sight of his men, and tugged.

"Let them say what they want now rather than fester later," she whispered. The tension leaving Ruairí's body was the only sign she received that he heard her.

"This is Senga MacLeod. She's my guest, and you will

treat her as such. I will treat any disrespect as though it were done to me."

Senga knew that meant the lash. For the men's sake, even though they weren't her friends, she hoped they were all wise enough to keep their thoughts to themselves. Ruairí looked to Kyle, who stood at the wheel and nodded. Kyle began barking orders for the crew to raise the sails and lift the anchor. Ruairí guided Senga to the stairs that would take them to his cabin. Once inside, Ruairí locked and barred the door before turning to Senga. She was already pulling her blouse over her head. Ruairí pulled her toward him as he loosened the waist to her skirt.

"For now, until I'm sure of my crew, you must lock and bar the door any time you're alone here. Promise me."

"Of course. Ruairí, this isn't my first time sailing. Besides, I grew up with men who spent more time on water than land. I know how they feel about a woman on their ship."

"I'm glad it doesn't bother you. However, I picked up some new crew just after my last raid in a smuggler's town in Cornwall. I don't know them well enough yet to trust them. Until I do, I don't want any of them near you." Ruairí tugged the ribbons at her shoulder, and the chemise fell to the ground.

"Undress, *mo chaiptean*."

"You call me your captain, yet you issue the orders?" Ruairí cocked a brow, but his seriousness faded when he couldn't help but smile.

"I thought you'd agree, unless there is something else you want to do." Senga paused as she rolled down one stocking. She stood up and looked around. "Do you have logbooks to fill?"

Ruairí growled before pouncing on her. "There is only one thing I intend to fill," he groaned, as he lowered his mouth to hers.

Their kiss was wild as they devoured one another. When they finished undressing, Ruairí lifted Senga, and she wrapped her legs around his waist. He sunk into her as her head fell back.

"God, the feel of you entering me is almost enough to bring me to climax."

Ruairí backed them against the door as he thrust over and over. He worried she might be sore from the night before, but she pressed her heels against the small of his back when he tried to slow. His hand grasped her breast and kneaded the supple flesh.

"Pinch. Bite," Senga panted, and Ruairí was only too happy to satisfy her request. He watched the pulse pound in her neck as her head fell back. Each pinch, each bite of her nipple seemed to drive her closer to the edge. Ruairí experimented with the pressure and the pain he would cause. He discovered she liked when he was rougher with her.

"Do you like the pain, little one?"

"Yes. After all this time, it makes me know I'm still alive. I can still feel."

Ruairí pinched her nipple while tugging on the other with his teeth, applying as much pressure as he dared not wanting to break the skin with his teeth. Senga's fingers dug into his shoulders as she moaned more and more, relishing the feel of the pain transforming into unparalleled pleasure. It was only a matter of minutes before Ruairí felt Senga's inner muscles grip his cock as spasms rocked her core. He spun them and walked to the table. He swept his arm across it and knocked mugs, plates, maps, and ledgers onto the floor before lying her down. She unhooked her legs and brought her feet to the edge, giving herself leverage to meet each of his thrusts. She couldn't keep from moaning as the intensity built again.

"Look at me, *leannán*."

Senga tried to keep her eyes open as she felt a wave of pleasure spread from the bottom of her belly out to her limbs. She failed as she raised her chin and screamed. The moment the sound died on her lips, she bit her tongue and her ardor dampened. She looked at Ruairí, sure he wouldn't want her announcing to the entire ship what they were doing. He leaned forward and ran his tongue over the whorl of her ear.

"I'd have them all know you're mine," he growled.

"I don't doubt they already know."

She relaxed once she knew vocalizing her pleasure didn't bother Ruairí. She rose and clasped her hands behind his neck as she kissed him. Ruairí felt his knees shake as he drove himself harder and faster as Senga begged for more. He lifted her from the table and moved to a chair. She straddled him and rode him as her hair hung down her back and swished about her hips. Ruairí fisted his hand in the raven locks and kissed her throat and collar bones as she set her own punishing pace.

"I'm close, lass." He lifted her from his shaft, and she gripped his cock as she stroked him to completion. They sagged against one another, their breathing ragged and hearts pounding. It was only when the perspiration chilled Senga's skin as they cooled that Ruairí felt the strength to rise. He walked to the bed with her in his arms and pulled back the covers.

"Sleep some more. You had a long night, little one. I'll be back when it's time for the midday meal."

Senga was fast asleep before Ruairí was done getting dressed. He was tempted to wake her and insist she lock and bar the door, but she was so peaceful, he didn't have the heart to do it. He did what he could by locking it from the outside. When he went on deck, he found one of the men who had been with him the longest and posted him as a guard outside his cabin.

# CHAPTER FIVE

R uairí took the wheel from Kyle as they stood beside each other. "She seems to have settled in quickly enough," Kyle waggled his eyebrows. Ruairí glared him, and Kyle took a step back. "Tread carefully. You saw her last night; she's not the usual tavern wench. She's not like any of the others. She matters to me." His gaze drifted to the stairs leading to his cabin, and he remembered the look on Senga's face not long ago as they raced to climax. Rather than just lust, another emotion Ruairí couldn't name filled his chest. It almost burned, but it wasn't painful. He welcomed it as once again, he felt the bitterness that had been his constant companion for so long being chipped away.

"But you barely know her. How could she be that important to you so soon?"

"I don't know. I truly don't, but there is something about her, between us. Call it divine intervention."

Kyle guffawed. "You've found God along with a bedmate. You did well for one night."

Ruairí gripped Kyle's collar and pulled him close. "You've been my closest friend besides Rowan. We've sailed together for years. Don't make me choose because, for once, you may not come out the winner." Kyle put his hands up in surrender, and Ruairí let go.

"I meant no offense, Captain." Kyle used his title since they were drawing attention. "I'm just surprised is all. I never imagined the Dark Heart would ever be anything but, well, dark."

"I'm realizing there is a time and place for each."

"In all seriousness, though, what're you going to do when we attack another ship? Do you still plan to pillage and plunder?"

"Of course. She knows who she came with. She knows what I am. I don't look forward to her seeing that side of me, so I intend to keep her under lock and key whenever we must conduct business."

Despite the years of sailing, first as a crew member aboard what he and his cousin started out thinking was a merchant ship, then as a captain of his own boat, he never liked to say out loud that he stole and killed for a living. A sliver of guilt that it would disappoint his parents if they knew still niggled at his mind when he spoke aloud of what he did as a pirate.

"I hope for her sake that she remains tucked away. Have a care when you decide who to board. She seems like a nice sort." That was the best compliment Kyle would offer, and the conversation seemed to end.

Ruairí remained at the helm until the sun was high overhead. Kyle had caught a few hours of sleep, and Ruairí handed command back to him before stopping by the galley to gather a tray. He nodded to his guard and knocked before unlocking the door. He opened it but didn't see Senga. For the first time in half a score of years, Ruairí felt a consuming wave of panic. He dropped the tray and spun around to see Senga standing wide eyed behind the door with a dirk in each hand.

"What's wrong?" she asked. Ruairí gawked at her before he understood her question.

"What's wrong? I walk in here, looking for the woman I

left asleep in our bed, and the cabin appears empty. What was I supposed to think?"

*Our? What the bluidy hell? This is still my cabin.*

But Ruairí knew that wasn't the truth. He already thought of the cabin as theirs, along with the bed and everything in it. The moment he came together with Senga against the very door he now slammed shut, everything had changed once more.

"I didn't intend to worry you. I know someone has been outside the door for hours, and when I heard more movement, I wasn't sure who was there. You warned me not to trust anyone and to be careful. I was."

"Do most intruders knock before entering? I told you I'd return at midday."

"I haven't a clue what time it is. The porthole is too small to tell where the sun sits. And again, you warned me to be vigilant." She stepped forward and looked at the meal strewn across the floor before looking back Ruairí. "I didn't mean to anger you."

Ruairí caught himself gawking again. "I'm not angry. At least not at you. Perhaps a little at myself. I felt the same fear when I couldn't see you as I did last night when I worried that I wouldn't get to you in time. Woman, you are shaving years off my life. More than pirating does."

Senga returned the blades to sheaths in her boots that Ruairí hadn't noticed. She embraced him and sunk into his chest as his arms came around her.

"I wasn't trying to frighten you. I took your words of caution to heart. Perhaps announce yourself next time, and I won't draw a blade on you."

He breathed in a scent he'd recognized the night before, lilacs and roses. He calmed as she ran her hands over his back, and he looked down at the meal that now sat on the floor. To their great fortune, many of the items were wrapped in oilcloth and weren't ruined from being on the ground. She stretched for a kiss before bending to gather up what could be salvaged. She looked around for a drying linen but had no idea where he kept them.

"I'll get something to sop up the wine. Don't worry, little one."

After Ruairí wiped away the puddle of wine that trickled beneath the table, Senga laid out their repast. She moved to pull a chair to the table, but Ruairí was quicker. He grasped her waist and pulled her onto his lap.

"I prefer this," she purred as she pulled out a bannock and broke it in half before feeding it to Ruairí. Senga popped the other half into her mouth. She opened the wrapping on several other items before finding a wheel of cheese. She smiled, eager to cut it into pieces. Senga passed several to Ruairí before sighing as she took an unladylike-sized bite. She closed her eyes and savored the strong flavor. Cheese was a weakness for her. She loved it and could make a meal out of it any day of the week.

Ruairí watched as pleasure spread across her face near to what he saw when they coupled. He fed her another piece as she looked eager for what was clearly a favorite. He fed her several more bites until she sucked his finger into her mouth and released it with a pop.

"I shalln't eat it all, though I could." She fed him several pieces before cutting an apple into sections. They were more than halfway through their meal before either of them spoke. Hunger of more than one kind kept them silent.

"I know you can't remain below deck forever. I'm happy to bring you up to the deck and walk or stand with you, but I don't want you to come above deck alone. You can without a doubt trust the man who guarded your door, Tomas, and my first mate Kyle. If I can't be with you, you may go with them. No one else. Not yet."

Senga leaned against his shoulder as she stroked the hair at his temple. "I know what you and your crew do, Ruairí. I know what you are. I saw for myself what type of man sails for you, and they're the same type that frequent the tavern. I'll be careful and use due caution, but I won't break knowing I'm aboard a pirate ship. I came willingly."

Ruairí captured her fingers and kissed each one before bringing her hand to his cheek. He leaned into her warm palm. "What a treasure I found," he murmured.

"One that wishes to be plundered," Senga had discovered she quite liked the various euphemisms she could use with her pirate lover.

"Of that you need not doubt. I'll gladly do that morning, noon, and night. But I don't want you to feel you're a prisoner here, or that you're little more than a bed slave. I may look like a Viking and at times act like one, but I don't want you to feel trapped."

"That you care and are trying to reassure me speaks to who I'm discovering you are. I've seen glimpses of the man I've heard so many rumors about. You're fierce and could scare even the most hardened pirate, but I see a side I don't think you show many others."

"You see a side I've never shown anyone."

"Do you fear your crew will think you've gone soft? Would you rather I not go above deck either so you don't have to show your kinder side, or so I won't see your Dark Heart side?"

"So you know of that moniker. I suppose most people do. I don't worry that they'll see me as soft. There should be little doubt in their minds as to my true nature."

"And that true nature is ruthless?"

"Aye."

Senga took in the statement said so flatly. She supposed he was right. He admitted that no one saw the kindness he showed her. His true nature wasn't the gentle lover whose lap she sat upon. His true nature was one that made him renowned for his merciless attacks on merchant ships and privateers. Senga hoped they could both come to terms with the opposite sides of his personality. She closed her eyes as she rested against his chest. Content where she was, she didn't want further conversation to ruin it. Senga ran her fingers over the stumble on his jaw. She liked the prickle, but she forced herself to curb her desire to rain kisses along his throat. The man had just admitted he could be cruel. It didn't seem the right time to show more affection.

Ruairí felt the shift in Senga as she became more reserved. She continued to run her hand over his face, but she seemed introspective where she'd been playful moments ago. He wasn't sure what to say. He'd been honest, but he'd intended on reassuring her that he wouldn't regret bringing her along. Instead, she retreated from him.

"I don't want you to fear me."

She sat up and cupped his face in both hands. "I don't. I told you, I know who you are. I understand what you do and how you must be."

Ruairí gripped her wrists, but his touch was soft. "Then why did you retreat from me? Why sink into a shell?"

Senga looked at him with genuine confusion. "I didn't retreat from you. I didn't think it was the time to be overly affectionate when you reminded me moments ago that you aren't soft nor weak, despite your kindness to me."

"I find I desire your affection as much as I do your passion."

"I feel the same," Senga leaned in for a kiss.

"I want you to feel free to show affection. I crave it, in fact. It's been so long since I've felt any," Ruairí trailed off. He could tell from her face that she was eager to hear more, but he already knew she wouldn't ask. He scrubbed a hand over his face.

"I suppose I should tell you how I came to be a pirate if you're to live with me. I don't want you to feel as though I'm keeping secrets or am keeping you at arm's length." Senga nodded and offered him an encouraging smile. "You've heard me speak of my cousin Rowan. Perhaps you've met him, and I'm sure his reputation precedes him as well." Senga nodded again but said nothing. "When we were six and ten, I went on a trading voyage with my father. He's Rowan's father's younger twin. Rowan's father was the laird of the MacNeils of Barra."

Senga nodded.

"While my father and I were away, Rowan's father forced him to go on his semi-annual tour of their lands. They went twice a year to observe the planting and harvesting. Rowan had been before, but that spring the weather had been worse than usual. He argued with his father that it was too danger-ous, since much of their journey would take them along rivers and inlets. Rowan relented after his father insulted him in front of their men. He called Rowan a coward, so my cousin had no choice but to save face."

"I can't believe his father would do that," Senga murmured.

"Halfway into their tour, they made camp near what was once a stream. With the spring thaw and rains, it was a surging river. When the other men went out to scout, they left Rowan and my uncle arguing once more. Rowan walked away until he heard his father and his father's horse scream. The embankment had shifted and fallen into the raging water, carrying man and beast away. Rowan ran to fish him out, but his father cracked his skull against a tree limb as Rowan pulled him to safety."

Ruairí paused as if picturing the past.

"He got them both out of the water and collapsed next to the laird. He woke to arguing and someone kicking him awake. His father was dead, and they were accusing Rowan of patricide. They bound him and forced him to ride with his dead father's body tied before him. It was a sennight's ride before they made it home. His mother spotted them and fell apart when she saw her dead husband. She never even looked at Rowan."

"I don't believe that. A mother wouldn't ignore her son like that." Senga was quiet but adamant.

"Regardless, they threw him first into the dungeon, then

into the oubliette. He spent a month down there before my father and I returned. We tried to convince the clan elders that the idea Rowan would kill his father was preposterous. It was to no avail. The council wanted my father to be the laird. They were mistaken to believe he'd be malleable and weak, that they could force him to bend to their desires. My father was the softer spoken of the twins, but he was far wiser than his brother."

Senga still held doubts about Rowan's mother's reaction, but Ruairí had continued on, and she didn't want to miss any of the story.

"The night we returned, my father sent me to rescue Rowan. I pulled him from the oubliette and practically carried him to a birlinn. He was skin and bones after a month in the pit. We'd been similar in size and build to what we are now. I almost didn't recognize him. We sailed that night, intending to meet my father in a few days, but a storm blew in. Rowan became deathly ill, and I missed the meeting point with my father. We put ashore and found a tavern where the owner was willing to let us stay until Rowan recovered."

The next part of the story wasn't one he wanted to tell the woman he'd just begun bedding, but it was an important detail. He tried to hide his grimace.

"The woman who owned the tavern, really more a brothel, took good care of Rowan until he was well. I think we both felt indebted to her, and we each developed a relationship of sorts with her." Ruairí paused to see how Senga would react to him admitting he was with another woman. It was one thing for it to go unsaid, it was another to tell her.

"Ruairí, you weren't a virgin last night. Neither was I. You've made no proclamations, and I've made no demands. I met you in a tavern where I know you'd been before, but I'd never seen you. I already figured out that was probably because you spent more time in a private chamber than the main dining room."

Ruairí found all of a sudden that he wanted to make

proclamations and wouldn't have minded if she demanded fidelity. He wanted to offer it to her. He'd have to revisit that notion later. He could only nod before going on.

"The woman recommended a merchant ship we could work aboard once Rowan was on his feet again. She not only ran a brothel, but she was a smuggler too. The merchant ship was a pirate ship. Rowan and I became indentured to the captain." Ruairí tipped his head back as he looked at the ceiling. Those had been the hardest years of his life. He saw and did things he never imagined his conscience would allow. He was sure it was when his conscience died. "It changed both of us. Neither of us recognized the men we became, but we had each other and kept each other alive."

Ruarí tipped his head forward and looked into Senga's eyes to see if she'd ask for more details, but she nodded once and waited for him to continue.

"We sailed together for three years before the captain traded me to another pirate. I'd killed one of his men in a fight, and by rights, he could claim me as compensation for losing his man. I didn't fare well on that ship, but I was a leader. I led a mutiny and killed the captain before the crew. I did it with such ease and cruelty, the name Dark Heart was born. No one aboard this ship has ever questioned my right to be captain. Not long after, the captain of the so-called merchant ship died. Rowan inherited it at the captain's will, and the crew elected to make him captain. We've sailed together and apart for ten years."

When he stopped speaking, Senga said nothing, so Ruairí wasn't sure if she was waiting for him to go on or was struck speechless.

"Are you repulsed to hear I killed a man in cold blood?" He wasn't sure he wanted to hear the answer.

"Would you be sitting with me if you hadn't?"

"Probably not."

"Then I'm relieved you did."

49

"You're not at all how I expected. You don't do or say the things I expect."

"That's good. It'll keep you interested longer."

Ruairí understood what went unsaid. He knew Senga assumed his interest would wane, and he'd turn her out. He wasn't so sure, but he knew it was prudent not to make any false or rash promises. "I'm already very interested."

# CHAPTER SIX

Senga shifted on Ruairí lap as she prepared to retell a tale she'd not told a single person other than Alex. She hadn't thought of the gruesome details of the day her parents were killed in years. Grief over the loss of her husband and son had consumed her for a long time, then eventually, all the hollowness and loneliness morphed into one aching pit in her heart.

"There is more to my own story." She waited until Ruairí nodded before she went on. "My father was the laird of the MacLeods of Lewis. I was my parents' only child. My mother nearly died giving birth to me and couldn't have anymore. My parents were a love match and doted on me. I told you my father carved the cradle before I was born, and he carved the cross for my baptism."

Ruairí nodded, encouraging her to go on.

"When I was three and ten, a sickness ravaged our clan and weakened it. The MacLeods of Skye seized the opportunity and raided us. They killed my father while he tried to protect my mother and me. He'd been fighting in the bailey but saw the old Skye laird rush into the keep. We hadn't always been enemies, and my father knew the laird was more familiar with the keep than most. My father knew the laird knew of the secret alcove in my parents' chamber. My father fought his way to his chamber, but a Skye warrior ran him through as he tried to stab the laird who'd just slit my mother's throat."

Ruairí attempted to hide his grimace, but he wasn't convinced he succeeded. He couldn't imagine watching his mother and father be murdered right before his eyes.

"I tucked myself away and went unseen in the alcove. It's the only way I survived, the only way they didn't rape me. I stayed in the hidey-hole until the next morning, when my uncle 'coincidentally' returned from sailing to Canna. He returned with men willing to live and work for our clan until we were back on our feet. That is how I met Alex."

It didn't feel right to refer to Alex as her husband when she sat upon another man's lap in his cabin aboard his ship. Her new circumstances didn't change who Alexander was to her, but much like not wanting to hear about the brothel owner, Senga didn't think Ruairí needed the reminder. Ruairí was struck by the similarities in their stories, but while they both had the better father between two brothers, it was Senga's father who had been killed. As far as Ruairí knew, his father was still alive.

"I knew what everyone else did. My uncle coveted the lairdship because he'd been my grandfather's favorite. My father was born to my grandfather's first wife, a woman he never wanted and refused to like. My uncle was born to the woman who was my grandfather's mistress but became his wife less than a moon after my grandmother died. My uncle arranged the raid with the MacLeods of Skye in exchange for my hand. My aunt had little say, but she threatened to involve the church if my uncle dared hand me over at only three and ten. My uncle beat her for it, but he knew she wouldn't bend. It's what saved me that time."

Ruairí ran his hand over her back and gave her waist a small squeeze when she paused.

"I grew to know Alex when he was at our keep. He traveled quite a lot between Canna and Lewis. When I was five and ten, I was sure I was in love with him and he with me. And we were, if only in puppy love. Alex took me away from Lewis only days before I was supposed to sail for Skye. As I told you before, he posted the banns on Canna to hide it from my uncle. My uncle ruled much the way your uncle did. I remember hearing stories about him."

Senga tried to hide her grimace, but it made her shiver instead. Ruairí wrapped his arm around her waist and rested his hand on her hip.

"It didn't take long for me to get with child, and before I gave birth, my aunt had the cradle smuggled to me. Someone had tucked it away in an old unused chamber in an abandoned tower for years. I couldn't believe it when I opened the door to see a man from my clan with it in his hands. He said, 'From your aunt,' and nothing else. He put it down and walked away. I haven't seen nor heard from anyone else from my clan since then. It's as though we don't exist to one another. I suppose much as you and Rowan feel about your own clan."

Ruairí was sure he and Rowan had a great deal more anger toward their clan, but he didn't interrupt Senga.

"I wasn't angry while I had Alex and then a bairn on the way. But once I lost both of them and had nowhere to go, I found bitterness eating away at my soul. I mourned the loss of everything. The family I made, the family I left behind, the clan I grew up with, the home that was no longer mine. All of it. It took me a year before I realized I'd put myself into an early grave if I didn't pull myself together. That was far harder than anything that came before it. I didn't really want to, but if I wanted to survive, I had to. The charity of my neighbors and my uncle had nearly run out. I had to take care of myself, so I began working in the tavern. Not much changed after that until last night."

Just as Senga sat quietly during Ruairí's tale, he did the same for her. He wondered if she might cry, but when he looked at her, her eyes were dry. He realized she'd resigned herself to her past, just as he had his. There was no more grief left but he'd hung onto his bitterness, used it to fuel him every day he stayed alive. Ruairí understood that it was acceptance that drove Senga to keep going. They were as different as oil and water in that respect.

"You haven't had it easy, little one. Tell me true, has any other man every attacked you before? Assaulted you?"

She shook her head but paused before speaking. "They weren't the first to try. Part of the reason Alex did ask for my hand was because my uncle cornered me once, and it was Alex's appearance that saved me. Some men on Canna tried to proposition me, and when I refused, they threatened me. Those nights, I urged other women to distract them and stayed near my aunt and uncle. I managed to go unmolested. Last night was the only night I was ever truly in danger."

Ruairí exhaled air he hadn't realized was trapped within his lungs. He'd felt the familiar sense of rage build within him as he waited to learn whether there were other men to kill. Senga ran her hands over his ribs and chest.

"Don't be angry. There is no one else to avenge." Her soft smile eased the tension from between his shoulders as he handed her a cup of wine. She took a sip before passing it to him. He took a long draw, then eased her off his lap.

"I shall arrange a bath for you. It will be me who knocks but still lock and bar the door." Ruairí left before Senga could say anything. She went to her chest and pulled out the things she needed, and it surprised her how quickly Ruairí returned. She still didn't trust a crew she didn't know, so she asked who it was before she lifted the bar. A troop of men arrived with a large tub and several steaming buckets of water. It amazed her that there was hot water. It meant there was a flame somewhere on the boat.

"I detest cold food every day, so I allow one fire, and it's in the galley," Ruairí explained.

Senga didn't care at that moment where the hot water

came from. She wanted to strip and hop in. When the men departed, she shucked off the robe she'd thrown on and was ready to climb in when Ruairí lifted her once again, and her legs encircled his naked waist as he slid inside her. He settled them in the tub where they coupled once more. Senga found the feel of the lapping water to be the most sensual experience she'd ever had. Ruairí squeezed her breast as she rocked against him, her nub rubbing against his pelvis. She felt the tightness beginning in her core as she tried to gain more friction, but their slick skin made it harder.

"What do you want, little one? Tell me what you need."

"You. I just need you." Senga ground herself against him as his hands on her hips pressed down, giving her the position she needed to edge closer to release. Her head lowered to his shoulder, her teeth grazing his skin as his fingers bit into her flesh. The harder they each pressed, the wilder they grew. Both enjoyed the fine boundary between pleasure and pain, finding one merged into the other. Her teeth sank into his shoulder as she moaned, her muscles clenching around him. He barely pulled out in time.

They eventually washed one another, and Ruairí poured fresh water over her hair to rinse out the suds. They dried off and chatted about the various places Ruairí had traveled and where Senga dreamed of going. Her knowledge of geography surprised him, but he reasoned that she'd lived among sailors her entire life.

Once dry and dressed, Ruairí assured her it would be fine for her to come above deck. He warned it was windy and pulled a MacNeil plaid from the bed. Senga hesitated a moment before accepting it. She'd only ever worn a MacLeod or Sorley plaid. She knew the statement it made if she wore Ruairí's, but it seemed pointless to deny she was his mistress. In the back of her mind, the thought niggled that not even mistresses wore a man's plaid in public. It was a claim of ownership to wear a man's plaid.

"I'd like you to wear it, Senga. I saw your other ones, but I want to see you wear mine. Not the one of a clan that forsook you, nor another man's."

She could see the importance of her decision in his eyes, and she realized she wanted others to know she was his. The only thing she was unsure of was whether he was hers. She wrapped it around her as an arisaid and belted it in place. She turned to look at him and caught his look of awe.

"Did you think I didn't know how to put on an arisaid?" She was confused.

He shook his head and swallowed. "No woman has ever worn my plaid before." He adjusted it to cover her shoulders. "I've never wanted one to. I don't know that I ever want you to take it off." He spoke more to himself than to Senga.

"You don't need the plaid to know I'm your mistress, Ruairí. Everyone on this ship knows that. If I go ashore with you, everyone will surely know it there. The plaid doesn't matter."

Something flashed in Ruairí's eyes, and Senga regretted her words. "It does matter. It matters a great deal to me. You know as well as I do what it means for a woman to wear a man's plaid, especially a woman outside of the man's clan. I'm staking my claim to you, Senga. And by me giving this to you, I hope you understand the claim you have to me." There. He'd said it. They both stood in shock at Ruairí's profession.

"Do you mean that?" Senga's voice cracked, and Ruairí nodded.

"I don't know what the future holds for either of us. I don't know if in a sennight you won't be able to stand the sight of me. I don't know if in a moon, I'll regret trapping you aboard this pirate ship. I don't know if in a year's time, you'll wish you never met me. But I know that right now and for the foreseeable future, I want no one else. I knew that last night when Agnes approached me. I know it now because my mind can't fathom another woman. You've bewitched and enchanted me. You're my own selkie come ashore to woo me. I just pray you don't disappear."

"I'm not going to disappear, and I'm proud to wear your plaid."

"No one has seen this plaid since I first boarded the merchant ship. Rowan and I practiced speaking to do away with our accents and hid our plaids to keep people from knowing which clan we ran from. Once this became my cabin, I was willing to lay it out. It was no longer a secret that I'm a MacNeil. But no one else has seen it. I like the idea that the first time it's worn again, it's worn by you."

Senga strained to reach his jaw and gave him a quick kiss, unable to reach any higher. "Then let us get some air and sunshine." Ruairí trailed after Senga, amazed how the sight of her wearing his plaid seemed as normal as the sun rising and the moon shining.

# CHAPTER SEVEN

They spent the afternoon together on deck. Ruairí introduced her to several deckhands, and it shocked him that they were on their best behavior. It stunned him to see the manners they could show when a woman other than a whore was nearby. Her easy smile and knowledge of sailing went a long way to make her welcome. She no longer was a mystery to the men, and most no longer found her a threat. They stood together at the prow as the mist sprayed onto their faces. He encircled her in his arms as one hand rested around her waist and the other braced them by holding onto the railing. They continued to talk about places Ruairí sailed and how far into the Mediterranean he'd been. Senga expressed curiosity about the women she'd heard of, those who wore veils and were owned by men for their pleasure. She knew someone could draw a comparison between these women's circumstances and her own, but she didn't feel like Ruairí's possession even if he showed some possessiveness. It was just enough for her to feel cared for rather than oppressed.

They returned to the cabin for their evening meal, but he had to leave soon after they finished for his turn at watch.

When he returned, he slid into bed next to Senga. She snuggled next to him.

"Cold," she muttered in her sleep before draping herself over him as if to share her heat.

Ruairí woke her in the middle of the night with an aching need to join with her. Senga couldn't force her eyes open, but she fully knew the way Ruairí made her body demand their coupling. He gripped her wrists, pinning them over her head as he pounded into her. His need and dominance had always spurred her arousal, but this time, he pounded into her with an urgency that kept his weight pinning her to the bed. She discovered she enjoyed the feel of Ruairí taking after he'd always been so sure to give. She welcomed the harshness of how he surged into her over and over, but she could do little to move beneath him. She wanted this coupling to be for him after all the times he'd ensured she climaxed over and over before he did. She found her release just before Ruairí could no longer hold on, pulling out to spill his seed onto the sheet. She was back asleep before Ruairí knew it. Her soft breathing lulled him back to sleep as he spooned her.

When they woke in the morning, once again need overcame them. Ruairí eased from their bed and stalked naked to a chest in the corner. He lifted the lid before rummaging through its contents. Senga tried to peer around him to see what he searched for, but his hulking body blocked her view. When he turned back toward her, she caught sight of four lengths of satin. They resembled the veils he'd told her the women in the Mediterranean wore. She didn't want to think about how he acquired them, and she had no time to.

"Roll over, Senga," Ruairí's tone was soft, but the order was clear. She shivered in anticipation as she suspected she would enjoy whatever Ruairí intended. "Spread your arms and legs wide, little one."

When she didn't move quickly enough for him, he snapped one of the swaths of satin over her backside. The sting tempted Senga to draw out his command in the hopes of receiving another one. When he pinched her backside then slapped her sheath after nudging her legs apart, she decided resistance was worth the risk.

"You're testing me, aren't you?"

"Mmhmm," Senga moaned.

"Then you shall see how a pirate plunders his woman." Ruairí caught hold of one wrist then the other, quickly binding them to the headboard then repeating the process with her feet at the foot of the bed. He trailed his fingertips over Senga's back, smiling when he noticed the goosebumps rising on her skin. He knew her shivers came from anticipation not the cabin's temperature. He kneaded the ample flesh of her backside before trailing his fingers down the cleft and to her rosebud. "Have you had a man here, little one"

"No. It would be yours alone, *mo chaiptean*. All yours." Senga raised her hips in offering as she called him "my captain".

"I shall take your offer. Senga, I wish to finish inside you. I won't risk getting you with child, but I hate having to pull out. I want us to enjoy our release together."

"I want that too, Ruairí. I hate the feeling of you stopping when we're so close."

Ruairí eased off the bed and returned to the chest he'd drawn the satin veils from. He returned with a vial of oil that he heated by rubbing between his hands. He climbed back onto the bed, straddling Senga's thighs as he dribbled oil on each globe of her backside. He rubbed it in as she moaned and shifted restlessly. He once again trailed his fingers along the divide, but this time he tapped a finger against her rosebud. He pressed the tip, and Senga made herself relax, accepting the slight intrusion.

"I must prepare you, little one. But you must stop me if it's too much. I could seriously hurt you, and that's not my intention. I want you to enjoy this, but don't take more than you can for my sake. If you lie to me, I'll take you over my knee. I won't risk it."

"I will. I promise."

Satisfied that she was telling the truth, Ruairí poured oil into his hand, coating his fingers. He eased one into her, giving her time to adjust to the foreign feeling. When she didn't flinch or show any discomfort, he slid a second finger into her, stretching and widening in preparation for his cock. As one hand worked her, his other fisted his cock. He stroked himself as he pictured the moment his rod would sink into her. He paused long enough to pour oil onto his cock, making his hand glide over the taught skin and reassuring him that his entry would be easier. He poured more onto his length before pressing the tip into Senga. She inhaled deeply, making herself relax as the initial intrusion burned. She trusted Ruairí implicitly and knew he wouldn't do this if he was the only one who would find pleasure.

Ruairí watched as the tip of his rod disappeared into Senga's rosebud. He clenched his jaw against the need to force his way in to the hilt. He wanted to bury himself and ride her arse, but he wouldn't do anything that might intentionally harm Senga.

"I can take more, Ruairí. I won't break."

"I know, little one." He inched his way into her, and Senga discovered that the more he filled her, the more the discomfort eased. Once he was settled to the hilt, Ruairí leaned his body over hers, entwining his fingers with hers. He rocked, flexing his hips as he thrust slowly. Senga's moan was almost more than he could withstand as she pressed her hips up to meet him. "Do you like this?"

"Mmhmm. So full." Senga could barely form a logical thought as her body grew accustomed to the strange and foreign sensation, but when Ruairí released one hand and slid his beneath her, searching for her nub, she lost any rational thought. She allowed the sensations to swallow her whole. Ruairí worked the bundle of nerves until Senga couldn't keep from rocking against his hand. He increased the tempo and force as he thrust into her. She responded immediately, and

Ruairí knew they'd found yet another way to bind themselves to one another.

The sun was well above the horizon when Ruairí slipped from the cabin, leaving a slumbering Senga in their bed and a guard posted outside their door once more.

They developed a routine that followed their first day. They joined several times throughout the day and night. Ruairí would slip from the bed in the morning while Senga continued to sleep off the exhaustion from the night before. She marveled at how he needed so much less sleep than she did. Ruairí showed her a small library of books he kept hidden in a trunk. As the daughter and nephew of lairds, they were both taught to read. It was a rarity for someone to teach a daughter, but Senga explained that since she was their only surviving child, her parents prioritized her gaining an education. She spent most mornings reading. They ate their meals together and spent most of their afternoons together on deck. While Ruairí couldn't always stand looking into the distance with her, Senga stood with him when he was at the helm. He let her have a turn holding the wheel while he gave her instructions. It became obvious to Ruairí that even though she let him give her directions, she was already an experienced helmsman. He pointed out as much, but she only grinned.

They sailed south for a fortnight, skirting the coast of France until they reached Portugal. They anchored for a night, and Senga was barely aware they took on new cargo before setting sail for further down the coast. Ruairí came to bed so exhausted that neither of them stirred the rest of the night. It was the first time he didn't wake her in the middle of the night, so she awoke refreshed while he snored. She climbed over him with care to look out the porthole. There was nothing to see but open water. It was still early, the last of the pink hues of dawn fading into the clear blue skies of daytime. Over the past fortnight, Ruairí had pointed out which men he trusted with her safety and those he still watched. Senga knew enough of the crew to feel comfortable around them without Ruairí at her side. She dressed in a pair of leggings the barrel man gave her. He wasn't a man, but a boy of about twelve summers who spent most of his time in the crow's nest. They were a similar height, so the pants fit well on Senga. She looked back as she lifted the bar and unlocked the door. Ruairí didn't move, and she had a moment of worry since he was the lightest sleeper she'd ever met. She felt badly that he was so tired that his only movement was to breathe. She made her way above deck and found Tomas and Kyle speaking together near the rail. They smiled as she approached.

"I hope I'm not interrupting," she said.

"Not at all, lass," Tomas replied. He was still the man who guarded the cabin door, and rather than be angry about the post, he took it as a position of honor. He was chuffed with himself that Ruairí trusted him with such responsibility.

Kyle looked around her but frowned. "Where's the captain?"

"Still asleep. I almost feared he was unwell, but I think he's just exhausted."

Kyle still frowned but nodded. "I take it he doesn't know you're up here."

Senga bit the side of her bottom lip. "Not exactly."

"Lass," Tomas warned as he too looked at the stairs leading to the captain's cabin. Trepidation was written across his face.

"No, he doesn't. Like I said, he's asleep."

"You better return sharpish," Tomas cupped her elbow and tried to steer her back the way she came.

"Are you both occupied right now? Is there no one who can act as my nursemaid?"

"I know what you're doing, Senga, and it won't work. You

64

can't bait us into putting our necks on the chopping block with the captain," Kyle responded.

Senga crossed her arms, but her eyes shifted to two figures circling one another. She recognized one as Braeden, the boy who lent her the leggings. The other was an older man she recognized as being approved by Ruairí, but she couldn't recall his name. She watched as the boy tried to pick up a sword that was much too long for him. He looked like a child trying to play with his father's sword. She cringed as he struggled to lift it vertically as the older man circled him again. The older man thrust his sword forward and narrowly missed the boy as he leaped aside and inadvertently dropped his weapon. The surrounding men guffawed, and one ruffled the boy's hair. Senga saw the boy's embarrassment as he tried to stand taller. She remembered that feeling when she was his age and her father insisted she learn to protect herself, but she was far smaller than the lads her age, who trained with experienced warriors. Only one had been patient with her: her cousin Alfred, the son of the man who later orchestrated her parents' deaths.

Senga spotted a large chest that sat open. Even from across the deck she could see it was filled with various swords and knives. She stepped around Kyle and Tomas, who still tried to convince her to return to the cabin. She made a beeline to the chest even though Kyle was close on her heels. Senga peered inside and spotted just what she wanted. She pulled a falchion sword that resembled a meat cleaver from the pile. It fitted her hand well, but she could see that the chips in the blade made it more dangerous for sparring than if someone sharpened it. She returned it and pulled a cusped falchion from the chest. It was just over three feet long and the right weight for her to manage. She eased several blades out of her way before finding another cusped falchion.

"Put those back, lass, before you harm yourself," Kyle barked.

"You whittle like an old woman." Senga waved away Kyle,

then the man who spared with Braeden. She handed Braeden one of the falchion swords. "Let it rest in your hand. See if you can find the point where it will balance. Once you do, then grip the hilt. It's slightly different for each person, depending on the size of your hand. It looks like ours are matching pairs, but my hand's smaller than yours, so I must grip closer to the blade."

Senga waited while Braeden copied her actions until the sword no longer wobbled in his palm. "You have the sword in your right hand, but I can see you favor your left. That means despite having the weapon in your right hand, you're more likely to leave that side undefended. Square your feet off and then step back with the right."

Senga demonstrated each direction she gave Braeden until she positioned him as she wanted him. She showed him different types of thrusts and parries as she explained how and when to use them. She explained scenarios where certain strikes would be most effective. As she walked him through each move, she told him what open spots on her body to look for and the hints her movements couldn't help giving away. By the time she performed every move and was satisfied Braeden could at least attempt them without someone hacking him to bits, the pair had drawn quite a crowd. Halfway through his training, Senga remembered the other man's name was Snake Eye; at least that was how he was introduced to her.

"Snake Eye, help me show Braedon what these look like when sparring for real. Braeden, move far to my right. Try to copy my moves as I spar with Snake Eye."

Her suggestions received several laughs until she pulled her knife from her boot and stepped forward. Senga watched for the moment Snake Eye raised his sword in anticipation and launched into a series of thrusts and swipes she knew Braeden couldn't hope to mimic, but it made the men aware she wasn't there to play or pretend. She slowed her movements as she shifted to her right, forcing Snake Eye to follow.

Senga now stood where she could see Braedon without losing focus on her opponent. Senga and Snake Eye went through several rounds of mock battle. All the while, she called out explanations to Braeden about both her actions and how she could anticipate Snake Eye's coming movement. It amused the crowd that she was on the mark each time she predicted each of Snake Eye's attempts to knock the sword from her hand. She counted herself lucky that he was a good sport, and she could tell he'd trained several others before Braeden. He knew to keep the tempo of their match slow so the boy could follow and practice. Senga was enjoying herself until a roar of such rage swept across the deck, she nearly dropped both her sword and dirk.

# CHAPTER EIGHT

R uairí awoke feeling refreshed as he stretched, but he soon noticed he was alone in bed. He hadn't awoken that way since Senga came onboard. He sat up and looked around, but she wasn't there. His gut clenched as he thought about her going above deck without him.

Ruairí pulled on leggings and boots but forewent his leine as he strapped his sword belt around his waist. He charged up the stairs as he took in the crowd that surrounded crew members he couldn't see. He scanned the deck but couldn't find Senga, but he spotted Tomas. Ruairí stalked toward the man until Tomas pointed toward the crowd and shook his head, looking defeated. It was only then he heard Senga's voice as she explained how to fight, of all things, that he breathed again. He heard her call out various moves and defenses he was never aware she knew. He assumed she was commenting on two of his men sparring, but when the opponents shifted, so did the crowd. An opening showed Senga battling a man who was one of his most seasoned sailors. He knew Snake Eye would be careful with her, but as she twisted and swung, he was uncertain she'd be careful with Snake Eye. He watched in horror as she waited until the last moment to dodge a strike of Snake Eye's sword that could have cleaved her in half before she came up with her dirk below his chin.

A soul-deep roar traveled from his gut up his throat. He tore across the deck, men moving out of his path before he barreled through them. He heard a string of curses come from Senga that made many heads whip back around. Ruairí hadn't imagined she knew so many blue words. When he reached her, she had the grace to lower her weapons and point them to the deck, but she had the temerity to grin.

"Good morning, Captain," she chirped. Her bright smile made the men scatter as Ruairí's face turned a shade of red none of his crew had ever seen. She leaned forward and whispered, "Did you sleep well? You seemed tired."

Ruairí growled as he lifted her off her feet and hefted her over his shoulder. Her braid swung around his knees.

"Ruairí, stop. Put me down." She tried to reason with him. "I'm fine. You're making a far bigger deal out of this than need be. You can see I'm hale. I was just teaching Braeden a few moves."

When Ruairí ignored her, and they neared the stairs leading below deck, she reached down and pinched his backside as hard as she could. She suspected she'd find a bruise later. She felt as though she were flying as Ruairí dragged her back down to the deck.

"Don't," he warned.

"I could say the same to you. You humiliated me in front of your entire crew. I spent the last hour showing them I'm not some defenseless chit, and you undo that all by storming away with me like a barbarian."

"You dare be angry with me?"

"Yes. I dare. I'm spitting mad now, so we're quite the pair. I know what I'm doing, Ruairí. I know you found me and rescued me twice, but I'm not incapable of defending myself. You said as much when you found me outside the tavern. That was without a dirk in my hand because of the pails. I'd already stabbed one man when you arrived at my cottage.

When you killed the man in front of me, I rolled free, grabbed my dirk from my thigh, and killed one of the other two. I might have been at a disadvantage with three men and only dirks, but I can hold my own. You'd know that if you hadn't carried me away like a naughty wean."

Ruairí watched the lightning streaks of green flash in her eyes as her temper flared with each word. She was magnificent, and he felt like an arse. Once more, he'd panicked where her safety was concerned. As he looked down at her now, his mind cleared, and he recalled the explanations she offered to the moves she and her opponent made. She hadn't sounded fearful or breathless. She sounded in control. Not only that, Ruairí recognized her words to be right for each thrust and parry.

"Who taught you to fight?" he wondered aloud.

A cloud passed over Senga's face as she remembered her time spent training with her father. "Da," she mouthed as she couldn't force any sound from her. Her chest ached, and she was tempted to rub the tightness from it.

"He did a good job." Ruairí took her hand and led her back to the place where she'd been fighting only minutes ago. He handed her the falchion and dirk that lay on the deck. He drew his own two-handed broadsword. Ruairí knew she could never manage such a large weapon, as it was as long as she was tall, but he also knew he'd insult her if he chose a smaller weapon.

"Wait," she said before turning back to the chest. She dug deeper into the chest and brought out another cleaver falchion in good repair. She looked to Braeden who stared at her and Ruairí with saucers for eyes. "These are both falchions, but very different styles. You can see this one looks like a meat cleaver. You can use in a similar manner. Both are the right weapons for people of our build."

Ruairí respected her choice of words as she avoided calling the boy small. He was the same height Ruairí had been at that age, but he was still smaller than most of the crew. He hadn't put on the bulk from training that Ruairí had when he was twelve.

Ruairí focused on Senga as they circled one another. He gave her credit for patience. She refused to go on the offensive even though she made several moves to trick him into it.

"One of us has to strike, Ruairí. I'll follow your leadership," she taunted.

"Ladies first." As soon as the words left his mouth, Ruairí wanted to draw them back in. Before her parents died, Senga was a lady. She would've held the title, but as an orphan who ran away to marry below her, she forfeited the honorific. Ruairí saw the pain register on her face, and it tempted him to call an end to the match before it started.

"Good thing I'm not one," she whispered, but there was an edge he hadn't heard before.

Ruairí could have kicked himself. The least he could do was honor her desire to show her abilities to him and his crew. If she couldn't earn their respect from a title, she could do it with her actions. Ruairí tested her with a wide swipe of his sword. He was unprepared for the invitation it signaled. Senga responded with a series of punishing blows that made Ruairí realize she was far better trained than he expected. Throughout their mock battle, Senga breathed with ease and spoke to Braeden as though she was explaining a child's game rather than how to maim or kill. Ruairí felt sweat break out across his forehead, but she seemed unfazed.

The longer they fought, the more willing he became to lend some actual force to his strikes. Senga blossomed under the challenge, and she caught Ruairí off-guard more than once using moves he'd never seen before. It disconcerted him how she read his moves and what he unintentionally telegraphed to her without much thought. The fight ended when they locked swords, and it was clear neither would have their sword knocked loose from their hand. Senga dropped her dirk and grabbed a handful of his leine as she pulled him down to her. She smacked a loud kiss before stepping back.

She dropped her sword and squealed as he once again lifted her over his shoulder. He smacked her backside playfully. "You have a reckoning coming your way, little one."

"Do you promise?"

They walked away from the gales of laughter that erupted after minutes of stunned silence as they watched their formidable pirate captain match wits and skill with a woman half his size. They lost none of their respect for him, but she gained more in their estimation.

Ruairí eased Senga to the floor of their cabin as he sheathed his sword. He pulled the sword belt from his waist and dropped it on the foot of the bed.

"Are you furious with me?" After the fierceness she showed, Ruairí balked at the timidity in her voice. He could tell her fearfulness was genuine.

"No. Not anymore. You need to stop making me panic."

"Or perhaps you shouldn't overreact. I'm not always in danger." Senga softened her words as she ran her hands over his chest. Her finger glided over the smooth planes of his bare skin, and she marveled at the feel of the muscles as they jumped beneath her touch. "I know we met under less than auspicious circumstances, and you took me away from Canna to keep me safe. You told me which men I could trust and which ones I couldn't. I've listened to you. Tomas and Kyle knew I was above deck, and they even tried to convince me to return here before you awoke, but they kept an eye on me nonetheless. I took pity on Braeden when I saw him struggle with a sword far too large for him. Snake Eye was patient, but no one would intervene and give him the right sword."

Ruairí covered her hands on his chest with one of his while the other tucked strands of hair behind her ear. She titled her chin up and smiled softly as his cornflower-blue eyes gazed into her hazel ones.

"I remembered how he must've felt when my father sent

me to train with the boys my age. I was smaller than them and struggled to hold my own until my cousin Alfred fitted me with the right sword. My father had trained me, but mostly with a wooden sword and more on how to use my knives in close proximity to my enemy. It was Alfred who taught me to use a falchion because it was a size I could manage. He gave me the confidence I needed to go against the boys my age. I came out the victor more often than not. After my parents died, I was filled with hurt and anger. Alfred's time training me was the only thing I had to look forward to when Alex was back on Canna. Alfred even took me raiding a few times, and he tested me more than once against a real enemy. I know what I'm doing, Ruairí. But I didn't mean to frighten you."

Ruairí was speechless as Senga revealed more of her past. Part of him wanted to hunt down her cousin Alfred and throttle him for encouraging Senga to think she could fight against men twice her size, and then the other part of him wanted to thank the man for showing Senga how to fight men twice her size. Since he could do neither of those, he pulled her onto his lap as he sat on the edge of the bed. She caressed his shoulder as she traced his tattoo. He'd discovered she found running her fingers over his tattoo as soothing as he found the feel of her hand upon him.

"We still have a lot to learn about one another. I don't want you to feel stifled or like you can't be yourself. I'd just ask that you warn me before you do something daring, and I'll try not to panic at the first sign of something wrong."

"Thank you, *mo ghràidh*."

They hadn't used many terms of endearment, but Senga wanted to. She tested out a simple "my dear" to see how Ruairí would react. The smile she received was almost too brilliant to look at. His face went from being uncommonly handsome to breathtakingly beautiful. Once again, he looked more like Adonis than a mortal man. He took her breath away, and she couldn't believe she was the woman he'd chosen. She knew by now that he'd never brought another woman on any ship he traveled aboard.

"*Mo chridhe.*" My heart. Ruairí's voice was little more than a whisper as he pulled Senga in for a kiss different from the ones they'd shared before. There'd been kisses of passion and desire; there'd been kisses of tenderness and hope, and there'd been fun pecks. This kiss conveyed the love that was blossoming between them. They both felt it as they leaned their foreheads together, but neither voiced their emotions.

Neither had broken their fast, so Ruairí fetched a tray. They breakfasted as they discussed their current location near the southern coast of Portugal. Senga wondered more than once why they hadn't attacked or been attacked and why they'd only anchored once. She broached the subject as they ate.

"Why haven't we seen any other ships? Are we not traveling in the shipping lanes?"

"We weren't. I unloaded half my cargo back on Canna, but I also brought things onboard. I had an arrangement with a merchant near Lisbon and couldn't afford to lose any of it. Now we will sail closer to Seville, and we will encounter other ships." He scrutinized her, but her face showed little reaction. "Are you worried?"

Senga shook her head. "Bored perhaps, but mostly curious about why I haven't seen you attack anyone yet."

Ruairí chuckled. "Bloodthirsty wench, aren't you? Don't let the crew hear you, or they might mutiny and replace me with you."

Senga shrugged as she bit into the cheese she'd saved for last. "I wasn't sure if you avoided attacking because I'm here. I don't want to interfere with your livelihood or that of your men. If you get yourself worked up when you don't find me in the cabin, I worry about how you'll act if we come under fire. Perhaps it isn't so good that I'm here."

Ruairí reached across the table and clasped her hand. "Don't say that again. I want you here, and yes, I have panicked more than once when I fear you're in danger. However, that has been when it has come unexpectedly. I can prepare as best I can before an attack. I can know you're locked in this cabin. I reinforced the door with the bar, and it's thicker than normal to make it nearly impossible to hack through. It's not the same as walking into my cabin or waking up not knowing where you are."

"Fair enough. Do you think you'll find a ship you want to board as we sail closer to Spain?"

"I'm certain of it. Among the Dutch, Portuguese, Spanish, French, and Arab traders, there is always plenty to find near the tip of Spain."

"You mention traders, but what of the pirates from Spain and France?"

Ruairí turned her hand over and placed his palm over hers. His hand appeared to swallow hers. "They're no laughing matter. British and Scottish pirates are quick about our business. We attack, we kill, we plunder, we leave. We know the Spanish and French to torture their captives, especially those from other pirate ships."

Ruairí's tone made it sound as though he knew from experience. Senga walked around the table and sat on his lap. It was her favorite place to be besides joined with him. He saw the questions in her eyes, but she didn't speak. "Yes, I know firsthand. You've never asked about my scar."

Senga knew which one he referred to. She'd felt it countless times, and the first time she saw it, she wanted to burst into tears. The raised mark ran from his right shoulder, across his back, and wrapped around to his left rib cage. "I figured you'd tell me when you wanted to. The wound must've nearly killed you. I didn't see a need to revisit something like that unless you brought it up."

Ruairí appreciated that about Senga. She listened to everything he had to say, but she kept her curiosity to herself. He'd lied to many women about how he came by the scar, making up a different tale each time, but none were as extreme as reality.

"Rowan and I had been sailing two years before we made it as far as the Barbary Coast of northern Africa. We'd heard tales of the corsairs and their cruelty, but neither of us knew what to expect until we encountered them as we sailed past Gibraltar. They seemed to materialize out of nothing, and the attack was so unexpected, we had little time to ready ourselves. They boarded us and swept through the crew as though we were carved figurines rather than trained marauders. Rowan and I fought beside one another, but when he moved to defend his back, it left an opening to mine. The blade landed against my ribs, and as I tried to spin away, it sliced up to my shoulder. It was so severe, the corsair assumed I'd die where I lay. Rowan was able to defend himself and then drag me to the galley where he hid me until the battle was over. It was Rowan's turn to hover over me as I teetered between life and death. It was weeks before I could move from the bedroll they gave me. Rowan just about whittled himself to death with worry. To this day, it's still the most gruesome battle I've been in. They were savages but fought with a skill unrivaled by any other pirates I've ever encountered."

"Have you fought any since then?" Senga's hushed tones spoke of her fear, and Ruairí held her closer.

"Yes. But none were like those. I've prevailed since then. Small nicks and cuts, but none as bad as that one."

Senga kissed each of his shoulders as she squeezed his waist. "I thank God for that. I've survived raids and even gone on them, but the thought of that battle makes it hard for me to breathe. To think I might never have met you." They held one another in silence, once again unwilling to put into words what they both felt.

# CHAPTER NINE

Over the next three days, Senga could sense the tension rising among the crew. It was a mixture of anticipation and trepidation. Everyone was eager for the thrill and profit of an attack. Ruairí handed Braeden's training over to Senga, and she even began to train some of the other men who had used bloodlust as their only tutor. Ruairí made time to spar with Senga every morning, and the time spent bantering brought them closer.

In the evenings, Ruairí showed Senga the maps he used to navigate the North Sea, the Atlantic, and the Mediterranean. They'd had a smooth passage through the Bay of Biscay near France, but Ruairí regaled Senga with tales of choppy oceans and gale-force winds. They shared tales they grew up hearing that made them both curious and fearful as children. Ruairí told Senga more of his childhood than anyone other than Rowan knew. In turn, Senga shared the loneliness of being an only child. While she had her cousin Alfred, it was clear Senga and Alfred were nowhere near as close as Rowan and Ruairí. Senga learned they'd been born less than an hour apart with Rowan arriving first, making them more like brothers than cousins.

The fourth day changed everything for both Ruairí and

Senga. The morning was overcast, and the crew was sure it was a sign of a storm brewing. Senga looked to the clouds but wasn't convinced. She argued the clouds would blow over, and it would be warm. The morning clouds made it difficult for Braeden to scout the horizon, so it came as a poor surprise when Braeden whistled a warning of the impending attack. He spotted a Spanish carrack riding low in the water. Ruairí's ship was armed with cannons, a new artillery device he had little experience with. His men ran to load the cannonballs and gunpowder as Ruairí bellowed orders for their black sails to replace their white ones. The clouds shifted, and the carrack came into view. The three cannons on each side were visible even from a distance, and Ruairí was thankful Rowan had convinced him to outfit his ship with them.

As his crew prepared to attack the merchant ship, he spotted Senga handing weapons to the crew. He stormed over to her and lifted her around the waist before hauling her toward their cabin.

"Haven't you any sense? You see us preparing for attack, and you're still standing on the deck. I told you, you were to go to the cabin and bar yourself in when the ship engages in a battle. Why were you still up there? A cannonball could land on the deck any minute, and it could kill you." Ruairí burst through the door and dumped Senga onto the bed before spinning around.

"Oh no, you don't. If you had the time to carry me down here, you have a moment to say a proper goodbye." Senga grasped his elbow and tugged until he turned around. "I didn't mean to worry you. I wanted to help and was handing over the last weapon before I planned to come below here. I don't want to be a distraction to you, but I also don't want you to fight without us saying goodbye." Her unspoken words hung between them.

Ruairí pulled her into his arms, and their bodies pressed together as they had so many times before, but this time there was an urgency born of fear rather than need. Senga cupped his jaw and held on as she smattered kisses over his cheeks before they came back together for another searing kiss. Ruairí let go and looked at her for a long moment before stepping back. Just before he walked through the doorway, he turned back to Senga.

"Stay here where you're safe. Senga, I love you."

He closed the door before Senga could respond. She stood there stunned but jumped when she remembered to lock and bar the door. Once she sat on the bed, she felt her world tip. At first, she thought it was the shock of Ruairí's declaration, but she realized it resulted from cannons firing from the holes along the side of the ship. The vibration rattled almost everything within the cabin, along with Senga's teeth. She moved to the porthole and was glad it was on the correct side of the ship for her to see the impending battle.

Senga didn't have to wait long before Ruairí's crew was swinging grappling hooks onto the deck and rails of the Spanish boat. She grasped the table behind her when she made ready for impact. Once the boat stopped rocking more than normal, she returned to the porthole. She watched with fascination as the crew laid planks from their ship to the Spanish deck and began running across. She saw Ruairí lead the way as he swung from ropes on the *Lady Charity* to the ship he was about to commandeer. The battle became a blur as Spaniards tried without success to board the *Lady Charity*. She strained to follow Ruairí as he moved about the deck, but she often lost sight of him. Senga forced herself not to panic when she couldn't see him, and she convinced herself to have faith that he'd survive this battle just as he had countless previous ones. As she watched the gruesome scene unfold, her mind echoed Ruairí's last words.

*I love you.*

Senga knew in her heart she loved him too, but the thought of saying it out loud terrified her. She knew it should be easy for her to respond. After all, she felt the same way, but the words lodged in her throat every time she thought about telling Ruairí when he returned to the cabin.

The battle felt interminable as it raged on now moving between both decks. Senga could hear the pounding of feet and the screams of pain from above. She walked to the corner where she kept her falchions. Ruairí had gifted them to her. Senga still had the two dirks she kept in her boots, along with the one strapped to her thigh. She pulled off the skirts she still wore whenever she wasn't sparring, then unstrapped the knife before kicking off her boots. Senga changed into the leggings and replaced the knife along her thigh high enough to be covered by the leine she pulled from Ruairí's chest. She swam in it, but it hid the knife. She pulled on her boots and found another belt in Ruairí's chest. When she began digging, she'd hoped she'd find the type where she could sheath more daggers. She breathed a sigh of relief when she found one, even though she had to improvise fastening it since she was much narrower than Ruairí. She knew where Ruairí kept more blades, so she sheathed three more dirks into the belt. Then she waited.

Senga heard feet clomping down the stairs, then boots stomping in the passageway before the sound of an ax struck the door. She would've pushed the table or chests against the door, but they were all anchored to the floor. When a second ax joined the first, Senga knew the door wouldn't hold forever despite being thicker than normal. Unsure of what type of weapons the enemy held, she was certain she didn't want to be visible when they opened the door. She crept across the cabin to hide behind the door. It wasn't long before the door splintered from the force of the dual attack. It swung open so hard, it nearly hit Senga. She held her breath as the first man rushed in. She counted to three to make sure he was in line with her before she launched two dirks at him, one sinking into his neck and the other between his shoulders. The man staggered before pitching forward. Senga pulled two more dirks out as the door slammed shut behind the second attacker. Senga leaped forward before the man turned all the way toward her. She aimed once more for the neck, and when she felt that blade wedge into the man's throat, she thrust the second dirk just below his sternum. She twisted as she levered the hilt down and pushed the blade up. Senga intended to do as much damage as she could. Despite having two knives embedded in him, the second attacker swung at Senga, coming too close to her right cheek. She recognized the sword as one Ruairí had called a scimitar. While it had a longer reach, it was hard for the man to maneuver in such close quarters. Senga pulled the dirk from her thigh and slashed at the man as she fumbled to reach one from her boots. Once armed with both, she slashed and struck with such ease, the man paused for a moment. It was just the time Senga needed to bury the two blades into his chest. His face showed his shock before his eyes turned sightless, and he fell to the ground.

Senga didn't move. She waited to see if anyone followed the men or if there was anyone else in the passageway. When she heard nothing, she pulled all her knives free and placed them back in their sheaths, not bothering to wipe any clean. Now that they'd breached the cabin, she knew she wasn't safe in such an enclosed space. She'd be safer finding somewhere to hide on deck. The hold was where the Spaniards would attempt to reach, so she had no intention of being in that enclosed space either. Senga pushed her braid beneath the collar of the leine she wore and tore a strip from the bottom to tie over her head both to keep her hair from her eyes and to hide it. She hoped it would make it less obvious at first glance that she was a woman. She grabbed both of her falchions before slipping from the cabin.

Senga inched her way toward the stairs and then crept to the deck. She waited and watched before moving forward slowly. She looked around and could see Ruairí's crew still had the upper hand, even though there were bodies strewn across the deck. Senga spotted Tomas a moment later, as he was a mountain of a man. He fought two Spaniards at once while Kyle kept another man from reaching the wheel. Senga looked toward the other boat and tried to find Ruairí. When she spotted him on the other ship, she ducked behind a stack of barrels and peered around, never taking her eyes off him. She felt like she was crouched there forever before time slowed to a stop, and her vision tunneled to where Ruairí fought two men. There was no way he could see the third man approaching from behind him. Senga was out from behind the barrels and across the deck before she thought about what she was doing. She leaped onto the rail and a plank as she pulled a knife out. She hurled it across the divide and watched it land in the man's throat, but not before the now-dead man's sword cut across Ruairí's ribs. Senga saw blood spread through the material of Ruairí's leine as he continued to fight the men in front of him. He didn't slow despite the wound, but Senga knew he couldn't keep up his defenses forever now that he was bleeding. She watched in horror as Ruairí stumbled backwards and a sword pierced him below his ribs. Senga's battle cry would be one the crew would talk about for years to come. Senga was across the planks and onto the Spanish ship before any of her victims realized what was coming. She struck without mercy as she fought her way to Ruairí's side. Senga cut down men twice her size with the confidence that years of training brought. She hadn't sparred during her time on Canna, but the few days spent practicing aboard the *Lady Charity* had been enough to remind her body of what it could do.

Ruairí's crew would later say she fought like the shield-maidens they were sure she was descended from. Senga felt the nicks and cuts from the various encounters, but she never received wounds like Ruairí's. She reached him as he sank to his knees, his neck wide open for attack. She swung her cleaver falchion down onto one of Ruairí's opponents as he raised his arm to attack. The man's forearm landed on the deck with a thunk as blood sprayed onto Ruairí's face and chest. Both the enemy and Ruairí turned to look toward her, stunned, as she parried with Ruairí's other opponent. She cut down both men and stood over Ruairí's body daring anyone to come near her. Many of the enemy took one look at her bared teeth, the blood splattered on her, and the determination in her eyes and chose other prey.

Ruairí could feel nothing but the searing pain along his ribs. He felt as though someone had cut him in half, and he wasn't sure he was actually still in one piece. He saw Senga jump in front of him and tried to reach for her, but his body was unwilling to cooperate. His head felt as though it floated a mile above him, and he shook it to clear the dizziness. He tried to call out to her, to tell her to hide rather than fight, but no sound came from his mouth as he lay prostrate at her feet. He turned his head toward her, so he could see every attack she warded off and every man that fell dead at her feet. He wanted to both praise and punish her for taking such risks. He'd told her to remain locked away in their cabin, and she'd disobeyed him. Now he couldn't protect her. The ironic thought she was doing a fine job protecting him crossed his mind before everything went black.

# CHAPTER TEN

The battle lasted less than an hour, but Senga was sure it lasted the entire day. By the end Ruairí's crew was victorious, but suffered serious casualties including their injured captain. As Kyle issued orders for the men to empty the hold and transfer all the booty to their ship, Senga issued orders for four men to move Ruairí to their cabin. He groaned enough while they carried him to convince Senga he wasn't dead. She entered before the men carrying him and swept the table clear before ordering him placed upon it.

"Get me any and all alcohol you can find. I need a candle lit and boiling water. Now."

She didn't look around to see who carried out her orders, she just heard running feet and the murmur of voices moving away from the cabin. Senga tore open Ruairí's shirt and wanted to heave when she saw how deep the wound was on his front. She stepped around him and managed to pull him mostly onto his side so she could see the wound to his back. That wasn't as severe as she imagined, even though it still bled profusely.

She pulled clean linens from the chest where Ruairí stored them and began cutting varying lengths of bandages. Snake Eye returned with an armful of jugs and bottles Senga knew contained whisky and ale. She glanced over at him before looking back at Ruairí.

"Thank you. I'll look at that gash on your head when I'm done with the captain."

Snake Eye only nodded as he stared at Ruairí. He moved aside when another man arrived with two pots of boiling water. While she waited for someone to light a candle, she said a prayer of thanksgiving that she'd brought her sewing kit with her. Until then, she'd darned some of Ruairí's clothes, but otherwise it sat unused in her chest.

Senga looked at the wound to Ruairí's back and decided that was the better one to start on. He'd have to rest on either his front or his back when she worked on the opposite side. She would rather he rested on his back than his stomach since that wound was far worse. Senga grabbed a jug and pulled the stopper loose. Senga looked at Ruairí as she took a long drag of whisky. She poured hot water into the wash basin and scrubbed her hands with soap. She had no idea why it mattered, but she learned from her mother that she should never tend a wound with dirty hands. Senga also knew she would have to put Ruairí in far more pain before she could ease his pain.

"Hold his arms and legs," she ordered anyone and everyone. She folded a strip of linen and put it between Ruairí's teeth. "He'll buck even if he doesn't awaken. You cannot let him loose."

Senga gritted her teeth as she rolled him back onto his side and the men took hold. She didn't even look to see who helped her before pouring a liberal amount of whisky into and around Ruairí's wound. He writhed in pain and groaned, but his eyes never opened.

"Keep holding him," she ordered as she wiped away the blood and grime from near the gash with linen she dipped into the boiling water. Senga spotted the lit candle and pulled a needle and thread from her sewing kit. She held the needle in the flame until it glowed then she passed the thread through the flame, too. She paused and tilted her head to the ceiling, eyes closed as she prayed. Without a word, she began to sew Ruairí closed.

Ruairí felt a burning unlike anything he'd felt since his battle with the corsairs years ago. He knew it should not have surprised him, since the ship they encountered was Spanish, but the crew were Barbary pirates. They were the same sort of men who had attempted to kill him years ago. *Apparently, they were back to finish the job.*

Ruairí struggled to open his eyes, but they refused to cooperate. He sensed people moving around him, but it was as though he had wool in his ears. He couldn't hear or see anything. The burning wouldn't stop, and his body tried to pull away, but something pinned him down. He willed his body to fight the weight so he could escape the pain, but both the weight and the pain were unrelenting. He tried to yell, but he was sure nothing came out besides a groan. Ruairí tried to focus on what was happening, but nothing made sense. His mind seemed to be telling him to float away as if on driftwood. As he tried to fight against it, he smelled the lilac and rose scent he'd forever associate with Senga. It wafted to him, and his mind won. He drifted into blackness.

Senga sewed as quickly but carefully as she could. She poured whisky over the wound several times as she created a row of even, small, and tight stitches. When she finished stitching his back, she placed a stack of bandages on the table and told the men to roll him back over. She wiped her brow and took another long swig of whisky before she moved onto the wound below his ribs. "Hold him tighter. This time will hurt even more. The wound is far deeper."

As she poured the whisky over the gaping hole, she could see further into the gash. She was sure she could see the tip of his rib. She swallowed the bile that wanted to rise in her throat. With no medicinal flowers or herbs, there was nothing she could do to pack the wound and prevent infection. She had to decide how she would stitch the wound closed. She knew it wasn't enough to just stitch the top layer of skin, leaving an open tunnel to his insides just below the surface. However, she feared sewing it so tightly that the flesh couldn't grow back properly causing his body to rot at worst or diminish his range of motion at best.

Senga once again tilted her head back as she looked to the ceiling. This prayer was far longer as she asked God to guide her in how to heal the man she undoubtedly loved. She pushed the thought of love out of her mind as a wave of regret tried to consume her. She wished she'd stopped him before he left and said it back to him. Now he might never know.

She worked through the afternoon as she took care stitching together what she could within the wound then the surface. When she was done, she fell into the chair Tomas rushed to push beneath her. He, Kyle, Snake Eye, and a man she learned they called Rollo had helped her throughout the surgery, doing any and everything she asked. She swept her tired gaze to Kyle before swallowing the tears that wanted to force their way out. She'd save that for when she had privacy.

"We have to go ashore somewhere, Kyle. I have to collect medicinals for him, otherwise, I fear we will lose him to infection."

"It may take us days to sail somewhere we can anchor," Kyle shook his head.

Senga was on her feet with a blade beneath Kyle's throat.

"You either find somewhere to sail to or don't fall asleep." She nicked his skin to make her point. "You saw me today. I know you did. Don't doubt my willingness to sacrifice you, any of you, for him."

Kyle pushed her wrist away before nodding. "I want him to survive too, Senga. He's my friend as much as he's my captain. I'll do what I can, but we aren't in friendly seas. You may not know it, but those weren't Spaniards. They were

Barbary corsairs. They buccaneered the carrack from a Spanish captain before we found them. We passed Gibraltar but are still close to the north coast of Africa. We must sail closer to Europe, but that'll bring about danger from Spanish and French pirates. Even if we go ashore, none of us speak the language well enough to ask for what you need. Our vocabularies are a mite more limited and specific."

Senga glared at him knowing he meant they only knew how to order drinks and women. She walked around to one of the maps she knocked to the floor earlier. She picked it up and held it out to Kyle.

"Where do you think we are?"

Kyle pointed to the map and the area near the southern tip of Spain. Senga bit her lip.

"It'll take at least six days to sail just to the south of England. We can't wait that long. He could be dead by then. Are there no bays or coves we could sail into? I could go ashore and look for the few plants I have to have. We wouldn't have to see or speak to anyone."

Kyle looked between the map and Senga who still held the dirk. "We can try."

"That's all I'll ask for."

# CHAPTER ELEVEN

Once the men helped her move Ruairí to the bed and left the cabin, Senga sank onto the chair beside the bed. She took his hand and breathed a sigh that it was neither too hot nor too cold.

"You can't leave me alone on this ship full of pirates, Ruairí. Stay with me. I need you, *mo chridhe, mo ghaol.*" My heart, my love. Senga clenched her eyes closed, but the tears still leaked from them. "Why did you have to tell me you love me then walk away? I never got to say it back. I didn't even get to think about it." Senga let the tears fall. "I don't even know if I can tell you. Every man I've loved or trusted has abandoned me to death. My father, my husband, my son, and now you might too. Ruairí, I need you too much. I can't let you go. But perhaps, if I don't love you, then you'll live. Is it my love that kills the men in my life? Am I a curse that brings nothing but sorrow? Live, and I'll leave you. Not because I want to, but if that's the sacrifice God demands, then I'll walk away knowing you're hale once more."

She bent to kiss the back of his hand, and she was sure she felt a meek squeeze of her fingers, but when she waited and watched, Ruairí did nothing else. The only movement was the shallow rise and fall of his chest.

The next four days passed with little to distinguish night from day as Senga refused to leave Ruairí's side. She fed him broth sip by sip and insisted he have water and nothing else to drink. She bathed his wounds with whisky, then linens soaked in more boiling water. She changed the bandages throughout the day and night. She kept vigil, praying he wouldn't develop a fever. She awoke early on the fifth morning to an inferno blazing beside her forehead. She'd fallen asleep once again leaning against the bedside, holding Ruairí's hand. She reached out to touch his skin but already knew what she'd find. She dipped a cloth into the basin of water and placed it onto his forehead before going to the door and calling for Kyle. Senga paced the cabin while she waited and nearly jumped out of her skin when Kyle walked in.

"He's developed a fever. We can't wait any longer to go ashore. I know we must be close to the north of France by now. There has to be somewhere we can go ashore. I don't need a village or town. I just need somewhere with an open field or trees nearby."

"It's not that easy, Senga." Kyle held his hands up as Senga reached for a dirk. "I'm not disagreeing with you, nor am I saying no. I'm just warning you it's not as simple as spotting land and weighing anchor."

"I know that. But you have to do something, or we will lose him." Senga did exactly the opposite of what she intended. She burst into body-wracking sobs as she sank to her knees. She hadn't sobbed in years. Senga believed most of her tears dried up when her husband and babe died. Now they flooded her cheeks and dripped from her chin. Kyle eased her to her feet and led her to a chair, but before she could sit, she heard a croak. She looked to Ruairí and saw he reached out his hand to her. Kyle helped her to the beside and pushed the chair under her.

"Sen--" Ruairí's voice was too hoarse to say more. Senga tilted a cup of cool water to his lips but only allowed him enough to wet his throat. "Senga."

He said no more but his fingers wrapped hers even if his grip was weak. Senga looked up to Kyle, pleading with her eyes. He nodded and left the cabin.

It took another day before Senga heard a call to drop anchor. She looked out the porthole but couldn't see land. Ruairí hadn't moved or said anything else since he whispered her name. She continued to speak to him throughout the day and night, even though she wasn't sure if he could hear her.

"I must go ashore, *mo chridhe*. I'll try not to be long, but I must search for anything I can use to bring down your fever. Don't go anywhere until I get back." She tried to infuse some humor into her voice, but it sounded more like begging to her own ears. Tomas rowed her ashore, but they had to wade the last few feet. "Bluidy hell, that's brisk," she grumbled to herself, but it gave her an idea.

Tomas helped her climb a natural path to the top of the cliffs they stopped near. She looked around and wasn't sure what she'd find. She'd seen trees as they approached, so she hoped she might discover something she could use. The pair moved in silence toward the trees, keeping their eyes peeled for anyone or anything that might alert their presence. When Senga arrived at the first few trees, she worried that she'd wasted everyone's time, but as she moved further into the woods, she could have whooped with joy. She spotted yarrow, which was the most important medicinal she needed. She found the wormwood that would work well with the yarrow to keep infection away from the wounds; Senga had seen small red streaks beginning to form around the edges of his front wound. She also found cloves, henbane, and angelica. They were all ingredients she could use to bring his fever down and help him fight infection from the inside out.

As she looked around, another thought came to her. She'd considered none of the items Ruairí's crew ransacked from the corsairs' ship, but she remembered something her mother once told her about. She'd explained to Senga that the myrrh spoken of in the story of Christ's birth could also heal. Her mother told her it came from far-away lands and had a distinct smell. Senga wondered if there'd been any in the cargo they plundered.

Once she gathered everything she needed, Tomas rowed her back the *Lady Charity*, and she set to work making possets and a tincture for Ruairí. Even in his unconscious state, his face scrunched as the horrible tasting brew slid down his throat. Another five days passed as they sailed further north. They made slow progress, with a headwind that forced them to keep their sails lowered. Senga added changing the possets and brewing the tincture to her routine. Senga also demanded that men bring buckets of seawater to the cabin along with the tub. She ordered Tomas and Snake Eye to help her get Ruairí in and out of the tub. She had him soak in a cold bath thrice a day for as long as she dared keep him in the water. Senga was desperate to get his fever down, but it continued to burn even though the red streaks had faded and neither the front nor the back wounds smelled putrid. Despair was setting in, and Senga turned away most of the food brought to her. She was coming to terms that the worst would happen when they turned a corner at last.

Senga dozed next to Ruairí, his hand in hers and her head resting on her other arm as she leaned on the mattress.

"*Mo ghaol*, what I wouldn't give for a bowl of lamb stew right now."

Senga jerked awake to find Ruairí looking at her. His eyes were clear, and his skin was no longer clammy. She stared at him as though he were an apparition, and he chuckled. Her arm swung out to slap him for laughing at her, but she caught herself and tucked it by her side.

"I'd hoped for a hug and a kiss. I've missed you."

"How could you have missed me when you've been unconscious for the better part of a fortnight?" Senga was already exasperated.

Ruairí's brow crinkled before he spoke, "I'm not sure, but I'm certain I could hear your voice even when I couldn't make out your words. I kept trying to call out to you, but you never seemed to hear me. I tried to squeeze your hand when I felt yours in mine, but my fingers never cooperated. The harder I tried, the deeper I seemed to fall into blackness."

"I'm so relieved you're awake. I---" she couldn't finish, and only shook her head.

Ruairí tried to raise his arm but felt his stitches tug. "Come to me, little one. I'd feel you next to me." Senga gingerly moved to the edge of the bed but didn't dare rest her entire weight on the mattress. "No. Not close enough."

"I don't want to bump your wound or jostle you."

"And I don't want to wait any longer to hold you." There was just enough space for Senga to lie on her side facing Ruairí. She stroked his cheek, and his eyes began to drift closed. He clasped her wrist and stopped her. "I'm not ready to sleep again. I've done enough of that. I'd look at you and hold you. Kiss me, Senga."

She brushed her lips against his, and the strength he had to deepen the kiss surprised her. Fear, frustration, passion, and love coalesced into a need that neither could control. Ruairí ran his hand over every part of Senga he could reach, and she skimmed her fingers over his chest.

"I need you, but I know I'm unable to do anything," Ruairí grumbled.

"I don't care. I can wait. I'm just thankful your fever broke. You've scared years off my life," her voice trailed off.

He kissed her nose. "After I make love to you until neither of us can see straight, I have a bone to pick with you." It was the first time either of them referred to their coupling as making love. Senga's hazel eyes stared into Ruairí's blue ones, and she knew what they shared was no longer about careless tumbles and tupping. It had become much more long ago, but to hear him say the words was as astonishing as his profession of love.

"A bone to pick with me? How about the one I have to pick with you for nearly dying?"

"We could easily have been in the same boat. I was awake when you came across those planks. I saw you fight those corsairs. You could've gotten yourself killed. I told you to remain here."

Senga pointed to the splintered door that didn't close all the way. "You must not have noticed that this cabin isn't as impenetrable as you believe. I killed two men here, knowing I couldn't remain in such an enclosed space. I went above deck to hide, but when I saw the man rush at you from behind, I chose you. I chose you over everything else." Senga felt the tears pool in her eyes. "Bluidy hell, I've become a watering pot since they injured you."

Ruairí wiped the tears and kissed her. "I would never have you shed tears over me."

"You're days late to stop that."

Ruairí smiled, "Tongue as sharp as ever. No mercy for an injured man?"

Senga tugged gently on his hair. "It ran out when you tried to worry me into an early grave."

"You look exhausted. The circles under your eyes are very dark. Have you slept at all?"

"A little here and there."

Ruairí ran his hands over her sides and then her bottom. "You've lost weight too."

Senga quirked a brow, "We both have."

"Senga," he warned.

"Ruairí," she mimicked.

They sank into another kiss until both of them drifted into a deep sleep.

# CHAPTER TWELVE

After a fortnight in bed, Ruairí demanded to go above deck. When Senga said she wouldn't allow it, she was certain the vein in his temple might pop. She acquiesced when he agreed to remain seated while he was on deck. He argued the fresh air and sunshine would do them both good, and Senga had to admit she agreed.

The wind had shifted, and they were making progress back along the coast of England. Senga and Ruairí agreed they'd sail toward Glasgow since it was time for Ruairí to pay his fealty to the Earl of Argyll. He and Rowan both sailed under the earl's marque when they needed an alibi and the disguise of being honest merchants. It was too late for them to sail up the other coast of the English isle, and he preferred Glasgow since it was a safe distance from the earl's far reach. Ruairí also knew Rowan was due to sail into port soon.

Senga watched the crew hoist the white sails once more as they approached the entry to the River Clyde. Ruairí sat beside her, but he was shielding his eyes and trying to see what looked like a blurred lump to Senga. He pushed himself to his feet, and Senga rose to hers. She put her arm out, but he stepped around it and walked to the rail.

"Young Braeden, is that the *Lady Grace* I spy?" Ruairí called up.

"I do believe so, Captain."

"How can you tell? I can barely tell it's a ship," Senga asked, stunned.

"Sixth sense I suppose, though Braeden has a clearer view than we do." He looked to Kyle, who stood at the helm. "We put ashore now."

Ruairí needed to see Rowan and explain what happened before they all arrived in Glasgow. A tremendous scene would unravel on the docks if Rowan saw Ruairí was injured. Ruairí knew his cousin would be livid and want revenge. Ruairí had to admit he rather wanted it too, but he was satisfied knowing that Senga was unharmed. Ruairí wasn't sure he wanted to keep her onboard knowing the danger, but he also knew he couldn't go anywhere without her.

It was a few hours later that Ruairí and Senga watched as a couple lowered themselves into a dinghy and were rowed ashore. They followed in their own dinghy. When they reached land, Ruairí climbed out first and gained his balance before reaching for Senga, but she'd already stepped onto the beach.

"Cousin!" Senga heard a voice that sounded remarkably similar to Ruairí's, and when she peered around his shoulder, it shocked her to see a man who could pass for Ruairí's twin.

"Rowan. And Caragh. It's a pleasure to see you again." Ruairí laughed as Rowan growled and Caragh turned a deep shade of red. Ruairí had met Caragh under less-than-honorable circumstances several months earlier. Ruairí reached a hand for Senga, and it was his turn to growl when he saw Rowan's appreciative look. But before either man could introduce the women, they ran to one another and embraced. A tangle of strawberry and raven locks blew in the wind as the women stood together.

"Senga?"

"Aye, Caragh. What are you doing with Ruairí's cousin?"

"I'd ask the same of you. How did you come to be aboard a pirate ship? Did you go willingly?"

Senga leaned back to get a clear view of Caragh. "Of course, I did. Did you not?"

"Well---"

Senga released Caragh and drew her blade as she turned to Rowan. Ruairí howled with laughter as Rowan put his hands up in surrender, and Caragh grabbed her wrist. Ruairí limped over to Senga and wrapped his arm around her. "She's fierce, Cousin. I'd be sure she hears the story from Caragh and not you."

"Senga, it's a long story, but I ended up on Rowan's boat after a night raid. I'm glad that I did. He's my husband now."

Senga stared at Rowan before smiling at Caragh. She put her blade away, and they embraced again.

"You know each other?" Rowan dared to ask.

"Yes. Rowan, you know how my mother was your mother's best friend. Senga's mother was my mother's cousin. They all grew up on the Isle of Lewis together. When my mother took me back to Lewis each summer, the same summers I went to Barra, I always played with Senga." Caragh waved Rowan closer, and the look of love they exchanged reassured Senga that all was well. The women were similar in build, and while their hair and eyes were different colors, their faces looked quite similar once they stood beside one another.

"Ruairí, what happened to you?" Rowan got around to asking.

"A run in with a Spanish ship filled with corsairs."

Senga watched as all the color leached from Rowan's face before rising in a shade she could only liken to burgundy.

"Don't worry," Ruairí assured him. "Between my crew and Senga, they're all dead."

"Senga?" Caragh and Rowan chimed.

"Aye, she's fierce and bloodthirsty. Bluidy Barbary corsair injured me, and she came to my rescue. Fought off I don't know how many men then nursed me back to health for the past fortnight."

Rowan turned to Senga and reached out his hand. She looked to Ruairí first before placing it in Rowan's. Rowan brought it to his lips and brushed a kiss on her knuckles. "You can see we are practically twins. He's as close to me as a brother. I thank you for keeping his arse in one piece." Rowan winked at her, and Ruairí growled, pulling her back to his side.

"Fair turnaround," Rowan muttered before Caragh pinched him. He pulled Caragh in for a kiss that rivaled any of Ruairí's and Senga's. "I'm sorry," Rowan whispered as he brushed his nose against Caragh's.

Senga looked up to Ruairí, but when she caught his eye, he flushed and looked uncomfortable. "A story best saved for when we are alone. And you can be angry at me in private." Senga's eyes widened, but before she could say anything, Caragh gasped.

"Ruairí doesn't know. Rowan, tell him. There is no way he could know."

"Know what?"

"Caragh, you shall go over my knee for that. And it won't just be my hand," Rowan's whisper wasn't low enough for Ruari and Senga to avoid hearing. Senga wasn't sure what to make of Caragh's grin of delight before she turned a remorseful face to Rowan.

"I'll explain that later too," Ruairí was better at whispering.

"I don't think the beach is the right place to tell this story. Either we continue on to Glasgow or we all return to one of our ships." Rowan grumbled as he tapped his wife's backside.

· · ·

They all returned to the *Lady Charity* since Ruairí had the larger cabin, and Ruairí, Rowan, and Caragh seemed uncomfortable with Ruairí going to their cabin. Ruairí only said in the dinghy, "Another part of the story for me to tell later." Senga was becoming both worried and annoyed at his secretiveness, but both couples were onboard before Senga could press Ruairí for more details.

Once tucked away in the cabin with a repaired door, Rowan took a deep breath and reached for Caragh's hand. She moved herself over to sit in Rowan's lap, and Senga felt a sharp twinge of jealousy, since she didn't think Ruairí was well enough for that. Senga yelped when she was lifted off her feet before she could sit. She found herself planted on Ruairí's lap.

"I'm tired of waiting to hold you," he breathed against her neck. "And I suspect I shall need your support with whatever Rowan is about to tell me."

"Ruairí, the morning following your visit on the *Lady Grace*," Rowan grimaced. "We went ashore at Bedruthan Steps, and I met Caragh's family. Caragh mentioned my mother and her mother were best friends. I hadn't a clue, but I remembered Caragh's mother's red hair from when we were children. You'd surely recognize her, too, if you saw her. Ruairí, she told me a story of my imprisonment that makes sense but is utterly opposite of what you and I have believed for a half a score of years."

Ruairí nodded, but his skepticism was obvious. Senga held her breath, unsure of what would come next.

"Catriona, Caragh's mother, told me she was there that day. The day I returned with my father's body on my horse. What I remember from that time in the bailey isn't what happened. My mother did wail when she saw my father on my horse, but they dragged me away before I could see all of my mother's reaction." Caragh squeezed Rowan's hand in one of hers as the other rubbed over his back and shoulders. When he paused to look at her, she smiled encouragingly. "Ruairí, she pulled my father's body from my horse, and when the shroud fell apart, she stabbed him. More than once. She stabbed his dead body. She was inconsolable, her rage consuming her. While they locked me in the dungeon, she pleaded with the elders to let her see me. She tried to bribe guards, but they always found her out. Caragh's mother witnessed all of this, and once they threw me into the oubliette, my mother begged Caragh's father to find your ship. She was sure your father could reason with the council." Rowan shook his head as Ruairí stared aghast at his cousin. Senga looked back and forth between the two cousins, then at her own cousin. "We both know what happened after that." Rowan looked to Senga then Ruairí.

"She knows everything, too. I told her just after she came aboard. We seem to have painfully similar family stories. Senga's father was the laird on Lewis before her uncle arranged for the MacLeod of Skye to lead a raid on her keep. Her parents died, and her uncle assumed leadership of the clan." Ruairí wouldn't tell any more of Senga's story, since he wasn't sure how much she wanted others to know.

"Senga," Caragh whispered. "I heard about your losses. I'm sorry I couldn't have gone to you." Caragh reached across the table and took Senga's hand. They gave each other a gentle squeeze.

"So, what do you plan to do now, Rowan?" Ruairí asked.

"We may go home before winter. Rather, we're going to see my mother. As Catriona tells it, my mother was never the same after that day in the bailey. She hasn't fared well and refuses to step foot outside the keep. Ruairí, according to Caragh's mother, Aunt Charity has done little better."

"Charity? You named your ship after your mother?" Senga questioned.

"Aye. My leaving our clan had nothing to do with my parents," he breathed. He didn't want to hurt Rowan by reminding him that his parents never wanted him to leave. "When do you plan to go back? Will you go after we settle with Argyll?"

"Most likely. Will you go with us?"

Ruairí shook his head. He wasn't sure he was ready to see his clan again. His anger and bitterness had faded since meeting Senga, but he felt it trying to take hold again. The injustices were done to Rowan, not him, but he felt them just as acutely as if they had been.

Rowan nodded before continuing. "We will make a run along the coast once more before heading north. We picked up cargo from Alane that we must unload."

Senga was sure she heard Caragh hiss. She looked at her cousin and was certain fire would leap from her eyes as she gave Rowan a seething look.

"The tavern owner I told you about. I can't believe he let Caragh meet her." Ruairí said as an aside to Senga, but the others heard.

"Oh, I met her," Caragh snapped.

"Enough," warned Rowan again, but his voice softened. "There was no other way, but I regretted it before we even went ashore. You know that, *mo ghaol.*"

Caragh sighed but nodded. She leaned against Rowan, and Senga couldn't help but smile to see her cousin had found someone who loved her as much as Ruairí loved her. That thought made a pit form in her stomach that remained there the rest of the night.

# CHAPTER THIRTEEN

R owan and Caragh returned to their ship, and Ruairí and Senga retired for the night. Ruairí was so persistent as he pled his case that Senga relented. They took their time making love as Senga straddled Ruairí's hips. She eased onto his length and rocked her hips. It had been weeks since they made love, and she still feared injuring him, but they both needed the reconnection.

The slow pace enabled them both to last far longer than usual. Ruairí ran his hands over her breasts as he watched her rise and fall onto his rod. She moaned as he pinched her nipples and threw her head back when he grasped her hips to brace himself as he tested his ability to thrust. Once Ruairí knew he could move too, neither of them lasted long. They pushed each other into release, and for the first time since they began coupling, neither tried to ensure Ruairí pulled out. They climaxed as one.

The following morning, Senga awoke before Ruairí. The night before had been too much for him, even if he'd never admit it. Senga dressed and slipped from the cabin to find Tomas or Snake Eye. She found both playing passe-dix, a game played with three six-sided dice, and it was clear Tomas was winning. She grinned and walked to them, hoping a winsome smile would set the right tone for her request.

"Good morning."

"Good morning to you, Senga," Snake Eye smiled and showed his missing teeth. Senga realized she rarely noticed the gaps anymore.

"I have a favor to ask one of you. Perhaps the loser, or even the winner of the next hand, might help me." Despite her sunny disposition, both men turned wary gazes toward her. She knew she had to tread carefully but pushed on despite growing nervous. "Could either of you row me over to the *Lady Grace*? I'd like to see Caragh and speak with her."

"Does the captain know you want to go?"

"The captain is fast asleep. Going ashore was a strenuous task yesterday, along with hosting his family, so he's catching up on his shut-eye." Senga refused to say more to keep Ruairí from sounding weak even if she trusted both men. Tomas shook his head.

"No, Senga. Without the captain's permission, I'm not taking you anywhere."

"Same," Snake Eye shook his head with more vigor than Tomas.

"Should I ask one of the other men?"

Both came to their feet.

"Absolutely not. You know Capt'n would have your hide and ours as well if you did that," Tomas looked around to make sure no one overheard them.

"Then help me lower the dinghy, and I'll take myself over there. The water's calm, and I've rowed plenty of times in my life."

Tomas and Snake Eye gritted their teeth before they each rolled the dice again. Tomas lost and was surly as he lowered the dinghy, then the rope ladder. Senga nimbly followed him into the dinghy, but Tomas refused to look at her as he rowed the small expanse between the boats. He called up to announce their arrival, and Senga saw Rowan run to the rail.

He looked anxious, and Senga realized that he must have been frightened that something happened to Ruairí.

"Is Caragh awake? I'd visit with her if she is," Senga called up and saw Caragh's face poke around Rowan's shoulder.

"Senga! Good morning. I'm here."

Senga scrambled up the ladder and hugged Caragh once she was on deck. "Rowan, don't worry. He's fine and was fast asleep when I left him. I haven't seen Caragh in so long, and we didn't have much time to speak just the two of us last night. I was hoping to visit with her."

"Of course, but I hope you let someone else know where you went. I can imagine what Ruairí will do if he awakes to find out you aren't aboard the ship," Rowan warned.

"Snake Eye knows Tomas rowed me over. Would it be possible to send Tomas back and have one of your men return me? I don't want to keep Tomas waiting or from his duties," though Senga knew he had none, since he was playing dice.

"That would be fine. Skinny can take you back."

Senga leaned over and told Tomas he should return. He looked doubtful, but when Rowan reassured him, he relented.

"Come below. We can talk in the cabin," Caragh offered.

It wasn't long before both women had swapped stories about how they came to be attached to two of the most feared pirates sailing through Europe. Caragh squirmed when she explained how she met Ruairí, and Senga couldn't believe how angry she grew toward Rowan. "Inauspicious circumstances" was an understatement, considering Rowan tried to trade Caragh to his cousin, and Ruairí nearly ended up coupling with Caragh before Rowan stopped them.

"He's different now though," Caragh puzzled. "When I met him, there was a coldness to his eyes. He scared me when I thought Rowan would give me to him. He's Rowan's mirror image, but anger was simmering below the surface."

"But you'd have gone with him." There was no accusation in Senga's tone even if jealousy nipped at her heels.

"If I hadn't any other choice. I would've made the best of another situation beyond my control. I'm just thankful that Rowan couldn't go through with it."

"And everything is resolved between the two of you?"

Caragh shrugged. "It improves every day, and I know I made the right choice marrying him. Speaking of marriage…" Caragh gave Senga a pointed look, but Senga couldn't meet her cousin's eye.

"That's what I came to speak to you about. I don't know that Ruairí will ever ask me to marry him. We've never spoken of it, but he said he loves me. He said so just before the battle, and he's alluded to it since he awoke." Senga rubbed her forehead. "I know I love him, too. And that's the reason I must leave him."

"What?" Caragh broke in.

"I prayed constantly while Ruairí was unconscious, and I pledged to sacrifice my happiness for his health. Caragh, every man in my life has either died or abandoned me. My father, my husband, my son. They all died. My uncle and even Alfred abandoned me. Neither my uncle nor my cousin cared for me, not really. I'm nearly convinced I'm a curse. Either way, I made that pledge to God, and I must honor it."

Caragh gawked at Senga for so long that Senga began to squirm. "That is the most ridiculous pile of shite, cousin. Not the part about your family dying; that's just a fact, and so is how your uncle treated you. Alfred had no backbone to stand up to his father. But the part about you leaving Ruairí because he's getting better is absurd. I believe you prayed, and I believe you think God healed Ruairí in answer to your promise. But I don't believe God would ever intend for you to make such a sacrifice."

"Whether or not you believe doesn't change my mind. Will you help me go ashore? I can't wait until we reach Glasgow. He'll be back on his feet by then. I won't be able to slip away."

"Do you even hear yourself? You don't want him to be

well yet. You have to slip away. Your own words show you know what you want to do is wrong. Senga, no."

"Caragh, it's easy for you to say 'no.' But you didn't see the man you love come close to dying before your eyes and then watch him fading away for a fortnight. I was sure I'd lose him. It was unwillingness to accept it that kept me going. I want him to live, but I don't want to be the reason for his suffering."

"Again, such shite. If anything, you're the only reason he isn't still suffering. I saw the way he looked at you, watched you the entire evening. The man is head over heels in love with you. What do you think your running away will do to him?"

"Keep him alive."

"Bah," Caragh waved her hand and stood up. She paced about the cabin as she kept looking over at Senga.

"Caragh, I'm going with or without your help. I figured the least I could do was let you know since we reconnected after so long. I didn't want to just disappear on you."

"You wouldn't do that to me, but you'd do it to Ruairí."

Senga clenched her hands into a fist and tried to remain calm. Caragh watched Senga and relented after debating with herself.

"Fine. I don't agree with you. I definitely don't condone this, but I'll help you. I'll speak to Skinny about taking us ashore. I should collect medicinals, just as you did. I haven't had a chance, but after hearing about the wounds sustained between Ruairí and his crew it would be wise for me to do that. Once we're on shore, we can decide what you'll do next."

Senga walked around the table and embraced her cousin. "Thank you," she whispered. The women were in the dinghy being taken ashore within a quarter hour.

Ruairí stretched, then groaned as he felt the stabbing pain of his stitches being pulled. He looked around the cabin, but Senga wasn't there. He smiled as he thought about the previous night. It had been wonderful to see his cousin and to know that things were working out for Rowan and Caragh. He liked the young woman, but he was thankful he hadn't brought her aboard his ship. He might never have met Senga, or if he had, he certainly wouldn't have invited her to come with him. His smile broadened as he thought about their love-making the night before. It was unhurried compared to their usual all-consuming need to come together. Ruairí knew he shouldn't have spilled his seed inside her, but the image of her standing beside the cradle was even more vivid than it had been in her cottage. Ruairí would ask her to marry him when he brought her back to the cabin.

Ruairí gingerly stood and pulled on his leine with minimal grunts. His leggings resulted in several curses and a moan, though he'd never admit to these. He braced himself against the bulkheads as he made his way to the stairs. His crew cheered when they saw him emerge onto the deck. Ruairí waved but searched for Senga. He spotted Tomas and Snake Eye playing dice while Kyle stood at the helm. He'd have to reward his first mate for doing such a fine job of leading the crew while he convalesced.

"Morning," Ruairí greeted Tomas and Snake Eye, but when neither man would look him in the eye, he searched for Senga again. "Where is she?"

This was a growl, not a question. He continued to scan the deck, but he knew he wouldn't find her.

"I warned the lass you'd get your dander up when you couldn't find her," Snake Eye muttered.

"Then you'd better tell me where she is."

"I took her over to the *Lady Grace*, Capt'n. She asked to see her cousin."

Ruairí gritted his teeth to keep from yelling. "And you're back now, playing dice. You just left her there."

"Your cousin said he'd arrange for one of his men to bring her back."

"And you thought I'd be fine with that. Some strange man in a small boat with my--" Ruairí didn't know how to finish his thought. He threw his hands into the air. "No, I'm bluidy well not fine with her being without someone I trust."

"You trust your cousin, don't you?" Tomas's eyes widened as he realized what he said aloud. "My apologies, Capt'n. I'll lower the dinghy and fetch her right now."

"I'll go with you. I have words for her that won't wait until we return." Ruairí almost bit through his lower lip as he climbed down the rope into the dinghy. He held his hand against his ribs, the pressure relieving some pain.

# CHAPTER FOURTEEN

I t surprised Caragh and Senga how easy it was to convince Rowan to allow them to go ashore with Skinny. Caragh was quiet for most of the way, lost in thought about what awaited her when she returned without her cousin. Senga, in turn, looked to the shore and tried to see if there was a town or even a village visible. The trio walked a couple of miles inland, the women gathering plants and placing them in a basket Caragh carried.

"What are you going to do now?" Caragh asked, looking over her shoulder at Skinny to be sure her voice didn't carry.

"I'm uncertain. Do you see the smoke against the clouds to the left? I think that must be a village. It's too much for one cottage. I can't stay there, but I can see if someone will take me further north."

"And you'll trust whoever you ask? What do you have to trade?" Caragh glowered at Senga to warn her not to include herself in the commodities she might have.

"I didn't bring anything of value with me when I left Canna. I have my knives from Ruairí's chest. Several of them have jewel-encrusted handles."

"Did he give those to you? Would you add thievery to your list of wrongdoings?" Caragh lifted something from around her neck. "Rowan has let me choose various pieces of jewelry from the chests he has kept. This one should bring you a fair amount if you can find a jeweler in a decent-sized town. Otherwise, use these rings."

Caragh pulled off two rings from her right hand and handed the three pieces of jewelry to Senga.

"You're getting too close to that village, my ladies," Skinny called out. "Someone may see us."

Skinny had given them privacy to talk, so there was quite a distance between the cousins and the pirate. Both women pretended not to hear him as they continued to wander and gather plants.

"We have to distract him long enough for me to slip away."

"You have to distract him. I'm complicit, but I'm not doing any more to aid in this insane plan of yours."

"Skinny?" Senga called to him. When he approached, she pointed to several trees near a deer path they could see. "Do you see the tree to the far right? I believe it's an alder tree. Could you help us by carving some bark from it? The trunk is hard, making it a difficult task."

Skinny looked between the two women and nodded his head. Caragh handed him a small sack from her basket. They waited until Skinny was within the tree line before Senga gave Caragh a tight squeeze and darted in the village's direction.

Ruairí could feel his temper rising with each splash of the oars. He saw Rowan wave as they approached his cousin's boat. "Where's Senga?"

"Good morning to you, too, Ruairí. She and Caragh went ashore with Skinny to collect medicinals. Caragh realized it was a good idea to have a stock on hand, and I guess Senga needed to replenish her supplies."

"You let them go ashore with only one man? Do you not

remember where we are?" Ruairí wanted to scream. They anchored off the coast of Inverkip, at what appeared to be a sleepy coastal village, but both Ruairí and Rowan knew it was a smuggling stronghold. One where they weren't welcome. Both had raised their white sails and the banners that showed they sailed under the marque of the Earl of Argyll for the express purposes of disguise. "I assume Caragh doesn't know where we are. I know Senga doesn't. What if they meet someone and mention who they're with?"

"I think both women know not to admit they sail with the MacNeil cousins."

"You think, but you don't know. Bluidy hell, Rowan. If anything happens to Senga, I won't forgive you."

"I'm coming down."

Senga looked back twice to be sure Skinny wasn't following her. The woods still hid him, and Caragh appeared to be looking at the ground for plants. Senga's legs burned, but she pushed herself until she reached the village outskirts, where she slowed to catch her breath. She looked around and spotted the tavern. She wouldn't go there immediately, but she knew she might have to if she could find no other sources of aid. As she approached the town square, she realized it was market day. She casually wound her way through the stalls until she found a jeweler who looked to know his trade and had items of similar value to what she carried.

"Good day," she spoke in low tones to hide her Hebridean accent. She must not have hidden it well enough, because the man's face took on a skeptical appearance.

"Good morning, lass. Is there something you're looking for?"

"Not exactly. I was hoping to make a trade."

"Trade or sale?" The man ran an assessing gaze over her.

"Sale. My husband passed, and now I'm in need of

funds." Both statements were true, even if she made them sound connected.

"Let's see what you have." Senga laid one ring on the stall. The man peered at it from various angles. "How did you come by such a fine piece? It looks French."

"It is." Senga prayed he wasn't testing her. "My husband traded there and brought it back." That was near the truth.

"I'll give you twenty shillings."

Senga smiled warmly, "Then you'll give it back, and I'll move on. Thirty shillings."

"Twenty-five."

"Done." Senga covered the ring with her hand until she received a pouch of coins. She discreetly tied the pouch to the laces of her skirt before hiding it within the folds of her arisaid. She'd been torn between which plaid to wear. Senga couldn't bring herself to leave the MacNeil plaid behind. She found she wasn't sentimental about her MacLeod or Sorley plaid, but she couldn't walk away without something from Ruairí. Senga moved on to several more stalls where she bought food and a wine skin. She kept an eye open for any merchant who seemed to be preparing to leave. Senga found an older couple who struggled to load their donkey cart. She walked over and helped without being asked.

"Lass, you're a kind one," the old woman offered her a gummy smile.

"It's my pleasure," Senga smiled back

"Would you like to pick something from our wares?" the old man asked. The man tempted Senga since the couple sold woolens, but she would rather they allow her to travel with them than consider stockings.

"I'm not in need of anything, but I appreciate your offer." She pretended to look at their crates. "From where do you hail? Where do you go next?"

The woman seemed happy to find someone to talk to when her husband only grunted at Senga. "Auchenbothie is our next market."

Senga hadn't a clue which direction the town lay, but she hoped it wasn't taking them closer to Glasgow. "Is that a busy market?"

"Nay. We came to the coast from Glasgow, but now head east and our home."

*East. That is the wrong direction. But Auchenbothie may be inland. If that's the case, Rowan and Ruairi won't be near the village.*

"Do you not stay along the coast?"

"Nay. We've already traded there and will go inland to make our way home sooner. Where do you go, lass?"

Senga racked her mind for any place she'd heard of near Glasgow that wasn't the city itself. She remembered a man who came to the Three Merry Lads who claimed to know the Earl of Argyll because he hailed from the village of Kilmacolm.

"Kilmacolm."

"Near to where we travel," the old woman responded.

"Aye. Perhaps I could be of help to you, since we travel in the same direction."

The husband chimed in at her offer of help. "That would be a fine thing, lass. We shall ride while you manage the donkey."

Senga helped the couple onto the cart and landed the switch across the donkey's rump. It brayed but moved forward. Senga didn't look back as she led the cart to the path that headed away from the coast. She couldn't bring herself to take one last glance, but it also meant she didn't see the men following her and the old couple.

# CHAPTER FIFTEEN

Ruairí tried to keep his knee still as his anxiousness grew with each sweep of the oars. The same sense that screamed for him to follow Senga to her cottage surged through him now. He had a sickening feeling that Senga was in danger, and he didn't know where she was. Ruairí and Rowan spotted Caragh and Skinny as they stood in the field arguing. Ruairí took off running but had to hold his side as he pushed himself. Rowan could have outpaced him, but Ruairí knew his cousin hung back for his sake.

"Where is she?" he demanded.

Caragh looked at her husband and cousin-by-marriage, but she refused to look them in the eye.

"Wife, you'd better answer now if you don't want to find yourself over my lap with a switch across your arse in plain sight."

A flash of defiance crossed Caragh's face as she looked at Rowan, but the distress on Ruairí's face made her relent. "She's gone, Ruairí."

He stood staring at the woman who looked so much like the one he loved and wanted to throttle. "What do you mean 'gone'?"

"She left. She's convinced she must uphold some pledge

she made to God when you were ill. She promised to let you go if you survived. Senga believes she's cursed since the men in her life always die. She thinks she's protecting you, Ruairí. Senga loves you."

"Loves me? Loves me? If she did, she wouldn't run away." Ruairí felt his world crumble around him. He swayed on his feet, and Rowan was quick to hold him up.

"Ruairí, I don't think you understand the depth of her love." Caragh's hoped her soft tone would calm the bereft pirate. "She's willing to live a life of hardship alone to give you the chance to live. You know she has nowhere to go and no one to help her. Wherever she settles, she'll have to make a life on her own, with no help from friends or family. At least when Alex died she already had a home on Canna."

"She could have a home with me," Ruairí croaked. He felt anger and bitterness creeping back into his soul. It had left him for the short time Senga had been part of his life. Now that she was gone, the void caused by her absence was rapidly being filled with the familiar feelings that had driven him since he ran away from home.

"Ruairí, you left everything you knew and loved to protect me," Rowan said. "Do you not see the similarities?"

"No," Ruairí barked. "It's not at all the same."

"But it is. I love you like my own brother. There's nothing I wouldn't do to protect you or to repay you for the sacrifices you made to keep me alive. She's willing to do the same. Misguided as she is, she's doing it because she loves you." Rowan attempted to reason with his cousin.

"Ruairí, I told her it was a ridiculous plan and a ridiculous reason to leave," Caragh cut in. "But she's deeply wounded by the things that have happened. Far more damaged than any of us could see. She believes she not only causes her own misery but is the cause of the deaths in her life. She's sure she's cursed."

"But I lived," Ruairí whispered. His throat felt as if it

would cinch closed, and he was close to crying for the first time since he was seven summers old.

"She's driven by fear, just like we were when we left Barra," Rowan reasoned. "Neither of us used much reason in those early months. We did whatever we had to. She's doing the same."

Ruairí blinked several times before looking toward the village. "I won't lose her." He began walking and assumed the others would follow. He felt like it took him years to limp into the village. He looked around, but the market day crowd was dense. "She could be anywhere."

"I can imagine where she went first," Caragh replied. She took Rowan's hand and dragged him into the crowd. Ruairí had no choice but to follow. Caragh paused at every jewelry stall until she found one she knew Senga would have chosen. "I have a very particular ring in mind, and I wonder if you have anything similar to what I desire," Caragh cast a shrewd look at the man. "It has a large ruby in the center with emeralds around it, as if to make a rose."

She squeezed Rowan's hand like it lay in a vice. She knew she'd have to add that to her list of transgressions, since he knew which ring she gave to Senga to trade. The jeweler brought out Caragh's ring.

"However did you have something like what I wanted?" Caragh asked, her charm on display. "Where did you find such a jewel?"

"A young woman traded it recently."

"Did she happen to have black hair?"

"Aye. That's the one."

"Hmm. I saw it last sennight and admired it. I wonder where she went. I should like to thank her for the opportunity to own such a beautiful bauble."

"I saw her leave to the east with an old tinker couple." Rowan slipped the man a few coins as they turned to leave. "But I doubt they made it far. I spotted some unsavory sorts following them."

That was more than Ruairí needed to hear to barrel through the crowd. He didn't care who he jostled or what bumped against his wounds. He pushed through until he reached the blacksmith's stall.

"I want a horse. Now."

"I'm sorry — You're Ruairí MacNeil." The man looked over Ruairí's shoulder and nearly wet himself. "And Rowan MacNeil."

"Aye, we are, and I said I needed a horse."

The blacksmith nodded and dashed to fetch any properly shod horses he could find.

Ruairí turned to Rowan and pulled him into an embrace. "This is where we part. You can't bring Caragh along if there might be a fight, and I know you won't leave her with just Skinny."

Rowan pulled a short sword from his belt and handed it to Caragh before grinning at Ruairí. "Do you not remember how you met my bonnie bride? She'd just killed one of your men. I'd put my money on her before anyone else. Just as bloodthirsty as your woman."

The three mounted their horses and raced out of town.

Senga knew they were being followed. She discreetly turned to look over her shoulder, but made it appear as if she were looking at the couple while the old woman nattered on. Four men followed them on horseback. They hung back, but there was no reason for them to do so unless they didn't want to overtake Senga and the couple. They were past the outskirts of town, and there was no way Senga could turn back without alerting the couple or the riders. She pulled the dirks from her boots and laid them in her lap. She wished she had at least one of her swords, but there'd been no way for her to bring them. Senga wished now that she'd stopped long enough to trade for a new one. She used the whip to hurry the donkey along the road, and for once, the animal sensed her urgency. She stopped the cart when they passed through a bend in the road. Senga pulled away from the road and put her finger to her lips when the old woman began to ask questions. The first rider made the turn, and Senga launched one of her dirks at the man's shoulder. It met its mark, and the riders pulled to a stop. Senga was ready for the attack.

"You bitch. You shall pay for that," growled the injured man.

"What do you want?"

"We know you came off the Dark Heart's ship. We saw you row over to the Blond Devil's ship, then come ashore with the other woman."

It was the first time she'd heard Rowan's moniker, but she had to admit it suited him as well as Ruairí's fit him. "So, what if I did?"

"Neither of those men take women on their ships. It's said the Blond Devil married some chit he kidnapped. You came from the Dark Heart's boat, so you must be his woman."

"If I were, why would I be riding away from him on a donkey cart?"

This made the men pause, but the man with the dirk in his shoulder responded first.

"What does it matter to us? He'll pay a ransom for you."

"Why would he pay for my return if he's already sent me away?" Senga hoped her lies would be convincing.

"If he doesn't, then we shall keep you for ourselves. Perhaps sample you before we hand you over."

"The only man sampling my woman is me."

Ruairí's voice seemed to echo in their surroundings. Senga whipped her head around to see Ruairí, Rowan, and Caragh galloping toward them. In the time it took for her to look away, one man grabbed her from the cart. She already had another dirk in her hand. She stabbed at any part of him she could reach, meeting her mark several times. The man released her, and she fell to the ground, rolling in an attempt to land clear of the horse's hooves.

"Senga!" Ruairí sounded like an enraged wild animal, and the men, as a one, looked back at him. Senga watched in awe as Ruairí raced toward them. His long blond hair had come loose from his queue. He leaned over the saddle as he swung his sword through one, then two of the men, nearly cleaving them each in half. "You touched her. You will die slowly for that."

Ruairí reined in and pulled the last man from his horse before dismounting. Ruairí leaped from the saddle, tackling Senga's attacker before clamoring back to his feet. He kicked the man in the bollocks before severing both hands with one strike of his sword on each side. The man hadn't pulled Senga's blade from his shoulder, knowing it would only make the wound bleed faster. He soon realized that leaving it was a far greater mistake than pulling it out. Ruairí leaned forward and twisted the blade as he pressed it to the hilt. It was only moments later that the bodies of the attackers lay strewn on the grass, dead where they dropped.

Senga watched in horror as she tried to hold both Ruairí's horse and the donkey in place. She wanted to run when Ruairí looked at her. She shrank back and bumped into the cart. Ruairí stalked toward her, and Senga could only shake her head.

"Don't you dare shake your head at me." His hushed tone was even more menacing than him yelling her name. He reached for her and pulled her into his embrace. "Don't ever, ever do that again."

Ruairí clenched his hands in her hair as he cradled her head and drew her in for a kiss that poured all his anger and love into one searing brand. Senga leaned into the kiss, cupping his jaw as their tongues dueled.

"You're mine," he breathed.

"I am."

They kissed again; the conflagration of emotions burned

through them as flames of desire flared between them. When they were both breathless, Ruairí ran the pad of his thumb over her swollen lips. Senga's eyes fluttered shut as she struggled not to fall apart in his arms.

"I only wanted to protect you," she whispered.

"I know. I know all about your foolish plan, what little there was of it. I shall relieve you of that foolhardiness when we return to our cabin, and I turn you over my knee. I should have done that ages ago. It would seem Rowan is far wiser than I am in that area. You might take a lesson from your cousin."

Senga peeked over his shoulder to see Rowan sat on a rock with Caragh draped across his lap and her skirt about her waist. She was receiving a punishing spanking, but she seemed no worse for wear. In truth, Senga was certain she was enjoying it, or at least not fighting it. "Our cabin?" she asked.

"Where else would we be going?"

"Not your cabin?"

"Lass, you aren't making sense."

"You still think of it as ours?"

"Of course," Ruairí noticed Senga's anxiety as she seemed to shrink into herself again. "I didn't come chasing after you just to let you go on your merry way. Senga, you're no one's curse. Not mine, not your own. You are, however, the most infuriating woman I have ever met, and the one I shall love for the rest of my life."

"I love you."

Ruairí was sure he'd heard nothing better than Senga sharing her feelings for the first time. "Will you marry me, little one? I intended to ask you in our cabin this morning, but alas, you sent me on a merry chase to earn your hand."

Senga fell against Ruairí but tried to pull back when she remembered his injuries. He anchored her in place, and she breathed the scent of sea air and pine that she'd always know was his. "I'll marry you. I'd marry you this very moment if I could."

"Then you won't be fleeing my arms again?"

"I wasn't running away from you so much as I was trying to outrun what I was sure fate would deliver. I love you."

"I shall insist upon hearing that several times a day and more often at night. I love you, *mo bhòidhchead*." Ruairí hadn't called her his beauty since early in their relationship, using other pet names instead. It reminded her of why she'd agreed to leave her home on a whim. She realized she was grateful for the intuition that said she should follow him. That intuition reared its head again, and she felt a calm settle over her as her soul seemed to speak for her.

"I want to marry you today, Ruairí. I don't want to wait."

"I'm glad to hear that because I already intended to take you to the kirk before returning to our ship." Ruairí saw her shock once more. "Yes, she's ours now. You'll be my wife and are already my partner, whether or not I said as much. I rely on you, and so you should have your own share of our enterprise."

"Pirates! They really are pirates!"

Senga had completely forgotten the old couple who sat on the donkey cart behind her. She laughed as she nodded her head. "I won't be traveling with you after all, but I thank you for your offer." Ruairí led Senga to his horse and mounted behind her. "I can't believe you haven't keeled over yet."

"I may very well do that the moment we get back to the *Lady Charity*. Until then, I have a wedding to attend."

Rowan and Caragh followed Ruairí and Senga into the kirk. It took little effort and a large sum of coins to convince the parish priest to marry them without the banns being read. Ruairí and Senga were married in less than a quarter hour, and the two couples rode back to the coast. None of them wanted to remain, knowing people had already recognized them. At the dinghies, they agreed to sail on to Glasgow to pay the earl his due before going their separate ways for a few weeks. Ruairí agreed to meet Rowan in two month's time to sail to Barra. They'd visit their clan together with their wives. Tomas rowed in silence as he counted his blessings that he might survive to see another sunrise.

Once aboard the *Lady Charity*, Ruairí introduced Senga as his wife to wild cheers. Even the most hardened and grizzled of his crew had fallen in love with Senga. He had few concerns for her safety now, and he granted the crew the right to a night of merriment while he planned to make merry of a different kind. Senga tugged at his hand and tilted her head toward their cabin.

They hurried below deck where Senga was undressing before Ruairí finished bolting and barring the door. She insisted upon inspecting Ruairí's wounds before letting him touch her. He grumbled that she was taunting him with temptation when he'd already suffered enough that day. Senga couldn't believe Ruairí hadn't torn any stitches and that he was still on his feet.

"I have reason to celebrate and reason to remain in the land of the living. I know I shall be sore in the morning, but I feel far better than I expected after making a mad dash after my wayward wife."

Senga had the good grace to look repentant at the reminder of the trouble she'd caused that day and the danger in which she'd place not only herself but Ruairí, Caragh, and Rowan. She didn't move when Ruairí approached. He led her to a chair and sat down without a word before guiding her over his lap.

"You said back in your cottage that you would've liked to be spanked." Ruairí couldn't bring himself to say her late husband's name or to even acknowledge she'd been married before him. "You shall get your wish now, little one. You talked your way out of a spanking when I found you sparring for the first time. You can't talk your way out now."

"Yes, Ruairí," Senga demurred. She shifted to find a better

position across his lap as she waited for her punishment to begin. The wait was nearly as much agony as she assumed the spanking would be. She glanced at Ruairí, but he was staring at her backside, appreciation clear on his face. He ran his hand over her bottom in a soft caress.

"You shall receive ten slaps on your pretty little arse, and you will count each one. You will thank me after each one. Thank me that I love you so much that I'd protect you from yourself." Ruairí drew back his hand and landed his palm across her bottom. He appreciated the way the skin rippled.

"One. Thank you, Ruairí."

"I love you, Senga. I'll do anything I have to, to keep you safe." He brought his hand down again.

"I know. Two. Thank you."

"I shall pinken your beautiful arse." Ruairí enjoyed seeing the color rise in Senga's backside. He loved the feel of her across his lap and the way her bottom felt each time his hand landed. He could feel himself hardening with each swipe across her globes. He landed spanks on each cheek and across where her thighs met her bottom. After the last one, he rubbed her stinging flesh until her moan was one of pleasure rather than pain. He nudged her legs apart and slipped his fingers between them. They were soon soaked with her dew that slickened the insides of her thighs.

"I think you enjoyed that punishment a little too much, little one."

"I admit that I did, Ruairí. I'm sorry for what I did, and I appreciate you loving me enough to want to protect me. But I won't apologize for how much I want you, how much I need you." Senga eased from his lap and came to kneel between his legs. She pushed them apart wider before drawing the laces of his leggings loose. "I would show you just how much I appreciate you."

Senga freed Ruairí's engorged cock and slid her tongue over it from root to tip, swirling and flicking her tongue as she made it twitch. She blew cool air over it before allowing her warm mouth to descend up on his rod. She moaned as she worked him, sucking hard enough to draw her cheeks in. She took him deeper than she ever had before, relaxing her throat as she nearly swallowed him. Ruairí grunted but forced himself not to push her head down further. She gripped the open waistband of his leggings as she continued to work him, sliding up and down as she hummed. Ruairí couldn't suppress the need to thrust. When he felt his need to climax threatening to end their interlude, he pulled her free and walked her toward the bed. Ruairí spun Senga around and pushed onto her hands and knees. His hand rained down several more spankings, but these were for their mutual pleasure. Senga rocked her hips back, wanting the pain and pleasure that only Ruairí could offer.

"Please, Ruairí. I need you. Please," she begged.

"I know, little one. And you shall have to do without just a little longer. You will know how I felt when I couldn't wait to be with you once again." Ruairí's hushed tones made Senga's sheath clench with a burning ache to be filled by him. When Ruairí knew Senga was on the cusp of desperation rather than arousal, they fell onto the bed in a tangle of arms and legs as their bodies fused together.

"I promise you shall only chase me to our bed from now on," Senga whispered.

The love they shared shone in every word they whispered and every caress they shared as day passed into night, and the sun rose again to shine upon their future.

# CHAPTER SIXTEEN

"**W**ife," Ruairí called down the ladderwell to Senga as the sun rose. When Senga appeared from their cabin, rubbing her eyes while yawning, Ruairí laughed. "I didn't keep you awake that long last night."

"The stars had already disappeared before I shut my eyes. Now the sun hasn't even realized it's daytime," Senga grumbled.

"I thought you wanted to bid farewell to Caragh and Rowan before we depart. It's been a sennight since we married, and much as I don't want to, we must set sail."

"I don't. I want to stay with them longer now that we've learned Caragh is expecting." Senga sighed, her exhaled breath blowing her hair away from her forehead. "But I understand we can't stay here forever. Where will we go after we report to the Earl of Argyll?"

It was Ruairí's turn to blow out a deep breath. He didn't relish telling Senga their next destination, but it wasn't any better than if they sailed to the Mediterranean like Rowan and Caragh had. He waited until Senga climbed the steps before offering her his hand as she stepped onto the deck. He led them to the rail, where they watched the pinks and purples inch their way above the horizon.

"We'll be making a run to Ireland after I trade in Glasgow."

"Ireland? That's bluidy pirate central!" Senga shook her head vehemently. "Why there? Neither the MacLeods nor the MacNeils are welcome there."

"The MacLeods aren't, which is no longer your concern—you're a MacNeil now—but Rowan and I are. We offer too much profit for the Irish to turn us away."

"But Ruairí, they're slave traders." Senga's eyes opened wide, but before she could speak, Ruairí snarled.

"I have never bought or sold a person in my life. My crew may come and go as they replace or are replaced, but I'm no slaver. Not after what happened to Rowan and me." Ruairí felt the bitterness that had been at bay for most of the time he'd been with Senga threatening to resurface. He turned a frigid glare on Senga, who looked anything but intimidated.

"I never said, never even thought you were. But you'd do business with those who are."

"We're pirates! Who the hell do you think I do business with?"

"Don't snap at me," Senga warned. "I told you when we met that I knew who you are and what you are. But that doesn't mean I have to agree with who you associate with."

"But you don't mind if I kill people and plunder their treasure."

Senga opened her mouth, then snapped it shut. She took a long moment to consider her wording before she laid her hands on Ruairí's chest. "It's not as though I haven't seen men die. It's not like I haven't killed men too. I've been on raids, and you witnessed me fight in my cottage. But there is something utterly repugnant about someone who can buy and sell other people. Knowing that someone forced my own husband into indenture makes my reaction all the stronger. I'm not blaming you so much as I'm angry at the situation. I would have killed Alane myself for what she did to you."

Ruairí pulled Senga into his embrace, laying his cheek on the crown of her head. The sense of security and peace she offered made the bitterness in his heart recede once more. He knew she was right, but he'd felt attacked and came out swinging.

"Senga, I know which men are the slavers, and I don't do business with them. I've attacked more than one ship with human cargo, and I've always done what I can to set them free. It was a pledge Rowan and I made to one another before I left the *Lady Grace* and its captain sold me to my predecessor here on the *Lady Charity*."

Senga wrapped her arms around Ruairí's middle and nestled further into his embrace, his arms and chest engulfing her in their warmth and protection.

"I think we've just had our first fight," Senga murmured.

"Aye, I'd say we have. Lucky for us, it was a brief one. I can accept we won't always agree, and that's fine, but please have a little faith that I still recognize some right from wrong."

Senga heard the plea in Ruairí's voice, and she felt guilty for having so little trust in her husband. She nodded before leaning back. "I do. I suppose there can be honor among thieves."

"Shall we row over to visit Rowan and Caragh before we depart?"

"Aye. I'd like that." Senga bit her bottom lip before gazing up at Ruairí. He could practically see the wheels turning in Senga's mind, but his mind and his stiffening rod were focused on the way her teeth sunk into her lower lip. He pulled it free before his mouth descended to hers. He tugged at that lip before sweeping his tongue within the silky depths. When Senga moaned, Ruairí's hands slid to her backside, pressing her against his arousal.

"Do you see what you do to me, wife? Do you feel it?"

"How could I not?" Senga laughed, but another moan escaped as Ruairi swooped in for another kiss. She felt drugged, as though she floated above the world upon a cloud, until she realized Ruairi had lifted her off her feet so they could see eye to eye.

"What are you thinking about, little one?"

"I disagreed with you. In public, where someone might have heard me. I questioned the captain and offered my opinion when it wasn't asked for."

"You did, but we're partners. The *Lady Charity* is as much mine as it is yours. You have a right and you have a say."

"But I did that in public. Someone could have heard my insubordination."

"Senga——" Ruairi's left eye narrowed as he examined his wife, tilting his head to the right. He bent his head to bury his nose in her hair and bring his lips to her ear. His warm breath sent a shiver down Senga's back. "Are you admitting to your crimes in hopes of punishment?"

Senga nodded but said nothing as Ruairi lowered her to the deck. He gripped her backside in a merciless hold, his hand hidden while Senga's back was to the rail. His fingers bit into her flesh as he pressed his rod against her mons. She fisted his leine as she looked into his cornflower blue eyes. He glimpsed the submission in Senga that they discovered after their wedding. It wasn't fear. He never wanted that. It was a pleading for his dominance. He'd noticed that the tension eased from Senga while he was punishing her. It was the opposite of what he expected. It was as if she found comfort in relinquishing control and letting him decide her fate. Ruairi realized he hadn't truly considered the hardship Senga must have faced after losing her first husband and son, along with the drain that working at the tavern was on her soul. She was tired of fighting alone, and welcomed Ruairi's control because it meant she no longer had to fend for herself.

136

"You shall have to wait until we return from the *Lady Grace* to learn of your punishment."

"Yes, *mo chridhe*. Whatever you say." The words were submissive, but Ruairí caught the usual fire that sparked in Senga's chocolate-brown eyes.

"And after I am done, how will you show your remorse, wife?" Ruairí's heart sped up as he waited for Senga to describe what he knew would happen. He held his breath, waiting for her response.

"I shall kneel before you, pressing my breasts together for you to do as you please. When you are ready, I will unlace your leggings and free your rod." Senga paused, her tongue darting out between her pressed lips, but it slid back into her mouth. "I will lick your cock before I take it in my mouth. I'm going to suck you."

Ruairí growled as he pounced. He pressed Senga back against the rail as his tongue flicked her earlobe before laving her throat from her collarbone to her jaw. He tugged on her earlobe before drawing it into his mouth. Senga's hand crept between them before cupping his aching rod. She rubbed her palm over it and felt it twitch within her hand. There were no illusions between them that Senga had as much power over Ruairí as he did her. Senga had the ability to bring Ruairí to his knees. He grasped her wrist, pressing her hand against him once more before pulling it away.

"We'll never visit with our cousins at this rate." Ruairí stepped away from Senga but didn't turn from her, knowing his arousal was on obvious display.

"I think you've just punished yourself as much as you will me when we return."

"Bluidy agony," Ruairí grumbled.

They took the dinghy across to where Rowan anchored the *Lady Grace* and spent much of the day with Rowan and Caragh. The men discussed their intended destinations before they would meet again to decide whether they would return to Barra. Caragh and Senga sat in the sun upon crates as they watched the men. They talked about everything and nothing as they enjoyed each other's company, knowing it would be several weeks before they saw one another again. When Senga and Ruairí could no longer delay returning to their ship if they were to make the tide and sail toward the Firth of Clyde, none of the four had dry eyes.

# CHAPTER SEVENTEEN

S enga entered the cabin before Ruairí, and by the time he had locked and barred their door, Senga already had the laces to her kirtle loosened. She observed Ruairí as he trained his eyes on her breasts, then her mound when the skirts dropped to the floor. She stood with her hands clasped behind her back as Ruairí meandered toward her, the anticipation making it hard for her to breathe. He stepped behind her and rested his hand on her belly.

"One day I will plant my seed and it will take root in here. It'll be my child that grows within." It wasn't often that Ruairí thought about the husband and child Senga had before him, but in moments like this, his possessiveness threatened to swallow him. He slid his hand over the curls nestled at the juncture of her thighs and dipped his middle finger into her sheath, drawing the dew over her bud. He circled it until Senga couldn't withstand the urge to squirm and drop her head back against Ruairí's chest. Ruairí purred beside her ear, "Wet for me already?"

"Always, *mo chridhe*."

"And what do you want?"

"My spanking, please."

"Anything else?" Ruairí asked lightly.

"To take you in my mouth. To pleasure you."

"Mmm. I think there's still something more that you want, little one. Tell me now, or I might not know there should be more."

"I want to feel your cock in my cunny." It wasn't often that they spoke so bluntly about their bed sport, but that evening it heightened their need and increased their restlessness. Ruairí wrapped his other arm beneath her breasts, cupping one in his hand. His finger dipped back into her sheath as he nudged her legs further apart.

"And just how would you like me to do that?"

Senga glanced at the bed, then the chair Ruairí would most likely sit on while doling out her punishment, and finally to the table.

"I want to see you, but I also want you to tie me to something."

Ruairí's eyebrow twitched just as his cock did. "You shall have your wish, but first we have your spanking to take care of." Ruairí led her to the chair where he sat down, then eased her over his lap. "Are you comfortable?"

"Yes, Ruairí."

As soon as the words left her lips, Ruairí's hand rained down a fiery storm of spanks, alternating sides. Some landed across the fleshiest part of her bottom, but several landed across the crease at the top of her thighs, pushing the globes up. He stared as the flesh transitioned from lily white to rosy pink to a deep blush, much like the hue he and Senga witnessed as they watched the sunrise. He hadn't understood Rowan's interest in erotic discipline until he experimented with Senga. He recalled that from the beginning that spankings interested her, and he'd known he was willing to try it if she wanted, but he never imagined that it would arouse him so much. He understood part of their happiness was due to his dominance; it was yet another means for Ruairí to express how much he loved Senga and wanted to care for her.

Throughout the spanking, Senga remained as still as she

could, one hand gripping the leg of the chair while the other clung to Ruairí's ankle. She forced herself not to kick her legs or try to shield her backside. She knew she'd asked for the spanking and that if she risked getting hurt by putting her hands behind her back, it really would upset Ruairí. She understood she risked never getting a spanking again if Ruairí believed he'd hurt her. As the blows slowed and decreased in intensity, Senga went limp across his lap. He rubbed the punished skin before dipping his fingers between her thighs. He discovered she was even wetter than she had been before they began the spanking. Without a word, Ruairí lifted Senga and carried her to the table. He sat her on the surface before retrieving the veils he'd used before. With a gentle kiss to her forehead, Ruairí eased Senga onto her back, drawing her arms overhead and securing them to the table legs with the satin. With her hips at the edge of the table, and her legs dangling, he bound her ankles to the other two table legs.

"Ruairí, I didn't show you that I'm sorry." Senga watched at Ruairí undressed.

"You will." Ruairí offered no further explanation, but Senga quickly understood when he came to stand behind her head. His superior height made it easy for him to press his rod against her lips. She raised her chin and opened her mouth in acceptance. It wasn't long before Ruairí withdrew, coming too close to his release. Senga spied him fisting himself as he walked around to her feet. She strained to lift her head, but the way Ruairí had restrained her arms made it nearly impossible. Her breath whooshed from her as Ruairí thrust into her, burying himself to the hilt as he gripped her hips.

Ruairí surged into her over and over as Senga willed her body to slow and not climax too soon. She wanted to enjoy this, drawing out each sensation that ricocheted through her as Ruairí drove her closer to release. Her eyes drifted closed when she could no longer fight the need to turn off one of her senses as the others remained overstimulated. Ruairí watched as Senga's eyelids drooped, understanding she was losing the battle to control her body. He leaned forward, taking one of her nipples into his mouth. As he suckled, she burst apart, her back arching off the table before she tilted her hips, offering a better angle. He was certain he had reduced his cock to nothing after the way his seed exploded from him. As soon as they both felt the tremors fade, Ruairí was quick to release Senga's arms, rubbing the circulation back into them. She wiggled her fingers before deciding she had enough feeling back to wrap her arms around Ruairí. They laid atop the table until Ruairí noticed Senga growing cold. He untied her legs and carried her to their bed. It didn't take long before they were snuggled beneath the covers and fast asleep.

# CHAPTER EIGHTEEN

Senga stood beside Ruairí at the helm as the city of Glasgow came into view down the Firth of Clyde. She shielded her eyes as they progressed along the inland waterway. There were other ships, mostly merchants and fishermen, who maneuvered around the *Lady Charity*. While the ship flew the banners that displayed the marque of Argyll, most recognized her for what she was: a pirate ship. Senga hadn't been on board the last time Ruairí sailed this close to a heavily inhabited area. When they put ashore just before their wedding, Senga and Caragh had to travel inland quite a way before they saw any sign of a village. From where she stood, Senga could see people moving along the coast and buildings formed into solid shapes as the Port of Glasgow came into sight.

"What will happen?" Senga caught herself whispering, as though her words might carry to someone on shore and alert the town to the pirates' approach. Though she spoke softly, Ruairí heard her, and responded.

"We will dock, and while the men unload what they can during daylight, I will pay my respects to the Earl of Argyll."

Senga nodded, unsure if she should ask to come along or barricade herself into their cabin, Ruairí seemed to read her mind. "I'm not leaving you here, Senga. I don't trust anyone in this city as far as I could throw them. I want you by my side where I know I can defend you. Besides, I have a rather bonnie bride I'm proud to have walking with me."

"If that's the case, it doesn't seem like we shall blend in," Senga pointed out. "You are a rather recognizable figure."

"And you are breathtaking." he smiled.

"Whose breath will you be taking if they look at me?" Senga grinned.

"Any and every man foolish enough to try." Ruairí pressed a kiss on her forehead as they drew closer to port.

In less than half an hour, Ruairí was assisting Senga onto the dock. She'd returned to their cabin and changed into the finest gown she had. Ruairí had a chest brought to their cabin after they married and insisted Senga select anything she wanted. Today, she'd opted for an intricately embroidered kirtle that complimented her ebony hair and dark eyes. She'd taken time to brush her hair and twist it into a stylish coiffure before draping a shawl over her head and shoulders to keep the wind from blowing her hair loose. Now she held Ruairí's hand as they walked along the dock. More than one woman approached Ruairí, but Senga's bared teeth halted them in their tracks. Ruairí chuckled until the first man leered at her, and Senga feared the man might die before he realized Ruairí would attack. She squeezed his arm and grinned at him.

"Not so nice, is it?" Senga cocked an eyebrow before sweeping her gaze over the women who plied their trade along the docks.

"No, it's not," Ruairí frowned, but his face relaxed when he caught the mirth in Senga's eyes.

"We're quite the piratical pair," Senga grinned. "Happy to plunder one another and possessive of our treasures."

"I'm a treasure, am I?" Ruairí teased.

"One I intend to plunder as soon as we return to our cabin."

"In that case, I shall hurry to conclude our business."

Ruairí scanned the gathering crowd, his arm wrapped casually around Senga's shoulders; however, she knew it was anything but. He was prepared to draw his sword in an instant if he perceived a threat. "We will need horses to travel the scant distance to Dumbarton Castle."

"I thought the earl's residence was Campbell Castle."

"It is, but the earl visits Dumbarton when his fleet, as he likes to think of them, sails into port. He collects a fee from all the captains, not just Rowan and me. We pay the most, thanks to our reputation, but it is a necessary evil to keep our heads attached to our necks. My fear is that with the delay, he will have grown impatient and departed. If that's the case, the best we can hope for is that he's gone to Inveraray instead of Campbell Castle."

"How long is the ride to Inveraray?"

"Only a couple of hours; not too bad a ride. If he's returned home, I'll have to find the man I've used as a messenger in the past. I'll take you back to the *Lady Charity* if that's the case. I'm not taking you to the place where I'd have to meet him."

Senga cocked an eyebrow and managed to narrow her eyes at the same time. "A brothel."

Ruairí halted and turned to look at Senga in surprise. "No. But even if that's the case, I would conduct my business and leave."

"Business of more than one kind?" Senga demanded.

"Are you trying to earn another spanking, or do you have such little belief that I can be faithful? Why'd you marry me if that's the case?"

Senga shook her head. "I don't know why I'm being so moody and contentious these days. Perhaps I need more sleep. We've just never been ashore together other than for you to chase me. I know what you did at the Three Merry Lads before we met."

"And you assume I'll return to my old habits the moment I'm out of your sight."

"I told you, I don't know why I'm being so moody all of a sudden. I just—" Senga trailed off. There was no rationale to her emotions. Ruairí had done nothing to make her fear he might stray. In fact, he was the most devoted husband she'd ever seen, but fear crept into her chest when he said he intended to take her back to the *Lady Charity*. "Ruairí, you told me you didn't feel comfortable leaving me behind on the ship. But now you're telling me that's where you'll take me and you haven't told me where you would be going. Where else would you be going if you don't want to take me?"

Ruairí saw the logic in Senga's fear, and he felt guilty for causing her distress. He pulled her into his embrace, not caring who witnessed the dreaded Dark Heart's affection toward his wife. He saw no weakness in loving Senga, nor did he experience any embarrassment for showing it.

"Senga, the man will undoubtedly be in the gaol. That's where I always find him. He was one of my men before he lost his arm. He couldn't work aboard ship, so he opted to retire from my service. He thought to find some work on land, but he's a drunkard on his best of days. I've offered to have him return, but he refuses, saying he doesn't need my pity. For all his faults, he's still one of the best horsemen I know, and I can trust him with my purse of coins. I don't want to take you where I'm certain I'll find him. I don't want you near that stench, and I don't want you to hear the things men will say to you. I don't want you to see such misery and suffering while I bribe his way out. I'd keep you from that because there are sights there that you will never unsee. I don't want you waiting outside for me, either, even with Tomas and Snake Eye to guard you."

"Hopefully, it won't come to that. And, Ruairí, I'm sorry. I shouldn't have jumped to conclusions so quickly. You haven't given me any reason to doubt you. I don't know that any man could be a more honorable husband."

"I understand your fear, little one. It's hard to overlook a reputation I rightly earned." He kissed Senga's temple before stepping back. "I don't regret for a moment that I'll earn a different reputation these days."

"And what's that?"

"A besotted husband who can't keep his hands off his bonnie bride."

"I rather like that reputation," Senga giggled as they came to the end of the pier.

Ruairí guided them through the crowded town until they came to the blacksmith. Spotting horses for rent was a tremendous relief to Ruairí. He hadn't been sure if there would be any available, and he didn't want to add horse thief to his lengthy list of transgressions.

"Is the Earl of Argyll still in residence at Dumbarton?" Ruairí asked as he clasped hands with a man he'd known for years. He'd come to this blacksmith countless times to have weapons repaired and to rent horses when he had to travel inland.

"Aye, as far as I ken. But I hear he is readying to head home. Ye made it just in time. He's been grousing that ye and yer cousin havenae held up yer end of the agreement. Been cursing yer name to anyone who will listen. Threatening to revoke yer marque and put yer head on a pike."

"Not a patient man, is he?" Senga mumbled.

The blacksmith turned an assessing eye on Senga, who returned his stare in equal measure.

"Bonnie lass ye have with ye, Capt'n."

"Senga is my bonnie wife." The steel in Ruairí's voice seemed to ring throughout the blacksmith's shop and into the stables. Once more, Ruairí's arm appeared to rest casually around Senga's shoulders, but there was no misunderstanding the menace in his glare as it swept across every man within earshot. He knew word would spread quickly and that his reputation protected Senga as much as it made her a target once again. Hopefully the warning in his glare would outweigh the bait.

"Then felicitations are in order. Ma regards, ma lady."

The blacksmith dipped his head, but Senga could tell he was still trying to assess her. She suspected he assumed she was a well-dressed prostitute, and Ruairí's snarl said her husband had come to the same conclusion. The blacksmith put up his hands in surrender. "I mean no disrespect, Dark Heart. Just curious is all."

"Aye, and curiosity killed the cat," Ruairí reminded. "Senga is from one of the smaller isles in the Hebrides. We met when I had to go ashore in her village." That was all Ruairí was willing to say. It wasn't an untruth, but he would never admit they met in a tavern, or there would be no way to change people's perception. He refused to have anyone confuse his wife for a tavern whore.

"Right. Ye'll be needing mounts, I'm guessing. Just two?"

"Nay, four. Tomas and Snake Eye are riding with us."

Senga kept quiet, though she was surprised to hear the two loyal sailors were ordered to accompany them. She wondered if Ruairí would have made the brief trip alone if she weren't with him. Senga glanced over her shoulder to see Tomas and Snake Eye lounging against the door frame, blocking the entrance for anyone who might attempt to enter before Ruairí concluded his business.

"Of course, Capt'n." The blacksmith called over his apprentices and sent the young men to saddle the horses while Ruairí paid. "I wouldnae waste a moment as word is, Argyll departs before the nooning. Ye're lucky he isnae an early riser."

Ruairí and the blacksmith shook hands as Senga realized that she and the local man had not truly been introduced. Ruairí then assisted her into the saddle. Senga hadn't ridden in years, but it came back to her as though it were still second nature. She tied her shawl tightly beneath her chin before they set off, and she was glad of it as they galloped out of the city. She hoped to preserve some of her polished appearance before they were presented to one of the most powerful men in Scotland.

Ruairí glanced over at Senga throughout the ride, both impressed and relieved that she was so comfortable on horseback. It wasn't often that he needed to ride these days, but should they ever need to escape by land, it was reassuring to know that she could keep up.

# CHAPTER NINETEEN

I t had been years since Senga stepped into the bailey of a castle, never mind one as enormous as this one. She hadn't had a reason to visit any nobility once she left Lewis. She'd made that one failed attempt to return home after her husband and son died. Beyond that, there was no keep to visit on Canna. Strangely, she felt both at home and on guard as she approached the castle's steps. She knew what to expect from a bustling keep, but she didn't know any of the people around her.

As armed as she knew Ruairí was, Senga had nearly as many weapons strapped to her. He'd teased her when she slid her dirks into the sheaths on her thighs and into her boots. She'd added the small, razor-sharp knife known as the sgian dubh to her belt along with wrist bracers she'd found in a chest not long after she boarded the *Lady Charity*. Ruairí jested, asking if they were to protect herself or him. His smile burst across his face as she hissed and pounced. She'd knocked him back onto the bed and reminded him there was nothing she wouldn't do to protect him.

Ruairí wrapped Senga's arm around his as a guardsman opened the castle's massive door. Her eyes darted over the floor, the walls, the passageways that led away from the entrance, and finally the Great Hall. She knew the man seated at the dais had to be the Earl of Argyll. There was an aura of arrogance that came from the generations of power and influence exercised by the Campbells. There were few clans who could rival the Campbells' power, or their dominance over the Highlands. Since the reign of Robert the Bruce, the Campbells' reach had spread across land that the crown ceded them as well as won in battle. No monarch had reeled in the Campbells, and they enjoyed their prominent position within the government and among Highlanders.

The man on the dais seemed the picture of gluttony. He grudgingly lowered the leg of mutton on which he chewed, licking his fingers before swiping his sleeve across his mouth. Senga had seen the same manners in the men who frequented the Three Merry Lads. She knew wealth didn't buy couth. As she and Ruairí approached, Senga wanted to squirm under the earl's lecherous gaze, but she refused to give him the satisfaction of her discomfort. Ruairí dipped his head but showed no other signs of deference. Senga curtseyed, but ensured she kept her back straight, lest she give the earl a view of her cleavage. She was determined to do nothing that could be seen as flirtatious or encouraging.

"It's about time you showed your face. You're late." The earl's voice boomed through the Great Hall. It was obvious that he was trying to shame Ruairí, who ignored the bait. Instead he stood in silence, waiting for the earl to continue. After a pause and a sneer when Ruairí failed to respond, the earl continued. "Where is your cousin?"

"He was unable to join us, but he sends his regards and his coins," Ruairí offered.

"Unacceptable," the earl sneered. "He was to pay his fealty to me in person."

"His wife has been unwell, so he asked that I represent the MacNeils. This isn't be the first time one of us appeared on behalf of both ships."

"Wife? The Blond Devil would never wed. And who is this

slut you've brought with you? Whores aren't welcome in the Great Hall."

Ruairí placed his hand over the hilt of his sword. No one had attempted to divest him of his weapons, a courtesy only paid to one of the most infamous pirates in the British Isles. "I wouldn't speak of my wife like that. Not if you want to live long enough to see your own whore," Ruairí's voice was so low that conversation ceased as many strained to hear the exchange. Before Senga understood what was happening, Ruairí whipped a dirk from his belt and sent it sailing toward Argyll's head. It whizzed past his ear, surely close enough to cut through his hair, and embedded in the screen behind the dais. Senga waited for guardsmen to seize her and Ruairí, but no one dared approach. Senga had met Ruairí in a smugglers' den where his reputation preceded him, but there he was among pirates and other criminals. She hadn't anticipated the power his reputation had among polite society.

"Wife? And what brothel did you find her at?"

"I wouldn't speak so of the MacLeod's niece. Her father was the previous laird."

"MacLeod? He has no nieces," the earl retorted.

"The one on Skye may not, but the one on Lewis does," Ruairí spat as he tossed another dirk into the air; it rotated before the hilt landed back in his hand. He continued to toss it as though the earl was boring him. Senga forced herself to move only enough to breathe. "The MacLeods of Lewis and Skye are allied these days. I don't think either sept would appreciate the foul words you're tossing at one of their own."

Senga prayed the earl wasn't familiar with her life story, or he might call Ruairí's bluff. She held her breath as she waited for the axe to fall, but the earl nodded. Ruairí sheathed his knife and drew a pouch from his waist that his cloak had hidden. He handed the pouch to a guardsman, who carried it to the dais. The earl peered into the velvet purse before dumping its contents onto the table. He pushed the coins around, even biting one to check that it was real. When he was satisfied that Ruairí had paid both his and Rowan's due, the earl nodded his acceptance.

"Perhaps you and your wife care to join me for a meal." Senga interpreted it as an order, not an offer, but Ruairí shook his head.

"We shall have to decline, my lord." It was the only sign of deference Ruairí had offered the odious man. "My wife and I will sail with the tide."

"And it isn't for several more hours." The earl offered a jovial smile, but his next word was a command. "Stay."

Ruairí was unaccustomed to taking orders, and he didn't trust the earl with Senga nearby. He wouldn't risk Senga's safety by causing a fight with any of the guardsmen, but he also refused to remain there for the man to insult his wife again, or to make the lusty offers Ruairí knew were inevitable. He'd known the earl for years, but the Campbell's reputation for mistreating women was blacker than his own for piracy. Before Ruairí could refuse again, Senga squeezed his arm and dipped into shallow curtsy.

"If I may, my lord," she smiled coyly. "Captain MacNeil has promised me time in the shops as a wedding gift. I also have medicinals to restock. My husband won't break his word to me, but I don't want to keep the entire crew waiting. You wouldn't have me upset such a group of sailors, would you? Unpredictable lot and all."

The earl's smile appeared more like a grimace as he nodded. "Very well, MacNeil. You have your wife to thank for being excused. One should never break their word to a lady. It is Lady Senga MacLeod, is it not? Even if your husband doesn't have the manners to introduce us properly, I recognize you. Your uncle is a good friend of mine. I shall be sure to pass along your regards when next I see him."

"Perhaps you could stop by my parents' graves while you're there. I'm sure they'd appreciate you passing along my regards to them. as well." Senga's voice was smooth and unassuming, but the earl flinched, revealing to Senga that the man knew how her uncle came to power. Ruairí didn't wait for the earl to respond. He dipped his head once more and spun them around.

"Do take care, Dark Heart. I hear there is rough water ahead," the Earl of Argyll called out to their retreating backs. Neither Ruairí nor Senga missed a step as they swept out of the keep. They both recognized the threat, but they denied the powerful man the reaction he hoped for. Ruairí and Rowan had spent a decade on the high seas, and had faced far worse foes than Argyll.

Ruairí ordered the *Lady Charity* underway as soon as he and Senga boarded, but they sailed just beyond the port and dropped anchor. They planned to wait until the cloak of darkness allowed Ruairí to unload the contraband cargo he didn't dare move during daylight. The rum and wine were worth a fortune, and he had no intention of having the earl claim Ruairí owed him more in taxes. Ruairí left Snake Eye behind to guard Senga in their cabin while he rowed ashore to complete his trade. Senga was already asleep when he returned, but she pushed her hair from her sleepy eyes as he sat on the bed.

"Did all go well, *mo chridhe*?" Senga's groggy voice had a rasp that went straight to Ruairí's cock.

"Aye. Better than I'd hoped. I received more than enough coin to make up for what Rowan and I had to pay. We also took on cargo the Irish will welcome."

"Dare I ask what?"

"Weapons. Swords, knives, shields. All things they desperately need as they continue to battle the English." Much like the Scottish, the Irish refused to silently accept English dominion. They'd been fighting the English for centuries, successfully sometimes, but more often taking heavy losses.

"Where do we sail to?"

"Rathlin Island, off the northern tip of Ireland. We will meet smugglers there, then sail to Ballycastle."

"That's two days sail from here, assuming the weather holds."

"Aye. Whatever shall we do to pass two days' time?" Ruairí leaned back and kissed Senga before twisting and capturing her beneath him, setting the tone for those two days. Kyle manned the helm most of the time, but Ruairí also took shifts, unwilling to ignore his duties completely as captain. As they approached Rathlin Island, Senga thought of Caragh and how her cousin had managed a smuggling ring. Caragh had lost half her men during Rowan's raid; her brother Eddie had died during Ruairí's attack. Senga didn't want to see any of the men she'd grown used to, even softened toward, come to harm. She prayed that history didn't repeat itself.

# CHAPTER TWENTY

R uairí scanned the beach as the dinghies approached. He saw wraithlike figures emerge from the caves, and he recognized the man with whom he'd trade. Aidan O'Flaherty was nearly as infamous as the Blond Devil and the Dark Heart, but unlike the cousins he preferred to stay closer to home and terrorize the waters around England. Ruairí only trusted Aidan out of necessity. O'Flaherty was more likely to plunge a dagger in a friend's heart than share any treasure.

"Stay beside me, Senga. I mean it," Ruairí whispered. Senga, dressed in leggings and a tunic with her hair tied back, was more than happy to comply with Ruairí's orders. She hopped over the side and splashed into the surf before Ruairí could help her. His scowl seemed to glow in the moonlight.

"I'm not going anywhere, but neither am I going to appear frail in front of these men," Senga insisted.

Ruairí nodded, but his scowl remained. He led the landing party ashore with his sword in one hand and a protective arm stretched out to keep Senga tucked behind him. "I was wondering if the Dark Heart had lost his way," came a voice that seemed far too loud for such a secretive meeting.

"O'Flaherty, you're a long way from home. Aughnanure

Castle is nowhere near here." Ruairí had explained to Senga that the man they planned meet preferred to stay near his home in Galway, on the western coast, whenever he wasn't on the water.

"Aye, well business calls, shall we say?" Aidan peered at Senga. The smile he offered was seductive and predatory as he approached. His inky hair gleamed like a raven's wing, and Senga was fairly certain his eyes were the blue of a midnight sea. He was the most handsome man she'd ever seen beside Ruairí, and Rowan, who was practically her husband's twin. She could understand how a man such as Aidan had the power to lead a woman to any manner of sin, but she wasn't interested. She felt Ruairí's anger mounting the longer Aidan stared at her, so she slid her hand along Ruairí's back and down his arm as she stepped beside him. She slid her hand into his, her possessiveness clear in her actions, and her understanding of Aidan's intentions clear upon her own seductive smile.

"Will you introduce me, *mo ghaol?*" Senga turned an inquisitive face toward Ruairí. She didn't turn to look at Aidan, or any other man as Ruairí spoke. She nodded, but she kept her gaze on her husband. She wouldn't have Aidan or any of the other Irish pirates presume they could lure her away.

Ruairí felt the anger rise within him as Aidan O'Flaherty continued to ogle his wife; much as he needed O'Flaherty's coin, he was tempted to run the man through. Ruairí decided, instantly and unequivocally, that he was retiring from piracy. He would take Senga back to Barra, or anywhere she'd be protected from the unsavory men he'd spent half of his life dealing with. He felt Senga squeeze his hand, and the resolute expression he could see in her eyes encouraged him, allowing him to relax long enough to remember that he couldn't gut Aidan. At least not at the moment.

"Aidan O'Flaherty, I'd have you meet my wife Senga MacNeil."

"Wife? Wonders shall never cease. I never took you for the marrying man."

"Aye, well, I wanted him and refused to let him go." Senga tucked herself under Ruairí's arm as she wrapped hers around him.

"A woman issuing you orders? And outside of bed at that. I never thought to see the day," Aidan crowed, but his lascivious grin hadn't slipped despite learning Ruairí and Senga were married, despite seeing how Senga clung to Ruairí. Instead, he seemed to take it as a challenge as he approached.

"Senga is my partner. And I had no desire to run once she captured my heart."

"Such sentimental drivel," Aidan spat. "Are you going soft?"

"There's nothing soft when my wife is near."

Senga was certain her face would go up in flames, but she understood the peacocking both men were doing. It wasn't about her so much as the posturing that both men did before the others. She remained close to Ruairí's side as the conversation between the two captains moved to business. She watched as the sailors from the *Lady Charity* carried crates onto the beach and pried open the lids. Aidan inspected each one, but Ruairí's men were quick to slap the lids down until Aidan signaled his men to carry out their own cargo to trade. There were several enormous chests that revealed coin, jewels, clothing, and even bottles of various types of alcohol.

Senga had never seen so many riches gathered in one place. She'd never paid attention to what the smugglers brought ashore on Canna. She purposely stayed far away from the caves at all times, and never went near the shore when pirates and privateers moored their ships off the coast. She guarded her reaction to Aiden's riches, but the treasure Ruairí received still impressed her. To Senga's mind, Ruairí had gotten the better end of the trade, but she understood it only proved how desperate the Irish were to defend their homes.

"Cross over to Ballycastle, and I shall offer you my hospitality." Aidan looked at Senga rather than Ruairí when he made the offer. She squeezed Ruairí's hand like a vice when he accepted. She didn't want to spend any more time in Aidan's company than necessary. Ruairí shot her a look that only she understood; he was asking her to have faith in him. It made her realize that business hadn't concluded despite dinghies loaded with bounty being rowed back to the ships.

The six-mile crossing seemed to take only a few minutes, and Senga stared up at the limestone cliffs upon which Kinbane Castle sat. She had to admit that she welcomed the warm fire that burned in the castle's Great Hall. The building was certainly more hospitable than Dumbarton. Aidan offered them seats at the dais.

"Do the MacDonnells know you're enjoying the MacAlisters' home as we speak?" Ruairí raised a chalice of wine to Aidan before taking a long quaff. Senga wasn't familiar with the politics among the Irish clans, but she assumed they functioned in a similar fashion to their Scottish counterparts. She wondered if the MacDonnells were as powerful in Ireland as the MacDonnells–a cadet branch of the MacDonalds–were in Scotland.

"They were no doubt aware of our meeting on their beach, and I assume they have lookouts here." Aidan shrugged as he poured more wine into his chalice. "The MacAlister men have gone hunting, and for reasons I cannot fathom, their noblewomen refuse to leave their chambers."

The hair on the back of Senga's neck rose with the threat that lay beneath Aidan's words. She refused to look at him as servants placed platters of food on the table. Ruairí placed a healthy serving before Senga, and while it was more than she normally ate, it provided a reason to keep herself occupied as conversation flowed between Ruairí and Aidan. But she couldn't ignore the man any longer when he addressed her by name.

"Lady Senga." She tried not to grimace at the use of a title she hadn't possessed in years. She'd given up the honorific with ease when she married Alexander, so hopelessly in love was she. Nowadays, it seemed ridiculous to hear it associated with her name after living in her small cottage and working in a tavern for five years. She nodded and finally turned her gaze to meet Aidan's. "My lady, perhaps you've heard the tale of how my crew and I found ourselves nearly stranded at Belmullet?"

Senga understood Aidan's intentions. The man was aware there was no way Senga could be aware of such an event, so when he forced her to admit as much, he would have the opening he needed to regale her of some impressive feat. She shook her head once.

"Ah well, it is quite a tale, my lady. My men and I were bound for Blacksod Bay before returning home to Galway. By our misfortune, we arrived at Broad Haven to find the waterways as dry as an Arabian desert. I thought to turn around, sail further around the coast in the open seas, but my men assured me they were strong enough. Do you know what they were strong enough to do, Lady Senga?" Aidan made her name roll off her tongue in a way that only an Irish accent could do. However, she much preferred her husband's Highland burr, which he was able to hide and that he shared only with her from time to time. "My men and I carried our ships overland. It might have been less than a league, but it was no simple task. But my men and I were up to the challenge."

Senga turned away when Aidan flexed his arms and chests as if to prove his strength. When she didn't offer him the 'oohs' and 'ahhs' he'd expected, he tried another tack. Senga sensed Ruairí's anger returning as Aidan flirted with her. She wished she could reassure him that this obnoxious man annoyed her more than anything else. The best she could do was grip his thigh under the table and make a quiet sigh of annoyance. She hoped Ruairí understood. He patted his hand over hers, then lifted her hand from his thigh. She glanced up at him and discovered Ruairí directed his anger at her. Aidan's knowing smile made Senga want to plunge one of her dirks into his eye.

"Do you know what my friends call me, Senga?" Aidan grew more brazen as he observed Ruairí's tension mounting.

"I wouldn't know, since we aren't friends," Senga snapped. "Until today, I didn't know you existed." But he was not deterred.

"That just means we must make time to become friends," Aidan pressed. "My friends call me *Naoise*." Senga wanted to laugh as she repeated the name in her head. Nee-sha. It didn't sound particularly masculine to her.

"Do you know what it means, Senga?" Aiden nearly purred.

"Some of your Irish Gaelic differs from ours." Senga hoped she sounded disinterested as she turned back to her trencher and took another bite of roasted fowl.

"It means warrior." Aidan grinned, proud of himself.

Warrior indeed. Arrogant prig seemed be a better name. Senga leaned toward Ruairí and whispered, "Can we leave soon?"

Ruairí narrowed his eyes at her as though he tried to read more into her words than she intended. She feared they'd have an argument once they returned to the *Lady Charity*, but she wasn't certain of the reason. She'd tried to disabuse Aidan of any sign that he held her interest. When he shook his head, Senga's heart sank. Her disappointment must have been too obvious, because Ruairí had a moment of doubt that he'd made the right choice in bringing Senga on land and to this infernal meal.

"What news have you?" Ruairí ended Aidan's self-gratifying storytelling.

"Those bluidy MacLeods are nipping at my heels once more. They're sailing too far to the west when they come into the North Channel. They act as though they own the bluidy ocean."

Senga tensed as she listened to Aidan speak of her former

clan, but she wasn't certain if he meant the MacLeods of Skye or Lewis. She glanced at Ruairí and sensed he wondered the same thing. She refused to speak again, so she prayed Ruairí asked for her.

"And which MacLeods are you at war with now?" Ruairí quipped.

"Those blighters from Lewis. Their laird is a pustule on the arse of a hog."

"Who's their laird these days? I haven't paid attention since we avoid that part of the Hebrides."

"Avoid it? I thought you sailed through regularly. Canna is a favorite of yours." Aidan shot Senga a wolfish grin as he waggled his eyebrows. Both she and Ruairí ignored his innuendos. When Aidan received no reaction from the couple, he carried on. "Neil MacLeod, the sodding bastard."

Senga pressed her lips together to keep from agreeing that her uncle was not only a bastard in deed but in truth. He'd been born before her grandfather married his mistress after her own grandmother's death. Despite his anger earlier, Ruairí pulled Senga's hand back onto his thigh and covered it with his much larger one. She spread her fingers out from under his palm, and the tension eased from between her shoulder blades when Ruairí entwined their fingers.

"What's he done now?" Ruairí inquired. "Besides sailing into *your* water." Ruairí taunted Aidan, knowing that a pirate from the western coast had no business claiming the waterway between eastern Ireland and southern Scotland was his. But pirates were wont to claim all the seas as their own, even those waters they'd never entered.

"His sniveling maggot of a son, Alfred, will be far easier to control. He doesn't have the same iron in his blood that his father does. It would be unfortunate for Neil MacLeod if he should die soon, and it would be unfortunate for the MacLeods of Lewis if Alfred should take the lairdship soon. But I fear fate has plans for just that." Aidan's laughter was rich and deep, and in another time and place, it might have stirred Senga's interest. But his patronizing manner and news about her family soured any warmth she might have found in it. "Lady Senga, if memory serves me, it was this very Neil MacLeod who orchestrated the murder of your father and mother, isn't that so?"

Senga's stomach clenched as her heart lurched. She didn't want to talk about her past, and she certainly didn't want to remember the second-worst day of her life. The only day that exceeded the pain of losing her parents was the day her son died. She nodded her head but kept her gaze lowered to the food on the table before her.

"O'Flaherty," Ruairí warned, but the Irishman threw his hands up in feigned innocence.

"I wasn't sure if the lass was aware of what's been happening in her home since she ran away."

# CHAPTER TWENTY-ONE

R uairí forced himself to remain seated and not draw his dirk as the Irish pirate baited him and Senga. It frustrated him that Senga opted to become shy that night, seeing how it drove Aidan to chase her, thinking she was playing a seductive game. The rational part of his mind realized that she didn't understand what her evasiveness and reticence was doing, but another part wanted to shake her and remind her of how that exact manner landed her in danger twice the very night they met. He wanted to bash Aidan's skull in for flirting with his wife underneath his nose and now taunting her. He never expected Aidan to be familiar with Senga's past, and it unnerved him when Aidan mentioned Senga running away from home. It meant Aidan knew more about Senga than sat well with Ruairí.

"Has the Dark Heart never heard the tale of the MacLeod lass who chose to be a common farmer's wife than marry a laird old enough to have sired her father? How the lass ran from her uncle when he tried to give her a poke?"

Ruairí placed both of his hands flat on the table before canting his head toward Aidan. To some, it might look like Ruairí had no intention of drawing his weapons, but Aidan shifted, recognizing a maneuver he'd used plenty of times to catch an opponent off-guard.

"Do you presume there is anything from my wife's past that I don't know? She is my wife, after all. We've had plenty of time shut away in our cabin to get well acquainted." Ruairí kept his hands on the table but leaned toward Aidan, the menace clear in his tone and his gaze. "If you want my support to fight MacLeod, come out and say it like a man rather than trying to humiliate my wife. Dead men don't fight, O'Flaherty. Where will your countrymen be when you no longer lead?"

Ruairí pushed back his chair and rose before assisting Senga from hers. He wrapped her arm around his bicep and guided her toward the steps that led down from the dais. Once they reached the floor, Ruairí spoke over his shoulder to Aidan. "Ask before we reach the door, and I will consider it. But if we leave and you don't, then not only will I never aid you again, I will kill you the next time we meet."

Senga forced herself to walk, even though Ruairí's longer stride nearly made her trot beside him to keep up. She kept her chin high, adopting the mien of a laird's daughter accustomed to others moving out of her way merely because of who she was. She realized being a pirate's wife wasn't so different from being the laird's offspring with the respect and fear it garnered. They were nearly to the door when Aidan's voice called out.

"Meet me at dawn, and we will plan what comes next. The O'Driscolls will want in." Aidan's words might have sounded like a command if there hadn't been a conciliatory tone in his voice. Ruairí nodded but didn't slow their pace as they exited the Great Hall.

"Do not speak until we reach our chamber, Senga," Ruairí hissed as they stepped outside. Senga kept her mouth clamped shut; her jaw ached from how tightly she clenched it. She understood Ruairí's anger directed toward Aidan, but she didn't understand why he directed any of it toward her. She had asked if they could leave ages ago, but it had been Ruairí who decided they would stay. Aidan had revealed nothing she hadn't shared with Ruairí on the night they met. It wasn't as though he discovered a secret she'd kept from him.

The rocking of the dinghy as Snake Eye rowed them back to the *Lady Charity* knocked Senga into Ruairí more than once, but he never wrapped his arm around her like he normally would. She shivered, but it wasn't from the cold air; it was from Ruairí's frigid demeanor. She followed his order, but the moment she heard the bar drop to secure their cabin door, she spun on him.

"What is the matter with you? What's happened?" Senga demanded. Ruairí barely glanced in her direction as he tore his leine over his head and threw it across the cabin. His long legs made pacing in the confined space difficult. He looked like a caged lion with his blond mane shining in the candlelight. His anger simmered, and Senga grew uneasy the longer he ignored her. She wasn't sure he even intended that; his mind seemed somewhere else. "What it is, Ruairí? You're scaring me."

Senga's softly spoken words permeated Ruairí's fog. He swung around to glare at his wife, but he had a moment of contrition when he saw genuine alarm in her gaze. Guilt niggled at him; he had sworn he would never do anything to incite fear of him in his wife, but anger once more got the better of him. He stalked across the chamber, backing Senga against a wall. He tunneled his hand into her hair, keeping her in place but not touching her in any other way. She had space to duck away, and he would let her if she tried, but she trembled before him even as her eyes met his.

"What's wrong? I watched my wife flirt with another man right before me tonight. Do you find him attractive, Senga? Do you want him?"

Senga narrowed her eyes, her own temper flaring. "Would you have me lie just so you can punish me? If I say I don't consider him attractive, then you'd recognize it for the lie it is.

Of course, I do. He is. But so is Rowan since you're practically twins, but never once have I desired him. So is Kyle, but I never once looked at him as anything more than a friend. I *do not* desire Aidan. I can barely tolerate him. I'm the one who asked to leave, but you decided to stay. What did that accomplish? Nothing but my own humiliation. Don't you dare blame me for this."

"So you don't believe your little performance when we arrived on the beach wasn't what started all of this?"

"What performance? I stood by your side. I assumed I made it obvious that I was only interested in you."

"By pressing against me and smiling like a dockside whore?" Ruairí slammed his mouth shut, knowing he'd gone too far.

The color drained from Senga's face so rapidly that Ruairí feared she might collapse, but then it returned in a fiery blaze. "How dare you speak to me that way? I swear to you, here and now, Ruairí. If you ever, *ever* speak to me like this again, I will jump overboard and swim back to shore like Caragh did. I'll take my chances on my own rather than remain with a man I love but who could speak to me like that."

"You are not going anywhere, Senga. You're my wife. Mine." Ruairí growled before pressing his mouth to hers. The kiss was punishing and brutal, but Senga opened to him. She was livid about his vile words, but she wanted Ruairí to claim her as much as she wanted to show him that she would never want a man other than him. He nipped at her bottom lip, taking it between his teeth and tugging enough to make her moan. He lifted her off her feet, and her legs wrapped around his waist as he pressed her back against the wall. "I'm going to fuck you, little one."

Senga ground her sheath against his rod, frustrated that several layers of clothing separated them. "Not until you take back those hateful words."

"You think to give me orders?"

Senga froze. She looked at Ruairí and suddenly understood where his anger that night began. Aidan had taunted Ruairí that he took orders from Senga. He'd belittled Ruairí's manhood from the start. She'd chalked it up to typical male posturing, but she suddenly understood that as the captain of a ship, a pirate ship, Ruairí couldn't risk anyone questioning whether he was in charge. She didn't doubt the men aboard the *Lady Charity* understood Ruairí was the absolute authority on their ship, but others might consider the *Lady Charity* was vulnerable to attack.

"No, Capt'n."

Ruairí's nostrils flared as he narrowed his eyes at Senga, unsure if she was taunting him now too. She lowered her gaze and rested her hands on his chest. Her sudden submissiveness made him doubt what was happening just as much as it made him want to thrust into her.

"Do you still demand an apology?"

"I want one, Ruairí. Your words hurt. They cut me deeply, and I don't think I've ever deserved them. But I do think I understand your anger. I don't think Aidan understood what I intended. I don't think you did either." Ruairí growled when she used the Irish pirate's given name. "I saw how O'Flaherty looked at me, and my intention was to show him and his men that I only want you, that I'm yours and no one else's."

"You made yourself look like a tavern wench. It infuriates me that anyone should see you as such."

"And that includes me acting in a way you don't approve of." Senga reasoned.

"You could have just stood still and silent. But no. You had to taunt Aidan with what he couldn't have. What I have and he doesn't. Don't you get that's exactly what makes a pirate attack? Then when you could have spoken up at the meal, you turned shy and evasive. He took it as you laying down an invitation to chase you."

"He might have, but you must know I wasn't." Senga fisted Ruairí's leine as though holding tightly would make him understand her sincerity.

"Maybe. Or maybe you liked the attention. Maybe you always liked the attention at the Three Merry Lads. You just didn't like it when you couldn't control it."

Senga released her legs from around Ruairí's waist and dropped to the floor. She tried to push him away, but he wouldn't budge. "That was uncalled for, just like your earlier name calling. I'm not arguing with a man who acts like a child. Move."

"A child, Senga? What child can stick his cock in your quim and make you scream his name?"

"You may have the body of a man, there is no doubting that, but you're acting like a spoiled wean."

"I'm acting like a man who watched another man drool over his wife all night."

"That isn't my fault!" Senga shouted.

"But it is, Senga."

"I have no more control over that bastard than I do you. We're all adults, or we are all supposed to be. We all choose how we react and behave. I can't change him any more than I can you, despite how much I might want to change you right now. Let go of me." Senga pushed away from Ruairí, and this time he moved. "I may have misjudged how to make Ai— O'Flaherty see I'm committed to you, but that doesn't mean I deserve what you're spewing."

"Your misjudgment, as you call, risked your bonnie little neck. Or rather, your bonnie little body. What happens when he tries to take you? And mark my words, he will. What if I'm not at your side when that happens?"

Senga froze and looked up at Ruairí. His words from a moment earlier echoed in her ears, and she suddenly understood Ruairí's anger. *You had to taunt Aidan with what he couldn't have. What I have and he doesn't. Don't you know that's exactly what makes a pirate attack?* It wasn't anger at all. It was fear. The anger and hurt drained from Senga, and her body weighed too much for her to hold up. She sank to the bed and hung her head. She patted the spot beside her, praying Ruairí would

170

take her invitation. Instead, he stepped before her and lifted her chin. She couldn't meet his gaze as she licked her suddenly dry lips.

"I didn't understand before, but I do now. You're the only pirate I really know, and you're different with me than with anyone else. I didn't think Aidan—well, I just didn't think like a pirate. I haven't learned how to. Your words tonight hurt me. Deeply, Ruairí. But I entered a situation with no experience and assumed I had control of it. I should have stood still and kept quiet like you said. I risked more than just myself, didn't I?"

"Yes, Senga. But you're more important than weapons and gold or fighting your blasted family or making deals with that pirating bastard. You played a dangerous game and understood none of the rules." Ruairí tilted her head back more until it forced her to look at him. "He angered me, but you scared me."

"I wish you'd just said that rather than everything else."

"I do, too. I'm sorry, Senga. You deserve that apology and much more. I never should have said such hateful things, but..." Ruairí shook his head as he ran his thumb over Senga's jaw. "I already felt weak compared to Aidan after I saw the look of appreciation you gave him when you first saw him. Rather than admit to my fear and how it made me feel even weaker, I lashed out."

Senga drew open the laces to Ruairí's leggings, but he covered her hands and shook his head. She batted them away until she was able to push the leggings down over Ruairí's lean hips. She moved her feet wider, so he could step into the space between her legs. She didn't hesitate to sink her mouth onto his rod, drawing him deep within her mouth. She moved along his length, humming with appreciation as he lengthened and thickened within her. Ruairí worried he might go cross-eyed from the sensation and view of her bobbing head as she worked his throbbing cock. When Senga tasted the first hint of his seed, she pulled away, grinning when Ruairí groaned in what sounded like agony.

"I believe you owe me a good fucking. At least, that's what you promised earlier. Are you up to it?" She stroked his cock twice before he yanked her to her feet. Ruairí spun her around, and she felt a brief tug before her leggings suddenly slackened around her hips. She glanced back to see Ruairí toss a knife onto the table. He tore the tunic from her, her the leggings following suit.

"Issuing orders yet again?" Ruairí's grin taunted Senga. She shivered as need coursed through her, leaving her core empty and achy. "Perhaps you have a lesson that needs learning."

"Yes, Ruairí. Will you teach me?" Senga clasped her hands behind her back, pushing her breasts forward despite the submissive posture.

"With pleasure—for both you and me. Lay on the bed, Senga."

Senga was quick to comply, scrambling onto their bunk and lying in the center of the bed. Ruairí kneeled between her legs, his arms bracketing her ribs before lowering his mouth to her breast. He flicked her nipple between biting down with an unexpected force. Senga cried out as her body bucked. Ruairí tugged and shook his head, elongating the punished nipple as Senga clawed at the sheets. She pushed her feet into the mattress, raising her hips in search of his cock.

Ruairí's hand cupped her mons, the heel of his hand rubbing against the nub that now throbbed. He plunged three fingers into her sheath forcefully enough that a wave of concern washed over him. He worried that he had been too rough, but Senga's moan and rocking hips reassured him that his wife wanted him to carry on. He slid lower on the bed before hooking her knees over his shoulders. His mouth feasted upon her, his teeth grazing the button of sensitive nerves before sucking hard. When he felt Senga's core begin to spasm, he pulled away, leaving her empty. She whimpered as her gaze flew to his. She gulped for air as a cool breeze circled around the heated flesh of her sheath. As she settled, Ruairí launched his attack again, repeating his assault and retreat until Senga was nearly insensate. She tried to reach for him, but each time, his hands pinned her wrists to the bed. She gave up and fisted the sheets as her body lurched toward the precipice, but Ruairí pushed her away from the edge each time rather than over it.

Ruairí watched Senga as she writhed in both pleasure and agony as his onslaught continued. He resolved himself not to give in to his own desire to bury his aching cock in her. They both tacitly accepted their dominant and submissive roles as Senga accepted Ruairí's form of punishment, which brought its own type of gratification to them both. When Ruairí sensed Senga's body was approaching the limits to her endurance, he flipped her over, spreading her legs as wide as she could. He shifted to kneel beside her before his hand rained down a punishing spanking that landed against her swollen and overly sensitive netherlips.

"You're mine, Senga."

Senga turned her head to gaze up at Ruairí. "I always have been. I always will be."

"And if another man wants to have you just as I do?"

"He can go fuck himself."

"You have a vulgar mouth that seems better suited to have my cock in it." Ruairí shifted his aim and spanked her round backside. "Naughty lasses don't get what they want."

"But you can take what you want." Senga wiggled her hips as she pushed them away from the mattress, bringing her bottom to his hand. He landed several more punishing blows before shifting once more between her thighs. He lifted her hips and thrust into her. Their sounds of relief as their bodies finally melded filled the cabin. Ruairí draped his body over hers, drawing her arms overhead as he entwined their fingers. He rocked into her, her body relaxing against the mattress. He shifted, worried that she would suffocate beneath his heavier weight, but her fingers squeezed his. "Stay."

Ruairí let go of his control, surging into Senga over and over, knowing the pleasure verged on pain, but the sounds he elicited from her only drove him wilder. As his approaching release drew his bollocks tight, he couldn't shake the sense that something was missing. As he ran his hands between Senga's creamy shoulder blades, he realized he wanted to watch her as she found her own release. He withdrew to her sounds of disapproval but flipped her over with ease, returning to the place he craved.

"Look at me, Senga. Let me see you."

Senga cupped his jaw and drew him down for a kiss, but before their lips met, she whispered. "I love you more than life, Ruairí. No one can ever change that." As their lips fused just as their bodies had, they both flew over the cliff and climaxed together. They laid joined, Ruairí stroking her hair as Senga's hands swept up and down his back.

"I am so sorry, Senga." Remorse for what he'd said slammed into Ruairí as though his body were being dashed against rocks. "I never should have said any of that. I didn't mean it."

"I know you didn't. That's why I'm still here and didn't hop overboard. I understand now, even though your words tore at me."

"Can you forgive me?" Ruairí feared that while they may have found pleasure together once again, the wounds he made might not heal.

"I already have," she reassured him. "You've never spoken to me like that before. Never. It upset you more than I imagined."

"That's still no excuse. As you said, we control our own behavior, and I didn't. At all."

"I've forgiven you, *mo chridhe*. If you let this consume you, the guilt might make you feel better in its own twisted way, but it won't make things better between us. Let it go. Don't do it again, just like I won't assume I know everything. I love you, Ruairí."

Ruairí nodded and smiled. "You're enough to make me believe in God again. There's no other way to explain why you came into my life. I've sought and plundered treasure near and far, but nothing so fine as you. Only God could have created such a gift."

Senga giggled. "I believe it was my mother and father doing something similar to what we've just done, but your flowery words are rather sweet." Senga shifted to find a better position. The movement made their breath catch and their gazes lock. Ruairí rocked into Senga with a gentleness that was the completely different than their last coupling, but it was what they both desired. The tenderness was the other half of the balm they needed. They spent the night wrapped into one another's embrace, only waking to make love.

# CHAPTER TWENTY-TWO

R uairí grasped the side of the dinghy as Tomas rowed him toward the surf break. He ordered that both his dinghy and the one that carried five other crew members should stop. He spotted Aidan moving along the beach with his entire crew behind him. Ruairí didn't intend to go ashore with only a handful of his crew while Aidan had all of his, and he had no intention of meeting Aidan on his ground again. If the Irishman wanted his help, Ruairí expected Aidan to meet him at least halfway, which put them in the bobbing surf in dinghies. Unlikely and unstable places to launch an attack, Ruairí's crew had conducted meetings such as these before, so they waited patiently for the other pirate captain to row out to them. None of them underestimated Aidan O'Flaherty or his sailors. Ruairí and his men all had dirks at hand, hidden under thighs and backsides but easily accessible.

As Ruairí expected, Aidan waited on the beach for five minutes before throwing up his hands and ordering his dinghies into the water. Ruairí adopted a bored expression, using his sgian dubh to pick invisible dirt from under his nails as Aidan approached. He yawned as the other pirate's boat glided to a halt beside his.

"Tired?" Aidan grinned.

"Aye. No peace for the wicked," Ruairí returned Aidan's grin, but smug satisfaction filled his expression as jealousy flashed across Aidan's face. "I haven't much time, so on with it. What do you want from the O'Driscolls and me?"

"Fionn O'Driscoll owes me a favor."

"Aye, killing his piece of shite father. I'm not convinced he'll jump at paying back that favor. I think he'd see you in Hell first."

"Right you are, but he hates the MacLeods and O'Malleys more than he hates me. Or you."

"And so you assume the enemy of my enemy is my friend. I can barely stand you, and I doubt Fionn O'Driscoll can do much better."

"You had no problem sitting at my table and eating my food last eve."

"You have better wine. And that was neither your table nor your food. Both belonged to the MacAlisters."

Aidan waved his hand in a dismissive gesture before glancing over Ruairí's shoulder at the *Lady Charity*. Ruairí once again grinned. Aidan could search all he wanted, but he wouldn't spot Senga. She agreed she shouldn't be on the deck where Aidan might spot her, but she'd argued against relying on the porthole in their cabin to show her what was happening. Senga perched in the crow's nest while Ruairí rowed out to meet the Irish pirate. She'd climbed up while it was still dark, knowing no one beyond their ship could see her. Aidan caught Ruairí observing him and grimaced. It only broadened Ruairí's grin.

"She's tucked away. It was a long night." Ruairí continued to clean his nails as though Aidan was of little consequence to him. "You still haven't given me a reason to help you. My wife is happy to never return to Lewis. She's a MacNeil now, not a MacLeod. She left that life behind years ago."

"You believe she wouldn't like to see the man who killed her parents?"

"I believe she's made her peace and looks to the future, not the past."

"Is that what you tell yourself, so you don't worry about her still loving the man she'd still be married to and whose son she'd be raising if not for a fever?"

"Once again, you seem to think there are secrets between me and my wife. Perhaps there would be if ever you trapped a woman into marrying your ugly mug, but I have no such worries. I know what Alexander and her son meant to her. I've never tried to replace them or make her forget. But that doesn't mean she wants to return to Lewis."

"But have you asked her?" Aidan pressed, eyebrow lifted imperiously. His expression made Ruairí want to drive his fist into the man's face. Aidan thought to trip Ruairí up or make Ruairí admit that he didn't know his wife as well as he assumed. But there was no chance of that.

"I never needed to. She told me as much when she shared her past with me. She knows how I feel about Barra, too. I told her everything."

Aidan's smirk faltered. Such openness and forthrightness were foreign to him after a lifetime of piracy. Because it was impossible for him to fathom such openness and honesty in his own life, he was incapable of imagining how Ruairí and Senga shared such.

"A man with no secrets left to hide doesn't live long," Aidan mused.

"I never said I have no secrets left." Ruairí snapped his mouth shut before adding that he just had no secrets from Senga. Admitting such made her a target for anyone who wanted revenge or thought he and Rowan had a treasure trove hidden away that Senga might lead them to. She'd never asked him what he had stashed away, and he knew she wouldn't. It never worried or interested her. He and Rowan had enough should the day come when they couldn't or no longer wanted to sail, but it wasn't the stuff of legends. However, he and Rowan had cultivated an image that there was a bounty as part of their fearsome reputation, but now that they both had wives, such a story threatened to be their undoing. "On with it, O'Flaherty. My interest wanes by the moment."

"Recruit the O'Driscolls to fight against the MacLeods of Lewis, and the Irish will no longer harry the Western Isles. We will oust Neil MacLeod and point our ships away from the Hebrides and Orkney."

"Why should I believe you?" Ruairí sneered.

"Honor among thieves?"

"Hardly where you're concerned."

"Very well. Your bluidy king intends to rein in the people of the isles by sending Lowlanders to homestead throughout the Hebrides. That's bad for business for everyone. We all need safe passage through these waterways without the royal navy breathing down our necks."

"I sail under the marque of the Earl of Argyll. My head shall remain attached to my neck."

"It might. But that doesn't mean you won't have your ship seized." Aidan cast a speaking glance at the *Lady Charity* once again. "Seized with your bonnie bride aboard."

Ruairí considered what Aidan said and what he left unsaid. Ruairí and Rowan knew that Lowlanders were moving to the Western Isles, but until they considered returning to Barra with their wives, it had meant little to them. If they were to return to Kisimul Castle, where he and Rowan grew up, he needed to ensure it was a safe place to retire with Senga. The notion of retribution against her uncle held an appeal too. He narrowed his eyes at Aidan as he considered the situation.

"I'll sail to Baltimore and the O'Driscolls, but before I offer my sword arm and agree to enter any battle on your behalf, I expect you to meet me in Dunluce with the plunder from your last run to Spain." Ruairí laughed when Aidan failed to mask his surprise. "Och, aye. I heard all about the jewels and gold you squirreled away. Coin you could spend yourself to recruit the O'Driscolls and I assume the MacDonnells, too. But you'd rather I provide you with weapons and an army—at my expense, no less. If you don't pay me, then I will turn the O'Driscolls and the MacDonnells against you and leave you for the O'Malleys to rip apart."

"You haven't changed in the least."

"Why would I? Did you expect taking a wife would make me into a new man? Hardly."

"The Dark Heart remains."

"He does. Play me for a fool, O'Flaherty, and I will cut your heart out while it's still beating. I'll shove it down your throat before I toss your carcass to the sharks." Ruairí glanced up from examining his immaculate fingernails. "Remember, the Blond Devil and I are a matched pair. You can't get to one of us without having the other on your arse."

Aidan nodded and stuck his arm across the distance between the two boats to shake Ruairí's, but Ruairí signaled for Tomas to drop the oars into the water. Ruairí sensed Aidan continued to scrutinize him, but he didn't glance back until he was climbing the rope ladder hoisted over the *Lady Charity's* rail. He ordered the ship to be under way. He called up to Senga, ordering her to wait until they'd pointed the bow to the south and Ballycastle was a speck behind them.

# CHAPTER TWENTY-THREE

Senga stood at the prow but watched Ruairí standing at the wheel. He was an imposing sight, nearly mythical in his Viking appearance and magnetic presence. She smiled as she considered the night before. They'd had a nasty argument, but their reconciliation seemed to strengthen them as a couple by the time they awoke that morning. She'd watched Ruairí being rowed toward Ballycastle, but she was relieved when he ordered Tomas to stop well before the waves broke onto the beach. She hadn't been able to hear what transpired between the two captains, but she'd been able to read Ruairí's body language. He never appeared to be out of control, and it was Aidan who shifted on his bench seat throughout the exchange.

Senga remained in the crow's nest for another half an hour after Ruairí returned to the *Lady Charity*; she wanted to keep out of sight just as much as Ruairí wanted her to. He'd lifted her down once she was within reach, and the kiss he pulled her in for drained the anxiety from her body. He'd patted her backside before turning to the helm. She'd been observing him off and on for another half an hour, exchanging smiles from time to time when their gazes locked.

Senga noticed he said something to Kyle before leaving the wheel to his first mate.

"Would that I could draw you as you stand there, little one. I would immortalize your beauty, my pirate queen." Ruairí slid his arms around Senga's waist as she stepped into his embrace.

"You're being sentimental, *mo chridhe*."

"I suppose. I would remember the sight of you on our ship when we grow auld and no longer have sea legs. I would show it to our wee grandbairns, regaling them with tales of how their grandmother once sailed the high seas with a band of wild pirates."

"Auld? Grandbairns? You are a wee sook," Senga giggled.

"Big softie, am I?" Ruairí nuzzled her neck as he pressed his hips forward. "What were you saying?"

"There's naught soft about your body, but you possess a soft heart, *mo rìgh spùinneadair*." Senga giggled once again as the man she called her pirate king playfully huffed, pretending indignation. "I take it things went well with O'Flaherty."

"Aye. As well as can be expected with a man I'll never trust. He wants me to sail south to Baltimore and recruit the O'Driscolls to aid his fight against your uncle." Ruairí held onto Senga as she tried to pull away, tucking hair behind her ear. "I know this isn't our fight, but I won't lie and say that vengeance against your uncle isn't tempting. Aidan has a bounty from three Spanish carracks he sank a few months ago. He'll trade the lot to me in exchange for my help to convince the O'Driscolls and MacDonnells to side with him."

"There has to be more to it than that. I never said anything about wanting revenge against my uncle."

"I know. The king is moving Lowlanders into the Western Isles, hoping to subdue the Hebrideans just as he hopes to subdue the Highlanders. Your uncle has put up a remarkable fight the last few years, but he's angered too many of his neighbors on both sides of the North Channel. Aidan promises the Irish will no longer harry the isles but will aid in the resistance to Lowlanders flooding our islands."

"Our? You haven't called Barra your home in ten years. I left Canna without looking back, and I haven't called Lewis my home in nearly as long as you've been absent from Barra. These aren't 'our islands.'"

"They might be sooner rather than later. One day we'll have bairns of our own, and that'll lead to those grandbairns I'd regale with our tales. But we can't do that if we die fighting for treasure we can't take to the grave. Caragh and Rowan are considering returning to Barra. I am too, Senga. I want a home that doesn't rock, one where we can start a family."

"And that'll be on Barra?"

"It might. I don't know yet." Ruairí tucked the same lock of hair behind Senga's ear that blew loose once more. "It'll be wherever you want, *mo ghaol*, but I will make sure we have all we need to survive on for a long, long time. When we meet up with Rowan and Caragh, I will make it clear to Rowan that I'm retiring. I'll give the *Lady Charity* to Kyle. I believe Rowan intends to give the *Lady Grace* to Keith. The brothers can take over from the cousins."

"And if I want to continue sailing?"

"Do you?" Ruairí's eyebrows shot up.

"No, but what if I did?"

"Then you'll have a fisherman for a husband. I won't continue a life where I put yours in danger every day that we're together. We finish this with the Irish, then join Rowan and Caragh and make our home near theirs. If you want to continue sailing, then it'll be with nets and rods, not swords and knives. It wasn't by chance that a set of cousins fell in love with a set of cousins. It was fate."

Senga pressed a soft kiss to Ruairí's lips before leaning against his chest, her ear over his heart. "Tell me what happens after Baltimore. What will you do once the O'Driscolls agree to sail with you?"

"You make it sound easy to convince them."

"If they dislike my uncle as much as Aidan does, then it shouldn't be hard to convince them. While you were talking to Aidan, I remembered my uncle mentioning the O'Malleys. I hadn't thought of it in years, but I recall him saying they were allies. Their agreement allowed my uncle free rein to sail near Ireland, and they helped him fight your people. It was the only way to win against—well, I suppose your father. He would have been laird when my uncle had my father killed. You and Rowan might be the dreaded pirates from Barra, but everyone in the isles knows not to underestimate the MacNeils. It's as though you were all born to the water, as though God intended your clan to master the waves. If I didn't know that your people descended from Vikings, I'd guess you descended from Neptune."

Ruairí chuckled at Senga's suggestion that any of his family were part sea god, even if he and Rowan resembled Vikings more than most Scots. He sobered as he recalled that he looked just like his father, and that his siblings and mother also had blond hair and blue eyes. He'd thought about his family more since meeting Senga than he had in the entire time since he left home. Concern replaced the humor in Senga's eyes as she leaned back to peer up at him, and Ruairí regretted growing serious. He kissed her forehead and offered her a warm, reassuring smile.

"We'll see if the O'Driscolls will join us, then we'll sail to Dunluce, where Aidan will meet us. He either pays me what we agreed, and I help him recruit the MacDonnells, too, or we go our separate ways. After I run him through."

"And assuming Aidan doesn't double cross you and the O'Driscolls, and the MacDonnells will ally with you and Aidan, then what?"

"That depends on what you want, Senga. Do you want to return to Lewis? Do you want to see your uncle overthrown and Alfred put in his place? Do you want to claim your birthright?"

"No."

"No? To which part?"

"All of it. I don't care if I never lay my eyes on Lewis again. I'll be the one to plunge a blade into my uncle if ever I run into him, and I will spit on Alfred for playing me as a fool. I understand now that he only pretended to be my friend, training me and even taking me on raids, all while sharing my secrets with my uncle. It's the only way my uncle could know that Alexander and I were growing serious and why he tried to rush the betrothal. I didn't understand any of it at the time, but I've had years to grow up and learn people's true nature."

Senga shook head before gazing at the open water. Sadness and anger warred within as she thought about her cousin. She wanted to have fond memories from the time she spent with her cousin, but his betrayal was more than she could overlook.

"Alfred won't be any better than his father. My cousin might not be a murderer, but he has no qualms about taking what he wants regardless of who it hurts. He was delighted to become the heir to my clan's lairdship. He never would've been heir if my father lived."

"Aye, your husband would have been."

Senga's eyes widened as she stepped back from Ruairí. Her throat tightened as she tried to choke out her words. "Do you want the lairdship? Is that what this is about?"

"Hardly." Ruairí's laugh was brittle. "I could have remained with my own clan if I wanted to be laird. Remember, I would have become the heir, too, in much the same way as your Cousin Alfred did. I only want to know what you want. If it's returning to Lewis and returning to what's rightly yours, then I will make it so. If you never want to step foot on Lewis again, never see its shores, then so be it."

Senga nodded, her heart slowing the rapid staccato that had made her chest burn. She closed her eyes, inhaling Ruairí's fresh scent of sea air and soap. "I shouldn't jump to conclusions. Thinking about returning to Lewis fills me with dread and anger. It'll never be my home again. Not now. That chance died the day my uncle refused to allow me in the bailey when I arrived as a childless mother and grief-stricken widow. I told you, if I catch sight of him again, it'll be my blade that kills him. I'd sleep soundly that night, too."

"Then I will do what I can to avoid sailing to Lewis once the Irish are allied."

"Thank you, Ruairí." Senga leaned her head against his chest once again as her calm returned. They stood together at the rail well into the early evening. They spent much of the time watching fish and dolphins swim alongside the hull. Senga pointed to a flock of seagulls that circled and dove off their starboard side as they made their way along the coast. They spoke about everything and nothing as they daydreamed about the family they hoped to start one day. They avoided any specific mention of where they might raise this family, but Ruairí made Senga choke on a gulp of air when he said he envisioned them having at least six children. He feared he'd gone too far when he suggested names. Never having learned her deceased son's name, he feared that he mentioned the babe's name. He'd never asked and hadn't intended to until Senga drew quiet as she noticed Ruairí withdraw.

"What's wrong? A moment ago, you were naming our children, now you won't meet my eye."

"I fear I've overstepped."

"Overstepped? We're planning our life together. How is suggesting names wrong?"

"Maybe I shouldn't mention so many lads' names. Maybe I shouldn't make you think about bearing bairns again."

Senga understood when Ruairí refused look at her but tightened his hold on her. She patted his forearms before sliding her arms around his neck. "You recall his name was Alexander." Senga no longer considered the man as her husband; it felt odd to say as much, so she avoided it. She'd been truthful when she'd described to Ruairí what she'd felt all those years ago was puppy love. She'd been little more than a girl when she'd married the first time. What she experienced with Ruairí, what she shared with him, was unlike anything she'd experienced with Alexander, and she doubted it was possible even if he hadn't died. She swallowed before whispering a name she hadn't said since she watched her infant son being lowered into his grave. "My son's name was James."

Senga blinked several times as memories from that day flashed before her eyes. She swallowed over and over, but the lump in her throat wouldn't dissolve. Ruairí's embrace kept her on her feet as she remembered the baby smell she'd treasured until the last moment. She'd lost Alexander and James within hours of each other. She'd believed that day that her life had ended, but she'd awoken the next morning and the morning after that, over and over until five years later, she met Ruairí.

"I no longer think about Alex every day, but James pops into my mind at least once each day. But the pain has eased over the years. No child will ever replace him, but neither do I want to go without feeling a bairn growing within me because I lost my first one. I want to feel the kicks and flutters. I'd bear the agony of childbirth over and over to have a family with you. I would put my bairn to my breast once again. That bond, that experience is one I can never put into words, and it's one that I never imagined experiencing again until I met you. Do you have any idea what I dreamed of that first night in my cottage?" Ruairí shook his head. "I dreamed of standing over the cradle my father built and looking down at our bairn, yours and mine—not anyone else's—sleeping in the cradle while I rubbed my hand over my swollen belly. I dreamed you stood behind me, your hands resting on my belly as our bairn kicked within me. That's how I was certain I should go with you."

Senga's words astounded Ruairí, his mouth opening and closing several times before he found his voice. "I had the same vision. When I watched you standing beside the cradle, I envisioned the same thing. That's why I asked you to come with me. I knew you were meant to be with me."

"Fate, *mo ghaol*," she whispered.

"Fate, *mo ghràidh*," he returned as he kissed her temple. "Shall we go and try to make that first bairn?"

Senga nodded and pulled his hand as she darted toward the ladderwell. They ignored the knock at their door when Snake Eye brought their dinner tray. They didn't emerge until the middle of the following morning.

# CHAPTER TWENTY-FOUR

The *Lady Charity* sailed along the eastern coast for the next five days. Fair weather and strong tides kept the *Lady Charity* at a steady clip, and Baltimore came into view during the middle of the fifth day. Senga stood beside Ruairí at the helm. He'd offered her the chance to take control of the wheel more than once since she joined the ship. She'd proven to have a keen sense of navigation and understanding of the sea. She loved the sense of freedom and control that came with such responsibility, and Ruairí found the sight highly arousing.

"Is that Baltimore Castle?" Senga asked as a bawn, or curtain wall, came into view atop a ridge.

"Aye, but they call it Dún na Séad." They neared the harbor, but Ruairí had already given the order to anchor beyond the natural inlet. He'd explained some of the history of Clan O'Driscoll to Senga; she understood why they were wary of any ship they didn't recognize. The O'Driscolls had taken control of the castle from the powerful McCarthy clan. While the O'Driscolls were smaller than the McCarthys, the people of County Cork had learned not to underestimate them. The castle they saw now wasn't the original structure, built by the Anglo-Normans. It was at least the fifth or sixth iteration, the previous castles having burned down and been rebuilt several times. The O'Driscolls had proven themselves once and for all when a feud with Waterford City merchants carried on for nearly two hundred years. They overcame the most recent sacking of their castle only to build and fortify the most impressive castle yet. Their persistence garnered a reputation for stubbornness and ruthlessness. They were not a clan to cross; they also did not ally with others easily. "We'll wait until we're invited ashore. Their most recent tale of woe was an attack from Barbary pirates. The blighters sailed all the way from Algiers and sailed off with more than a hundred captives, who are now probably slaves."

"So they're not ones to offer strangers a warm welcome." Senga nodded as returned her gaze to the harbor they neared.

"Nay. Fionn O'Driscoll is the least trusting man in my acquaintance. He's fearsome looking, with nasty scars across his forehead and down his left cheek and he's missing half his teeth. He has Aidan and his men to thank for that. Aidan killed Michael O'Driscoll a few years back, and while that allowed Fionn to become chieftain, it left him with constant reminders that he's indebted to Aidan for it. That's the only reason Fionn will hear me out." Ruairí turned to his crew and called out, "Hoist our sails. The marque of Argyll is more likely to earn us cannon fire than a place by the fire. Raise our red flag." Ruairí and Rowan sailed with their signature red flags emblazoned with crossed golden basket-hilted swords.

Senga stood at the rail as the crew dropped anchor and unfurled Ruairí's pirate sales. A breeze made the canvas billow, and the Dark Heart's flag flapped above them. It wasn't long before the O'Driscoll banner hung from a top window of the keep. Senga made out a large ship and three rabbits stitched upon it. At her expression of confusion, Ruairí explained, "The rabbits represent their ties to King Conn Cead-Cathach, the ruler of the ancient kingdom of Connacht. The ship depicts the clan's ties to the seas. They seem a bit of an odd combination, but it marks them as descendants of kings."

"Don't most Irish clans claim they are descendants of kings?"

"Aye. There's bound to be some truth to the tales, but the Irish are more notorious bards than the Scots." Ruairí grinned before ordering the crew to lower the dinghies.

"I will remain quiet this time, Ruairí. I promise." Senga kept her eyes lowered and her hands clasped before her. The couple hadn't discussed the incident with Aidan, nor had they discussed whether Senga would go ashore. Ruairí simply told Senga that morning to prepare to meet the O'Driscolls. As the time to disembark drew nearer, Senga experienced a rush of nervousness that compelled her to reassure Ruairí that it wouldn't be a mistake to take her with him.

"I know you will, little one. But Fionn is not the same type of man as Aidan. His wife died a number of years ago during a Waterford raid, and he's lived like a monk since. But he's a man filled with rage and vengeance. I doubt he'll take notice of you as a woman, but he will be suspicious of you as a stranger."

"I'd prefer that." Senga offered Ruairí a tentative smile.

"Senga, we may have settled into a new dynamic with me more dominant and you more submissive, but I never want you to be timid. Not with me and not with anyone else. If you fear me or how I will react, we end these roles and return to how we were before we married."

"Yes, Ruairí," Senga's words were once again submissive, but the hint of mischief in her eyes told Ruairí that the spirit he adored persisted. A deep rumble in Ruairí's throat signaled his approval before he pressed his mouth to hers, swiping his tongue across her lips. When she opened, he dominated their kiss, and Senga happily gave in. She clung to him as the kiss carried on, her body pressed as tightly against his as were their mouths. When they heard the splash of the last dinghy, they pulled apart.

"I shall have to be a patient man, little one, because all I want to do now is make love to my wife."

"That's all you ever want to do," Senga teased.

"Can you blame me?"

"Hardly, since all I ever want to do is make love to my husband."

"No wonder we're so good together." Ruairí tapped her backside before guiding her to the rope ladder. Once again, she wore leggings and a tunic. Senga reasoned that if things soured between Fionn and Ruairí, then she needed to be dressed to fight or to run. A kirtle wouldn't allow her to do either easily. It was only a matter of minutes before Senga once again hopped over the side of the dinghy, but the atmosphere on the Baltimore beach differed vastly from the one only days ago at Rathlin. Local fishermen continued their work as if a band of pirates hadn't arrived onshore moments before. Senga supposed it was a familiar sight for most of the locals. As they made their way along the dock, Senga spied the same people that a visitor expected in any coastal village. The dockside whores smiled and shimmied for Ruairí, but he took no notice as he strained to spot Fionn O'Driscoll, who he knew would never come to greet him. O'Driscoll expected nothing less than for Ruairí to go to him. Senga glared as more than one woman attempted to take a step toward them, and she drew her dirk when one had the audacity to bare her breasts. The woman snapped her blouse back into place when she caught the gleam reflected off Senga's blade. Ruairí chuckled. "I'm glad to have you protecting my virtue, little one."

"It appears someone has to," Senga huffed, then grinned. "I'm no more possessive than you are."

"Then no one will ever get near either of us." Ruairí glanced down and offered his own broad smile. "O'Driscoll is just ahead, where the path twists toward the keep."

Senga whipped her eyes forward, but she struggled to see anyone. It wasn't until they were nearly upon Fionn that she spotted him. He was exactly as Ruairí described. If she hadn't recognized the blankness in his eyes that only grief could create, she would have been justly terrified. Instead, she sympathized with the man. Speaking of children the night before had flooded Senga with memories, alternately warm and horrifying, of her time with Alexander and baby James. She'd forced herself to relegate them to the corner of her mind where they usually resided. She hadn't lied when she confessed that she thought of James at least once a day, but it was usually a brief glimpse of a cooing baby rather than one ravaged by fever. She'd awoken in the middle of the night drenched in sweat, trembling. Ruairí had settled her against his warm body despite remaining asleep. She'd drifted back to sleep immediately once she was wrapped in Ruairí's protective embrace.

"Fionn, come out and greet me and my wife. You are known for better hospitality than that." Ruairí's voice carried and seemed to bounce off the nearby cliffside. The scarred man stepped forth and offered what Senga assumed was a smile. He waited for the couple to approach, rather than meeting them halfway, proving Ruairí's prediction was true: he wouldn't offer a warm welcome. But, Senga reasoned, at least he wasn't hostile toward them. When they were almost within sword's reach, Ruairí stopped and dipped his head. "Fionn O'Driscoll, I would have you meet my wife, Senga MacNeil. Senga, this is Fionn O'Driscoll, chieftain of Clan O'Driscoll."

Senga stood in silence beside Ruairí but offered the warmest smile she could muster. The man swung his vacant gaze toward her and nodded before turning to walk up the path. Ruairí and Senga followed behind with Tomas and Snake Eye bringing up the rear. When they neared the keep, guards seemed to materialize from nowhere. They flanked the couple and their men. Guards ordered Ruairí, Snake Eye, and Tomas to remove their swords before entering, but they fooled no one: the men were still well armed. Senga's tunic covered the dirks strapped to her thighs, and the sleeves covered the knives in her wrist bracers. The hilts of the dirks in her boots didn't show beneath her leggings. Senga's eyes swept the Great

Hall, estimating the number of people within and checking for potential means of escape. She caught sight of more than one pirate hiding in the shadows, prepared to attack if Fionn gave the signal.

Ruairí didn't trust Fionn any more than he did Aidan, but entering the keep and taking the noon meal in the Great Hall were necessary to prove the *Lady Charity* arrived in peace. To refuse the offer would insult Fionn and his clan. He kept his arm around Senga's waist, offering her a chair that placed her in the corner. He wasn't keen on the seat since it meant she might be trapped if a fight broke out, but it kept her back protected and made approaching from the sides more difficult. It was the safest seat available. Snake Eye and Tomas found spots on benches below the dais. They talked quietly between themselves and offered their best manners to the serving women.

"What brings you to Ireland, and more specifically, what brings you to Dún na Séad?" Fionn wasted no time as he poured himself a chalice of wine before passing the ewer to Ruairí. Ruairí did the same thing as he'd done at Ballycastle. He waited for Fionn to finish his first goblet, then drank his own. When neither man keeled over, he refilled the chalice and offered it to Senga.

O'Driscoll continued, "You have the makings of a good husband, though I can't imagine why the lass ever married you? Did you kidnap her?"

Ruairí laughed, "No. That's how Rowan met his wife. Senga came willingly."

Fionn peered past Ruairí, passing an assessing glance over Senga before looking back at Ruairí. Senga realized Ruairí hadn't exaggerated. The man showed no more interest in her than he would any stranger. He barely seemed to notice she was a woman.

"Did O'Flaherty send you?"

"Do you have second sight?" Ruairí countered.

"Not in the least. I wish that I had." Fionn grimaced

before taking a long drag from his chalice, and Ruairí wished to take back his words. He was sure they only reminded him that Fionn had been unprepared for the Algerine attack, and he'd been unprepared for his wife's death at the hands of their Waterford enemies. "Nay. I assume that bastard still thinks I owe him."

"He may have said something along those lines when he suggested I sail down here."

"What dealings have you had with him? I thought you swore never to cross tides with him after he tried to attack you the last time you stopped at Canna."

Ruairí felt Senga tense, and he slid his hand over her knee beneath the table. He'd never shared that there had been an attack before Ruairí and his men arrived on Canna. Part of the reason he'd agreed to allow his men a night in the tavern was as a reward for the fight they put up against Aidan and his crew. It was also when Ruairí agreed to the trade of weapons for the chests of gold and coin. Aidan claimed he attacked because he learned the weapons were part of the cargo the *Lady Charity* carried. Ruairí had spared Aidan his life in exchange for a future trade, which had happened the week earlier. Both Aidan and Ruairí recognized Ruairí came out with a far more valuable bounty than Aidan, but Aidan obsessed over fighting the MacLeods and O'Malleys.

"Aye, he did. He wanted weapons for his war against the MacLeods. He thought to steal them from me, but I had them stashed elsewhere." Ruairí wasn't about to admit to Fionn that the weapons had been onboard all along and hidden in the false bottom of the hold. "He's agreed to leave the Western Isles and Orkney to the Scots if I asked you to fight alongside him."

"And why would I do that?" Fionn muttered around a mouth full of pottage.

"Because doing away with Neil MacLeod would make passage through the North Channel easier, and the O'Malleys would have one less ally."

"My argument isn't with the MacLeod. He leaves me alone since I threatened to share his secret."

Senga had relaxed with Ruairí's calming touch, but she tensed once more. She shifted in her seat but stilled, fearing Fionn sensed her eagerness. She covered her anxiousness by leaning forward to reach the pitcher of wine. She sneaked a quick glance at Fionn, but he was intently looking at his food.

"And what secret would that be?" Ruairí inquired.

"It'd hardly be a secret if I told you, now would it?" the O'Driscoll smirked.

"And what does the man have on you if you're willing to stay quiet? It's got to be more than being left alone." Ruairí took a risk that he prayed paid off. "Did I mention that Senga was a MacLeod before she became a MacNeil?"

Fionn nodded, then swallowed a mouthful Senga feared would choke him. "You look like your da, lass, but those are your mother's eyes." Fionn's words shocked both Ruairí and Senga, but she recovered faster.

"You knew my parents?"

"Aye. I did quite a lot of trade with your father before his bastard brother had him killed. I was glad to hear you escaped marrying the auld MacLeod from Skye. A nasty dragon, he is."

"Is that the secret? That you're aware my uncle orchestrated that raid?"

Fionn put down the hunk of bread he was about to bite into and looked at Senga, then Ruairí. He lowered his voice before speaking once more. "Nay, lass. I'm aware he tried to rape you, and that your young Sorley took you away from Lewis to protect you. I also know word spread of why you left. The MacLeod of Skye was livid when he discovered you'd not only escaped but gotten yourself married. He prepared to attack Lewis, but your uncle came here before the MacLeod of Skye had the opportunity to sail. He hid the dowry he was supposed to pay auld MacLeod close to here. I've told no one but you. It's a small fortune that I've guarded in exchange for the MacLeods of Lewis keeping their distance from my ships and my shore."

"Why're you telling us this?" Senga leaned around Ruairí, but shrank back when she realized she was being outspoken. She glanced at Ruairí, but his nod gave her the confidence to look back at Fionn.

"Because I may have been glad that my father died, even if it weren't by my hand, but your ma and da didn't deserve to die. Family shouldn't kill family. They were good people, and you were still a young lass when it happened. I have no tolerance for men who force themselves on women." Fionn stared out into space, seeming not to see the crowd before them. "It changes the woman forever. She loses a piece of her soul." He shook his head as though he might clear the maudlin thoughts and remember who he spoke with.

"You recognized who I was even before Ruairí introduced us." It was a statement, not a question. Senga tried to recall if they'd met when she was a child, but she drew a blank.

"Nay, my lady. We never met," Fionn offered the first sign of warmth since they arrived when he smiled at Senga. "I met your ma before you were born. She sailed with your father often, and as I said, I traded with your father often. It's why Neil thought he'd find an ally in me."

The trio sat in silence for several minutes before Fionn cleared his throat. "I will fight alongside O'Flaherty, but you will join the fight, MacNeil. I don't trust that bastard not to run me through in the middle of the battle. And I'll return the dowry to you, my lady. It should have been yours all along. That's what your father would have wanted. I don't care a whit about the Western Isles or Lowlanders invading your precious Highlands. I'll fight Neil MacLeod in honor of your mother and father, Lady Senga. Your mother was kind to my wife many moons ago."

It was the first time since she escaped her uncle and the isle of Lewis that Senga didn't experience discomfort from the honorific. It felt sincere coming from Fionn O'Driscoll, which shocked her even as she appreciated it. While she wasn't eager to return to Lewis—she'd only felt disinterest, at best, when Aidan spoke of sailing to her former home—she was filled with a new sense of purpose with Fionn O'Driscoll at their side. Ruairí squeezed her thigh, and she understood the question in his eyes. She gave a quick nod, and Ruairí turned back to settle the agreement with Fionn. They returned to the *Lady Charity* with the agreement to meet Fionn at dawn to retrieve her hidden dowry. Then the crews of the *Lady Charity* and the four ships that made up the O'Driscoll fleet intended to sail north with the tide.

# CHAPTER TWENTY-FIVE

A storm off the coast of Dublin forced the ships to drop anchor as the gale blew in from the northeast. It marked them as easy prey as they sat in a cove with the sails lowered and hatches battened down. The last of the wind had barely settled before the sound of cannon fire erupted just before dawn. Ruairí awoke with a start, but as the *Lady Charity* shuddered and listed to port, he understood they were under attack. Senga was already awake when he shook her shoulder. She rolled out of bed and donned her clothes as quickly as Ruairí. She strapped her falchion to her belt and hurried to fasten her bracers. After the last attack, Ruairí admitted that the door wasn't as secure as he'd always assumed. He didn't want Senga trapped in the cabin again, so he'd told her that she was to find a crate or barrel on deck to hide within. He even ordered her to use the freshwater barrel if needed.

The couple emerged on deck as a cannonball whizzed over the bow, striking the water within spitting distance of the ship. Senga swept her eyes across the deck and noticed none of the men appeared injured. She squinted, trying to catch sight of the O'Driscoll ships through the smoke and predawn haze. She counted four, but one seemed off-kilter, and she feared a cannonball had struck it. She glanced up at the cliffs that towered above the inlet where they'd spent the night. There were two cannons that Senga spotted, and both appeared to have smoke rising above them.

"Ruairí, look!" Senga pointed toward the mouth of a sea cave. She doubted any of the captains had spotted the cave the night before, in the driving rain and under the black cloud cover. Four small but fast ships emerged from the mouth of the cave. Senga didn't recognize any of them. "What are those?"

"Bluidy hell," Ruairí growled. "The low-profile ship with oars and sails is a fuste. They're popular with Barbary corsairs. We didn't recognize the Barbaries when they attacked because they weren't in their regular ships. The other three are French corvettes. Those are the ones we must keep our eye on because they usually have anywhere from four to eight small guns on the deck."

"Who are they? Are they O'Malleys?"

"Aye. Senga, we need to get you hidden. They'll try to board us." Ruairí guided Senga toward a barrel he knew was empty. It had been a freshwater container, but they'd emptied it a few days earlier. He pulled the lid off and lifted Senga into it before she said a word. They exchanged an all-too-brief kiss before Ruairí ordered Tomas, Kyle, and Snake Eye to surround the barrel with him. He understood he was running the risk of the O'Malleys figuring out there was something—or someone—of value within the container. But Ruairí refused to take the risk of one of the Irish pirates taking the barrel and discovering Senga as the real treasure. Senga watched in horror through a hollow knot in the wood as the battle ensued. The crew of the *Lady Charity* defended their ship valiantly, and more O'Malleys fell into the water than boarded the vessel, but the battle waged on.

"These rats must have climbed out of the woodwork," Kyle called out as he and Tomas fought back to back, preventing anyone from approaching Senga's hiding place from the port side.

"They'll all be drowned rats soon enough," Snake Eye puffed as he swung his sword in a wide arc, then thrust his dirk into the man who prepared for the sword strike instead. He had no chance to say more as two O'Malleys rushed toward Snake Eye. Tomas shifted to come to Snake Eye's aid, but it left Kyle's back unprotected. Senga covered her mouth in horror as a man thrust his sword at Kyle's ribs, the blade slicing through the first mate's tunic and flesh. Kyle bellowed in rage as he turned toward his enemy. Blood poured from his wound, and as the minutes dragged on, Senga witnessed Kyle's strength waning.

Senga shifted to find where Ruairí fought, discovering that he was battling two opponents. Tomas and Snake Eye were both enmeshed in their own fights for survival. Kyle wouldn't make it if someone didn't come to his aid. From what Senga's limited vision allowed, there was no one able to come to Kyle's defense. Beside Rowan, Kyle was Ruairí's closest friend and had been his confidante for years. As angry as Ruairí would undoubtedly be if she helped Kyle, it would devastate him if Kyle died. She was confident that she could assist Kyle, then find another hiding spot. She knew there was a space between the mast and a stack of crates. It was what Braedon used to give him a higher start when he climbed the mast to the crow's nest. If need be, she knew she and Braedon could both fit in the small perch above the deck.

Senga didn't wait to make her move; she refused to reconsider the choice that would undoubtedly land her across Ruairí's lap, and not for their pleasure. She pushed the lid free and leaned all of her weight away from where the fighting took place. She scrambled out of the barrel and came to her feet. She leaped over it as she drew her falchion. She swung the sword high overhead, using momentum to add force when she brought the blade crashing down onto Kyle's opponent's neck. Blood geysered from the wound, and the man collapsed on the deck.

"Thank you," Kyle gasped.

"You need to apply pressure to that wound, or you'll bleed to death." Senga ran to Kyle's side. "You have to go below to—"

"No. I'm not running away from battle."

"I wasn't suggesting that. I was going to say, go below and get something to bandage your wound. Tightly. Then come back to fight. If you don't put pressure on that, you will die. Are you going to put Ruairí through that?"

Kyle gave her a long look before he nodded once and bounded toward the ladderwell that took him to his quarters. Senga had no time to watch Kyle disappear below deck before her next opponent was on her. The man grinned as he approached.

"I shall enjoy killing you, *leannán*. But first I think I shall find a wee bit o' privacy where I can bend you over first." The man leered as he lunged for Senga, but she was quicker than he anticipated. She flicked a dirk from her wrist bracer and flung it at the man's crotch.

"You won't be rutting anything now." She followed through by plunging her sword into his groin, withdrawing it, then thrusting it into his sternum. She pulled her dirk loose as Ruairí's voice roared her name.

"Punish me later, Ruairí. You need all the sword arms you can get." Senga spun around and spotted a man reaching for the mast. He had his dirk between his teeth as he prepared to climb the rigging. She wasn't sure if the pirate intended to saw through the sails or go after Braedon, but she wasn't willing to risk either. She threw the dirk in her hand, watching with satisfaction as it embedded in the man's throat. She pivoted as she spied movement in Ruairí's direction. She watched her husband fell an enormous man with skin like the midnight sky. She'd seen no one like him during her time sailing with Ruairí in the Mediterranean. But she had little time to ruminate on the stranger as two more men ran toward Ruairí. Senga didn't hesitate to rush to her husband's back. She crouched as one of the O'Malley sailors shifted to take her on, while the second man focused on Ruairí. She and Ruairí had sparred with each other for countless hours after he discovered she knew how to fight. They'd grown used to one another's movements and were compliments to one another's prowess as they moved with synchronicity. Husband and wife defended one another like a choreographed dance.

"You shall have a red bottom that you won't be able to sit on for a month of Sundays when this is over," Ruairí growled.

"Aye, Capt'n."

"Now you can obey?" Ruairí failed to keep the amusement from his voice despite his anger that his wife purposely ignored his order to remain hidden. Again.

"Not very well, but I can," Senga puffed. "You should've learned the first time that I wouldn't leave your back unprotected. You can turn me over your knee after I celebrate your survival."

"Senga!" Ruairí's bellow warned Senga that he didn't appreciate her sense of humor. She opted to remain quiet as they twisted and turned, thrusting and parrying against their opponents. Movement at the corner of her periphery had her whipping her head around in time to notice a man pulling Braedon down the mast. When they landed on the deck, the pirate lifted his sword to Braedon's throat.

"I have to help Braedon," Senga yelled over the sound of swords clashing.

"Go," Ruairí nodded. Senga didn't wait another moment before she ran toward the man as he pressed the blade against Braedon's skin. She witnessed the first drop of blood bloom on the polished metal, and all reason left her mind. She swept up a short sword as she passed it on the deck. The blade was wider and flatter than her falchion; it made cleaving the man's head from his neck much easier than it would have been with the thin blade of her own sword. Braedon staggered when the hold on him suddenly disappeared.

"Go back up, Brae. I'll stay below. No one will touch you again. I swear it," Senga panted as she pushed the boy back toward the rigging. She climbed atop the crates she had once thought to hide behind. The superior height gave her leverage that even the tallest man didn't have, and most of the enemy had already seen her fight. None approached her or the mast. She remained on guard, protecting both Braedon and the sails until the fighting ended.

# CHAPTER TWENTY-SIX

Senga watched as the crew of the *Lady Charity* tossed the dead bodies of the O'Malleys onto the fuste that had come alongside their boat. When the last one landed on the deck with a thud, the men severed the grappling hooks from the ropes, keeping the metal grips while throwing the ropes into the water. The O'Driscolls fared the same as Ruairí's crew, but the ship Senga had seen earlier listing to one side was slowly slipping beneath the surface of the water.

"They may have lost that one, but they gained two corvettes. Fionn won't be too disappointed," Ruairí observed as he dumped a crew member's body over the rail. One of the corvettes had abandoned the fight and returned to the O'Malleys' lair with a skeleton crew that had survived the fight against the O'Driscolls. None of the O'Malleys who boarded the *Lady Charity* survived. Senga was in the middle of pouring whisky over Kyle's wound as he cursed under his breath. She offered him some of her own, some that made even the toughened pirate blush. "Wife, you have a foul mouth," Ruairí observed.

Senga grinned unrepentantly. She knew this was the least of her transgressions, and it distracted distracted Kyle from the pain as she stitched him up. She teased Kyle that the ladies in the next port would vie for the chance to minister to his needs. He begged that she not make him laugh as he gripped his ribs below his wound. When she finished with the first mate, Senga moved on to other crew members who needed suturing. They spent the rest of the afternoon setting the deck to rights, disposing of dead bodies, and tending to their wounded as they sailed north and away from the unprovoked attack. When Senga finished tending the last man, she swiped her sleeve across her sweaty forehead and tipped her head from one side to the other in an attempt to loosen the stiff muscles in her neck. She squealed when Ruairí slung her over his shoulder and carried her toward the ladderwell.

As they descended out of sight of the crew, Ruairí didn't wait to rain down painful swats to Senga's behind. They entered their cabin, and Ruairí kicked the door shut so hard that the frame rattled. He lowered Senga to the floor and narrowed his eyes. She didn't meet his gaze, instead pulling her belt loose and dumping the sword and knives on the table. She kicked off her boots and lowered her leggings without a word. When she was bare from the waist down, she stood with her hands clasped behind her back and her head lowered.

"You're prepared to receive your punishment?" Ruairí drawled as he stalked toward Senga. When his booted toes brushed against her bare ones, he reached around her and grabbed her backside in one hand and her braid in the other. He tugged her braid, bringing her chin up and giving him access to her mouth. The kiss was hungry and uncontrolled, and Senga met him with equal measure.

Fear and anger melted away while they clung to one another, needing the solace and reassurance that they had both survived yet another threat against their lives. When the initial frenzy calmed, the kiss turned tender and languid until they both pulled away, needing to breathe. Ruairí took Senga's hand and led her to the chair where he administered most of her spankings. Senga draped her body over his lap before he had the chance to speak any instructions. She pulled the tunic out of the way, bunching it high around her ribs.

"Senga, you disobeyed me when I ordered you to stay hidden for your safety. I won't deny that you saved Kyle's life, and probably mine and Braedon's, but I can't ignore how willingly you put yourself in danger when you fight men twice your size with far more experience in battle. It's not that I don't believe you are skilled and able to defend yourself, but your opponents aren't there to spar. They're trying to kill you, and that thought makes the blood in my vein turn to ice. I see stars and break out into a sweat picturing you lying dead on the deck of our ship. I'm of two minds as to whether you deserve this punishment. I'm torn between wanting to thank you and throttle you."

"Can you not do both? I don't mean throttle me, but can't you punish me for disobeying you but thank me for loyalty and devotion to you and our crew?" Senga attempted to look back over her shoulder as Ruairí rubbed his large, warm palm over her backside.

"Aye, I can, little one. That's exactly what I shall do. You shall receive your spanking, and then I intend to spend the rest of the voyage to Rathlin worshipping your body." With that, Ruairí lifted his hand before bringing it down across Senga's flesh. "You will receive twenty spanks, Senga. You will count each one. You will thank me for loving you so much that I'll do anything to protect you, even if that's protecting you from yourself."

"Yes, Ruairí." Senga braced herself for the twenty blows to begin, silently thankful that it was Ruairí's hand and not a belt or whip. The next spank landed across both cheeks and made her yelp. "One. Thank you, Ruairí."

Ruairí ran his hand over the pickening flesh, rubbing away some of the initial sting. The next five landed squarely across both globes, just as the previous ones had. The next ten alternated sides, while the final ones landed where her thighs met her bottom. Ruairí took care not to use more strength than

Senga could tolerate, but the spanking was not like the many playful ones that were preludes to making love. Spying Senga springing from the barrel had terrified him. While he was proud of his wife's skill and bravery, those were the same characteristics that made him most fear for her life. He'd been truthful when he told Senga how he felt seeing her fighting men who had no qualms about killing a woman. He knew he didn't need to state the obvious: any of those men would take pride in killing the Dark Heart's wife. It was that knowledge that drove him to ensure Senga understood these battles were not like the raids she experienced with her cousin. She may have been one laird's daughter and another laird's niece, but neither of those endangered her as much as being his wife. His guilt gnawed at him that he was the one who endangered Senga, first by bringing her aboard and then by marrying her.

When Senga counted the last blow, Ruairí ran his hand over the heated skin, bending low to place a tender kiss on each globe. He helped Senga to stand when she shifted. He obliged when she pressed his knees apart and sank to hers, careful not to press her tender flesh against her heels. She unfastened the laces of Ruairí's leggings with one hand while the other stroked his hardened rod. He'd seen her arousal grow as the dampness between her thighs increased with each spank. He captured both of her hands in one of his and leaned forward to dip his fingers into her sheath. He thrust into her as his thumb rubbed lazy circles around her bud.

Senga tried to shake Ruairí's hand from hers, but he clamped his palm over hers. "Please, Ruairí," she begged. "Please let me. I need to." Her mouth ached just as her core did to feel the press of his cock. He relented and used his hand to hold back her hair instead. She rushed to free his cock before diving to take it into her mouth. Ruairí thought he would spill that very moment as the tip brushed the back of her throat. When her hips pressed forward, searching for more friction and depth, he pulled his hand away. Senga's whimper nearly had him giving in to pleasuring her, but as much as she might beg for it now, she would regret giving in to her pleasure before she'd atoned for her transgressions. She hummed as her mouth slid over Ruairí's engorged rod, her cheeks hollowing each time she lifted her head. When Ruairí knew he had little willpower left and was about to spill his seed, he lifted Senga under her arms and pressed her backwards toward the bed. She shucked off her tunic as Ruairí rushed to undress. He fell onto the bed and across her body as she opened her arms and legs to him.

"I love you more than anything, Senga. I don't know that I could live another day without you, and I will do everything I can to protect you. I need you to accept your limitations because I can't live in fear of losing you every time danger is near." Ruairí sank into the warm depths of her core as her arms and legs wrapped around him. He dropped his head and shuddered as the depth of his emotions took hold. Senga held his large frame against her as they lay joined. "I can't avoid fighting your uncle if I'm to deliver the O'Driscolls to Aidan's side, but I don't want you going ashore. That is the last battle I will ever fight as the captain of the *Lady Charity* and as the pirate Dark Heart. I can't do this anymore. I can't live with the constant threat that you might die because you married me."

"Ruairí, I understood from the start what I risked leaving Canna to sail with you. I knew the danger, and I accepted it because you drew me to you. I won't ever regret fighting to defend you and our home, our friends, and our crew. I don't do it to anger you or to scare you, but I can't imagine living without you either, and I'll be damned if I hide while you die. Punish me over and over for disobeying you, for risking my life, but I won't ever stop if it means we can lie together again just as we are now. You are my present and my future, and I will always fight to protect that. But, *mo ghaol*, I will take care not to endanger myself needlessly or to be a distraction to you. I can admit to my limits." Senga pressed a kiss to his lips. "If you wish for me to remain in our cabin when you go ashore on Lewis, you'll get no disagreement from me. I owe you that much."

"I love you, *mo ghràidh*, with all that I have and with all that I am." Ruairí once again captured Senga's mouth in a kiss, pouring every bit of love and devotion into it that he could. He felt her return the sentiments as their bodies moved together. Neither fought the crest of pleasure as it crashed over them. When they once more gazed into one another's eyes, they knew that if they hadn't created a new life within Senga before, they had surely just done so.

# CHAPTER TWENTY-SEVEN

Ruairí breathed a sigh of relief when Ballycastle came into view a week later. The battle against the O'Malleys resulted in the loss of several crew members, and it forced each person aboard the *Lady Charity* to carry out double the work. The O'Driscolls fared about the same, even with the addition of two new light, and speedy ships. They'd taken heavy casualties, but Fionn still had enough men to be a strong fighting force against the MacLeods. The delay made Ruairí concerned about their provisions. They needed to put ashore for more freshwater and food. Hardtack and bannocks weren't enough for anyone, let alone the men recovering from injuries sustained during the battle.

Braedon spied movement on the beach and called down to Ruairí. The captain didn't need to look to guess the MacAlister men had returned from their hunt, forcing him to endure not only Aidan O'Flaherty's overinflated sense of importance but Padraig MacAlister's insufferable whining. He grimaced as they drew nearer the dock, and Ruairí recognized both men. Senga came to stand beside him at the rail, but waited for Ruairí to speak first.

"Don't leave my side, Senga. Aidan is bad enough, but

Padraig is cruel to women. I don't want him backing you into some dark corner." Ruairí wrapped his arms around Senga, wishing it was possible to wave hello and goodbye without leaving his ship. He didn't trust Aidan or Padraig not to send men for Senga if she remained on board, so he had little choice but to bring her along.

"I won't say anything this time, Ruairí. I'll observe and listen from the start."

There was no more time to talk as crewmen threw ropes onto the docks and bounded over the rails to secure the *Lady Charity*. Pulling into the harbor and docking relieved Senga; she found the jostling of the dinghy made her feel nauseous, even though it never bothered her before. She supposed the current differed on this side of the North Channel. Ruairí steadied her once they both stood on the deck. He'd informed Senga that they could dock in port rather than anchoring in the bay, but she still opted for her leggings and tunic. It offered her easier access to her knives, and she was unconvinced that they wouldn't have to make a dash for the ships.

She watched as Aidan and a massive bear of a man approached. He was nearly as wide around the middle as he was tall. Senga knew enough Hebridean sailors and High-landers not to underestimate the strength of a man, even if he appeared corpulent. Significant force came from a body that large, and she had no intention of discovering how much. Ruairí wrapped his arm around her shoulders, much as he had when they'd first met Aidan. But this time, Senga merely angled her body against his, waiting for the men to meet them.

"Ruairí MacNeil, you're a sight I hoped never to behold again," Padraig bellowed.

"You're no prized bull yourself, Padraig MacAlister."

"O'Flaherty says you've brought a wife with you. Why'd you go and do that? I have whores aplenty here for you."

"You may enjoy the pox, but I enjoy more pleasant company. I prefer my wife. Senga MacNeil, this is Padraig

214

MacAlister. And you recall Aidan O'Flaherty." Ruairí made the introductions, and Senga nodded but remained silent.

"Senga, you're so quiet this time. Cat got your tongue, or did Ruairí order you to remain silent?"

Ruairí squeezed Senga's shoulder, willing her to understand that inevitably she'd have to speak. He agreed with her assessment from the last time they met Aidan. She couldn't appear weak.

"I hadn't heard anything worth responding to. I prefer my husband keep me company, too." Senga notched up her chin as she stared each man in the eye.

"Padraig, leave the lass alone, you worthless sack of shite." Fionn O'Driscoll's voice carried from the end of the dock as he approached. His ship moored on the other side of the dock from the *Lady Charity*. "If I'd known you were in residence, I'd have stayed home. At least there's decent whisky there."

"Fionn, kill any more men to keep your chieftain seat?" Padraig tossed back at Fionn.

"Aye." Fionn answered with one word, but the sneer he directed at Padraig said more than anything spoken out loud.

"Shall we take our business inside where there aren't so many big ears and wagging tongues?" Ruairí intervened.

As the group approached the curtain wall, Senga noticed something shift on the battlements. She squeezed Ruairí's hand and nudged her chin in the gatehouse's direction. The tips of several arrows were barely noticeable, but Ruairí and Senga recognized what they were. Ruairí returned her squeeze and shifted their angle so his body blocked hers. Senga bit her tongue to keep from muttering that it wouldn't matter much after the first arrow struck him. They passed into the bailey, which seemed more subdued with the MacAlister chieftain in residence than when only pirates roamed the grounds. Senga got the impression that Padraig may have been a feared leader, but he wasn't a respected one. Once inside the Great Hall, it was a relief for Senga to see other women moving about where there had been few the last time she was there. Both noblewomen and serving women seemed in abundance.

"Padraig has three unwed sisters, his mother, his wife, and four unwed daughters. They were the ones hiding from Aidan."

"Understandable. But that's far too many women in one household. Good God." Senga's eyes bounced from one woman to another, noting most appeared as unwelcoming as Padraig.

"Lady Senga, do you care for refreshments?" Aidan appeared at her elbow.

"No, thank you. Ruairí and I broke our fast together before we came ashore." Senga glanced at Aidan only long enough to keep from being rude, but she returned her attention to the people moving about the Great Hall.

"Perhaps one of the MacAlister women might show you the gardens. I'm certain you're happy to be on land once again."

"I prefer the sea. But once again, thank you." Senga stepped closer to Ruairí, but when Aidan made to follow, she flicked her wrist so her tunic sleeve fell back to reveal the dirk secured in her wrist bracer. Aidan nodded once but kept quiet, deciding to stand near Fionn.

"You handled that well, little one," Ruairí's mint-scented breath wafted across Senga's face, making her relax muscles she hadn't realized stiffened while Aidan was near. "Do you want refreshments or that tour around the gardens?"

"Not at all. I'm not leaving your side, and I'm not eating or drinking anything here until I see the MacAlisters do it first. Something feels off."

"I sense it too. If you prefer to sit, then I will take a seat with you. Aidan, Fionn, and Padraig are the ones who have business with one another now. I'd be on our way if it were possible. I'd sail out of port this minute and agree to meet them on Lewis on their designated date." Ruairí kept his tone low and casual, making it appear that husband and wife were making small talk rather than assessing their predicament.

"Do you think we'll be able to return to the *Lady Charity* with no one questioning us? Or do you think they'll suspect you will run off?"

"The latter in Padraig's case. You've charmed Fionn, and I think you may be the only person the man trusts at the moment. Aidan won't give up the chase, so he'll maneuver in every direction to get you alone with him."

"I told you, I'm not leaving your side." Senga settled her eyes on Ruairí's chest, wishing it were appropriate to lean against him for support. Something troubled her, but she couldn't identify what made her so uneasy. Senga observed as four young women she assumed were Padraig's daughters set their sights on Ruairí and approached like a pack of lionesses. Senga ground her teeth as they each cast her a smarmy smile before directing their attention to Ruairí.

"Captain Dark Heart," the eldest cooed. "It has been too long since you've paid our clan a visit."

Ruairí remained silent, his expression disinterested. Senga wanted to shake him and remind him that women took disinterest as an invitation to chase just as much as men did.

"Ruairí, if I recall correctly, you promised me a dance the last time you were here." The youngest was brazen enough to step forward and reach out her hand, but Senga slipped in front of Ruairí.

"Touch my husband, and you'll come away short five fingers." Senga kept her voice low so only Ruairí and the MacAlister sisters caught what she said. "None of you appear dimwitted, so I assume you've either heard or deduced that I'm the Dark Heart's wife. Do you know what type of woman a man like the Dark Heart would want to marry? Can you imagine?" Senga narrowed her eyes and ran the tip of her tongue along the bottom of her top teeth.

"Our apologies, Lady, uh, Dark Heart," one of the previously silent sisters muttered. "We meant no offense."

Senga cocked an eyebrow but said nothing. Her expression displayed she knew those words for the lie they were. Her hand rested casually on the hilt of the falchion that remained at her waist. While the guards stripped the men of their swords, the guardsman standing before Senga merely chuckled when she reached for hers. The man assumed she was no threat, so Senga opted to keep the weapon on her. She figured there was no reason to relinquish it if no one made her.

The four young women backed away until there was enough room for them to spin around. They scattered like baby chicks searching for their mother hen. Senga glanced up at Ruairí, expecting to see ire after she failed to remain quiet, but Ruairí struggled to keep from laughing. He eventually relented and chuckled.

"Lady Dark Heart. I rather like that, *mo chridhe*. I shall remember that for tonight when you plunder and pillage me."

"Someone has to protect you," Senga giggled but sobered when she feared someone might overhear them.

"MacNeil, bring your arse over here," Fionn called. Ruairí took Senga's hand as they rejoined the group. His gaze hardened when Padraig glared at Senga.

"Can't she manage on her own for a while? There are enough bitches in here to keep her company."

Ruairí's dirk pressed against Padraig's throat before anyone, including Senga, realized what was happening.

"I don't give a rat's turd how you speak about the women in your family, but insult my wife again, and your clan will have a woman sitting in your seat by supper." Ruairí pressed the blade against Padraig's Adam's apple, causing him to gulp, then choke, when the nodule didn't move easily. Ruairí leaned close enough that only Padraig could hear. "I don't give a fuck what you mean to anyone. I will hack you to bits, then leave you for the wolves to eat. But not before I cut off your cock and balls and shove them down your throat while you're still breathing. Do I make myself clear?"

"Abundantly," Padraig rasped. Ruairí knew he was taking a risk humiliating the man in his own home, but of the four men gathered, his reputation exceeded them all, and it was based on truth. The rumors of his wealth might have been exaggerated, but the stories told of his brutal punishment paled compared to reality. He was confident no one dared cross him. He straightened and cast a warning glare at Aidan, who threw up his hands and backed away from Senga, who he'd inched toward when Ruairí wasn't looking.

"I've agreed to fight alongside O'Driscoll as part of the terms to get him to sail with you. That's all that was expected of me, and now I will be on my way." Ruairí reached for Senga's hand and turned them toward the door. His patience was evaporating, and he needed to escape before he killed Aidan or Padraig while they continued to gawk at Senga.

"We need the MacDonnells before we can sail," Aidan blurted.

Ruairí turned slowly and smirked. "The MacAlisters owe their fealty to the MacDonnells, send Padraig sniveling on his knees to ask his overlord for help. That's not my problem. I have your agreement, Aidan, to trade what I wanted for getting the O'Driscolls to join you. I've pledged my sword arm to the O'Driscolls in return for their joining you. I have naught to do with the MacAlisters nor the MacDonnells."

"And what will Lizzie MacDonnell say when she learns you've been all the way to Rathlin and Ballycastle without paying her a visit?" Padraig called out. Senga ground her teeth as she glanced at Ruairí. When he appeared unfazed by the mention of another woman's name, Senga dug her nails into the back of his hand.

"I haven't a clue what Lizzie MacDonnell would say, nor do I care. I may have tupped her a time or two, but she was as good as the next. Aidan can have her, if he wants her. She holds no interest for me. But I warned you, MacAlister, about how you speak of my wife. That includes trying to humiliate her." Ruairí whipped out the dirk he'd returned to its sheath and sent it sailing into Padraig's throat. Blood surged from the gash, spraying Fionn and Aidan. A woman screamed from somewhere behind Senga, and the sound of feet running echoed in the hall, but she kept her eyes on Ruairí. He stomped over to Padraig as the wounded man sank to his knees before keeling over. Ruairí withdrew another dirk and slashed Padraig's groin. "You're lucky I find I don't have the stomach to actually touch you. You'll die without sucking your own cock."

Fionn clapped Ruairí on the shoulder and grinned. "Thank you. I couldn't stand the bluidy bastard. I just wish the blood was on you and not me. I'll be drawing flies soon."

Aidan stepped in front of Ruairí, not appearing as pleased as Fionn. "You just ruined any chance of the MacDonnells joining our cause."

"Your cause, not ours. I told you that before. I don't care whether or not you fight Neil MacLeod because it doesn't matter to Senga. O'Flaherty, you may not understand this, but you need to accept it: my wife is the only priority I have. I will do anything to defend her, and I'll turn away from everything else."

"You'll care now that you've agreed to fight alongside Fionn. When the MacLeods outnumber us, you'll care then."

"If you don't believe you can win, don't enter the battle. I'm no sacrificial lamb."

"So what if you couldn't stand Padraig? You took care of that. Lizzie MacDonnell was an excuse to embarrass you, and we all see where it got the arse. She's not a reason to avoid recruiting the MacDonnells."

"You don't seem to understand, O'Flaherty. I'm not worried about seeing Lizzie or any other woman from my past because it's obvious to everyone that that's what it is. My past. I love my wife, and she knows I'm devoted to her. But it matters not because I'm not interested in recruiting anyone else to this. You want more allies, make them yourself. I'll show up at the appointed time." Ruairí turned back to Senga and wiggled his fingers within her iron grasp. She hadn't eased her hold on him since the other woman's name was first mentioned.

"Then do it for your son," Aidan declared.

Ruairí glanced at Senga and saw the devastation on her face before he lunged at Aidan. He grasped the man around the throat and shook him like a rag doll before driving him backward into the wall, his head smashing against the stone wall with a sickening crack. Ruairí plowed his fist into Aidan's face, cracking his jaw.

"That child is yours, and anyone with at least one good eye can tell. He has black hair and blue eyes and is the spitting image of you. Just because that bitch tried to trap me years ago doesn't make her lies true. Anyone who can count to nine knows I didn't father that lad. I was in the bluidy Mediterranean when you sired him. Do right by the lad. Don't fob him off on me. And if you try anything more to get between me and my wife, to try to lure her away, I will gut you. What I did to Padraig will be considered a mercy kill compared to what I'll do to you. Don't believe I've gone soft just because I have a wife." Ruairí drove his fist into Aidan's gut before dropping the man to the ground. Aidan O'Flaherty was a sizable man who'd clearly fought more than one battle, but Ruairí made him appear like little more than a child compared to him. Ruairí took Senga's hand and led them out of the keep. Neither said a word until they arrived in their cabin.

# CHAPTER TWENTY-EIGHT

R uairí had a pounding headache as they boarded the *Lady Charity*, and Senga only made it worse when she slammed the door.

"You might have told me there's a rumor you sired a child," she hissed. "The only person to humiliate me there was you. How could you not tell me there's a chance you have a son?"

"Because there isn't a chance. You heard me. The child is Aidan's, and any halfwit knows it with one glance. Besides, I wasn't anywhere near Lizzie when she conceived that child. She was Aidan's bluidy mistress!" Ruairí kicked the chair away from the table and sank into it. "I never said anything because I never think about that. I was always careful with the women in my past. You're the only woman I've spilled in. Or rather, the only one I've risked planting my seed in."

"Risked? Is that what it is?"

"It was before we married," Ruairí growled. Senga backed away, shaking her head, her eyes narrowed. Ruairí leaped from his chair, pouncing. "Oh, no, you don't. Don't retreat from me. You wanted to accuse me of something I already explained I hadn't done. And yes, it was a risk before we wed. How did I know you wouldn't want to leave? That you

223

wouldn't try to leave? What if I had sired a child on you and you left? I would never allow a child of mine to grow up as a bastard. I never would have brought you aboard because I'd be married and miserable with Lizzie if the lad was mine."

Ruairí tunneled his hand into Senga's hair, keeping her in place. She fisted his leine, unsure if she wanted to push him away or pull him against her. Ruairí decided for her, when his hand slid to her lower back, and he brought their bodies flush. He nuzzled Senga's neck, and she was unprepared for the gentleness. Ruairí eased his grip and kissed her behind her ear. It wasn't a kiss intended to seduce her. It came across as more like an apology.

"I'm sorry that Padraig and Aidan humiliated you, and I can understand how horrid hearing those things must have been. But I need you to have faith that I would never keep such a secret from you. After what happened to Rowan, I'd don't have it in me to turn away from my own child. We may know now that it was a misunderstanding, but Rowan and I spent half a score of years assuming his mother abandoned him. My fears before we married were as real as yours were now. You did try to leave." Before Senga had the chance to defend herself, Ruairí pressed a soft kiss against her lips. "I understand why you did it, and I'm no longer angry or hurt, but what would have happened if we had created a child and you left? I would never have known. I would never have seen the child I've wished for with you."

"Wished for?" Senga asked. "You make it sound as though this is something you've thought about for a while."

"I told you my vision from the night we met; it was the same as yours. I've wanted to have a bairn with you since the very beginning, but we weren't in place to do that. Now we are, and we've been trying very hard."

Senga ran her hand over Ruairí's hair as he bent his head to once more kiss the sensitive spot behind her ear. Her core clenched as she swayed toward him. "It was humiliating, but it hurt so dreadfully much to think you'd kept such a secret from me. You know all about my past, but there is so much that I've never asked about yours, and you've never volunteered it. I didn't want to know the details about the gruesome side of your business, but now I wonder how much of your private life I should have inquired about. Lizzie may have been Aidan's mistress, but did you love her? Did you want her for yourself?"

"Absolutely not. Did I strike you as the type to fall in love when we met?"

"Actually, yes. You did with me."

"Because it was you. I didn't earn the name Dark Heart by being sentimental and caring. Senga, before you, anger and bitterness consumed me because of what happened on Barra all those years ago. I clung to it and let it fester. I even nurtured it. I was incapable of moving past how fate forced Rowan and me into piracy. And I couldn't accept my role in what I became. There wasn't a speck of room in my heart for anything but coldness and fury. At least, not until I met you. You melted all of that away in an instant. The night we met I experienced a calm for the first time in years. You've been a balm I never wanted before I met you. I haven't told you the unsavory details of my years sailing and pirating because I wish to spare you that. You know what I got up to when I came ashore. You told me you knew as much, but it was enter-tainment. It was a satisfying way to pass the time. That is not how I see us. I've never seen us that way."

"I love you, Ruairí. I think I have since that very first day. It crushed me to think you shared a family with another woman."

Ruairí gazed into Senga's eyes for a long time before he decided to say what had plagued him since they met. "I've been jealous of a dead man ever since Shamus told me you were married before. We both lived a whole lifetime before we met, but I'm jealous that my bairn isn't the first you'll carry, that you've had that family before me. I'm jealous that you've loved a man other than me." Ruairí swallowed the lump that

225

threatened to choke him and blinked away the tears that pricked the back of his eyelids.

"Ruairí, a part of me wishes you were the only man I'd married, the only man to father my child. But I can't undo that, and I'll never regret having James. But how I feel about you couldn't be further from what I experienced with Alexander. Yes, I loved him, but it was much like a friend. It was the physical attraction that made me think it was more than that. Aye, I enjoyed him bedding me as much as you enjoyed your time with other women. But the consuming need to be with you, to protect you, to make you happy, to comfort you, to share everything with you, was never there before. I try not to imagine the number of women who have enjoyed you like I have, but it's hard not to sometimes. I get jealous, too."

"Senga, it wasn't the same with them."

"I can understand that, but it's still hard, especially when I see how women look at you. I suspect you'll always be the handsomest man in any room or on any dock or any ship. Anywhere. Women will always want you, and most will never care that you have a wife. You might not do anything to encourage them, but it's still hard."

"We're a right pair, little one."

"That's why we work." Senga grinned as she stretched to kiss Ruairí, and the fire sparked between them. It had been an eventful and draining morning, and both needed to clear the air as much as they needed the restorative touch. The kiss continued until they both grew restless. They pulled apart, but Ruairí rested his hands over Senga's when she moved to untie the laces at the neck of her leine.

"Little one, there's still the matter of how little faith you had in me, how you assumed the worst of me."

Senga lowered her hands and dipped her chin. She'd suspected she wouldn't get off that easily. While they'd cleared the air and made declarations they each needed to hear, Ruairí was right: she'd questioned him and made up her mind before hearing anything he had to say. He led them to the side of the bed and sat on the edge. "Lower your leggings, Senga."

She didn't hesitate to comply, kicking off her boots before pushing her pants down over her hips. They pooled around her knees, making her shuffle toward him. She arranged herself across Ruairí's lap, her breasts pressing against the outside of one thigh with her mons rubbing against the outside of the other. She bit her lip to keep from moaning as the friction already aroused her. Ruairí reached down and found Senga's nipple. He rolled it between his fingers until it became a puckered dart that he tugged, twisted and pinched. The pain filled her breast with an achiness that only his mouth could satisfy, and her core burned with need for him to fill her.

Ruairí pressed his fingers between her thighs, discovering she was already dripping. When his attempt to spread her legs wider failed, he yanked the leggings the rest of the way off and flung them across the cabin. His fingers caressed her netherlips with the lightest of touches before dipping within her just enough to coat his fingers. He drew them along the crease between her rounded globes until they grazed her rosebud.

"All of this shall be mine today, Senga. I'm going to take you hard, and I'm going to take you tenderly, but I am going to take you." Ruairí's hand rained down the first spank, and Senga bucked, unprepared for the sting.

"One," Senga began her count without being told. Ruairí's hand landed with a ringing crack that seemed to bounce off every surface in the cabin. "Two."

"Trust may be something that I must earn, but I thought I already had." Smack.

"Three."

"You're far too quick to assume the worst about me, and that pains me, Senga. I'm a jealous and possessive man when it comes to you, but I don't assume the worst about you." Four more spanks came in rapid succession as Ruairí alternated sides. Ruairí continued to torment her nipples as each strike pushed her nub against his thigh. "Don't you dare climax while you take your punishment, *mo chridhe*. That will not please me."

"Yes, Ruairí," Senga panted. The spanking was at the point where it was still painful, and her body wanted to buck and escape. Senga took a deep breath and forced her mind to settle into the place it went where she relented and accepted the punishment. She ceded control to Ruairí, and her body relaxed. The spanking was no longer painful, even if it hurt. When Ruairí's hand swept over her chest and along her throat with a softness that belied the force being used on her backside, she tucked her chin, trying to catch hold of his fingers. Ruairí understood her intention and brushed his fingertips over her lips, so she opened and sucked his first two fingers into her mouth. She mimicked the action she intended to soon as her punishment ended.

Ruairí perceived the moment Senga released control and gave herself over to him and the punishment. His hand stopped spanking and rubbed the reddened flesh. He feared he might spill when she took his fingers into her mouth. The sensation of her breasts swinging against his thigh along with her pressed against his groin and his fingers dipping into her sheath with several of the strikes made him as hard as a pike. He leaned over and kissed each cheek, his sign that the spanking was complete.

Senga slid from his lap and kneeled between his legs. She looked up, and when Ruairí nodded the permission she sought, she unlaced his leggings and took his cock in her hand. She stroked it thrice, then lowered her mouth onto him. She worked his rod until his head fell back, and his hips thrust forward. He fisted her hair and pressed her head down as he surged into her mouth over and over, brushing the tip of his cock against the back of her throat. He controlled the speed and depth with which Senga sucked, but she hummed and moaned throughout. She rolled his bollocks and stroked the length she couldn't manage when Ruairí allowed her reprieves. Ruairí usually lifted Senga from his rod when he sensed his release approaching, then joined their bodies, but he intended for her to pay full restitution this time.

Senga swallowed over and over as Ruairí's seed sprayed within her mouth. It wasn't often that he finished like that, so she was unprepared, and some of the viscous fluid spilled past her lips. She lapped it off her cheeks before cleaning Ruairí's cock with her tongue.

"Take the leine off then onto the bed, face down," Ruairí ordered, and Senga was quick to comply. Ruairí pushed her legs wide before pushing her knees up, giving himself a view of Senga's sheath. The position forced her hips to rise, making it easy to press his tongue against her core as he settled between her legs. He alternated pace and pressure as he tortured Senga with his skills, taking her to the edge before pulling away. She whimpered as her endurance for pleasure and pain waned. Ruairí mumbled, "Not yet."

Senga buried her face in the covers as she clawed at them, so she was unprepared for Ruairí to thrust into her. His rod seemed larger than usual, but Senga wasn't sure if that was the case or her need for him to fill her led her to feel like this. Ruairí ground his hips against her backside and thrust twice more before spilling again. He'd been fisting his cock the entire time he'd feasted upon Senga. His fingers dipped into her entrance as he coated them, then pressed against her rosebud. She drew her knees under her and offered without reservation her most sacred space. Ruairí pressed his fingers within, readying her as he once again stroked himself. His ability to harden a third time amazed even him. He wasn't a callow youth who became aroused by the wind blowing in his direction. He worked his cock until he was stiff enough to press into Senga's core once more. Senga whimpered as he coated his cock with her dew. She cried out when he pulled away, leaving her with an emptiness that made her want to sob. Ruairí was careful to slow his pace and be gentle as he pressed into her rosebud. Once seated to the hilt, he rocked his hips, giving Senga a chance to adjust before he thrust. He kneaded the still-red flesh as he brought himself to release for a third time.

"Do you ache for me, Senga? Do you need to come?"

Senga sobbed as Ruairí eased her onto her back. He feared he'd pushed her too far when he saw her tearstained cheeks, but she opened her arms to him, silently asking for his embrace. She curled into his arms as he kissed her forehead and stroked her hair. They lay together, Ruairí dropping light kisses as his hand ran over her hip and backside, soothing away the last of the sting. Senga was nearly asleep when Ruairí's cock stirred. She glanced up at him, and when he nodded, she stroked his length. When he was certain he had the stamina to go again, he rolled Senga onto her back. Easing into her slowly before pulling nearly all the way out before surging into her. Senga shattered as her nails dug into Ruairí's back. He thrust into her over and over until he was certain her body was too wrung out to climax again. Senga drifted to sleep before Ruairí pulled out. He smiled as he settled beside her.

# CHAPTER TWENTY-NINE

It was midafternoon when Kyle pounded on the door. Senga remained asleep through the morning and past the noon meal, but Ruairí had slipped from their bed and examined maps of the Western Isles. He knew the region like the back of his hand, but the maps he studied showed the shifting tides by season, which told him the times of high and low tides. It had been years since he approached Lewis, having purposely avoided the MacNeils' greatest rival. Ruairí opened the door enough to slip out before Kyle could see into the cabin and spy a naked Senga still stretched out on their bed.

"O'Driscoll is here to see you. Says you've had enough time to make it up to your bride."

"There is never enough time," Ruairí grumbled. "Tell him I'll be on deck in just a moment." When Kyle turned away, Ruairí crept back into the cabin, but Senga was already seated, brushing hair from her face. He walked to the bed and lifted her onto his lap, tipping her to rest on her hip, careful not to put weight on her abused skin. He was certain her backside would still be sore.

"I'll order you a bath, little one. You can soak as long as you like. O'Driscoll is here. I must deal with the fallout from earlier, and discover whether Aidan survived meeting with Fionn alone."

"I might come with you, but that bath sounds lovely." Senga grinned as she kissed Ruairí. "I want more of that. Much, much more, but I know duty calls."

"I will make it as quick as I can. Perhaps I'll be back in time to wash your back," Ruairí shot Senga a cheeky grin as he helped her stand.

"Be back in time to wash a lot more than just my back." Senga tossed back as she pulled a robe on.

Ruairí stepped out of the cabin and found Tomas, ordering him to have a bath filled for Senga. He made his way above deck and found O'Driscoll waiting by the mast, his back to the tall wooden pole. Ruairí smothered his grin. O'Driscoll remained as untrusting as he'd always been, but Ruairí couldn't fault him. He stood with his back guarded too when he went aboard any ship other than his own or Rowan's.

"Is there one dead body or two?" Ruairí called as he approached.

"Only one for now. The whelp had the good sense to listen to a man who's been sailing since before his father fucked his first whore."

Ruairí only nodded. There wasn't much he could say to contradict Fionn since he spoke the truth. Fionn appeared old enough to be Aidan's or Ruairí's father, and it was no secret that Aidan's mother had been a tavern wench who became the mistress of the O'Flaherty clan's chieftain. As the chieftain's only surviving son, presumably the title would one day pass to Aidan.

"What did you decide, and how upset are the MacAlisters?"

"Upset? I'd say they're rightly furious that you murdered their chieftain in their very home before their very eyes. But I doubt anyone will miss the man. You have left them with no clear successor, though. The MacDonnells will have to decide, and that is where the trouble will come from. I doubt they'll be eager to see you or agree to aught you ask once they learn what you've done."

"Would you have let him get away with what he said?"

"You know I wouldn't. Aisling meant as much to me as your lass means to you. But that won't matter to the MacDonnells."

"Then I'll gladly remain aboard my ship while you and O'Flaherty negotiate. Or better yet, I'll cross back over to Scottish water."

"And bob about as a sitting duck? You're safer over here."

Ruairí drew in a deep breath. Fionn was correct that he was safer surrounded by Fionn's and Aidan's ships than anchoring on his own closer to home. "I'm not going ashore until you have the MacDonnells agreement, and I know Senga won't be left a widow."

"Very well," Fionn grinned. "O'Flaherty is already aboard his *Baile Diabhail*." Devil's home. Ruairí had always thought it a fitting name for the man's ship, even if his moniker, *Naoise*, meant warrior. Fionn clapped him on the shoulder before walking to the rail, tossing over his shoulder, "We sail within the hour."

Ruairí watched the older captain make his way across the dock to his ship the *Aisling*, named for his wife. Fionn no longer sailed looking for bounty or loot, but he remained fearsome. He fought battles with equal ease aboard his ship and on land. Ruairí shook his head as he turned toward his cabin, grateful that Fionn O'Driscoll chose his side. Ruairí returned in time to help Senga wash her hair, and even though she'd already used a linen square to scrub herself from top to bottom, Ruairí insisted they be thorough as he lathered up the soap.

⚓

Senga felt the boat rock as the anchor rattled onto the deck. Not long after, she and Ruairí made their way onto the deck as they headed south once more. Ruairí explained it should be less than a day's sail to Dunluce, where the MacDonnell sept most likely to support Aidan lived. While MacDonnells occupied Rathlin Island, the MacDonnells of Dunluce had grown more powerful. As they stood together at the rail, Ruairí shared the Irish tale of Nessa, a warrior princess.

"She was named Assa, or gentle one, and she was a great scholar blessed with twelve foster fathers. But one day she caught the eye of the druid chief Cathbad, who fell in love—or rather in lust—with her upon first sight. He is said to have had her foster fathers killed, so he could have her. So great was her anger and pain that she became a warrior and known as Ní-assa."

"Not easy or gentle," Senga murmured. She remembered something of this myth from her childhood. "Did Cathbad trick her when he discovered her bathing alone? She had to marry the man who orchestrated the death of her foster fathers."

"Aye, that is part of it." Ruairí opened his mouth to continue, but Senga interrupted.

"That sounds rather familiar. I was supposed to marry the MacLeod of Skye, the very man who attacked and killed my parents."

Ruairí froze, wanting to kick himself for not thinking through what he said. He'd intended on telling Senga a well-known Irish story, but instead, he reminded her of her loss. He straightened from leaning his forearms on the rail, but Senga laid her hand on his arms, staying him.

"Keep going," she murmured.

"Her father was king of Ulaid, so he gave the couple land where they made their home. The story goes that Cathbad demanded a drink from the river, but when Ní-assa returned, the water contained two worms. Cathbad insisted she drink it instead, and some insist that's how she conceived her child, Conchobar. Others claim she had a lover, Fachtna Fáthach, despite being married already. They say Conchobar was his son."

"One of the greatest, and cruelest, kings ever to reign in Ireland."

"That would be him. It's said that after Cathbad died, she remarried Fergus mac Róich and convinced him to abdicate his throne for a year in favor of Conchobar, which he did. Nessa, as they called her, turned out to be more cunning than either of her husbands. She whispered in Conchobar's ear, guiding him to give wealth and gifts to their people so that when the year ended, the people refused to take Fergus back as their king."

"I remember now. Wasn't Nessa also the mother of Deichtine and Findchóem?"

"Aye, and some say she was also the mother of Conchobar's son, Cormac Cond Longas. But others claim that his wife, Clothru, fathered his son."

"I'd rather think the latter, but naught in fairytales surprises me."

"I wouldn't let any Irishman hear you call their history fairytales. The fae have their own stories to be told." Ruairí chuckled.

"At least my story turns out to be much happier and doesn't involve incest."

"True, little one. Though I foresee a great tale to be told one day of how a set of piratical cousins fell in love with beautiful cousins, one English and the other Scottish."

"The tale must include how the cousins, both MacNeils and descended from the O'Neills of Ireland, were born to the sea, sailing from the great Hebrides to the coast of Africa."

"As long as it includes the part where the MacNeil of Barra charms the lovely MacLeod lass from Lewis and how they fell madly and passionately in love."

"That's my favorite part."

# CHAPTER THIRTY

Ruairí paced the deck in the dark while Senga sat on the stacked crates by the mast. She watched as his hulking shadow passed back and forth, but she remained quiet. She understood Ruairí's anxiety over Aidan and Fionn meeting with the MacDonnells. Padraig's death had been unplanned and unexpected, but Senga had no sympathy for the man. Ruairí warned him, but Padraig chose to test Ruairí's resolve and came out the loser.

However, Ruairí worried that the tenuous truce between Fionn and Aidan might crumble once the MacDonnells heard what happened. If they refused to aid Aidan's cause, there was no reason for the O'Driscolls to remain. Ruairí didn't want his deal to fall through with Aidan, but that was inevitable if the alliance collapsed. And while he didn't want Senga anywhere near Lewis or Skye, he admitted to himself that taking a pound of flesh from Neil MacLeod held a great appeal. He would fight to avenge the life Senga's uncle stole from her, even if Senga remaining on Lewis meant they never would have met.

The stars appeared while Ruairí continued to pace, but his hand went to the hilt of his sword when he heard the splash of oars. He glanced at Senga, who was invisible against the mast, but he was certain she hadn't left her spot. Ruairí strained to see who approached, but as he leaned toward the rail, he noticed dinghies rowing toward Aidan's and Fionn's ships while one pointed at his. He'd observed Aidan and Fionn rowing ashore earlier and recalled that neither captain took more than one dinghy. He resigned himself to accepting a visit from Dónal MacDonnell.

Senga inched closer to Ruairí, remaining behind him, so he blocked the view of her from the approaching boat. "Do you want me to go below?" she whispered.

"Aye, for now. If it's safe, I'll send Snake Eye for you." Senga darted across the deck and down the ladderwell, but she remained at the bottom rather than going to their cabin. She heard Ruairí's voice after the last splash of the oars. "Come to pay a visit, Dónal?"

"Aye. Seems you've sent my cousin to the devil. I'm not sure if I should thank you or run you through."

"I'd prefer your thanks," Ruairí quipped. He didn't offer a rope ladder to Dónal, nor did the man ask for one. "Why'd you row out here?"

"To let you know I hold no hard feelings. O'Flaherty began the tale of woe, but Fionn cut him off and told me a version I believed. The prig insulted your woman. You're the Dark Heart." The chieftain shrugged in the dark. "It was easy to figure out what happened before Fionn got to the part where you drew your dagger the first time. If my mother didn't threaten to skelp me alive, I'd have done the job myself years ago."

"Aye, well, I still wasn't sure how you'd receive the news."

"With bells on. I couldn't stand him. If you're concerned that your actions will make me refuse to aid O'Flaherty and O'Driscoll, then put your mind at ease. The MacDonnells will join in. We have no love for the MacLeods of Lewis, bluidy thieves, and anything that rankles the O'Malleys makes for a good day for me."

"Is it that simple?" Ruairí was skeptical that anything

could be as easy as a brief conversation with Dónal MacDonnell.

"I want half of what O'Flaherty promised you," Dónal was quick to reply.

"Fine."

"That simple, Ruairí?"

"Aye. I never wanted to be a part of this, but I am. I don't need what O'Flaherty promised, and I'm not greedy enough to sail into battle with my wife on board without a force equal to the one we attack."

"That's reasonable. But if you have a wife now, why sail to Lewis at all?"

"Don't play daft. I'm certain you've heard who I married. I respect O'Driscoll, and I'll avenge my wife's family. But O'Driscoll drew me into this battle as part of the trade between O'Flaherty and me. O'Flaherty refused pay without O'Driscoll's pledge to fight, and in turn, O'Driscoll refused to fight unless I agreed to join them."

"That's quite a tangled web of friendship."

"Friendship?" Ruairí barked a laugh, and Dónal chuckled.

"Perhaps not friends. But it still makes for odd bedfellows," Dónal conceded.

"The only person in my bed is my wife. If I suspect any of this will fall apart, I will leave all of you blowing in the wind. She's the person least interested in going to Lewis and fighting her clan."

"It seems the lass is the only one of us with any sense. I won't gut you, MacNeil. Come ashore in the morning, so we can strategize and be underway. The sooner we leave, the sooner I return home."

Ruairí grunted his agreement as MacDonnell's man pushed the dinghy away from the side of the *Lady Charity*. When the MacDonnells were an inky blip moving toward the shore, Ruairí called, "You can come out, Senga."

Senga eased her way to Ruairí, unsure of whether she'd angered him by not locking herself in their cabin. "You're not in trouble. Come here." Ruairí held his arm out to Senga.

"That seemed to go well. Do you trust what he said?"

"About as much as I trust Aidan, but if we can speed things along, we can be on our way to meet Rowan and Caragh. It's been nearly a moon, and our meeting draws nearer. I'd rather sail with them than this Irish rabble."

"I'd take Rowan and Caragh over the Irish any day of the week and twice on Sundays." Senga gazed at the keep that sat upon the cliffs. The stars shone over it, making it glow. She wondered what manner of men belonged to the Irish MacDonnell clan. If they were anything like their Scottish brethren and the MacDonalds, they would be fierce fighters, but their priority would always be themselves.

Ruairí spent a restless night in bed beside Senga, who sensed his unease in her sleep and tried to comfort him by wrapping an arm around his waist. It calmed him for a while, but it was never long before he shifted again. It was before dawn when Ruairí abandoned sleep and climbed out of bed. Senga grumbled, but her eyes didn't open.

"Come back to bed, Ruairí. The sun isn't up, and it's too soon to go ashore," Senga mumbled.

"Sleep, little one."

Senga sat up, rubbing her eyes and pushing hair from her face. She watched Ruairí as he completed his morning ablutions. She doubted she'd ever tire of watching the muscles in Ruairí's back bunch and ripple as he bent over the bowl and ewer. Her eyes slid to his backside as he moved to get dressed. "But I was enjoying that," she complained as he pulled his leggings over his first leg.

"Enjoying what, *mo ghaol?*" Ruairí asked, but they both knew he was aware Senga watched with appreciation. She slid from the bed and stretched, her back arching and her breasts rising. Ruairí stalked back toward her, his leggings forgotten. He wrapped his arm around her, his other hand going to her breast, pinching her nipple. "Tempting me?"

"Maybe. Perhaps this is what you need to fall back into bed and catch a little more sleep," Senga seductive smile dropped as she lifted her hand to run the pad of her finger under his eye. "You have raccoon eyes. You haven't slept well in days. I worry about you, *mo chridhe*."

"I have time to sleep when I'm dead."

"That will be all too soon if you're exhausted before you even show up for the fight. Please, Ruairí. We have at least another two hours before we normally rise. It will set my mind at ease if you at least try to get a bit more sleep."

Ruairí relented and climbed back into bed, pulling Senga into his embrace. It wasn't long before he noticed his eyelids were drooping. He realized that he would have slept better if he'd been holding Senga as he did once they returned to bed. The sun had been up at least an hour when Ruairí's eyes opened again. He could tell Senga was awake, but she was still, understanding he slept so well because of their position. He kissed her shoulder, a wave of tenderness washing over him as he considered how fortunate he was to have found a woman who cared enough about him to lie beside him, presumably bored, just so he could sleep.

"I love you, Senga."

Senga rolled over and ran her fingers over his tattoo. Having memorized the pattern, she could have traced it with her eyes shut. She found it soothing, and Ruairí enjoyed the touch. She'd been the first and only woman whose tracing his tattoo put him at ease. It had always annoyed him in the past.

"I love you too, Ruairí." Senga eyes narrowed as she assessed Ruairí's expression. "You say that as though you need to remind me in case you don't have an opportunity to later. What's going on?"

Ruairí shook his head. "I intend to live a long life telling you that every day. Many times a day, in fact. I didn't mean to be maudlin. I suppose I was being sentimental," he chuckled. When Senga cocked an eyebrow, he relented and explained. "You've been awake for a while. I can tell, but you remained beside me just so I could rest. You take care of me when I never thought I needed it. You're good to me and for me. I love you."

Senga wasn't sure what to say. Ruairí never lacked displays of affection and desire. He even told her several times a day that he loved her. But the admission that he understood how much she loved him, even if it was as simple as remaining in bed beside him, touched her. "I do with all my heart."

Ruairí offered her a smile that dazzled and made him look like anything but the Dark Heart. She pressed a kiss to the corner of his mouth before rolling to get out of bed. Both of them accepted that it was past time to rise. They hurried to go ashore, where they joined Dónal and the two other pirate captains to break their fast. Senga noticed a comely woman sitting beside Dónal, and she assumed she was the lady of the clan. When the meal ended, and the men moved to Dónal's solar to strategize, Senga moved to a seat on the left of the woman, avoiding the laird's chair on the other woman's right.

"Good morn," Senga ventured.

"Good morn," the woman's voice was tentative and her smile shy, but she was receptive.

"I'm Senga MacNeil." While her surname was still new to her, neither MacLeod nor Sorley ever felt so natural.

"I'm Moira. I'm pleased to meet you." The woman appeared younger than Senga, as though she was barely out of girlhood. Senga couldn't tell if the woman was shy by nature or just around strangers.

"I'm happy to speak to another woman. It has been a while." Senga smiled warmly, and the woman appeared to relax. "Have you been married to the MacDonnell for long?"

"Oh, Dónal's not my husband. He's my brother." Moira chuckled and blushed as she swept her gaze across the people who remained in the Great Hall. Senga got the impression the woman went unnoticed most of the time. She wondered if it was by choice or by Dónal's mandate.

"I have to admit I wondered since you seem quite a bit younger than him. I worried you might have been a child bride."

Moira's face fell as she shook her head. "I've never married, and I'm not as young as I appear. I'm past my twentieth year. No one has accepted any of Dónal's offers for my hand."

Senga glanced about the keep and over the food that remained on the high table. Her eyes swung to the tapestries on the walls, the hearths, and the candelabras overhead. "It's obvious you're a well-trained chatelaine. You have a well-kept home."

"Aye, and thank you, but it's because Dónal is miserly. He's not willing to pay a decent dowry, so I'm unconvinced I'll ever marry. He won't let me marry any of the men in this clan, and no one outside of it wants me. He says marrying anyone who isn't of noble birth is beneath me."

"I've heard that before," Senga mumbled before offering another smile.

"Are you a noblewoman, too?" Moira's tone was timid, and Senga could tell she didn't want to insult Senga.

"I am again now. I wasn't for several years. I did marry beneath me, according to my uncle."

"But they say Captain MacNeil once was the nephew of a laird."

Senga wasn't sure how Ruairí would want her to respond to that, but she'd just admitted to being a noblewoman once again. "I was a laird's daughter, then a laird's niece, but my first husband was a farmer. He died several years ago, and Ruairí comes from a noble family. I don't think of myself as a lady, considering where I live."

"You mean aboard a pirate ship," Moira bluntly stated.

"Aye, aboard a pirate ship," Senga grinned. She wasn't

243

embarrassed of her husband, and she would never allow anyone to assume she was.

"Do you care to join me for a walk in our garden?"

Senga's gaze darted toward the chieftain's solar. She didn't want Ruairí to come looking for her and assume she'd disappeared. She was certain he would lose his temper before he asked questions. She knew she'd be foolish to trust anyone at this keep, even Moira. But she wanted the fresh sea air without the rocking motion of the ship. She considered the seven dirks she had strapped to various parts of her. Unlike at the MacAlisters, the guards insisted Senga remove her sword before entering the keep. With some hesitation, she nodded her head.

# CHAPTER THIRTY-ONE

The two women moved through a dimly lit passageway, and Senga kept her hands on the dirks on either side of her belt. She pulled them halfway out of their sheaths, so she was prepared if someone attacked. It wasn't until they stepped into the daylight that she pushed them back in, but her hands remained near the hilts as she scanned the garden. She searched the branches in the orchard, then the bushes within the flower garden, and finally to the rows of flowers and vegetables. She eased her hands away from her knives, but she didn't relax her guard. Something about the MacDonnell keep put her nerves on edge. She hadn't felt this degree of unease since she went to Skye as a young woman to meet her potential betrothed.

"Would you like to see my lavender? It's my favorite," Moira suggested.

"That sounds nice. It's a favorite of mine, too," Senga smiled once more, but she scanned the garden to orient herself before they stepped forward. She wasn't pleased to realize the lavender was at the far side of the garden, toward a shady section. She had no view of the other side of the trees or what lurked behind them. Moira offered lavender sprigs, but Senga had nothing to carry them in. As Moira chattered, becoming more confident, Senga spied the entrance to the lists across from the garden. She could see most of the training field. It shocked her to realize there were far fewer men practicing their fighting skills than she expected. It was midmorning, and the grounds should have been teeming with warriors.

"Your roses are beautiful," Senga mused, pointing toward the red, white, and pink bushes. She stepped in their direction and hoped Moira followed. The bushes brought Senga to the path that separated the gardens from the entrance to the lists. She bent over in the pretense of sniffing the flowers, but she assessed the warriors in sight. They were skilled, and it was clear they were experienced, but there just weren't many of them. "I learned there are the MacDonnells of Rathlin, and you're a MacDonnell of Dunluce. Is your clan spread out even more?"

"Aye. We have people at Kinbane and Dunaneeny. Kinbane, where the MacAlisters live, is about a two-hour ride east of here, and Dunaneeny is only a little further. They're both a hop, skip, and a jump to Ballycastle. Those are the ones in this region, which we call Antrim. There are others, since we share our roots with Clan MacDonald."

"Same as in Scotland," Senga mused as she continued to observe the lists. "Are your branches as fractious as the MacDonalds in Scotland? Do you fight in one another's battles?"

"Sometimes. We don't have a good history with the O'Neills, but we've put most of that to rest as several generations ago, the clans intermarried. We've never taken issue with the Scottish MacNeils though. Similar name, but very different people."

"We say the same for the MacDonalds on either side of the North Channel. The MacNeils aren't as large a clan though. We've fought the MacLeods of Lewis and Skye many times."

"You really think of yourself as a MacNeil, don't you?"

"Aye. I have no ties to the clan of my birth."

"But your husband has no ties to his clan of birth either. How can you be so loyal to the MacNeils?"

"It's not loyalty at all. I am a MacNeil now, and so it is their history that I claim. I haven't said a prideful thing about either clan, only the truth of how much they dislike one another." Senga glanced at Moira as she straightened. "The MacLeods of Lewis and Skye live separate lives but are allies." Senga was growing tired of trying to illicit information from Moira, who didn't seem evasive; rather she did not seem all that astute. "Will the other MacDonnells join this fight?"

"Nay. I doubt it. My brother is more concerned with the coast and sailing than the other branches. He holds a grudge against your uncle for sinking three of his ships after they boarded and raided them. But he might," she shrugged, and Senga tried not to grow irritated.

"Are those men sailors too?" Senga tilted her head toward the lists.

"Most."

"Are they like the MacNeils of Barra and MacLeods of Lewis? Do they prefer to fight their battles on the sea rather than land?"

"I don't know. We lost many of our men the last time we fought the O'Neills. It's been a few generations, but our sept has been slow to grow. While the clan as a whole is powerful, our branch has sought aid from our Scottish allies in the meantime."

"It is interesting how connected the Scots and Irish are. I hadn't realized that before now." Senga told the truth, but she also wanted to finish their conversation before Moira grew suspicious. She knew she needed to return to the Great Hall before Ruairí tore it apart searching for her. "Shall we return? My husband shall wonder where I've run off to."

"Does he get angry easily too?" Moira's concern amplified her obvious fear. Senga liked Moira, and her heart broke as she suspected her earlier guess was correct.

"About some things, but almost never at me. Even when

247

he's angry, I don't fear him. I'm certain he would never strike me."

Moira nodded but remained quiet. She told everything to Senga when she unconsciously rubbed her upper arm as if to rub away a bruise. The two women returned to the Great Hall in time to hear an almighty roar.

"Where the bluidy hell is my wife, MacDonnell?"

"Probably off with my insipid sister," Dónal tossed back, apparently unconcerned. Senga rushed forward and grabbed Ruairí's arm as he readied to swing at Dónal. She tugged downward as hard as she could, knowing she was no match for Ruairí's strength if he punched Dónal.

"I'm here! I'm well, Ruairí. I visited the gardens with the MacDonnell's sister, Moira." Senga shot Ruairí a quelling glance and tilted her head toward the doors that lead outside from the Great Hall. She needed to get Ruairí alone and tell him what she'd learned. She feared Dónal might exaggerate the force he intended to provide, forcing them to sail to Lewis at a disadvantage. Ruairí turned toward Senga, the angry haze clearing from his vision when he recognized his petite wife hanging from his arm. "I'm fine."

Ruairí took a deep breath but returned his glare to Dónal, as if to warn him that he wouldn't be so patient the next time. Ruairí had no intention of backing down despite his overreaction. Dónal wasn't a man to show weakness before; he would attempt to exploit that weakness. He nodded to Aidan and Fionn, who stood at the sidelines. Aidan appeared surprised, but Fionn grinned; the older man was familiar with a protective husband's nature. Ruairí wrapped his arm around Senga's waist and kissed the top of her head. While he refused to apologize for overreacting, he had no qualms showing the MacDonnells that Senga was precious to him. It was a silent warning.

# CHAPTER THIRTY-TWO

The three pirate captains and Senga left the keep and walked back to the harbor in silence. Before returning to their ships, Aidan, Fionn, and Ruairí shook hands. Senga once again wondered if there was a pirate code of honor. She had deduced there was some honor among thieves, but she hadn't figured out the dynamics of piracy with regard to alliances. She presumed all truces ended if the battle turned away from their favor. It would be each captain for himself and his crew. Once aboard the *Lady Charity*, Senga motioned toward their cabin.

"What happened with the MacDonnell?" Senga went straight to the point.

"Not much. He agreed to sail with us in return for the largest portion of any spoils we take from Stornoway. Senga, I will take anything that was yours or that you want. I made that provision with all three of them. It was your home and your people for more of your life than it wasn't."

Senga shook her head. "There is nothing left there that I want. I have my father's cross. It was all that I took from Stornoway, and it's all that I took from my cottage."

Ruairí twisted his mouth as he considered whether he should share a secret now, or wait until the time came when he wouldn't need to hide the surprise. He opted for now. "The cross isn't the only thing you have. Senga, I had the men bring the cradle, too. It's stored in the hold wrapped in sailcloth to protect it."

Senga's mouth dropped open before she launched herself into Ruairí's arms. He staggered backwards until his legs hit the table. Senga pressed him onto it as she brought their lips together. Ruairí was unprepared for the intensity of the kiss. There was giddiness, thankfulness, and a heavy dose of passion. He spread his knees for her to step further into his embrace. She drew back and wrapped her arms around his back as she rested her head on his chest.

"Thank you. I never thought I'd see it again. I admit it was hard to leave it behind, but there seemed to be no reason to take it, and I didn't want to ask to use the space in the hold."

"It seemed wrong to leave it behind. It was clear how much it meant to you, and after my vision of you standing over it, I knew it had to come with us. Even if we never fill it with a bairn of our own, it's an important part of your past."

Senga cupped his jaw, this kiss short and light. "I am the luckiest of women to have a husband like you. You're better than any other. I'm sure of it."

Ruairí grinned as he tucked hair behind Senga's ear. "Don't let our cousins hear that. I would venture Caragh and Rowan disagree." He dropped a quick kiss on Senga's cheek. "But I'm certain no other woman could ever bring me the peace and happiness that you do. You have freed me from the emotions that drove me for so long. I was a prisoner to them, and so I deserved the name Dark Heart."

"Shall I call you *cridhe blàth* from now on?" Senga giggled.

"You may call me warm heart or anything else you'd like, so long as you call me."

"I shall hold you to that, *cridhe blàth*. But Ruairí, I need to talk to you about what I saw and learned while I was in the garden. The MacDonnell force is small. It doesn't seem like there are many men to spare if Dónal plans to keep his home protected while he's gone. Moira said they suffered heavy losses before they made peace with the O'Neills, but their branch hasn't grown nearly enough to offer a real fighting force. He might fill two ships, but that's a stretch. Fionn filled three and still left a strong guard at Dún na Séad."

"Did you notice anything else? Did they appear well-trained?"

"Aye. They all appeared experienced and able to fight. It concerned me how few of them there are. What type of ships do the MacDonnells sail? Sails or oars?"

"Sails. I wouldn't have agreed to seek their help if they rowed. I don't want his warriors, regardless of how many or how few there are, exhausted before the fight begins."

Senga nodded. Much of her anxiety eased as she listened to Ruairí. It was clear he appreciated the information she shared, but he didn't appear surprised.

"Are you all right with having so few men?"

"I bring the least amount. Aidan will have another ship join us on the way, Fionn has his three, Dónal will have two, and I only bring one."

"But I've seen your men fight. They're all worth three of anyone one else's men."

Ruairí beamed. "I shall have to tell the men that, and I'll give them extra rations. That's high praise coming from you, little one." It was Senga's turn to grin. She squeezed Ruairí once more before they went above deck, Ruairí to speak to his men and Senga to the stacked crates by the mast.

The day dragged on, and Senga didn't understand why they weren't underway. She wanted to sail to Lewis, survive the battle, and then meet Rowan and Caragh. She wanted to learn when they would sail to Barra, if they sailed there at all. She was fairly certain that they would. She'd seen Ruairí change during the time they were together, and she understood he no longer wanted to sail as a pirate. He would always belong on the water, but she suspected he'd be happy to finally be a merchant.

She observed Ruairí as he talked to his men, his authority clear for anyone to recognize. Not for the first time, she wondered if Ruairí could settle back into a clan lifestyle where he would have to follow orders from a laird, most likely his father or even his younger brother. She feared it would rankle and that Ruairí would grow restless. Her brooding must have shown because Ruairí moved toward her with concern etched on his face. He ran the pad of his finger over the deep grooves between her eyebrows. Senga's face relaxed, though she hadn't realized she furrowed her brow.

"What troubles you, little one?" Ruairí smiled as he offered Senga his hand. She hopped down from the crates, and they walked to the rail where they gazed out at the open water. She wasn't sure which thoughts to share: her remaining concerns about having too few men or her concerns about making a home on Barra. Ruairí solved it for her. "Tell me what concerns you in the here and now, then we can talk about Barra."

"How'd you know?" Senga gasped.

"Because our minds are very similar, and those are thoughts that concern me," Ruairí shrugged.

"It makes me uncomfortable sailing into battle with so few men. My uncle has hundreds of men at the ready. Between those who live at Stornoway and those he can summon as soon as they spot the ships, he will have a veritable army. Do you and the others intend to lay siege? I don't know how else you'll be able to prevail. Going head-to-head will almost certainly guarantee failure. Ruairí, this is the first time I've ever feared you won't come away victorious." Senga trembled as she whispered, "I'm scared."

Ruairí wrapped his arms around her, and Senga settled into the shelter of his embrace. The sound of Ruairí's steady heartbeat under her ear calmed Senga, and she let her eyes drift closed. She absorbed Ruairí's heat as her body gradually released its tension until she leaned heavily against him. Ruairí ran his hand over her back as he rested his cheek on the crown of her head. He refused to keep secrets from Senga, but he chose not to disclose how he shared the same fear she did. They stood together as the boat rocked against its mooring; the sounds of the crew working filled the surrounding air, but their world shrank to the two of them as they gained strength from one another. They drew apart when Kyle approached as the sun dropped low over the western horizon.

"It appears O'Flaherty and O'Driscoll are going back ashore," Kyle reported. "Do you need the dinghy lowered?"

Ruairí nodded. He didn't relish having to return to the keep or MacDonnell's company, but there was no avoiding the man's hospitality without driving a larger wedge between the two. Senga's scowl made both men raise an eyebrow.

"The bluidy bastard beats his sister. Ruairí, keep me away from him, or I will gut him like you did Padraig. She's a sweet lass, and he's a bully. She'll never stand up to him; she can't. So he will continue to mistreat her."

"He'll marry her off soon. She looks nearly old enough," Ruairí reassured.

"She's more than twenty summers. She told me her brother won't pay a decent dowry, so no one's asked for her hand." Senga shook her head. She knew there was nothing to do about it, but she wasn't eager to break bread with a man who took advantage of those who depended upon him and were so much smaller. Moira appeared to be in need of several solid meals.

"She doesn't seem that old," Kyle mused. "I thought she was perhaps fifteen, at most."

"That's what I thought, too," Senga admitted. "She's sweet but naïve. I feel bad for her. She reminds me of me when I was fifteen. I ran away as fast as I could, but I had a reason to. I had someone to protect me and a good life to begin. I don't think she has any of that." Senga sighed as she stared at the keep. With a shrug, she let the matter drop. She and Ruairí went ashore with Tomas and Kyle, and she found she was happy that Moira greeted them in the bailey. Senga didn't miss the appreciative expression on Kyle's face as his eyes swept over the young woman.

"Lady Senga, please come inside," Moira invited as she linked her arm through Senga's. She leaned close so only Senga could hear. "Who's the man with the red hair? There's something about him that scares and intrigues me at the same time. It's unsettling."

Senga kept her eyes straight ahead, fighting the temptation to glance at Kyle and grin. "That's Kyle; he's Ruairí's first mate." Moira nodded but said no more.

Conversation flowed during the evening meal, but Senga found the noise gave her a headache, and she struggled to stay awake as the evening progressed. She refused the extra ale and wine Ruairí offered, and she sensed he grew agitated when she picked at her food.

"Nothing's wrong," Senga whispered. "I'm extremely tired suddenly. That's all."

"We've eaten and drunk the same things. Do you think they've drugged us?" Ruairí's gaze shifted toward Dónal, who drank heavily while speaking to Aidan. Ruairí had seen the man's chalice refilled from the same pitcher that filled his own cup.

"No, not drugged. Just tired." Senga was about to ask to return to their cabin when a dark-haired little boy ran toward the dais.

"Da!"

# CHAPTER THIRTY-THREE

Senga watched as the boy grinned at Ruairí, then her eyes shifted to the beautiful woman who followed a few steps behind. Senga's stomach clenched as she understood in an instant that the woman was Lizzie MacDonnell. Senga hadn't been forced to encounter any of Ruairí's former bed partners since they left Canna. The woman who neared the dais was tall, willowy, and blond. Her fair skin was the creamy alabaster Senga's had been before spending long days in the sun aboard the *Lady Charity*. The woman moved with a grace Senga was certain she'd never possessed, and her smile matched her son's. Both smiled at Ruairí.

"Don't, Senga," Ruairí hissed. Senga tore her eyes away from the woman and child when Ruairí's punishing squeeze of her hand made her wince. "I know you've figured out who they are, but don't. Look at the lad. He is the image of Aidan. She and Dónal only want me to claim them because they assume I'm a better connection than Aidan. They're manipulative and greedy."

The boy bounded up the steps to the dais and ran to stand between Ruairí and Senga. While Ruairí smiled back at the child, he turned his glare on Lizzie, and she faltered. Senga recognized the glare. She'd seen it plenty of times, but had only been on the receiving end once. The dreadful night she met Aidan.

"Da, you've come back!" The boy beamed. Senga feared she would be ill. Even though she recognized the truth–that the boy was the spitting image of Aidan–to see and hear another woman's child claim Ruairí as his father threatened to overwhelm her. When the boy turned his bewildered gaze on Senga, she forced a smile she didn't feel. It wasn't the child's fault that he'd been lied to, nor was Senga going to be the one to set him straight. She raised her eyes and met Ruairí's.

"Sean, you know I'm not your father. I wish your mama and uncle would stop saying such things," Ruairí infused as much calm and gentleness into his voice as he could muster when he wanted to bash Lizzie's and Dónal's heads together.

"Uncle?" Senga gasped. "She's his sister?" Senga's gaze swung toward the beautiful woman who stared at her, her eyes narrowed and hatred oozing from them.

"Sean, go down to see Aidan. You know he's your da even though your mama told you to come to me. You'll hurt your da's feelings if you ignore him."

"But you're the great pirate Dark Heart. I want to be like you when I'm a man."

Senga feared her heart would break. The little boy's face and tone were so earnest, but her hurt and envy became a vice in her chest. The air felt thick, and she struggled to draw her breath. Her hand clung to the arm of the chair as spots danced before her eyes. She forced herself to take several deep breaths, and the stars faded away. When she glanced up once more, she found Ruairí's concerned gaze upon her rather than Sean. Ruairí stood and stuck out his hand for Senga. "We're leaving," he mouthed.

"Sean, your da is a great sea captain, and the man who will teach you to sail and train you to fight." Ruairí turned Sean toward Aidan and nudged him forward. The little boy tried to hang back, but even with a gentle touch, he couldn't hold his ground when Ruairí guided him toward Aidan. He glared down at Aidan when he stood beside the other captain. "Fix this."

Senga clung to Ruairí's hand as they walked away from the dais. She had to swallow the bile that rose in the back of her throat when Lizzie stepped toward them.

"Touch me, and I'll cut out your heart," Ruairí warned as Lizzie raised her hands to touch his chest. "Stop lying to the lad. I won't have him growing up convinced I'm his father who abandoned him. He'll realize your lies when he notices he looks more and more like Aidan each year."

"Ruairí," Lizzie began, her attempt at a seductive voice made Senga's nerves stand on edge.

"Look at my husband again, and I'll be the one to cut out your heart, you bitch." Senga flicked a knife from her wrist bracer. "You know who I am, and you dare approach us as though he'll leave my side to go fuck you. I'll cut you down before your entire clan and sleep peacefully tonight."

Lizzie's expression was that of a woman who was willing to take the challenge in order to win the coveted man. "He may have married you, but I bore his son."

Senga's brittle laugh cracked through the air. She stepped toward Lizzie, releasing Ruairí's hand. While Lizzie's eyes followed the dirk Senga held, she didn't notice the one Senga drew from her belt. The sgian dubh pressed against Lizzie's belly, piercing her clothing until it touched skin.

"Spew your lies again. I dare you," Senga voice was deceptively calm as she added more pressure to her knife. "Do you still claim my husband sired your son?"

Lizzie's bravado slipped, and she darted her eyes to Ruairí, pleading for him to intervene. He crossed his arms and leaned back on his heels, content to let Senga resolve a matter that plagued him for years. His wife's endurance, even when ill, impressed him. There was no trace of weakness in her voice or her stance. She was a pirate queen.

"I'm waiting," Senga's hushed tones filled the air as the MacDonnells turned to ogle.

"He might have married you, but he keeps coming back. I wonder why that is," Lizzie challenged.

Senga laughed once more as she stepped so close that the hilt of the sgian dubh pressed against her stomach. "You're a prideful eejit. He fucked you, and now you assume you understand him. Did he invite you aboard his ship and to sail with him? I'm certain he didn't. Who did he choose to live with? Who has been at his side while you remained here? Alone. Without him. No one could conceive of the Dark Heart marrying, but he did. Who did he marry? Me, not you. Has he pledged to love you, to care for you, to grow old with you? I can see you want to argue with me, claim he never said those things, but there are plenty of witnesses who can tell you he's said all of that and more. Now, do you still want to argue? Do you want to leave your son without a mother? Because don't think for a moment that I'll hesitate to kill you if you try to come near my husband again."

Senga waited as Lizzie's eyes once more pleaded with Ruairí to help, but he refused to interfere. He understood Senga would never leave a child without his mother, but he wasn't about to reassure Lizzie. She'd been the bane of his existence each time he sailed to Ireland ever since she gave birth to Sean. She had spies and turned up at Ballycastle and Rathlin unannounced. At first, he'd accepted it as a terrific coincidence that the lusty and skilled woman greeted him after long stretches as sea. But once she became pregnant and claimed he'd fathered her child, Ruairí avoided Ireland whenever he could. Unfortunately, demand for Irish wool and whisky made visits unavoidable. He'd made the foolish choice of availing himself of her more than once, even after Sean was born and the lies began.

Senga raised her other hand and pressed the tip of her dirk to Lizzie's cheek. "Perhaps I will let you live but cut out your tongue. You won't spew more lies if you can't talk. But you can suffer." Senga nodded as if she agreed with her own idea. "Aye, I rather like that plan better. Open wide."

Fear entered Lizzie's eyes as she accepted Senga refused to back down. Self-preservation took hold as she stared at her family on the dais, none of whom came to her rescue. She glanced at Aidan, who distracted Sean, but turned withering glares at her throughout the standoff. Her peripheral vision told her none of her clan seemed surprised that she was being threatened. Several even appeared amused.

"You can keep looking around. No one is coming to save you, and I'm tired of waiting. I told you: open wide." Senga pulled the blade away from Lizzie's belly to use that hand to force Lizzie's mouth open. She pried her tongue forward, using her greater height and strength to her advantage. Lizzie bucked away, and Senga let her go, but not before she wrenched Lizzie's tongue.

"Fine. Fine. I admit it. Ruairí is not Sean's father. Aidan is."

"That's not good enough. You fooled no one with those lies even though you insisted. Promise you'll stay away from my husband. And if you think to make that pledge while plotting against me, know that just as the Dark Heart doesn't sail alone, neither do I. My cousin married the Blond Devil after she left the smuggling ring she ran. Would you take her on, too?"

Lizzie's eyes widened as she shook her head. "I pledge to leave Ruairí alone. I will not interfere anymore."

Senga returned her dirk to her wrist bracer but kept the wickedly sharp sgian dubh in her hand. She nodded before stepping around Lizzie, but the woman struck out at Senga, hoping to take her by surprise. Senga slashed her knife across Lizzie's chest, and blood pooled through the linen tunic. "You shouldn't have done that, but now you have something to remind you that I protect what is mine, and I don't share." Senga drew back her fist and drove it into Lizzie's stomach.

"Ruairí?" Lizzie pleaded.

"You brought this upon yourself. This is years in the making. How many other husbands have you bedded? You're lucky to still be alive." Ruairí took Senga's hand and led her out of the keep and through the gate. When they were beyond the sentry's sight, he swept Senga into his arms as her legs buckled. She was in tears by the time they reached the dinghy and sobbing when they reached their cabin.

# CHAPTER THIRTY-FOUR

Ruairí had grown concerned throughout the meal as Senga's energy flagged. Then he'd been livid when Lizzie appeared with Sean. He'd expected her to do it, but it didn't diminish his anger when it happened. He'd been nervous when Senga and Lizzie argued, fearing what Lizzie might say. He was proud of Senga for standing up for herself and for them. It was her fight, both as his wife and as a woman who lived aboard a pirate ship. He couldn't afford for anyone to underestimate Senga and try to kidnap her, holding her hostage against him. He'd known all along that she never intended to hurt Lizzie, but the woman caused her own injury when she lunged at Senga.

As he carried Senga's trembling body to the dinghy, he realized that her fight-or-flight response had worn off, and the already-exhausted woman barely hung on. Her sobs tore at him as he cradled her in his arms as he sat on the bed. She hadn't sobbed like this since the night they met. He was ill-equipped to console her, so he settled for rocking and cooing in her ear.

"Ruairí," Senga whimpered. "I don't understand what's going on with me. I was so tired one moment and ready to murder her the next, and now I can't stop crying."

"You're still new to life at sea. Even without working the rigging, it's tiring to be in the wind and sun all day, bracing yourself wherever you walk. You've been through more battles than any woman I know, and you've been a victorious warrior each time. That's a lot of strain on anyone, especially someone who's had so little time to adjust."

"I was certain I'd gotten used to it. I thought I was strong enough to be your wife." Senga's sobs began once more, and Ruairí tucked her head against his chest.

"You're the strongest woman I know. You've endured losing your parents only to live with the man who arranged their murder. You avoided his advances and fought for a better life. You lost a husband and child at the same time. You fended for yourself for years, and then you joined a pirate crew. I'm not an easy man to love or to live with, but you've braved this new life."

"Ruairí, falling in love with you was the easiest thing I've ever done. When I feared you were dying, there was nothing I wasn't willing to do or give up to save you. I haven't had to face your past until now. Not your past with other women. Lizzie is so beautiful and graceful, even if she's a liar. I understand why she drew you to her, but the envy and insecurity made stars dance before my eyes. I understood, I mean really understood, what you told me about being jealous that I've already had a child with another man. To be confronted with the claim that you'd fathered a child, and that he was standing before me with the woman who insisted she shared that with you, I wanted to curl up and die. It was nearly as bad as losing James all over again. Then I remembered how I've already lost one husband, and the certainty I'd had that I couldn't live without Alex. My fear that you would choose Lizzie was utterly irrational, but that sense that my life couldn't go on became more extreme than what happened when Alex died. I don't understand why I reacted like that. You've never once given me reason to fear for our future together. You've been the one steady point in all of this, but I panicked. What's wrong with me?"

Senga shrank into a tight ball in Ruairí's lap, as if she didn't want any part of her out of his reach or that if she became tiny enough, there wouldn't be a part of her that he couldn't protect. He ran his hand over her back as his other tightened around her. He felt out of his depths to console Senga, but he understood what she meant. She reacted to what she perceived as an imminent threat, but he'd experienced the same emotions on a low simmer since they met.

"Nothing's wrong with you, *mo ghaol*. You said you truly understand the envy I held, and I'm certain that you do. But Senga, my fears didn't evaporate just because we talked about them. I fear I'm not as good a husband as Alex was because all I provide you with is danger. I haven't given you a home and security like a husband should. What if my seed never takes root in you, and I can't give you the children you want? What if I'm not as good a father as Alex would've been, and you regret having a bairn with me? These thoughts still plague me, but I'll never be forced to meet Alex. I will never come face-to-face with your past, but there's always the chance you'll contend with mine. I'm so sorry for that."

Senga sat up and twisted to look at Ruairí. She cupped his jaw and laid a soft kiss against his lips before they tilted their foreheads until they rested against one another. When it became unbearable to wait another moment, Senga lifted Ruairí's chin and pressed their mouths together, opening for him. The kiss was passionate, but it bloomed into an exchange of love and a need for acceptance.

"I'm not upset that you had a life before me." Senga offered a half smile. "There is much I wish I had the power to spare you from, but you don't need to apologize for what you did before we met. I'm sorry I overreacted. I was ready to gut her. I'm certain you're convinced I wouldn't, not when she has a son—regardless of who fathered him. But I would have. I wanted a reason to press my dirk into her belly. I've never had such consuming rage and need to be violent. I've never felt so protective or possessive of anything except for when I had James. That's the only time. When he became sick, I would've murdered someone with ease if it meant I could protect him."

Senga's heart lurched. She counted back the number of weeks since she'd met Ruairí, and she realized that she'd missed her courses since they married. She should have had them the week before, but she had no sign that it would come. She wanted to keep her suspicions to herself until she became certain, but she knew Ruairí would worry if he feared she was unwell or hiding something from him.

"Ruairí, it's possible I might be with child. It's the only thing I can come up with to account for my moodiness and protectiveness. Even the queasiness when I'm in the dinghy. My courses haven't come since before we wed. You remained careful not to spill in me before then, but they haven't come, and they should have last sennight. I don't know for sure, but maybe that's why I'm acting like this."

Ruairí sat stunned as he absorbed Senga's suggestion. His chest tightened, but it wasn't anger or fear. He recognized those emotions. This was the joy that only Senga created. He beamed as he held Senga against him until he realized he must be suffocating her. He pulled back and laughed when he caught sight of her trepidation.

"Senga, if you are, then I'm overjoyed. If you're not, then we'll work through whatever is causing you upset. As long as you're safe and well, then we will face the future together. I love you, Senga."

"I love you, too, Ruairí. My future is wherever you are." Their next kiss proved an erotic prelude to how they spent the next hour before Senga dropped into a deep sleep.

# CHAPTER THIRTY-FIVE

Senga stepped onto the deck the following morning, appreciating the cool breeze and bright sunshine. She'd slept much later than usual, and Ruairí had been silent when he slipped from the cabin. She was surprised to discover they remained moored in the harbor; she had thought they were on their way. The surf was rough enough that she'd assumed the rocking motion was from them sailing. As she scanned the sky, the sunshine came to an abrupt end, and a wall of black clouds moved toward them. She wanted to groan, knowing there was little likelihood of them sailing into a storm if they could avoid it.

"I've been keeping an eye on them for an hour, and the storm is moving quickly," Tomas spoke from behind her shoulder. She turned to find the weathered sailor rubbing his elbow as he often did before it rained. "My arm aches something fierce, so it will be a gale."

Senga nodded as she gazed at the cloud cover. The first drops of rain began even though the sun still shone. Ruairí came to join her, offering her half of his bannock. She hadn't realized she was hungry until she ate. She'd been too anxious and tired the night before to eat much at the evening meal.

"We won't be leaving, will we?" Senga didn't attempt to hide her disappointment.

"Nay, little one. It looks to be a bad one. I will order the men to batten down the hatches, then we're going ashore."

Senga shook her head and stepped back. "Do we have to? After last night, I don't want to show my face again. What if I'm not wanted?"

"My lady, maybe you couldn't hear the whispers while you were—ah—talking to Lizzie, but her clan isn't fond of her. More than one woman was happy to see you take her to task for trying to steal away your husband. I'd say the tides have shifted for her. I suspect people won't accept her conniving and manipulative ways," Tomas explained. "Beside no one will say boo to a goose after they saw you stand up for yourself. I'd wager a few women will ask you to teach them how to wield a dirk."

Ruairí nodded, though Senga didn't appear convinced. "Senga, last night might have embarrassed you, but I prefer people have a healthy dose of fear when it comes to you. It'll keep them away from you and keep you safe. No one's likely to challenge you now that they've seen you won't back down." Ruairí's smile set Senga at ease, and she returned his nod. "Pack a satchel with what you need for a few days. I'm guessing this squall will be worse than the one we encountered on the way here."

Once Senga packed a bag for each of them, the crew went ashore. Only a few men would rotate watch while the rest of the men took shelter within the bailey wall. Senga kept her chin up and refused to cower as she returned to the Great Hall. She caught women smiling at her and nodding as she walked past. Men who had starred a little too long the day before averted their eyes. Ruairí squeezed her hand as they approached Dónal, Fionn, and Aidan.

"Looks like *fuath* have woken," Fionn grinned. When he noticed Senga's bewildered expression, he explained, "They are sea monsters who prey on sailors. The word itself means 'hate.'"

Senga nodded as she caught sight of several older clan members shrink away at the mention of the mythological creature. She was not a superstitious person by nature, but she knew plenty of the Irish were, much like the Scottish. She flinched when Sean ran to Aidan's side. The little boy took the pirate's hand and grinned, looking like the mirror image of Aidan when Senga met him. The man became uncomfortable with the child clinging to him, but he didn't send the boy away.

"Mayhap it's a *dobhar-chu*," Sean suggested as he continued to beam at Aidan. Senga was certain she failed to hide her shock when Aidan scooped the boy up and tickled him before placing him on his hip.

"And what do you know about a creature that's half dog and half otter?" Aidan chuckled. Senga's gaze shifted between the two, hoping that if she was with child, that it would be a little boy who was Ruairí's likeness. When her husband squeezed her hand once again, she peeked up to find longing in his eyes as he regarded Aidan and Sean. It wasn't a longing for Sean, but a longing for a family. He wrapped his arm around her shoulder as she leaned against him. Fionn cast them a knowing expression as he noticed but said nothing.

"It's a horrible, horrible beast that feasts on people's skin," Sean explained, his face crinkling in disgust before he giggled.

"Aye, that's right. And what do you plan to do if you meet one?" Aidan adopted a curious expression.

"Hold a dirk to him like Lady Senga did to Mama last night," Sean crowed. Senga gasped and wished to flee, but Ruairí anchored her against him. "Mama wasn't being nice to Lady Senga last night. I think her words hurt Lady Senga's feelings, and then she was mean when she tried to hit Lady Senga." Sean gazed earnestly at Senga before continuing. "Lady Senga, I'm sorry my mama was being nasty to you. I think she wishes she could play with Capt'n Ruairí, too."

Several chuckles carried from those eavesdropping nearby, and Dónal had the temerity to laugh loudly. Senga wished she could melt into the floor, but Sean wasn't finished yet. "I like Capt'n Ruairí. Mama said he's my da, but I don't believe her. I know I look like Capt'n Aidan. And he slips me sweets and lets me curse. And I like him," the young boy chirped. "Capt'n Aidan is here more often too. I'd like him to be my da."

The adults stared at Sean as he spoke the truth like only a child could. While Senga was still uneasy, the others relaxed. Aidan carried Sean into the kitchen to find some of those sweets, and the child's voice carried as father and son sang a song entirely inappropriate for a five-year-old.

"About time that mess got sorted," Fionn said as though it ended any more discussion. "I suspect this storm will keep us ashore for a few days. I'm not interested in losing another ship."

"Aye. The weather can't be changed. I'll send messengers over land to Kinbane and Dunaneeny, telling them that we sail when the storm ends and that I expect them to be ready to join us. The Rathlin MacDonnells will learn of it as soon as the MacAlisters get their summons, too."

It shocked Senga to hear that Dónal intended to order the other MacDonnells in their sept to join them. It relieved her to know they ventured to Lewis with a better fighting force, one large enough to pose a threat to her uncle rather than a mere annoyance. Ruairí shifted, and Senga sensed the news relieved him, too. He'd tried to reassure her the night before, but learning of the additional sailors and warriors made both Ruairí and Fionn visibly relax.

The weather remained ominous until the next day, when the heavens opened. It was a fortnight before the weather calmed enough for Dónal to send out a messenger. He'd suggested sending men into the storm, but Aidan, Fionn, and Ruairí convinced him to wait. It was another sennight before the MacDonnells from Rathlin, Kinbane, Dunaneeny, and the

MacAlisters from Ballycastle arrived. The harbor had a fleet anchored off its shore. The first sennight spent with their days and nights in the keep was uncomfortable for Senga, but by the second week, she accepted that no one intended any animosity toward her. Lizzie's admission finally set in motion an opportunity for Aidan to be a father. No one was more shocked than he to discover that he enjoyed having Sean as a near-constant companion. Lizzie shifted her attempts for attention to Aidan and barely cast Ruairí a glance. She was an opportunist at heart.

By the time the fleet was ready to embark, Senga didn't fear arriving in the Great Hall each morning. She was also fairly certain that she was expecting. She needed naps at least once a day and barely kept her eyes open through the evening meal. Her breasts were sensitive and certain smells turned her nose up. Ruairí doted on her, often rubbing her back until she fell asleep. When she'd discovered she was expecting James, Alex had been too busy working in the fields to tend to her. Senga was grateful for Ruairí's support, knowing there was a possibility that she might not be expecting, but rather contracted some withering disease. They agreed not to say anything or decide anything until they knew whether Senga missed her courses again. The sun beat down on the deck as Ruairí guided the *Lady Charity* into the open water of the North Channel and set course for Scotland.

# CHAPTER THIRTY-SIX

The crossing to the Hebrides was uneventful after the tempest that battered the northeastern Irish coast. As they drew closer to the islands, Senga wavered between the calm that came with familiarity and fear of returning to people who cast her out. She knew it was her uncle, not her clan, who had expelled her, but she doubted a warm welcome awaited her when she arrived on a pirate ship with a crew intent upon attacking.

Ruairí and Senga agreed that Senga would remain on the ship with Braedon, Tomas, and Snake Eye. They grumbled about being left behind until they learned Ruairí tasked them with guarding Senga. All three understood the trust Ruairí placed in them, and they appeared to gloat before the rest of the crew. Senga agreed without complaint to remain secured in their cabin during the attack. She wasn't eager to cross paths with her uncle and cousin, and she refused to endanger her life or that of any bairn. She did, however, hold a dirk to Kyle's throat, threatening to geld and disembowel him before chopping off each of his fingers and toes and feeding all it to him as haggis if he allowed Ruairí's back to go unprotected. Kyle pledged to fight alongside Ruairí and pledged lifelong fealty to Senga if she agreed not to chop him to bits before the fight began.

They dropped anchor off the coast of Stornoway during the dead of night. Ruairí and the other captains ordered the dinghies to take the crews ashore, where they hid along the cliffside until the sky lightened before dawn. Senga watched the men move like ants along the hillside until the warning bells rang to signal the attack. There was no way for Senga to view what happened along the bailey wall and beyond, so she and Braedon barricaded themselves in the cabin while Tomas and Snake Eye stood guard, one outside the cabin door, the other at the top of the ladderwell.

"How long do you think it'll take?" Braedon wondered. The youth was accustomed to sea attacks that were short compared to land battles.

"Most of the morning, if the keep doesn't fall immediately. The bells will warn the villagers to come within the curtain wall if there's time. If there's not, they'll flee out past the fields. Some men from the villages will come to join the fight. My father insisted that even the farmers learn to fight in case of this very type of attack. When I left, my uncle was still carrying on the practice. We must wait and see."

The morning dragged on as Senga and Braedon played dice games, and Senga told him stories of her childhood on Lewis. Braedon told her tales of the voyages he was on before Senga joined Ruairí aboard the *Lady Charity*. The sun was well overhead before she caught the sound of a shout and Snake's Eye's voice called down to Tomas. The latter knocked on the door and told them a dinghy approached but to wait while he and Snake Eye learned of the battle's outcome. Senga peered out the porthole, but there wasn't much that she could see, so she went to stand beside the door. When she recognized Kyle's voice but not Ruairí's, she flung open the door and flew up the steps to the deck.

"Why the hell are you here without Ruairí? Where is my husband?" Senga demanded, a dirk in each hand. Kyle threw his up in the air before pointing toward the beach. She spotted Ruairí waving to her, but when she returned his wave, he turned back toward the keep.

"Senga, he couldn't leave. He's dealing with your uncle and cousin, but he wanted me to reassure you that he's fine. Barely a nick on him. Your clan was unprepared for the attack, so we breached the gate and wall with ease. The fight was long, but we gained the upper hand early. Your uncle nearly lost his head, but Ruairí lowered his sword at the last moment. Once we captured the MacLeod, it wasn't long before your cousin conceded. The capt'n wants you to join him before he decides what to do with your uncle and cousin. He found your aunt, and she's demanding to see you for herself. She's safe," Kyle reassured as Senga's face blanched. She hadn't cared what happened to her uncle or Alfred, but her aunt had protected her and shielded her until she could leave with Alex. The woman had done her best to step in as a mother when Senga lost hers.

"Take me ashore," Senga murmured, but she was already moving toward the rail. She discovered she had more energy than she'd had in weeks as she dashed along the path that took her from the beach to the keep. Kyle and Snake Eye accompanied her, and she pushed them to keep up. As she passed through the gate, she spotted Ruairí with ease, her eyes always finding her husband even in a crowd. Next, she caught sight of her family. Neil MacLeod had a nasty gash along one cheek, and he held his ribs as though someone broke at least one. Alfred's sword arm was bandaged, and he had several scratches visible even from a distance. But she wasn't interested in any of that once she recognized her aunt.

"Senga!" The woman called as she tried to push past members of Ruairí's crew. When Ruairí turned to her, she nodded. Her aunt lifted her skirts as she ran to Senga, who met her halfway. The women collided in a tight embrace while Neil spewed curses at Senga for daring to return. Senga opened her eyes in time to witness the hilt of Ruairí's sword make contact with Neil's temple. The man crumpled. Alfred lunged toward Ruairí, but halted when Ruairí lifted his sword, prepared to cleave him in two. He wobbled and lost his balance, landing in the dirt beside his father.

"Aunt Christina? You're all right? You weren't hurt?" Senga stepped back and surveyed her aunt, but the woman appeared unscathed.

"Your man found me before the fighting even began. He burst into my chamber and told me to hide. He told me you would come for me when the battle was over and that I was to protect myself until he returned to get me. He said not to come out unless it was him, personally, who fetched me. I don't even know his name. Someone called him the Dark Heart."

Senga listened as her aunt explained, but her eyes were glued to Ruairí. She guided her aunt to Ruairí but stopped listening as soon as he was within reach. She flung herself into his arms, and he lifted her off her feet. She gazed at him, searching his eyes for reassurance that he was as well and unscathed as he appeared. When she found what she searched for, she cupped his jaw and kissed him, relief washing over her.

"She's still a whore," Alfred cried out.

Senga waited until Ruairí lowered her to the ground, but her aunt didn't. The slap she laid across her son's cheek echoed. "Don't you dare call your cousin something so vile. Just because she didn't choose you doesn't make her that horrid word. She never would've been yours, and you know it. Your father never would've broken the agreement with the MacLeod of Skye. She married Alexander Sorley and lived an honest life until his death. Your father refused her return. Blame him not her, but from the ring on her finger," Christina pointed to Senga, then Ruairí, "and the one on his, I'd say she's remarried. The only one running around coupling out of wedlock is you."

Senga stood in shock as she listened to her aunt castigate

her son. She'd never heard such a tone from Christina, and it stunned her to witness her aunt dressing her cousin down for all to witness. Senga suspected it only happened because Neil was still unconscious, and she felt protected with Ruairí nearby. Alfred grumbled before sneering at her. Senga stepped away from Ruairí and stood in front of Alfred. She bent over him and tsked.

"Time hasn't been kind to you, Alfred. You're as bitter as your father. I suspect you've grown as cruel and immoral as him. You played me for a fool, building my trust, training me as though you respected me, all so you could spill my secrets to your father." Senga glanced back at Ruairí, who fought to restrain his temper while Christina and Senga took control of the situation. "I'd take care, Alfred. My husband is overprotective and possessive. If you wish to live, mind your words and your tone. Your mother won't be able to save you again. I'll be the one handing my husband a sword to cut out your tongue."

"You couldn't sink lower if you tried, cousin," Alfred jeered. "First a farmer, and now a pirate. You lay with men beneath you." Alfred spat at her feet, but when Ruairí lunged forward, she put out a restraining arm.

"The only man laying beneath me is my husband. Every chance I get. A position you may have wished for, but you'll never get. Your mother makes it sound as though you're the whore, but that can't be, can it? Or did things improve over the years, and now you can raise your sail?" Alfred stuttered as he struggled to his feet. "Women talk, Alfred. And I listened. You may have spilled my secrets to your father, but I kept yours for a rainy day. I think it's going to pour."

Ruairí lunged again, but this time it was toward a man he'd observed creeping toward them. The warrior inched forward to not draw attention, but he lifted his sword to charge Senga. Ruairí thrust his through the man's middle, but it was Alfred who bellowed.

"So, Harrold is still your lover? Even after all these years. I

275

suppose that means you can be faithful." It appeared as though time stopped as everyone froze at Senga's revelation. "Och aye, I told you I knew your secrets. Perhaps I should have been clearer about what I asked. Are women now able to raise your sail? Because I know which men already have. Some of them are still breathing from what I can see. Many of them even let you bugger them by choice."

"You've changed, Senga," Christina whispered. A moment of guilt made Senga hesitate. She regretted hurting her aunt, not humiliating and endangering her cousin.

"I have. They," Senga pointed at Neil and Alfred, "were willing to send me to the bed of a man who intended to beat me and probably kill me, as he did his previous wives. My own uncle conspired with that man, and if you hadn't protected me, he would have to wed me to the monster when I was but three-and-ten. Uncle Neil tried to rape me, but it was Alexander who saved me. Alfred told Uncle Neil about Alex, told him about how I loved him, told him that we wanted to get married. Alfred is the reason Uncle Neil beat me right before Alex took me away. Alfred tried to make me—but thank God he couldn't," Senga shuddered.

Ruairí pulled Senga back as he stepped toward Neil, whose eyes fluttered open. "Do you make it a habit of beating women? Or was it just my woman?"

"She wasn't yours back then," Neil spluttered.

"Wrong answer." Ruairí thrust his sword into Neil's neck, and blood drenched Alfred. He spun toward Senga's cousin, raising his sword to below the man's chin. "I don't give a bluidy damn who you bed, but my wife is right. Insult her again, and you will learn that I'm not an impetuous man by nature. Just the opposite. I'm very patient while I torture a man."

Senga watched Christina as Ruairí ended her husband's life, and she was certain she saw relief in the older woman's eyes. "Aunt Christina, I had to make a life for myself, alone, for five years because I wasn't welcome here. I had nowhere to go, so I stayed on Canna until I met Ruairí MacNeil. I'm not that girl of five-and-ten anymore. I've watched my husband and son die. I've buried them, then burned everything they touched after a fever took them. I've lived aboard a pirate ship for months now, and I love my husband more than anything or anyone. I will never be Senga MacLeod again."

Christina nodded as she watched her son attempt not to tremble as Ruairí held the tip of his sword beneath his chin. "Alfred, for the love all that's holy, keep your gob shut. Our fight is lost. Do right by our clan, and make peace with these men, so they will leave. Senga, you are welcome here as long as I draw breath, but I understand why you won't come back." Christina drew Senga into a hug, and Senga had a moment of peace that she hadn't had since she was a child and her mother embraced her. Christina tucked a lock of hair behind Senga's ear before kissing her cheek.

"I think we will live on Barra soon," Senga whispered. "You can always visit me there. Ruairí will ensure your safety, I promise."

"I'll think about it, lass." Christina shifted her eyes to Ruairí, her gaze hardening. "If you do anything that upsets her, even causes her a moment of distress, what you did to my husband will be considered mercy compared to what I do to you."

Ruairí nodded, but the corner of his mouth twitched, "And they call the MacNeils bloodthirsty." Ruairí gave in and smiled. His good looks made Christina blink several times as his charm dazzled her, but when she regained her senses, she returned the smile. "Senga, do you wish to find anything that was yours? My lady, do you have anything that Senga might wish to have?"

Senga and Christina shook their heads, both saddened that there was nothing left to remind Senga of her life with her parents. "Ruairí, I have my cross, and you made sure I have the cradle. There really isn't anything else. I'd like to visit my parents, though."

Ruairí arranged with Fionn and Aidan that they decide Alfred's future as long as they spared Christina and the other women and children. Fionn's face went red as he reminded Ruairí that he didn't make war on the innocent, and Ruairí felt like an arse for reminding the man once again of how he lost his wife. Aidan's newfound honor as a father made it easy for him to agree. It wasn't until Ruairí and Senga walked toward the postern gate that they discovered Dónal lay bleeding beneath a MacLeod. Ruairí called men over to help the chieftain before he and Senga made their way to the cemetery. He offered to wait outside the gate, away from consecrated ground, but Senga insisted she wanted to introduce him to her family.

They spent the rest of the afternoon at her parents' graves as she told them about her life on Canna and her life with Ruairí. She reminisced about her childhood as she shared more stories with Ruairí, now able to point to places in the tales. It was dusk when they returned to the *Lady Charity*. The crew cracked open several casks of whisky they found in the cellars. Senga and Ruairí retired to their cabin to the sound of drunken revelry. More than one man raised his cup in her honor, her losses vindicated by the men who pledged their loyalty to their pirate queen.

# CHAPTER THIRTY-SEVEN

Ruairí covered their sweat-dampened skin as he settled on his back, and Senga cuddled next to him. They'd returned to their cabin, where Senga helped Ruairí scrub the grime from his hair and body before they fell into bed. Senga traced her fingers over Ruairí's tattoo, relief flooding her for the umpteenth time that he'd survived. She accepted that much of her anxiety came from not fighting alongside him and having to trust that he could defend himself. She recognized the notion was ridiculous since he'd fought countless times before they met, so she kept it to herself, but she accepted that she was as overprotective about Ruairí as he was with her.

"Does it seem anticlimactic to you, little one, since you weren't there for the fight?" Ruairí surely read her mind.

"A little. I was more concerned with your safety than the outcome. Once I walked through the gates, I was certain I would never consider Lewis home again. I think a wee part of me hoped it might be possible, but I always knew it wasn't to be. That's why I haven't wanted to return. But now I know. Being a MacLeod is a part of my life that is finally over. I hold no animosity to my clan, but neither do I hold any ties."

"I suspect I shall have my own revelations soon enough.

Senga, I want us to join Rowan and Caragh if they go to Barra. I want to see if that part of our lives is over, too. I want to see my parents and brother and sisters at least once more, even if the clan rejects Rowan and me."

"What if they try to imprison you or kill you?" Senga bit her bottom lip as a knot formed in her stomach.

Ruairí chuckled. "You really think you and Caragh would let that happen? I believe the MacNeil clan faces a violent end on Barra before you and Caragh let them harm a hair on our pretty heads."

"So very pretty, and that's how I should like it to stay." Senga stretched to kiss his cheek. "But seriously, Ruairí, I am scared of what they might do to you. At least we didn't fear my clan arresting me."

"I know, *mo ghaol*. Rowan and I will talk about it with you and Caragh before we make any decisions. We will meet them near Canna in a sennight."

"What will we do until then?"

"There's a tiny isle with a cove where we can wait out of sight. It'll give the injured men time to heal, and we could all do with a rest."

"That sounds heavenly. I could still sleep for a month of Sundays. I'm not as exhausted as I was before, but I still need for a nap every day."

"Once we decide whether we're staying on Barra or if we need to move on, I'm finding a midwife to examine you."

Senga nodded, blinking several times, trying to keep her eyes open. She stifled a yawn, but Ruairí drew her closer. She smiled as her eyelids drooped. "Good night, *mo chridhe*."

"Good night, *leannán*."

Senga stretched as she yawned, looking toward the porthole. She stirred earlier when Ruairí left their cabin, but she rolled over, falling back to sleep. Now the sun shone into the cabin, making it impossible to ignore the new day. She rose and dressed, glancing again at the horizon. She smiled, knowing they were underway and would soon meet up with Rowan and Caragh. Their journey through the Minch was smooth the first day, but as they entered the Little Minch and spent two days navigating the hundreds of rock formations and tiny isles, the water grew rougher. Senga experienced her first case of seasickness as the boat rocked, and her stomach followed the unsettling rhythm. That morning, she woke without a need to hang her head over the chamber pot. She smiled to herself as her anticipation grew, excited to get together with Rowan and Caragh that day. They'd spent three days bobbing off the coast of Sandray. They were less than half an hour's sail from Canna, and they planned to rendezvous with their cousins at sunset.

"Are you excited, little one?" Ruairi greeted her when she approached the helm.

"I am. I really miss Caragh. We went so long between seeing each other, then we haven't spent nearly enough time together since we reconnected."

"You should have plenty of time with Caragh over the next two score years or so," Ruairi grinned.

"Have you decided whether we're staying on Barra?" Senga's brow furrowed. The last they talked about the immediate future, Ruairi assured Senga that he wouldn't decide for them, but she wondered if he'd changed his mind.

"We can't be sure until we go ashore, but I hope we can. For your sake and Caragh's. I hope we can make our home where there are other women who can help care for you and Caragh when your times come."

"Are you certain I'm increasing?" Senga giggled. "Are you a midwife, and I didn't know?"

"Hardly. But if you are with child or you ever are in the future, I want you well cared for. If we can't stay there, then we will sail together until we find somewhere to settle together. I'm certain Rowan feels the same as I do. Neither of us want to continue as we are now that our priorities have changed. Our wives matter more than anything else, and Rowan knows he'll be a father soon, and perhaps I will be too."

"Then I'm excited for this evening when we can discuss our plans." Senga's smile slipped as she glanced north. They'd circumvented Canna on their way to Sandray, but she could see it in the distance. Knowing she was close to her former home made her anxious. The memory of the attacks returned as though they'd just happened. Ruairí was aware of what she was looking at and sensed her growing unease as he guided her back down to their cabin. She spent the rest of the day sewing and reading until it was time for them to meet their cousins aboard the *Lady Grace*.

"Senga, what's the matter?" Caragh murmured as they embraced.

"It's nothing. I'm a wee uneasy about being so close to Canna again. I didn't leave with good memories, and seeing the isle again makes my stomach ache." Senga glanced toward the porthole in Rowan's and Caragh's cabin and shrugged. "The sun will set soon, so I won't have to see it."

"Stay here while Rowan and Ruairí go ashore. Keep me company, and I'll keep your mind off of where we are. When they return, we can have a late supper together."

"I'd like that," Senga embraced Caragh once again before they said goodbye to their husbands.

Ruairí and Rowan rowed ashore with their crews, who hurried to retrieve bounty hidden in the caves on the uninhabited side of Canna. Ruairí looked toward the village where he met Senga. His heart thudded in his chest as he recalled the fear he'd experienced twice that night when he intuited that she was in danger. He closed his eyes as he forced memories of their first night making love to replace the horror of seeing her attacked.

"Do you ever think we're making the wrong decision having them sail with us?" Ruairí spoke under his breath, ensuring only Rowan could hear him. His cousin nodded as both men turned to look back at their ships. Their men didn't take long to load the dinghies, and by the time they were ready to return to the *Lady Grace*, Ruairí and Rowan had decided to return to sailing together, whether it was the short trip to Barra or further afield. But both captains agreed that their retirement was imminent. Neither wanted their wives to give birth on pirate ships. Ruairí struggled with a surge of doubt when they discussed returning to Barra.

He'd been convinced that it was the right decision, but when he told Rowan about the battle on Lewis and what happened when Senga returned to Stornoway, doubt niggled that going home might not be an option for Rowan and him. Rowan admitted he had doubts too, that he'd even considered taking Caragh back to England to make their home there.

"We don't have to stay, Rowan." Ruairí sighed. "But now that we've learned how things really happened, don't you think your mother deserves to see you? To know you survived. I know my parents do. My father was set to meet us. We could've tried to find him once you were well, but neither of us would swallow our pride. Look where that led. We were never just merchants. We might have been, and my father could've helped us. Instead, we've spent the last half a score of years killing and stealing. It doesn't sound like such a grand adventure anymore." Ruairí sighed once more as they reached the *Lady Grace*.

# CHAPTER THIRTY-EIGHT

Before they climbed the rope ladder onto the *Lady Grace*'s deck, they agreed to set a course for Barra, but they decided not to say anything to their wives until they had a better plan in case their arrival was unwelcome. The evening meal was subdued as they chatted, but no one brought up the subject of their next destination, and both women grew tired soon after the meal ended. Senga bit her tongue as they rowed back to the *Lady Charity* and remained silent until they reached their cabin.

"Are we going to Barra?" she blurted as soon as Ruairí locked the door. She bit her bottom lip, unsure if she should have kept the question to herself. Ruairí pulled her lip free and offered a soft smile.

"You never need to fear asking me where I intend for us to go. We're partners, and I won't keep you in the dark about where we're going. But Rowan and I haven't decided on what's best when we arrive."

"I don't suppose you'd let me and Caragh go ahead to see if you'll be welcome?"

"I'm not even going to answer that."

"So it's a yes?" Senga wiggled her eyebrows. "Should Caragh and I go in one of our dinghies or one of theirs? We don't need anyone to row us ashore. We're both strong enough to do it alone, if we had to."

"Senga," Ruairí warned as he scratched his palm.

"What?"

"It's been several days since you've been over my knee. I think you're trying to bait me into spanking you."

"Is it working?" she grinned.

"No." Ruairí regretted the answer the moment he said it. The sparkle in Senga's eyes spoke to the mischief that surged through her mind.

"I'm a strong swimmer, you know. Caragh and I learned how to swim in the Minch. She claims the water in Cornwall is much warmer. I used to tell her that if she could survive the water in the Hebrides, then the water in England must be like a bath."

"Neither of you is going for a swim." Ruairí growled.

Senga pushed her kirtle to the floor as she winked at Ruairí. "You'd have to catch me first." Ruairí pounced, wrapping his arm around Senga's middle and lifting her off her feet. He pulled her across his lap once he settled on the chair. Senga squirmed until the first spanking landed, her body jerking in response.

"I know you know what your wiggling body does to mine. You won't make this go any faster by making me hard."

"Maybe not, but I can enjoy your cock pressed against me while I take my punishment."

"Enjoy?"

Senga grimaced as she realized her mistake. Ruairí stood so abruptly that she nearly tumbled to the floor. He caught her and bent her forward over the table after he stripped her of her chemise. She gripped the far side of the table as she draped her body across the hard surface. She steeled herself for the first spank, but it took her breath away as her skin stung.

"One. Thank you, Ruairí." Senga's voice was muffled as she rested her forehead on the table, but her back arched and her head whipped back as the next three spanks landed in rapid succession.

"Little one, this may be how you receive all of your spankings in the future. I'm the one who gets to enjoy your body pressed against mine. You are not to find enjoyment while being punished."

"Yes, Ruairí," Senga groaned, but they knew Senga enjoyed every moment of her spankings, be they for pleasure or for punishment. Ruairí nudged her feet wider apart. He stepped between her legs and thrust his finger into her entrance, tut-tutting when he inevitably found her core drenched from anticipation.

"You don't seem very repentant, Senga. I think you're close to climaxing already." As if to prove his point, one hand rained down several sharp blows, alternating sides, while the fingers of his other hand worked her pearl and the surrounding heated flesh. She moaned and writhed as she tried to press her body closer to his. "Now the punishment begins, little one."

Senga mewled as her body reacted to the torment Ruairí made her endure. With each spank, her body lurched forward, pressing her pubis against the table, the friction pushing her closer to release. As her body relaxed between blows, Ruairí's fingers drove her back toward the edge. She banged her fist against the table in frustration as Ruairí brought her close, but refused to allow her to climax. When he recognized she had reached her limit, he stepped back and eased her off the table. She sank to her knees, tugging on the laces to his leggings, desperate to take him into her mouth. She moaned with relief and pleasure as she sank down over his rod. Ruairí watched as her head bobbed, but soon he had to close his eyes, the image too erotic to remain in control. He pulled away, lifting Senga off her feet once again. He tossed her onto the bed, careful not to be too rough. His body covered her as he entered her with one thrust. He circled his hips as his teeth skimmed her nipple.

"Ruairí!" Senga came apart in his arms, but he wasn't ready to stop. He rolled them over, so Senga could take control. The sight of her swinging breasts as she rode his cock mesmerized him, but when she leaned forward and nibbled on his earlobe, his restraint failed. His cock pulsed as they climaxed together, their heavy breathing filling the air.

Ruairí tensed as Senga's hand slipped between his legs and cupped his bollocks. They stood in Rowan and Caragh's cabin the next morning, and he and Rowan were discussing their plan for going ashore the following morning. Caragh and Senga had been chatting, but he and Rowan could tell the women strained to hear their conversation. It shouldn't have surprised him that Senga grew impatient, but he was unprepared for her to seduce him in front of their cousins.

"Minx, I know what you're up to." Ruairí hissed over his shoulder.

"I could say the same," Senga teased as she patted his bollocks.

"I think I shall take a lesson from my cousin." Ruairí swung around, catching Senga unprepared. She squealed as his hand landed on her backside over and over. He was certain it had to be sore from the night before. "You'd like to hear our plans and hope to take advantage of me to convince me to tell you."

"Take advantage." The huskiness in Senga's voice was like an arrow to his cock. It pulsed within his leggings, and he wished they were in their own cabin, so he could press her against the wall and sink into her. "I rather like that idea. So, what's the plan?"

Senga didn't back down; instead, she pressed her body against Ruairí's. When Ruairí's arousal pressed back against her belly, she stretched to flick his earlobe with her tongue. Ruairí fisted her hair as his mouth crashed down onto hers.

The kiss was hungry and punishing, but neither he nor she gave quarter. Both sensed Rowan and Caragh moving about the cabin, but neither was interested in anything beyond their kiss. When they gasped for air, they turned to look at Rowan and Caragh, who stared back at them. Ruairí watched a predatory gleam creep into Senga's eyes, and when he glanced at Caragh, he saw a matching expression. His head whipped back around when Senga pulled the laces loose at his waist. She sank to her knees as she freed his aching rod. Ruairí glanced back at Rowan and Caragh. His cousin's large frame blocked any view of Caragh, but from the way Rowan's head fell back, Ruairí guessed Caragh and Senga were like-minded.

Ruairí leaned forward and braced his hands on the wall as Senga's satiny mouth slid over his cock again and again. He couldn't take his eyes off Senga as she drew him close to the precipice, but he refused to let it end so soon. He drew Senga off her knees before spinning her around. He gathered her skirts and pushed them into her hands.

"You are going to get the spanking you deserve, little one. You couldn't be patient for a few more minutes. You knew Rowan and I would tell you and Caragh everything, but you refused to wait until we were ready. Your cousin is as guilty as you are, and from the sounds of it, she's getting the spanking she deserves." Ruairí tipped Senga over his arm and knee, bracing his foot on the bedframe. The sound of his palm making contact with Senga's backside was in harmony with the sound of Rowan's hand striking Caragh's bottom. Neither woman struggled to get away or begged for lenience. After ten spanks, Ruairí pinched Senga's tender flesh as he glanced once more at Rowan, who lifted Caragh and carried her to the table. Ruairí lifted Senga, and she wrapped her legs around his waist, clinging to him as her mound rubbed against his cock. He pressed her against the wall and sank into her. When he was seated to the hilt, he paused, reveling in the sensation of being joined with his wife. But need soon got the better of both of them. Their bodies rocked together as desire took control.

"I'm too close, Senga," Ruairí whispered. "I can't last much longer. If you're not close, then I have to slow down. I won't finish before you."

Senga fisted Ruairí's hair and tugged as her mouth covered his. She met each of his thrusts as her body sped toward release. Her body turned rigid as her core spasmed around Ruairí's length. She squeezed her legs and clung to Ruairí as pleasure crashed over her, threatening to consume her. Ruairí pressed her head against his chest, smothering her scream. He grunted as he spilled his seed, stars dancing before his eyes.

Afterward, Ruairí and Senga set their clothing back to rights and waited for Rowan and Caragh to do the same. It wasn't the first time Ruairí and Rowan coupled with women in the same room. They'd shared women many times over the years, even at the same time, but neither of them imagined their wives would consider making love while in the same cabin. Senga and Caragh shrugged as their husbands watched them, unsure what to do next.

"We still want to learn what you're planning," Senga spoke first. She locked gazes with Ruairí, challenging him to answer. The two couples spent the next hour planning various ways their arrival could play out. Senga and Caragh both balked at the suggestion that the women stay behind while the men ventured ashore first. Caragh spun away from Rowan, then turned back and glowered at him.

"No!" Senga exclaimed. "You are not leaving us behind to fear they've killed you." She imagined standing on the deck of the *Lady Charity*, watching an arrow pierce Ruairí's chest as he approached the shore. She trembled as she thought of how terrified she'd been while Ruairí fought at Stornoway, and she had no way to know whether he'd been killed.

"And you think we'll take you with us to face the same threat?" Ruairí countered. "Not bluidy likely."

The women listened as Rowan explained their reasoning that it would be safer and easier for the two men to escape if things turned out badly; it was far more dangerous and difficult if the four of them traveled ashore together. Senga recognized the hard glint in Ruairí's eyes from when they first met. She accepted that nothing she said would shake his resolve, but she wasn't ready to give in.

"Very well," Senga nodded. "We'll wait. On deck."

"No!" Ruairí and Rowan bellowed together.

"You'll wait in one of our cabins until we return for you or order the sails hoisted." Rowan ordered.

"Do you intend to lock us down there?" Caragh stood with her hands on her hips as she tapped her toes.

"Yes." Both men responded in unison once more.

Ruairí pulled Senga into his arms as Rowan and Caragh spoke in hushed voices. He stroked Senga's back as she trembled. "I need you to trust me on this, *mo ghaol*. Rowan and I have spent half a lifetime keeping ourselves alive in places where we aren't welcome. I need to rest assured you're safe on one of our ships, or I won't go ashore at all."

"I'm scared," Senga choked. She struggled to breathe as she fisted Ruairí's leine in her hands. "It was different at Lewis. Yes, you were going into battle, but it wasn't as personal for you as it will be on Barra. The stakes were different. If they'd captured you, I might have been able to bargain for your life, but here, well, I mean nothing to the MacNeils. I'll have no way to help you or protect you."

"Senga, let me worry about this. You can't control what will happen any more than I can, but you can let me shoulder this burden. Let me be the protector this time."

"You're always protecting me. Always," Senga wept. "I feel so useless since I can't protect you."

"Useless? I recall two occasions where I would have died if you hadn't protected me. The crew says you were a cutthroat on that Barbary ship. They claim to fear you more than they ever did me. Senga, do you not realize that you've been in danger since the moment you came aboard the *Lady Charity*? Even before that, you were in danger. I nearly didn't get to you in time the night we met. Please, let me keep you safe. I'll breathe easier if you remain on the ship." Senga sensed the urgency as Ruairí pleaded with her. She nodded as the fight drained from her, and she relied on Ruairí's strong arms to keep from collapsing.

# CHAPTER THIRTY-NINE

Senga shivered as the dinghy fought against the surf in the early morning light. They'd spotted a blond woman on the battlements who disappeared moments later. Ruairí explained that the woman was Rowan's mother. He and Rowan relented about keeping the women locked in a cabin, but insisted the women remain in the dinghies just before the break in the surf. Ruairí's arm kept Senga pinned against his side as they bobbed over the waves. While he watched the beach, he whispered to Senga, but his words trailed off as two women and an older man raced down the path to the sand. He recognized his parents in an instant, and he was certain the other woman was his aunt. Before the dinghies reached the break in the surf, Ruairí and Rowan ordered the men to stop rowing. He pressed a kiss to Senga's forehead before swinging over the side and dropping into the thigh-deep water. His mother lifted her skirts to her knees as she waded in to meet him. She stumbled, and Ruairí lurched forward to catch her, knowing he couldn't reach her. His heart slowed when his father braced her against his side, but they continued to wade toward him.

"Ruairí!" Lady Charity cried. "*Mo mhac, mo mhac.*" Ruairí's mother chanted "my son" over and over until she wrapped her arms around that son for the first time in a decade. A moment later, Angus MacNeil engulfed his wife and son in an embrace that threatened to suffocate both Charity and Ruairí. The three clung to one another as the time apart slipped away.

"Mama, Da," Ruairí breathed.

"*Mo ghille*," Angus choked. Ruairí blinked away tears, hearing his father call him "my boy" as he had until the day Ruairí and Rowan fled Barra. "You're finally home."

"Home?" Ruairí repeated. "Am I welcome here?"

"I'll kill anyone who says otherwise." The vehemence in his mother's voice took Ruairí aback. He peered down at the tiny woman who'd both scolded and comforted him. "Are you here to stay?"

Ruairí expected the question was coming, but he wasn't prepared for it so soon. He glanced back at the dinghy and spotted Senga gripping the side. "That depends on whether it's safe for my wife. I won't go any further if you can't assure me that Senga will be safe. Rowan won't agree either if Caragh is in danger."

"Your wife?" Angus grinned and clapped Ruairí on the shoulder.

"Senga?" Charity leaned around Ruairí and gasped. She tried to push past the two hulking men who kept her from being knocked over by the surf. "Senga MacLeod, is that you, lass? I don't understand. The last I heard——" Charity trailed off as she shook her head.

"Your brides are safe with us. Bring them ashore where they aren't getting sprayed by the surf," Angus ordered. Ruairí and Rowan exchanged a glance before they returned to their dinghies to retrieve their wives. The men carried the women ashore, but Charity pulled Senga into her embrace before Senga's feet touched the sand.

"Senga, is it really you?"

"Aye, Lady Charity."

"Ruairí's aunt has told me so much about your mama."

Charity froze as she strained to see Rowan and the woman who spoke to Laurel. "Ruairí, did you say Caragh? As in Caty and Henry's lass?"

Angus roared with laughter when Ruairí and Senga nodded. "You mean, cousins married cousins?"

"Aye, Da." Ruairí grinned as he peered down at Senga's upturned face.

"You called Rowan's mother Laurel. I always assumed her name was Grace, that he'd named his ship after his mother like you did," Senga whispered.

"No," Ruairí murmured in response. "He said the ship moved through the water with the same grace his mother did, like a queen."

The three couples and Lady Laurel made their way to the keep, but Senga stood in stunned silence as an older man suddenly accused Rowan and Ruairí of being outlaws. Her hand hovered over the hilt of her dirk, and she noticed Caragh made the same move. Neither of them wore swords, but Senga was confident her cousin was as well armed as she was, with knives strapped to various parts of her. A collective gasp ran through the bailey as Lady Laurel stepped forward to defend her son and nephew. Senga was aware Laurel hadn't left the keep since the day they brought Rowan back with his dead father's body slung over his horse. She sensed Laurel's outburst stunned many, but she understood the woman's vehement defense of her son. Laurel appeared ready to tear the man to shreds until Angus intervened. Before Senga understood what was happening, the man was being dragged away, with an order to lock him in the dungeon.

"I'll explain later," Ruairí whispered. "Let's get you inside."

Senga accepted the chair offered to her, but she turned away when food was placed before her. The smell was so overpowering that she feared she'd be ill in front of everyone. When she glanced around and realized no one else was offended by an odor, she realized it was her. Ruairí nudged her shoulder, a frown marring his face when she stared blankly at him.

"I wasn't seasick, Ruairí. I had morning sickness," she whispered. "My sense of smell is overly sensitive. It was this way when I was carrying James. I can't eat much, or I will be ill."

"Can you manage some bread and watered ale?" Ruairí offered, and when Senga nodded, he poured her a chaliceful, then broke off the heel of a loaf. "Just nibble, if that's all you can manage."

Senga sat back and followed Ruairí's suggestion. After a few bites, she felt more herself as she listened to the conversation swirl around her. She and Ruairí answered questions from Ruairí's sisters, Sinead and Saoirse, and his brother, Rab. They attempted to distract his siblings when they pressed to hear how Rowan and Caragh met. Senga gushed over Ruairí's bravery when he came to her rescue. Sinead and Saoirse, both hanging on every word, murmured how romantic their brother was.

By the time the meal ended, both Caragh and Senga appeared exhausted. Lady Laurel had already noticed Caragh's rounded belly, and Senga sensed that Caragh had deduced she was carrying too. Senga didn't doubt Lady Laurel and Lady Charity realized she was expecting as well. She followed the two older women to a chamber abovestairs while Rowan and Ruairí met with Angus.

"How do you feel, *mo ghràidh?*" Ruairí sat on the edge of the bed as Senga stirred. He dropped a kiss on her forehead as she blinked to clear the sleep from her eyes. "Did you sleep well?"

"I did. How long have I been up here?"

"A couple of hours."

"How did things go with your father?" Ruairí shook his head, but his face broke into a smile that turned his handsome face into a masterpiece. She reached out and ran her fingertips over his cheeks before twirling a lock of his blond mane around her finger. "Are you going to tell me, or will you keep it a secret?"

"My father asked Rowan to take on the lairdship."

Senga's mouth dropped open in shock. "What did Rowan say? How do you feel about that? Rab told us earlier that he was glad to no longer be the heir, but that would've made you next in line."

"I've never wanted to be the laird. I teased Rowan about it over the years when we were children. Even though we were born within an hour of each other, as the younger of the two of us and as his cousin, I gloated that I'd never be stuck listening to bickering farmers and angry fishwives. I bragged that I intended to spend my days in the lists with the other men while he'd sit in his chair and get soft around the middle."

"It amazes me that you remained friends," Senga pursed her lips until she could no longer contain her smile. "What did Rowan say?"

"He said he would consider it, but he refused to decide until he spoke with Caragh." Ruairí picked up Senga's hand and entwined their fingers. "Are you disappointed that I won't be in line to be laird? That you won't be the lady of the clan?"

"What? Of course not. I stopped thinking about being the lady of any clan when I was five-and-ten and ran off to marry a farmer. When we met, all I knew was that you were a pirate. I have no aspirations, but I'll support Caragh as she learns her new role. My mother trained me to be a chatelaine, and I haven't forgotten how, but I don't want to be one myself." Ruairí sighed with relief. He'd expected Senga's response, but it relieved him to hear it. He didn't want to disappoint his wife by denying her a position of respect within the clan. "But Ruairí, you've governed over your crew and been in charge of your ship for years. Will it bother you to take orders from Rowan?"

"Not in the least. It's what we grew up believing would be our future. Rowan is not the type to abuse his position, and I'm happy to be his second. That's how it was supposed to be. It's the most normal thing to happen since we left here."

"If this is what you want, if this is what will make you happy, then I'm all for it." Senga wrapped her arms around Ruairí's broad frame as he nuzzled her neck. He stretched out beside her as they held hands, and Ruairí told her stories about how he and Rowan used to hide beneath the bed when they got in trouble. He laughed as he recounted how one time his mother and aunt were on the hunt after he and Rowan pinched three pies from the kitchens when they were supposed to be milking cows. The mothers knew the boys were hiding beneath the bed, but the cousins refused to come out. The boys screamed and rolled out from under the bed when the women climbed onto the mattress and jumped over and over. Their mothers terrified them, making them think the bed was about to collapse on top of the boys.

"Mama and Aunt Laurel are a lot like how you and Caragh are together. Or at least they used to be. I hope Aunt Laurel improves now that Rowan is back."

"I think she already has." Senga replied. Then they spent the rest of the afternoon under the covers until it was time for the evening meal where Angus announced Rowan's new position.

Ruairí toasted his cousin and their homecoming as he surveyed the clan members who sat before him. While Kisimul Castle didn't feel like home yet, neither did it feel foreign. The familiarity was a comfort to Ruairí as he settled into the idea that he and Senga would build their future within those walls. The last shard of ice melted from the Dark Heart's soul as he watched his wife charm the MacNeils, her hand resting lightly over her belly where a new life grew.

# EPILOGUE

"**R**uairí? Ruairí! Are you listening to me?" Senga huffed as she twisted in her husband's arms. The sun's last rays gave the sand a pink hue as they stood with their toes in the surf. Their evening ritual of walking along the beach together was one of the few times they could be alone outside their bedchamber. Senga ran her fingers over the tattoo that lay hidden beneath his leine, just as she had for the past twenty years. She gazed at the laugh lines that bracketed Ruairí's sensual mouth. She recalled that the grooves were just starting to show when they'd met, but then they had been from his intense scowl. Since returning to Kisimul, the last vestiges of Ruairí's anger and bitterness had disappeared, and the lines around his mouth and eyes came from the many smiles and laughs they'd shared. "You're not listening, are you?"

Ruairí lowered his mouth to hover above Senga's. "I'm listening, little one, but soon I'm going to be tasting." Ruairí's kisses drugged Senga the same way they had from the very beginning. His hands slipped to her backside as he cupped the generous swell of her buttocks. She wasn't as lithe as she had been when they met, having borne six more children since leaving the piratical life behind. But Ruairí's body still had the same immediate, visceral reaction. "Tell me later."

Ruairí tugged Senga's hand as they raced along the beach to a cave the rest of the clan knew they shouldn't enter. It was the couple's escape, and they'd come to it too many times to count over the past twenty years. A plaid waited for them, folded on a rock and away from the damp walls. Ruairí struck a piece of flint, and a torch soon blazed. He placed it in the wall sconce he'd fastened to the rock face years earlier. Senga melted into her husband's arms as they pressed their bodies together. Ruairí unbound Senga's hair, running his fingers through the thick strands now laced with gray. His need for his wife, both in and out of bed, had only grown with time. Ruairí relied on and trusted no one more than he did Senga, and she swore the same was true for her.

"We can't be down here long. Kyle and Keith will arrive with their wives and families soon. If we're late, then Callum and Malcolm will ask why, and unless you want to explain what happens between a man and woman to your youngest sons, I don't want them demanding answers."

"You don't answer to a five-year-old and a seven-year-old, Senga," Ruairí grumbled.

"You're right, I don't. You do. I explained to the lasses what goes on between a wife and her husband, but you still have two sons left to tell. And I remember how well it went with Shamus and Dougal."

Ruairí growled as he nuzzled Senga's neck. "Senga, our children are aware of exactly what happens between a man and a woman. If not from catching us one too many times, then from finding Caragh and Rowan doing exactly what we're about to do now. Now hush and let me make love to you." Ruairí captured Senga's mouth in a passionate kiss, the fire between them as scorching as it had been the first time they came together in her tiny cottage on Canna.

"Hurry before Ellie comes searching for us again." Senga hummed with appreciation as she lifted Ruairí's plaid and ran her hands over his rod. "Tina won't forgive us if we're late. She claims she's been waiting her entire life for you to announce her betrothal to Tadhg."

"I can't believe my wee lass chose my first mate's son," Ruairí grumbled again. "I'll cut off the lad's cods if he upsets her even once."

"You will not," Senga giggled, but it turned into a moan as Ruairí lifted her, and she wrapped her legs around his waist. There were no more words as he slipped into the one place he was certain was more glorious than Heaven. Years of sharing passion and love showed in their movements. Duties, chores, the entire outside world slipped away as husband and wife became one. They clung to one another until their bodies surrendered, and release crashed over them both. When Senga caught her breath enough to speak she whispered, "I love you, Ruairí, now and forever."

"And I love you, little one. My heart is dark no more."

Discover how Moira MacDonnell winds up as a stowaway on the infamous Red Drifter's ship when she encounters Kyle MacLean on the high seas in *The Red Drifter of the Sea*.

# THANK YOU FOR READING THE DARK HEART OF THE SEA

Celeste Barclay, a nom de plume, lives near the Southern California coast with her husband and sons. Growing up in the Midwest, Celeste enjoyed spending as much time in and on the water as she could. Now she lives near the beach. She's an avid swimmer, a hopeful future surfer, and a former rower. When she's not writing, she's working or being a mom.

Have you read *The Highland Ladies Guide?* Learn all the behind the scenes details from my flagship series! This FREE book is available to all new subscribers to Celeste's monthly newsletter. Subscribe on her website.

**<u>Get Celeste's freebie</u>**

Join the fun and get exclusive insider giveaways, sneak peeks, and new release announcements in Celeste Barclay's Facebook Ladies of Yore Group

# PIRATES OF THE ISLES

*The Blond Devil of the Sea* **BOOK 1 SNEAK PEEK**

Caragh lifted her torch into the air as she made her way down the precarious Cornish cliffside. She made out the hulking shape of a ship, but the dead of night made it impossible to see who was there. She and the fishermen of Bedruthan Steps weren't expecting any shipments that night. But her younger brother Eddie, who stood watch at the entrance to their hiding place, had spotted the ship and signaled up to the village watchman, who alerted Caragh.

As her boot slid along the dirt and sand, she cursed having to carry the torch and wished she could have sunlight to guide her. She knew these cliffs well, and it was for that reason it was better that she moved slowly than stop moving once and for all. Caragh feared the light from her torch would carry out to the boat. Despite her efforts to keep the flame small, the solitary light would be a beacon.

When Caragh came to the final twist in the path before the sand, she snuffed out her torch and started to run to the cave where the main source of the village's income lay in hiding. She heard movement along the trail above her head and knew the local fishermen would soon join her on the beach. These men, both young and old, were strong from days spent pulling in the full trawling nets and hoisting the larger catches onto their boats. However, these men weren't well-trained swordsmen, and the fear of pirate raids was ever-present. Caragh feared that was who the villagers would face that night.

*The Dark Heart of the Sea*

*The Red Drifter of the Sea*

*The Scarlet Blade of the Sea*

# THE HIGHLAND LADIES

*A Spinster at the Highland Court*

**BOOK 1 SNEAK PEEK**

Elizabeth Fraser looked around the royal chapel within Stirling Castle. The ornate candlestick holders on the altar glistened and reflected the light from the ones in the wall sconces as the priest intoned the holy prayers of the Advent season. Elizabeth kept her head bowed as though in prayer, but her green eyes swept the congregation. She watched the other ladies-in-waiting, many of whom were doing the same thing. She caught the eye of Allyson Elliott. Elizabeth raised one eyebrow as Allyson's lips twitched. Both women had been there enough times to accept they'd be kneeling for at least the next hour as the Latin service carried on. Elizabeth understood the Mass thanks to her cousin Deirdre Fraser, or rather now Deirdre Sinclair. Elizabeth's mind flashed to the recent struggle her cousin faced as she reunited with her husband Magnus after a seven-year separation. Her aunt and uncle's choice to keep Deirdre hidden from her husband simply because they didn't think the Sinclairs were an advantageous enough match, and the resulting scandal, still humiliated the other Fraser clan members at court. She admired Deirdre's husband Magnus's pledge to remain faithful despite not knowing if he'd ever see Deirdre again.

Elizabeth suddenly snapped her attention; while everyone else intoned the twelfth—or was it thirteenth—amen of the Mass, the hairs on the back of her neck stood up. She had the strongest feeling that someone was watching her. Her eyes scanned to her right, where her parents sat further down the pew. Her mother and father had their heads bowed and eyes closed. While she was convinced her mother was in devout prayer, she wondered if her father had fallen asleep during the Mass. Again. With nothing seeming out of the ordinary and no one visibly paying attention to her, her eyes swung to the left. She took in the king and queen as they kneeled together at their prie-dieu. The queen's lips moved as she recited the liturgy in silence. The king was as still as a statue. Years of leading warriors showed, both in his stature and his ability to control his body into absolute stillness. Elizabeth peered past the royal couple and found herself looking into the astute hazel eyes of Edward Bruce, Lord of Badenoch and Lochaber. His gaze gave her the sense that he peered into her thoughts, as though he were assessing her. She tried to keep her face neutral as heat surged up her neck. She prayed her face didn't redden as much as her neck must have, but at a twenty-one, she still hadn't mastered how to control her blushing. Her nape burned like it was on fire. She canted her head slightly before looking up at the crucifix hanging over the altar. She closed her eyes and tried to invoke the image of the Lord that usually centered her when her mind wandered during Mass.

Elizabeth sensed Edward's gaze remained on her. She didn't understand how she was so sure that he was looking at her. She didn't have any special gifts of perception or sight, but her intuition screamed that he was still looking.

*A Spy at the Highland Court*

*A Wallflower at the Highland Court*

*A Rogue at the Highland Court*

*A Rake at the Highland Court*

*An Enemy at the Highland Court*

*A Saint at the Highland Court*

*A Beauty at the Highland Court*

# THE HIGHLAND LADIES ALWAYS

*A Sinner at the Highland Court*

**BOOK 1 SNEAK PEEK**

*I hate him. I hate him. I hate him. How can he do this to me? How could he pick her over me? That fat sow. Kieran will regret this till the day he dies. He and she both. This is her fault. All her fault. I hate her too.*

Madeline MacLeod felt the four walls of her tiny convent cell closing in upon her. Her brother, Kieran, had dragged her from Robert the Bruce's royal court at Stirling Castle and dumped her at Inchcailleoch Priory earlier that week. She refused to accept that any of her words or actions had caused her fall from grace. She'd only spoken the truth each time she told Maude Sutherland how unconventionally curvaceous she was. Why her brother wanted to marry a woman who looked more like a tavern wench than a lady was beyond Madeline.

*He just wants a good rut. He'll realize what a dreadful mistake he's made when he takes her home to Stornoway. He will realize that tupping her won't be worth the humiliation of having such a plain-faced, round as a barrel, heifer for a wife. He could have had Laurel Ross!*

As Madeline listened to the bells toll for yet another Mass, she grimaced. All she seemed to do was pray these days, but God certainly wasn't listening because she remained at the priory despite her fervent appeals. She kneeled among the other novices, postulants, and nuns eight times throughout the day and night as they followed the Liturgy of Hours. The bells in the background signaled Prime, so she knew it was still very early. She'd already attended Matins in the middle of the night and Lauds at sunrise.

Madeline glanced out the narrow window set high in the wall, thinking that the masons must have designed it so the women couldn't escape. The sunlight, weak and dismal, matched Madeline's mood. When she lived at court, six o'clock in the morning was an hour she'd never seen. Now that she lived at the convent, she'd already been awake for an hour and a half.

Madeline dragged herself from her cot and her introspection. She could feel her anger simmering below the surface, and if she wanted to avoid another outburst—which would result in two days of wearing a hair shirt for penance — she would do well to calm herself. She splashed freezing water from the washbasin onto her face. It was refreshing, but it only reminded her of the austerity she now faced daily. Already dressed in her postulant's dark gray gown, she'd tucked her roughly shorn hair beneath her wimple, and a large wooden cross hung around her neck. The undyed wool of the dress made her skin itch, and it chafed the open cuts upon her back. But it was far better than the hair shirt they forced her to wear the third day she arrived. She'd lashed out at another postulant who bumped into her as they entered their pew. The postulant was formerly a lesser noble, and Madeline reminded her that she, Madeline, was the sister of a laird and a former lady-in-waiting to Queen Elizabeth de Burgh. Madeline's voice carried, but the other woman was more discreet in her own set-down, as she pointed out that Madeline's brother was the one to banish her from court.

*A Hellion at the Highland Court*

*An Angel at the Highland Court*

*A Harlot at the Highland Court*

*A Friend at the Highland Court*

*An Outsider at the Highland Court*

*A Devil at the Highland Court*

# THE CLAN SINCLAIR

*His Highland Lass* **BOOK 1 SNEAK PEEK**

She entered the great hall like a strong spring storm in the northern most Highlands. Tristan Mackay felt like he had been blown hither and yon. As the storm settled, she left him with the sweet scents of heather and lavender wafting towards him as she approached. She was not a classic beauty, tall and willowy like the women at court. Her face and form were not what legends were made of. But she held a unique appeal unlike any he had seen before. He could not take his eyes off of her long chestnut hair that had strands of fire and burnt copper running through them. Unlike the waves or curls he was used to, her hair was unusually straight and fine. It looked like a waterfall cascading down her back. While she was not tall, neither was she short. She had a figure that was meant for a man to grasp and hold onto, whether from the front or from behind. She had an aura of confidence and charm, but not arrogance or conceit like many good looking women he had met. She did not seem to know her own appeal. He could tell that she was many things, but one thing she was not was his.

*His Bonnie Highland Temptation*

*His Highland Prize*

*His Highland Pledge*

*His Highland Surprise*

Their Highland Beginning

# THE CLAN SINCLAIR LEGACY

## *Highland Lion* **BOOK 1 SNEAK PEEK**

Liam Mackay gazed at the bustling Orcadian village of Skaill, on the isle of Rousay. He thought of how it reminded him of his clan's village, outside the walls of Castle Varrich in the Scottish Highlands. As he crossed the dock, he noticed the massive longboats that Norse traders sailed to conduct trade on the island. With his father's jet-black hair and emerald eyes, few would believe Liam had Nordic heritage, but it had connected his family to Orkney for ten generations. He swept his eyes over the crofts nearest the marina of sorts. He watched as a tall blonde woman stormed out of a house and slammed the door shut. The fury on the woman's face made him think of his mother when she was angry with Liam and his younger brothers and sister. But the woman before him, statuesque and voluptuous, couldn't resemble his petite brunette mother any less. Her tall stature belied her curves until she leaned forward to fill a bucket at the well.

"Elene, come back here. We are not through speaking," an older woman called from the doorway to the croft Elene Isbister left. The younger woman continued to fill the bucket as though no one spoke to her, but Liam watched her face grow red, and it wasn't from exertion. His path carried him toward the well, but he could have continued past to reach his destination. Instead, intrigued by the stunning blonde and the scene playing out before him, he stopped at the well as the woman finished raising the bucket. She poured the contents in her own pail before letting it drop back into the cavernous pit. Unaware of Liam, she jumped when he stepped forward and grasped the crank.

Liam's emerald eyes met deep sapphire, the shade of the Highland sky in autumn. Liam observed the surprise, then wariness, in her gaze as she stepped away. He drew the full bucket to the ledge and dipped the community ladle into the cool water. As he sipped, Elene took two steps back before turning away, disconcerted by the handsome stranger. However, her feet grew roots as the older woman stormed toward her. Liam kept his head down as he lowered the bucket, chiding himself for his nosiness but unwilling to move away. The older woman glanced at him dismissively before settling her attention on Elene.

In Norn, the language of Orkney, the woman continued her chastisement. "I didn't tell you that you could leave. We were in the middle of talking."

"No, Mother. You were in the middle of talking, and I was in the middle of not wanting to hear any more. I cannot believe you're considering marrying him."

"Not considering. I've already decided. When Gunter returns in a sennight, we will wed. Then we will all move home with him."

"Home?" Elene scoffed. "Norway hasn't been our people's home in ten generations. And you are a fool if you believe he will allow me to remain."

"You're old enough to marry."

"Getting married is a far sight different from being sold!" Elene made to step around her mother, but the older woman was just as quick.

"You exaggerate."

"And you believe a slave trader over your own daughter."

"Gunter is not a slave trader. You would smear his name because you aren't getting what you want, you selfish child."

Clearly not a child, Elene stood to her full height as she gazed at her mother, who was at least two inches shorter than her daughter. "Selfish," she repeated her mother. "I hadn't realized Katryne and Johan raised themselves."

"I am their mother."

"But I raised my brother and sister. I lost my chance to marry while you lost yourself in barrels of mead." Elene swung her glare at Liam, who'd remained near the arguing women while he spoke to his two ship captains. Despite speaking Gaelic, Liam sensed Elene knew he understood her conversation with her mother. It explained her accusatory glare.

"That was my grief."

Elene released a dismissive puff of air. "That was your habit. You haven't missed Father in years. You welcomed Petyre into our home almost every night, and Father hadn't been dead two moons."

"We need a man to provide for us," the older woman sniffed defensively.

Elene gawked at her mother before she laughed. "We do not need a man to provide for us. You might need one because you can't stand to be alone for more than a day. But I work our fields and hunt out supper. Petyre, and now Gunter, come into our home and eat the food I provide. I should have accepted Duncan's offer before he grew fed up with waiting."

"You didn't love him."

"You mean like you love Gunter?"

"I do love him," Elene's mother insisted.

"More fool are you," Elene muttered.

"Come inside. You're causing a scene."

"I'm not the one yelling. And I can't. I must bring Bess this water, feed the chickens, muck out the stalls, then milk Bess. I haven't time to argue when I know you refuse to believe me."

"He is not going to sell you!"

"He will. Or he'll force me to bed him. He will not feed and clothe another adult without getting something in return. He told me."

# VIKING GLORY

## *Leif* **BOOK 1 SNEAK PEEK**

Leif looked around his chambers within his father's longhouse and breathed a sigh of relief. He noticed the large fur rugs spread throughout the chamber. His two favorites placed strategically before the fire and the bedside he preferred. He looked at his shield that hung on the wall near the door in a symbolic position but waiting at the ready. The chests that held his clothes and some of his finer acquisitions from voyages near and far sat beside his bed and along the far wall. And in the center was his most favorite possession. His oversized bed was one of the few that could accommodate his long and broad frame. He shook his head at his longing to climb under the pile of furs and on the stuffed mattress that beckoned him. He took in the chair placed before the fire where he longed to sit now with a cup of warm mead. It had been two months since he slept in his own bed, and he looked forward to nothing more than pulling the furs over his head and sleeping until he could no longer ignore his hunger. Alas, he would not be crawling into his bed again for several more hours. A feast awaited him to celebrate his and his crew's return from their latest expedition to explore the isle of Britannia. He bathed and wore fresh clothes, so he had no excuse for lingering other than a bone weariness that set in during the last storm at sea. He was eager to spend time at home no matter how much he loved sailing. Their last expedition had been profitable with several raids of monasteries that yielded jewels and both silver and gold, but he was ready for respite.

Leif left his chambers and knocked on the door next to his. He heard movement on the other side, but it was only moments before his sister, Freya, opened her door. She, too, looked tired but clean. A few pieces of jewelry she confiscated from the holy houses that allegedly swore to a life of poverty and deprivation adorned her trim frame.

"That armband suits you well. It compliments your muscles," Leif smirked and dodged a strike from one of those muscular arms.

Only a year younger than he, his sister was a well-known and feared shield maiden. Her lithe form was strong and agile making her a ferocious and competent opponent to any man. Freya's beauty was stunning, but Leif had taken every opportunity since they were children to tease her about her unusual strength even among the female warriors.

"At least one of us inherited our father's prowess. Such a shame it wasn't you."

*Freya*

*Tyra & Bjorn*

*Strian*

*Lena & Ivar*

Made in the USA
Monee, IL
15 May 2025

17545757R00184